AN EXTRAORDINARY LORD

ANNA HARRINGTON

sourcebooks
casablanca

Published by Sourcebooks Casablanca, an imprint of Sourcebooks
P.O. Box 4410, Naperville, Illinois 60567-4410
(630) 961-3900
sourcebooks.com

Printed and bound in Canada.
MBP 10 9 8 7 6 5 4 3 2 1

Dedicated to Dance Tonight Chattanooga
for teaching me how to waltz.
And to Valkyrie Axe Throwing for teaching
me how to throw a Viking battle axe.
(Because an unmarried miss never knows what kinds
of skills she might need for the marriage market.)

One

Late October 1816
London

BLOODY HELL. THE PRINCE REGENT HAD MADE HIM A BARON.

Blowing out an aggravated breath that left a cloud of steam on the damp midnight air, Merritt Rivers quickened his pace through the rain-drenched back alleys and narrow passages between Lincoln's Inn Fields and St Paul's. He flipped up his greatcoat's collar against the ice-cold drizzle, yet he was thankful that tonight's rain had prevented another riot from breaking out and kept the City relatively quiet for once.

A barony. *Christ*. If he'd known that the infamous Mrs. Fitzherbert had been in the carriage he'd saved from attack last month, he'd have fled in the opposite direction as fast as he could run.

He grimaced. No. He still would have rescued her, but he would at least have had the foresight to give a false name.

Maybe that was what he needed, he considered as he continued to scan the foggy darkness around him. A secret identity. An easier way to separate his daytime career as a barrister from his nighttime activities on the streets. After all, didn't he already become a different person when he put on his black clothes, armed himself for battle, and headed out into the night? *Had* to. It was the only way he could survive.

The Night Guardian…the City Watchman…

"The Black Baron," he muttered.

He rolled his eyes. *Bloody hell.*

He turned south toward the Thames. There was plenty of time left before dawn to search the area and find the contacts he kept within London's criminal underworld, to question them about an escaped convict named Ronald Chase. The Home Office was certain the man could provide information on the recent spate of riots that were raining havoc across the City, and they had asked Merritt to catch him.

He'd agreed, but not to support the Home Office as much as to give himself an excuse for stalking the streets tonight and burning off the tension coiling inside him.

An excuse for hunting.

As with most nights, sleep wouldn't be forthcoming anyway. *Especially* tonight, when restlessness pulsed in his veins like poison and gripped every muscle like a vise. He'd never be able to simply lie still in the darkness and close his eyes without the ghosts coming to—

A shout broke the stillness, followed by a smashing of wood and the sounds of running footsteps.

He bit back a curse. So much for a quiet night.

Merritt ran after the noise, dodging down a passageway in almost pitch-blackness. He broke out into a fog-banked alley and skidded to a halt, staring at the scene in front of him. *What the hell…?*

A large man stood with his back pressed against the brick wall. His hands rested at his sides; his eyes were as large as plates and his face pallid. A small barrel lay broken on the cobblestones beside him, its contents spreading around him in a dark puddle. Less than ten feet away, the door of the shop hung splintered on its twisted hinges. So…a burglar.

But it was the person who'd caught him who stole Merritt's attention, who even now stood in front of the man with the tip of a knife pointed at his chin. *A woman.* And one unlike any Merritt had ever seen.

She held the knife with its tip pressed lightly into the soft flesh beneath the man's jaw and at such an angle that its sharp blade would slice through his throat if he dared try to shove it away. Not a trace of fear showed anywhere in her. But then, what else would he expect from a woman dressed in a man's black work shirt beneath a tightly cinched waistcoat made of thick leather and metal studs, black breeches, and short boots? Two short knife sheaths were tied to both forearms, with a pair of handcuffs dangling from her right hip and a small sword strapped to her left. Thick, coppery red curls were tied back at her neck with a black ribbon, yet stray curls as wild as she was had slipped free and framed the sides of her face. Good God…who *was* she?

"Thank you for coming," she called out, her eyes never leaving the man in front of her. A faint foreign accent Merritt couldn't identify thickened her voice. "But I'm not in need of rescue."

Well, he could certainly see *that*. He arched a brow and leaned his shoulder against the wall, settling in to watch whatever happened next. "Who says I'm here to rescue *you*?"

Her sensuous lips curled with amusement. "In that case, he's mine. I got to him first."

"I would never attempt to pull rank." Not with a woman. And certainly not one armed to the teeth. Good Lord, was that a gladius sword sheathed at her hip? "But I'm a bit foggy tonight, so you'll have to explain to me why I would want him."

"He broke into the shop."

"I see." Actually, he didn't have a clue. "And you are…?"

"Rich man, poor man, beggar man…thief," she mused, chanting out the beginning of the old children's rhyme. With a slow smile, she added, "Taker."

He narrowed his eyes on her. The streets were filled with thief-takers these days, lurking about in the wakes of the riots to arrest opportunistic men who used the confusion and destruction to cover their own crimes. Low-hanging fruit. Merritt had no patience for them, knowing they were profiting off the riots as much as the men they captured. But this one… *Sweet Lucifer*.

He'd never seen one like her before. Hell, he'd never seen a female thief-taker at all.

His boring night had suddenly turned interesting.

"So as you can see, I don't need your help," she reiterated.

Apparently not. "Good. Because I wasn't offering it." He ran a deliberate and assessing gaze over her. "I didn't realize Bow Street employed women."

"*Bow Street?*" Keeping the knife lightly pressed under the burglar's chin, she turned sideways to shoot Merritt an expression of such disgust that he wondered for a moment if he'd sprung a second head. "Do I look weak and corrupt to you?"

"Not at all." Actually, she looked...*magnificent*. And deadly.

"Bow Street," she muttered in an aside to her prisoner. "He thinks I'm a runner. No honor among thieves with that lot. Did I behave like a runner to you?"

The thief stiltedly shook his head, afraid to move more for fear of slitting his own throat.

She slid her eyes to the criminal. "Did I ask you for bribery money to turn you loose or make an offer to split the profits of what you've stolen? Of course not." She scoffed a snort of revulsion. "Bow Street...*please*."

"Then who are you?" Merritt asked.

"You first."

Damnation. Where was a good false identity when he needed one? He *really* needed to work on that. The first name that popped into his head—"Mrs. Fitzherbert."

"And I would have guessed you were Lady Jersey."

It was her turn then to finally scrutinize him with a good long perusal. If she were surprised to see him looking like a wraith in the night, the hilt of his own sword visible beneath his open greatcoat, she didn't show it, and her expression remained as enigmatic as ever.

She arched a brow. "Prinny's tastes in women have definitely turned unique, I daresay."

His lips pursed in mocking insult. "Are you saying I don't look feminine enough to entice a prince?"

"Not at all. Only that you look...*younger* than I would have assumed."

He sent her his best rakish grin. "It's not the years. It's how you wear them." And speaking of wearing... He nodded toward her sword. "That's an interesting choice of fashion accessory."

"My dressmaker was all out of matching parasols."

"Really."

"I'd show you what she substitutes for reticules, but I'm not certain you'd survive."

Good Lord, she was sharp. So were all three blades she carried, he'd wager. "What—no pistols?"

"A weapon that's useless up close, has to be reloaded after a single use, and kills more people who pull the trigger through misfires than those whom the barrel is pointed at?" She shook her head with only slightly less disdain than she'd expressed at being confused for a Bow Street runner. "Where's the fun in that?"

She took a step toward Merritt and sheathed her knife on her left forearm. From the curious way her gaze journeyed over him, she couldn't quite fathom him or what he was doing lurking in the rain-soaked streets so far from any place respectable. But then, he could barely understand it himself.

Her eyes drifted down from his shoulders and across the black tunic he wore instead of a shirt and waistcoat, then down his black trousers. His cock flexed shamelessly when her attention landed on his crotch.

He grimaced. *That* look was certainly more likely done to note if he carried a pistol tucked into his waistband than because this unusual encounter was arousing her. Disappointingly.

Behind her, the burglar moved to step away from the wall and run.

"Stay." With a lightning quick reflex, she drew her sword and pointed it at the man's chest, not looking away from Merritt.

The burglar froze like a well-trained dog.

She cocked her head as she studied Merritt. "Who are you? Who do you work for?"

She'd said earlier that she'd beaten him to the burglar. She must have thought him a fellow thief-taker. He didn't correct her. That omission was far better than the truth.

Like her, he looked nothing like a thief-taker. He looked nothing like a baron either. *Thank God.*

"I'm a peer of His Majesty's realm." Merritt could still barely say that without laughing. Or wanting to flee.

She shook her head. "Claiming to be Mrs. Fitzherbert was more believable." She kept her sword pointed at the burglar, who was too afraid to flee. "As you can see," she pointed out, "your assistance is unnecessary."

In other words, he could go rot, and she could be on her way, criminal in tow, to the nearest watchhouse.

But Merritt wasn't ready to saunter off just yet. Not once had he experienced a night like this since he'd returned to England last year, taken up at the bar again by day, and been compelled to patrol the streets at night to keep from going mad. The Home Office's mission for him tonight suddenly fell out of favor. Who needed an escaped convict to distract him when a woman like this stood before him?

"You think I'd dare try to steal credit for your arrest with the night watch?" He feigned offense. "What kind of gentleman would I be to do something like that?"

She shrugged. "A thief-taker."

"That's where you're wrong. I leave the thief-taking to better men." And better women, too, apparently. "I'm the exact opposite, in fact."

Good Lord, was he ever. In his daylight profession as a barrister, he encountered more thief-takers than he could shake a stick at, and God knew how much he wanted to take a stick *to* the corrupt, lying lot of them. As far as he was concerned, only the foot patrols had worth. Men who walked the streets to look for crimes as they were happening, to arrest the criminals right then rather than hunt them down after the fact the way most runners did. After all, wasn't that what he did himself almost every night, patrolling the streets to protect innocents?

She must belong to one of those patrols.

And clearly didn't believe him. "Then why would you be out on a night like this, prowling the dark streets at this hour?" She sardonically clucked her tongue. "A defenseless thing like you might get hurt."

I'm hunting. And not just for an escaped convict.

"I could ask the same of you," he dodged, pushing darker thoughts from his mind. "I've never met a female thief-taker before."

"Then we're even," she shot back. "I've never met Mrs. Fitzherbert."

With a lazy grin, he let that pass. There was no good response to that, and he had more important things to focus on at the moment. Or at least more pointed things.

He nodded at her sword. "Do you truly know how to use that thing without hurting yourself?"

"Do you?" She gestured at his.

He pushed back his greatcoat to fully reveal his sword. "Want to find out?"

She studied him for a silent moment, her eyes flickering eagerly at the temptation. "Are you asking me to dance, my good sir?"

Dance, fight…anything else she felt like doing with him. "Yes." *Oh yes.*

Her attention flicked to the burglar as she weighed her options, then she conceded. "All right." She lowered her sword and stepped back. "It's your lucky night," she told the burglar. "*Leave.*"

The man turned and ran, stumbling over himself and the

cobblestones in his scramble to vanish into the darkness of the passageway.

Slowly, she stepped into the middle of the alley. The challenge Merritt had tossed out now tingled like an electric storm between them, and the deserted street came to life beneath the cold and damp night.

Who the devil *was* she? The desire to find out coiled in his gut.

Merritt pushed himself away from the wall and deliberately drew his sword in a controlled slide from its scabbard. He didn't know her, didn't know how she'd been trained or how skilled she was, how controlled in her reactions and emotions. The last thing he needed was for her to startle at any quick movement and decide to run him through.

But that worry quickly turned baseless. Judging from the way she circled him, now assessing him openly with the cool detachment of an adversary, the woman possessed control of emotion, body, and weapon that wouldn't have faltered even under cannon fire. A well-trained and experienced soldier. Each fluid, graceful move she made reminded him of a lioness stalking its prey.

He stood still and let her circle him, his sword drawn but pointing nonthreateningly at the ground. He followed her path with a glance over his shoulder. "You've had significant training, then?"

"I have." Her boot heels clicked softly against the cobblestones, and every breath she took sent up a cloud of steam on the cold air. "I've studied under some of the best fighters in Spain and France."

"What a coincidence." He turned his head to glance over his other shoulder, keeping her in sight as she completed her circle. "I've killed some of the best fighters in Spain and France."

She stopped in front of him. "Then you might possibly offer a challenge."

An amused grin tugged at his lips. Oh, he was enjoying this! "Possibly."

She dragged her gaze over him one last time. "Until I skewer you."

"*Very* possibly," he returned, deadpan.

Light laughter bubbled from her lips, and the inscrutable mask she wore splintered to reveal the humor beneath, the amused glimmer in her eyes, and the tug of her lips into just the start of a faint smile.

But immediately, her world-weary mask fell back into place, all her emotions once more controlled. What a damn shame, too, because he would have loved to have seen what she looked like with a beaming smile on her face.

"Shall I call off?" She stepped back until they were arm and sword's distance apart.

He raised his blade in front of his face in salute. "Please do."

With an edgy smile registering her mounting excitement—the same anticipation he felt pulsing inside himself—she returned the salute. "*En garde.*"

They took their positions, as if on a refereed piste instead of a slippery cobblestone alley half obscured by thick fog and haze. Their well-practiced stances of seasoned fencers only added to the absurdity of this sparring match. And to the fun of it.

"*Prêts?*"

"Oh yes," he drawled. More ready than he'd been for any match in months.

"*Allez!*"

Instead of charging, she feinted, surprising him by retreating instead of attacking. But then, nearly everything she'd done so far had surprised him. The simple move forced him forward on the offensive, and he obliged by charging her. The clash of steel against steel jarred loudly through the quiet streets and reverberated off the stone buildings. The noise gave the foggy night an otherworldly feel, as if he'd fallen into a bizarre dream.

He pressed forward with testing thrusts of his sword to gauge her skill and study her movements. Damnation if she wasn't doing the same to him as she continued to fall back in a circling retreat, every parry and deflection a chance to assess how he fought.

She lunged. Her blade pushed his to the side and ran down the steel shaft toward the hilt. But he dodged to the left before she could score such an easy touch.

There would be no blood drawn; both of them were too well controlled to accidentally prick the other. The match would only be won when one knocked the other's sword to the cobblestones. Which he had no intention of allowing to happen to his.

She was good, he'd admit.

But he was better.

To prove it, he launched a series of thrusts that forced her to turn her dominant side to him, leaving her weaker left side unguarded. A side he exposed with a lightning quick slash of the flat side of his blade to her leather waistcoat. A spank meant to put her in her place.

"So we're playing like that, are we?" she panted out, her eyes gleaming with unveiled excitement. "All right, then."

She let loose an offensive of thrusts and slashes that had him parrying her blade from all directions. Then she dropped into a crouch and swung her sword in a wide slash at his lower legs.

He jumped, and the blade passed harmlessly through the air beneath.

"So we're playing like that, are we?" he repeated. He lunged, catching her blade with a hard slash of his. The strength of the thrust knocked her arm far to the side and forced her to stagger back half a dozen steps to regain her balance and once more find her fighting stance. He leveled a hard look at her. "Then do it."

With a sound that was half exertion, half pleasure, she ran at him, hacking and slashing in a flurry of movement, not to cut him but to force him to parry each move so that he'd leave himself open to attack. So that each hard and quick thrust forced him to swing slightly wider, putting him increasingly off-balance and leaving his sword arm exposed. What she'd unleashed wasn't at all the controlled, tight movements taught to dandies at fencing academies but the tactics of a fierce fighter.

"You're in the streets every night," he forced out breathlessly between parries and thrusts, still holding his ground despite her attack. *Not* a question.

"Yes." Her answer came just as breathlessly as she dropped back a stride, only to charge again. "Aren't you?"

He caught her sword with a twist of his wrist and strode forward, deflecting her blade to the side and closing the distance between them until they were less than an arm's length apart. A deadly position he never would have taken with any other adversary, but with her, one he felt confident enough to claim.

"The riots have been increasing," he stated and seized the opportunity to turn their match into an interrogation.

"Yes." Her chest rose and fell with her rapid breaths of exertion, her face deliciously flushed and her green eyes gleaming. "Every night."

"But not tonight."

"No. It rained." With a twist, she freed her blade, stepped back, and thrust.

He easily parried. "No. It drizzled." He parried a second thrust to the opposite side. "What kind of rioters have you ever met who would let a little sprinkle stop them?"

His question caught her by surprise. For a split second, she froze, just long enough for him to advance, twist his arm around hers, and hold both swords pressed immobile between them.

"That's why you're out here tonight," she mused with a frown. Her voice emerged as a smooth drawl that wrapped around him like a blanket. "The riots."

"What do you know about them?" Her face was framed by the crossed swords between them, and he leaned dangerously closer, even as their arms began to tremble from the exertion of keeping their swords pressed so fiercely together.

"Nothing."

Deception flared in her eyes, and his pulse stuttered. What did she know? What was she hiding? "You're lying."

Taking a moment to gather herself, she licked her lips. "They're just riots."

His eyes darted down to her mouth. Good Lord, how kissable she looked. How delectable. The fight had knocked loose the black hair ribbon, and now her hair cascaded over her shoulders and down her back in a mass of riotous copper curls. Her eyes shined bright; her lips were ripe and red and invitingly sensuous. Each panting breath she took to gather back air into her lungs made her bosom rise and fall tumultuously beneath the leather waistcoat she wore instead of a corset.

If they weren't holding swords just inches from each other's throats, he would have said she looked…aroused. God knew he was becoming exactly that himself, helped along in no small part by the tension pulsating between them so strongly that it buzzed like electricity. The air around them practically sizzled.

"Who are the leaders?" he pressed, keeping their grappling close by shifting his stance so that he pressed a shoulder and hip against her to keep her still.

She couldn't back away now without dropping her sword and letting him win. Something he knew she would never do. "I don't know."

He leaned closer, bringing his face so close to hers that he could feel the warmth of her sweet breath stir across his lips. The attraction between them was as palpable as the cold drizzle dripping across the city. "Then tell me this…who are *you*?"

Delight sparkled in her eyes. "Now, now, Mrs. Fitzherbert." Her voice turned husky. "What kind of lady would I be to confide such personal information to a stranger? One wielding a sword, no less." She clucked her tongue like a scolding governess. "Who knows what kind of wickedness such disclosure might lead to? I'm certain the archbishop would not approve."

"I often find myself at odds with His Grace in matters of wickedness." His mouth lingered achingly above hers, so close that he could kiss her with just a tilt of his chin. And if he did, she might very well run him through with her sword for it.

Her brow inched up. "More scandal, less sacred?"

"His Grace would surprise you."

She curled an amused smile at the archbishop's expense. "Not as much as you."

That low and throaty admission played down his spine like seeking fingers of seduction. *Sweet Jesus…*she was liquid fire in his veins, tensing every muscle in his body. He couldn't remember the last time such immediate attraction struck him the way it did now with her, the last time his gut tightened with such animal arousal at a first meeting. Irrationally, he wanted to bury himself between her thighs and claim the ferocity inside her…raw and wild and intense.

"I'm Merritt. *Tell me your name. Dear God, please tell me your name and how I can find you again…*

A light laugh fell from her lips, tickling his. "Of course you are," she mused, her voice lowering into a throaty whisper. It was a siren song that had him hanging on every word even though he knew she had the skills to skewer him. Her lips twitched mischievously. "Like an honor to be won?"

Not when he'd gladly surrender to her. The defeat would be exquisite.

"Who *are* you?" His eyes trailed over her beautiful face, engrossed by the fine lines of her cheeks and the creamy smoothness of her warm skin, captivated by the light in the depths of her eyes. And by the way, even now, she refused to give up the fight, continuing to press her body against his so strongly that any slip of his attention might send the sword slicing into his throat. "At least tell me your name."

She hesitated, then capitulated, still holding the swords locked between. "Veronica Chase." The smile she gave him corkscrewed into his gut. "My friends call me Roni. *You* can call me Miss Chase."

Good God. It was impossible. *She* was impossible. But he knew…damnation, he *knew*.

Carefully, he eased back the pressure of his sword until he could shift his hip and shoulder away. When he barely held her blade with his, he stepped back to safely retreat out of thrusting range and lowered his sword.

Their fight—and the moment of elation it had brought—was over.

She lowered her own sword, bewildered yet obviously pleased that he was giving up. "You're surrendering?"

"No." He bit back a curse. At that moment, he hated the Home Office more than he could have ever expressed. "I'm arresting you."

Two

VERONICA SAT HANDCUFFED ON A LARGE WOODEN CHAIR THAT would have looked right at home in a medieval castle. Fitting, since she seemed to be sitting in the middle of a fortress.

She trailed her gaze slowly over the room around her. Richly decorated walnut-paneled walls, a massive stone and marble fireplace, pieces of heavy leather and wood furniture...this place would have made every gentlemen's club on St James's Street weep with envy, right down to the Aubusson rug and gas lighting. Except that the windowless brick walls rising around her in an octagonal central tower were at least ten feet thick, and no gentlemen's club she'd ever heard of had twin portcullises guarding the entrance. And when the man from the street and his friend had stripped off her knives and sword, it wasn't because they didn't already have enough of their own apparently. Not when what looked like half the small arms of the Household Guards decorated the walls of the adjoining room.

Where on earth had they brought her?

"Well, I have to admit," the dark-blond friend mused as he pulled up a chair in front of her and sat, "you're not at all what I expected."

She tilted her head slightly and returned his curious stare. "And what did you expect?"

"A cock."

At that brusque interjection from across the room, she swung her narrowed gaze to the man who had arrested her. The same man who had sparred with her so brilliantly. He now guarded her, leaning against the wall with a steely expression on his face and his arms crossed over his chest.

"Imagine my surprise not to find one," he drawled.

She quirked a brow. "A common complaint of yours, is it, Mrs. Fitzherbert?"

His jaw clenched even more tightly when the blond man was unable to quash his grin at the man's expense.

But she found nothing at all amusing about her current situation. Dismissing the man she'd liked so much better when he'd simply been hacking at her with a sword, she turned her attention back to the one in front of her. "Who are you?"

"Major Clayton Elliott, Home Office Undersecretary." He nodded toward Mrs. Fitzherbert. "And that's Merritt Rivers."

She sliced a sideways glance at him. "So your name really is Merritt." Next, she supposed he'd be attempting to convince her that he truly was a peer of the realm. "How allegorical of your parents."

"Veronica," he volleyed back. "How Catholic of yours."

She smiled tightly. He didn't have a clue... "So now that we know who everyone is, you can release me, and we can all go home."

"Not quite." The undersecretary gestured at her. "We were expecting a man. Ronald Chase, escaped convict from Newgate."

"Ah yes. *Him.*" She forced a curt laugh. "The fault of a court clerk who accidentally wrote down Ronald instead of Roni when he transcribed the trial record." In that, at least, the record had been correct. *Veronica Chase* hadn't done what the conviction was for.

"I don't believe you." Merritt Rivers shook his head. "Everyone in the courtroom could have seen that you were a woman."

"Yes, *if* they were in the court, but the clerk who transcribed the record wasn't," she corrected. "Mistakes occur all the time in the court records—wrong dates, wrong directions, wrong names. Surely, you know that." She dismissed him and turned back to the undersecretary to explain. "The trial lasted less than ten minutes, and I was in Newgate within the hour." She shrugged. "By then, there was no point in the courts wasting time and ink to correct the record when no one cared one whit about me."

"I'm certain they cared when you escaped," the undersecretary drawled. "The prison guards described you as a man."

"And *I'm* certain they didn't want to admit that they'd been outsmarted by a woman."

The man's lips curled faintly.

"How do you know what was in the court records?" Merritt Rivers interrupted.

"I know people in high places." When neither man replied to that, she corrected herself. "All right, I know how to *bribe* people in high places."

"A court clerk?" he drawled sarcastically. "Not exactly a high position."

"The man who controls the word controls the world." She lifted a knowing brow. "I didn't go to university, yet even I know that."

The two men exchanged another silent glance.

All kinds of private communication had been passing between the two since she'd arrived here…wherever here was. The mark of an old and close friendship. They'd placed her in this chair, then they'd huddled together at the side of the room for a long while, speaking in murmurs and whispers. But they couldn't conceal their surprise whenever they'd glanced in her direction. Or their dismay.

"You were convicted of theft and the fencing of stolen goods," the undersecretary stated.

"Among other things." Things she'd never done but would let the world believe she had.

"The judge sentenced you to five years imprisonment."

"Yes."

"According to the records, you thanked him for it," Merritt interjected. "Why?"

"He was lenient." She faced straight ahead, not daring to take a direct look at him. Sparring with him had been a foolish mistake—an absolutely exciting, heart-pounding, blood-coursing mistake. One she'd gladly make again in a heartbeat. "He could have transported me." Or ordered her to swing. Yet how many times during those six months in prison had she thought hanging would have been more merciful than the hell of Newgate?

"After six months," the undersecretary continued with his quiet interrogation, "you managed to escape."

"Yes." From the corner of her eye, she saw Merritt's mouth twist. Was that a grimace or grudging admiration?

"How, exactly?"

She had no intention of answering that. She'd find herself back there soon enough, and—

"She might need to escape that way again, so she won't tell you," Merritt answered for her, as if reading her mind. Oh, he was sharp. Of the two men interrogating her, he was the more dangerous. "There's no point in asking."

Wisely, the undersecretary left that question alone. "You escaped, yet you remained in London. Why?"

Because I had no place else to go. What she'd wanted since she was a girl and lost her mother and home was to find a place where she could belong. This city and the existence she'd stumbled into here wasn't it, she knew that in her bones. It would never be a true home. But Filipe was here, so she'd stayed.

"What better place to disappear than a city like this?" she dodged. *An overcrowded, impersonal rabbit warren of alleys and passageways…where everyone comes and goes and nothing ever seems to be permanent?*

"So you became a thief-taker," he murmured thoughtfully, his eyes narrowing as he studied her.

"I had to support myself somehow. You'd rather I went back to stealing?"

The two men exchanged another glance, another private communication. But this time, Veronica had the feeling that the undersecretary had somehow gained the upper hand over Merritt Rivers.

"How does that work, exactly?" He leaned back on his chair and gestured casually toward her to tell her story, as if they were simply making pleasant conversation. "An escaped convict walking another criminal into the watchmen's house for arrest doesn't seem the best way to avoid attention."

"That's why I don't." Both men's curiosity settled on her, and she explained, "I work with a man named John Fernsby, a former—"

"A former thief-taker with Bow Street who cut his teeth for years as a guard at Newgate before he became a runner," Merritt finished.

A chill passed through her in uneasy warning. How did he know Fernsby?

"One of the few thief-takers who wasn't corrupt." He frowned. "But he's old and arthritic now, can barely walk from one end of Hyde Park to the other."

"He doesn't have to," she corrected. "I bring the criminals to him. He delivers them to the watch, and we split the reward."

"Seems an odd way to make a living," the undersecretary half mused. "You risk being caught yourself."

"I trust Fernsby." *And he knows I'm innocent.* The man told her what she'd needed to know to escape Newgate, for heaven's sake. She trusted him.

"Why not do what most thief-takers do?" Merritt interjected. "Bribe the criminals yourself to let them go and not bring Fernsby and the watch into it at all."

"And destroy all honor among thieves and thief-takers?" She tsked her tongue at him with mocking exaggeration. Then she answered honestly to the undersecretary, "I do it because it helps Fernsby." That wasn't completely a lie. But it also wasn't the only reason. "He has no other way to earn income, and I won't let an old man starve on the streets. Or hurt his pride by simply giving him blunt."

"Told you so," the undersecretary muttered to Merritt, although his eyes never left her.

Merritt said nothing, but his chest rose and fell in an irritated breath beneath his still-crossed arms.

Unease pricked at Veronica's nape. What *exactly* had the two men been discussing about her? She didn't like where this interrogation was going.

"Still seems like an awfully dangerous career for so little in potential reward," the undersecretary considered. "After all, if the criminal you apprehend protests that Fernsby didn't catch him, that it was a woman who did, you'd never be able to appear in court to testify. He'd be set free, and you and Fernsby wouldn't receive your reward."

"What man would publicly claim he was bested in a fight by a woman?" She glanced at Merritt over her shoulder. "I beat you tonight, Mr. Rivers. Did *you* tell your friend that?"

The undersecretary cleared his throat to keep from laughing. "Now that we've established your character—"

"We've done nothing of the sort," Merritt grumbled.

"Now that we've established your character," he repeated, ignoring the interruption, "let me be blunt. While I might not have known you were a woman, I know exactly who you are." His piercing gaze fixed on her. "You're part of a criminal ring in Cheapside that specializes in theft and burglary, stealing goods from the warehouse docks and then fencing them in the market and local shops."

Not at all. She might live among thieves, but she played no part in breaking the law.

"You broke into a storeroom owned by Winslow Shipping and Trade."

No, she'd been arrested long after the storeroom had been burgled, the goods sold, and the money distributed to the poor. After Filipe had been arrested and was awaiting trial, when she'd begged Fernsby to help prove her guilty instead so Filipe would be set free. Then she walked into Bow Street and turned herself in.

"You were tried, pled guilty—you should have hanged."

"Yes." Yet she'd been willing to sacrifice herself for the people who lived with her at the Court of Miracles, those people who had become like family to her. She would have done anything to keep them fed and protected by Filipe and his men, including surrendering her own life. She would gladly do so again.

"But the judge has a personal grudge against Henry Winslow, so he sentenced you to five years in Newgate instead just to irritate the man."

"Lucky me," she replied, deadpan.

With a frown, Merritt interjected, "When you escaped after six months, you returned to Cheapside and took right back up with the same criminals."

"And then, Mrs. Fitzherbert, you caught me and brought me here." She ignored the aggravated darkening of his expression. "But this place isn't Newgate." She cast a glance at the octagonal room around her and the tower that rose overhead before leveling her eyes at the undersecretary. "And it's certainly not the Home Office. So what do you want with me?"

"I want your cooperation with one of our investigations."

She scoffed. "Why should I help you?"

"Because you'll be granted a pardon," Merritt said quietly.

A pardon. Veronica's belly tightened into a knot of longing so fierce that she struggled to hide her wince. Was he serious? God's mercy, she'd do anything for that!

Returning to Newgate would end her.

Merritt Rivers knew it, too, damn him.

She flicked a glance at him. He still stood in his original position against the wall, but now he stared glumly at the rug, not giving her a single look, as if he couldn't stand the thought of what the Home Office was offering. But she knew his attention was riveted on her. Her skin tingled with awareness of it.

"You live among the criminal underworld," he said to the floor.

Well, that was a nice way of calling her a thief.

"Which means you have contacts who can give us information about the men who are inciting the riots."

"What makes you think I can help you with that?"

"Because these aren't normal riots."

She turned in the chair as far as her handcuffs allowed to look directly at him. "What do you mean?"

His brows drew together, distracted. "Riots all have an initial reason for starting, some cause they want to draw attention to, even if the mob strays into sheer destruction once it's underway. But these don't." He pushed himself away from the wall. "Not one of the rioters who's been arrested has pled a greater moral cause in an attempt to persuade the jury toward innocence or used the docket as a pulpit to further his cause."

"Maybe those men who were arrested simply joined in after the riot started and didn't care what its cause was," she argued.

Shaking his head, he slowly came forward, drawn into the interrogation. "Riots have targets. The Gordon Riots targeted papists. Last year's riots over the Corn Laws targeted Parliament and the MPs. The riots this spring in Ely and Littleport targeted shops where the rioters broke in to take food to feed their families. Hell, even those so-called patriotic riots a few years ago attacked houses where the owners didn't illuminate their front doors in honor of war victories. They *all* had targets. But these rioters are randomly attacking anything they come across."

She darted a glance at the undersecretary, whose inscrutable expression gave away none of his thoughts. But he also wasn't looking at her; he was studying Merritt. Very closely.

"There should also have been a trigger."

She blinked. "A trigger?"

"An event that set off the riot that first night, that continued to generate every subsequent riot. But there wasn't any." He blew out a harsh breath. "These riots are unpredictable in their targets, seemingly with no reason but starting as if on cue and dissipating too rapidly... None of it's natural."

"So you're saying these riots are being orchestrated? Why would that be?"

"That's what we need you to help us figure out."

Something about the grim way he said that made her heart stutter. She wanted no part of this. Yet they'd promised her a pardon, a way to both protect Filipe and ensure she'd never go back to the hell of Newgate... She pulled in a deep breath. "What exactly do you want me to do?"

"Work with us to track the movements of a criminal organization we've been following whom we believe is responsible for the riots."

Wariness licked at the backs of her knees. "Which organization?"

"Scepter."

Her body flashed ice-cold, her breath strangling in her throat. Somehow she managed to force out in a fear-driven rasp, "You're out of your bloody minds!"

Merritt joined Clayton Elliott on the other side of the room. "I hate it when you think you're right."

"Because you know I usually am. Including this time." His old friend slanted him a knowing look. "She gives money to a destitute old thief-taker so he won't starve on the streets." Clayton's mouth twisted ruefully. "She's not a hardened criminal."

At that moment, Merritt didn't have any idea what the hell she was.

He'd certainly never seen another woman like her, and not just because of the men's clothes or the arsenal of weapons she'd carried. There was a depth to her that belied her age, a sharp edge and quickness of wit that were nearly as fast as her swordplay. Then there was her intelligence. She was well educated, no doubt about that. Not with the way she spoke, the passing references she'd made…the accent that hinted that English wasn't her first language and lingered just faintly enough that he couldn't place it. She certainly hadn't grown up near the docks on the east side of the City or the rookeries to the west.

So who the devil was she? That is, besides the physical manifestation of everything he'd spent his professional life fighting against and his personal life detesting—a criminal, hardened or otherwise.

"What makes you think she's innocent?" Merritt asked.

"I didn't say innocent," Clayton corrected.

"You're thinking it."

Clayton blew out a breath of irritation that Merritt knew him so well. "What I *think* is that she's not an average criminal. We can use that to our advantage if you still want to go through with this."

"I do." He was determined to find whoever was leading the riots, yet he was distracted by this woman and the unanswered questions about her that swirled in his head. There were too many puzzle pieces he simply couldn't make fit. About both of them.

"You truly think Scepter's involved?" Clayton pressed.

Scepter…a criminal organization that the men of the Armory had all vowed to stop after it attempted to harm two of their own and the women both men cared about. What they'd discovered, though, was that the group's final aims weren't criminal but revolutionary. Scepter wanted to destroy the regency and put an end to what they saw as the monarchy's moral and financial corruption.

But riots fermented among the lower classes. Why would Scepter be behind those? Mobs were too uncontrolled. Too bottom-up. Too…*French* for a group that wanted a revolution led by the aristocracy. Yet the recent riots possessed all the hallmarks of Scepter's involvement.

"I don't know," Merritt muttered, half to himself. "But I'm certainly going to find out." *And stop them before any more innocent people are hurt.*

Clayton turned his back to Veronica. From the bored expression on her pretty face, she didn't care one whit what they were discussing. But both men knew she was alert and paying attention to every move they made, no matter how small.

"Are you doing this because of Scepter?" Clayton shot him a hard look, the same one he'd honed to perfection on the battlefield and now used on his agents in the Home Office. But despite the grim expression, concern laced through his voice when he asked, "Or Joanna?"

Her name hit Merritt like a gut punch. For a moment, he couldn't breathe. He'd never told Clayton about his late fiancée or how she'd died, had never told anyone from his army days—

Brandon Pearce…*Christ.*

He'd told his best friend—once—when they were on the Continent, when he'd been so blasted drunk that he didn't know what he was saying or how his lips had functioned enough to even form the words. Pearce must have told Clayton. *Damn him.*

"Pearce had no right to tell you," Merritt growled.

"He's worried about you." A meaningful pause. "Quite frankly, so am I."

"Well, you can stop worrying. My interest in the riots has nothing to do with Joanna." That was a damned lie. He loved his friends like brothers, yet he didn't want them intruding where they had no business being. "Her death was an accident. The carriage was in the wrong place at the wrong time. The crowd frightened the team, they bolted, and she hit her head." If he told himself that lie enough times, perhaps he could finally come to believe it and push those horrible images of her murder from his mind. "Besides, that happened over five years ago."

"Five or fifty—no difference when it comes to losing the woman you love."

Merritt kept his gaze straight ahead. Unfortunately, that meant looking straight at Veronica. "I think the best way to honor Joanna's memory is to stop the riots and keep others from being hurt, don't you?"

"If that's all you're doing. But if you're doing it out of some sort of revenge—"

"I'm not."

"*If* it's revenge," Clayton repeated, "then you need to give it up right now, because you'll never find it."

An invisible fist squeezed Merritt's chest. He forced himself to breathe slowly, to keep the darkness from his face.

"Five years, a mob of people, an accident—" Clayton shook his head. "You'll never find the people responsible, and even if you did, there's no way to punish them for it now."

Oh yes, there was. He currently stood in the center of an armory, for God's sake, surrounded by a cache of swords and pistols. There were hundreds of ways of punishing the man responsible once Merritt found him.

"Even if you did," Clayton repeated quietly, as if reading the dark thoughts whipping through Merritt's mind, "it won't bring her back."

He knew that. Christ, how he knew that! He was there when she died, and he'd watched three days later when her coffin was lowered into the churchyard. Two weeks after that, he went to the church on the morning of what would have been their wedding day to stare at the empty and silent nave that should have been filled with family and friends. When he'd left the church, he'd gone straight to purchase an army commission. Bribes were paid to secure one as quickly as possible, and within a sennight—and against his father's wishes—he was on his way to the Peninsula, haunted by thoughts of Joanna and how he'd been unable to save her.

After five years, he was still haunted by her. Most likely he always would be.

"It isn't revenge," he repeated.

No, it was far more than that. But he couldn't say what he'd truly been doing in recent months. That he'd been out every night not since the riots started but long before, since shortly after returning from the wars. That it wasn't only the riots that plagued him but all the crimes that needed to be stopped before they happened. That being a barrister wasn't enough, because he wanted to bring the kind of justice to victims that no courtroom ever could. That he was sick and tired of dealing with criminals only after the crimes were committed, after innocents were harmed.

Yet if he revealed all that, Clayton, Marcus, and the other men of the Armory would try to stop him and start a new fight he certainly didn't need.

"Despite what you hope," Clayton warned quietly with a nod at the woman, "you might not be able to convince her to cooperate."

"She wants a pardon." He'd never been more certain of anything in his life. "I saw it in her eyes." The same look he saw in the eyes of desperate men brought before him in court.

"But she also knows about Scepter and what they're capable of."

Of course she did. A criminal turned thief-taker who lived among the worst of London by day and prowled through the streets by night—most likely she'd already seen firsthand the evils they'd committed. While Scepter might have moved on from committing crimes to starting a revolution, they'd begun this latest initiative in the crowded rookeries and gin-soaked alleys of the poorest parts of the city. The parts she would have known by heart.

"Leave her to me." He assured Clayton, "I'll convince her to work with us."

"How?"

When she glanced at them, he boldly met her stare full on. "However it takes."

Three

THE UNDERSECRETARY LEFT WITH A LOUD RATTLE OF METAL doors that vibrated through the old stone building as hard as Veronica's heartbeat slammed against her ribs. Merritt Rivers stared at her silently. He waited for the second clang of the outer door in the courtyard to announce the man's complete departure before approaching her.

He turned the chair around and straddled it, resting his forearms across its back. "So...thief-taker."

She lifted a brow. "Mrs. Fitzherbert."

"Merritt," he corrected.

"Veronica," she conceded grudgingly.

"There. That wasn't so difficult, was it?"

More than he realized. She should never have allowed such familiarity. But they needed each other's help, and maintaining strict formality between them would only work to keep them at odds. He was sharp enough to realize that, too, which was why he'd just forced it upon her.

"Now that's been settled," he said and leaned forward on his forearms, "let's have a nice little conversation, shall we?"

"I've told you. I want nothing to do with Scepter."

"Me either. But it doesn't seem we have much of a choice. I want to stop them from hurting any more innocent people, and you don't want to return to Newgate."

Her eyes narrowed. Why would he care about Scepter? "Are you with the Home Office, too?"

He chuckled. "Only one of us here is mad enough for that." He paused as if to gauge her reaction. "I'm a barrister."

She nearly laughed. He expected her to believe that? "Since when do the Inns of Court provide instruction in swordplay?"

"You'd be surprised at what you can hide beneath those robes and wigs." Another pause, this one with grim undertones, and he admitted, "I learned to fight in the army. With the Coldstream Guards."

"His Majesty's army doesn't teach its soldiers to fight like that."

"No, but some of the best fighters in the world are among its ranks."

"Who have nothing better to do than teach barristers how to fence *a passata sotto*?"

"Lots of time on your hands in the army, you know." A quiet distance invaded his voice. "Mostly long stretches of unbearable boredom punctuated by moments of sheer terror. Learning to fight fills the downtime." He tossed the conversation back at her. "Where did you learn to fight?"

"With His Majesty's army," she flippantly replied. Sometimes nothing hid the truth better than the truth. "Lots of time on my hands. Boredom. Sheer terror." She shrugged, and the shackles on her wrists clinked softly. "You know."

His sensuous lips curled into a tight smile. But she knew he didn't find her at all amusing.

Yet that smile twisted through her, right down to her toes.

He was certainly attractive, all right. It would be a damn shame if something happened to ruin that handsome face of his, so she screwed a hard look of warning on him. "Do you really know what you're getting into with Scepter?"

His smile faded. "Yes." He pushed himself off the chair and crossed to a side table along the wall where a dozen bottles of various golden liquors waited on a silver tray. "Scepter first came after my friends about six months ago." He paused to correct himself. "No, it was two years before that, right when their organization began." With a grim expression, he selected one of the crystal decanters, removed the glass stopper, and turned over one of the half-dozen waiting tumblers. "That was when they'd killed General

Marcus Braddock's sister because she'd learned Scepter was using prostitutes to extort money and favors from powerful men who they then used to increase their operations. Then six months ago, they came after the woman who became the general's wife."

A cold tingle crawled up her back like a spider along her spine. "A personal grudge against the general, then. One that's not worth you riding into the fray and losing your life over."

He smiled grimly at the glass. "Not just the general's family, but my best friend Pearce and his wife as well. Scepter blackmailed her brother into making government appointments that put their men into positions within the government."

"Criminals in the government's employ," she mocked. "I'm aghast."

His mouth tightened at that. "Not to work for the government." He looked up to meet her gaze as he splashed the caramel-colored liquor into the glass. "To start a revolution."

She couldn't possibly have heard... *"Revolution?"* A nervous laugh of disbelief fell from her lips. "You're bamming me."

"I wish I were." He replaced the stopper. "That's why Clayton's involved. The Home Office takes threats of sedition very seriously these days." Carrying the glass with him, he returned to her and once more straddled the chair backward. "Unlike the French, English aristocracy doesn't fancy being separated from their heads."

"No," she muttered, trying to absorb all that he was telling her, "I suppose not."

"So yes, I know all about Scepter and what they're capable of doing," he finished. "And no, I won't turn my back on my friends or my country."

He was either the bravest man she'd met in a very long time or an absolute fool. Right then, she wouldn't have placed a bet on which.

"Clayton wants Scepter at the gallows," he continued, "I want the riots stopped, and you want a pardon. The Home Office, the criminal courts, and the thieves—the perfect unholy trinity, don't you think?"

He held the glass out to her.

In reply, she held up her shackled wrists.

With one hand, he unscrewed the metal cuffs that bound her wrists. They loosened enough that she could slip her hands free and let them drop to the floor with a muted clatter on the rug.

She accepted the drink and took a slow swallow, aware of his stormy blue eyes on her throat as it undulated gently. "Thank you."

"Something told me you'd prefer brandy to tea."

A slow smile unfolded at her lips. "Ah, Mrs. Fitzherbert, how well you know me."

"I'd like to know you better."

Her heart skipped, followed by an immediate stab of self-recrimination. How pathetic she was! He certainly didn't mean his words as a flirtation. Yet a foolish part of her wished they were.

She rose to her feet and turned away before he could see the flush he put into her cheeks. Good God, a blush! She felt like an idiot, being well beyond girlish coquetry. In every way.

But then, he *was* a most unusual man.

Taking another sip to cover any emotions straying across her face, she slowly circled the large room. Stretching her legs felt good after sitting for so long. So did the brandy. And very fine brandy at that. As the warm liquid moved smoothly down her throat, she craned her neck to look up into the darkness of the tall tower, the large gas chandelier overhead unlit. Then she trailed her fingertips along the stone mantel of the massive fireplace as she slowly passed it. The turn about the room was simply a delay tactic to give her time to settle her whirling mind. But with the way he sent little thrills crackling inside her as his eyes followed her, she doubted there were enough hours in the night to put her at ease in his presence.

She stopped to contemplate the shield above the mantel. A

matching one with the same Latin inscription decorated the outer entrance. "*Ubi malum timet calcare*?"

"Where evil fears to tread," he translated, not moving from the chair except to swing around on it to watch her. He was still studying her every move, the same way a fighter observed an opponent. "It's our motto."

"Of course," she murmured dryly. "In Latin. About evil." Then, more loudly, her bewildered mind unable to take it all in, "What *is* this place?"

"This is the Armory." He cast a glance around the room as if attempting to see it through her eyes. "Think of it as a gentlemen's club of sorts for former soldiers returned from the wars."

The light from the gas sconces fell into the adjoining room just far enough to reveal walls decorated with all manner of weaponry. "And the claymores?"

"A gentlemen's club with its own weapons cache," he amended wryly.

"I see." Actually, not at all. But she'd never admit that.

Leaning back in the chair, he kicked out his long legs and crossed them at the ankles. The perfect posture of a gentleman at ease. But she knew he'd pounce in a second if she dared to sprint toward the door.

"The building was originally an old armory established by Charles II in the mid-seventeenth century," he explained.

"And what is it now?"

"A sanctuary."

When she faced him at that puzzling comment, his gaze drifted up to the shield.

"Marcus Braddock, former general and now Duke of Hampton, originally purchased it to use as a warehouse," he continued. "But he decided to renovate it instead."

"With walnut paneling, imported rugs, and a supply of expensive liquor inside ten-foot-thick stone walls?"

"Twenty, actually."

Her lips parted, stunned.

"Home sweet armory," he said drolly. "The general knew it would serve a better purpose as a place where his former subordinates could come to get away from their new lives back in England."

"Is that why you come here, Merritt?" she asked, thinking of the people she lived with in the Court of Miracles and how most of them would do anything to be able to escape that existence. "To get away from your life?"

He paused as if considering an answer. Then he blatantly dodged, "The general's planning on hiring a butler and house-keeper for the place."

"Ah. Roughing it, then, are you?"

An amused smile played at his lips. "There's a kitchen in the basement. Shame to let it go to waste. Might as well put it to use in roasting pheasant dinners." He shrugged. "And the general thinks having someone here watching over us will keep us from running over the settees during fencing matches. He's tired of finding boot prints on the leather."

"Will it?"

"Unlikely."

Hiding her amusement, she gestured toward the adjoining room. "Nice weaponry."

"Thank you."

He said that just arrogantly enough that she couldn't help muttering, "I've always said you can tell a lot about a man from the size of his sword."

"And a woman by hers."

She slid him a knowing glance, just in time to catch the gleam in his eyes.

"Where did you learn to fight?" he persisted. "The truth this time."

Well, he certainly wasn't going to get *that*. "Lots of places, all kinds of instructors…" She finished circling the room and stopped directly in front of him. So close that she could tap his boot with only a small kick of her foot. "Is that why you're offering me a pardon if I help you—because I'm a good fighter?"

"Partially." Then he admitted, "Clayton thinks you might be innocent."

A jolt of electricity snapped through her. The two men couldn't possibly know the truth about her past. No one did, except for Fernsby and Filipe. "And you don't?"

"Not at all."

Her belly tightened, all its tiny muscles ensnarling themselves into a pulsating knot. What this man thought of her shouldn't matter at all. Yet strangely, his answer cut.

Not breaking eye contact with her, he pushed himself to his feet and came to his full height in front of her. And what a height indeed. Surely six feet tall and well over a head above hers, with a lithe and lean body of all muscle and hardness. His dark-brown hair fell carelessly over his forehead as if he couldn't be bothered to trim or brush it. A faint growth of beard darkened his face, except for his bright blue eyes that reminded her of the sky after a summer storm. He was a fighter; every inch of him confirmed it.

But he was also sharp. Quick. *Dangerous.*

He took the brandy from her hand, lifted it to his mouth, and finished off the glass with a single swallow.

"This is the offer," he told her bluntly. "I'll provide whatever resources and guidance you might need, and you'll do the actual groundwork by finding out who's responsible for the riots."

"Reconnaissance, you mean." Acid rose on her tongue. She'd had more than enough of doing that for Allied soldiers on the Peninsula during the wars. She'd sworn to herself she'd never do it again.

"Call it whatever you want. If you agree, you'll work to give me the names of the mobs' leaders, and I'll secure you a pardon."

"And if I don't agree?"

"Then I take you back to Newgate right now."

She would *never* go back to that hell. This devil knew it, too, based on the knowing gleam of his eyes as he waited for her answer. He'd backed her into a corner, damn him.

But she wouldn't be his pawn.

"You'll do what *I* say, every step of the way, understand?" She moved closer and had to tilt back her head to glare up at him, but she wouldn't be cowed. "It's my world you're attempting to infiltrate. I know how it works, what the boundaries are, how to maneuver inside it. If anyone there discovers who you are, you're dead. They'll slit you open from throat to bollocks."

She'd meant to jab a finger into his chest to emphasize her point. But the hard muscle rippled against her fingertip, and beneath that, she felt the steady and strong beat of his heart. The strength of him momentarily took her breath away.

"I won't risk my life to protect yours." Damn her voice for emerging as a throaty purr rather than an icy warning!

"Trust me." Amusement danced across his face. "You don't need to worry about me."

"Trust you?" she echoed. A barrister? *Never.* "That's the first thing that has to go. There *is* no trust in my world. The sooner you learn that, the better off you'll be."

He dropped his gaze to her hand, still at his chest. "So we're agreed, then?"

She yanked her hand away as if she'd touched a hot stove. "Yes." She moved back, desperately needing air and space. "We'll start tonight."

"Good."

"But I'm going to need a coat." She waved a hand at her fighting clothes to indicate that they needed to be hidden. "Because first, I'm taking you shopping for better clothes."

He crossed his arms over his chest...to keep her from touching him again? "What's wrong with my clothes?"

"Nothing, *if* you're trying to resemble a priest." She cast a dubious eye over him, taking in the solid black that allowed him to fade into the night but wouldn't do at all for where she planned on taking him. "Believe me when I tell you that the men I'm going to introduce you to would as likely shoot you dead for being a priest as a barrister."

"Well then," he drawled. "Let's definitely find new clothes."

"Don't worry. I'll make you blend in." She patted his shoulder as she walked past him toward the door and flashed the taunting smile of a crocodile. Right before it snapped its jaws on its prey. "Trust me."

Four

MERRITT GLANCED UP AT THE DERELICT WAREHOUSE IN Saffron Hill that Veronica had brought him to. Three stories tall, the brick and stone building had been exposed to the soot of London coal fires for so long that its façade was dulled beneath a layer of permanent gray. It sat back from the street just far enough to reveal the old loading ramps where wagons had once waited to move goods, its wide loading bay doors now chained and padlocked. Tall, mostly broken windows fronted the building, and splintered boards that had been nailed to the main door to bar unwanted trespassers had been pried off and tossed aside.

"Where the hell have you brought me?" he muttered and readjusted on his shoulder the sacks of apples, oranges, and root vegetables she'd made him purchase at the market.

"Exactly." Veronica started forward into the building. She unbuttoned the greatcoat he'd given her to wear, letting it fall open now that there was no reason to hide her clothes. "Hell."

With a grimace, he followed after her through the doors and into another world.

Inside, the warehouse had been scrubbed clean and white-washed. The sunlight that slanted down from the brief parting of clouds and through the rows of windows brightly lit the place. The open floors that had once been used as storage space for barrels and crates had been broken up into room-like spaces by sheets of old sailcloth hanging from ropes strung between the building's giant supporting posts. A breeze blew through the missing window glass, and the sheets billowed into motion like a marching army of white ghosts. A strong gust blew the sailcloth up far enough to reveal pallet beds laid out upon the old plank floor, pairs of shoes and boots…a doll.

He caught up with her and stopped her with a touch to her elbow from behind. "People live here?"

"*I* live here." She didn't attempt to hide her indignation at his thoughtless question.

Damnation. He'd assumed she was bringing him to nothing more than a warehouse for stolen goods or a storefront for thieves and criminals. He hadn't expected this.

His chest clenched at this glimpse of life in a rookery, and one of the worst in London, too. He'd often prowled its streets during his nighttime patrols, knew the struggles of the people who had no place else to call home. Yet seeing it in broad daylight and being forced to acknowledge the children and elderly who lived here was a completely different experience.

Once more, frustration ate at him that he couldn't do more to help. "I didn't mean—"

"Yes, you did." She shot him a reproachful glance, then slumped her shoulders as she acquiesced. "But you're not wrong. I wouldn't wish this existence on my worst enemy."

She turned away from him then and walked on, and wordlessly, he followed her deeper into the warehouse.

"We call this place the Court of Miracles, after the slum in Paris," she told him as she stopped and reached to take the sacks he carried. She set them on the floor at their feet. "There, the name came from all the beggars who would pretend to use braces and crutches to make people feel sorry enough for them to give them money when they begged. When they returned home at the end of the day, they'd put down their crutches and walk." She drawled mockingly as she opened the burlap sacks, "Miraculously healed."

"Why do you use the same name here, then?" He hadn't seen evidence of that kind of begging ruse being perpetrated here. "What miracles does this place claim?"

She answered quietly, not looking at him, "The simple miracle that any of us have found our way to the safety of this place."

She cupped her hand to her mouth and sent up a call.

People emerged from behind the sailcloth walls around them; others hurried down the wide steps from the floors above. Old men, women of all ages, children...all of them in dirty clothing that was haphazardly mended, some in stocking feet, some truly missing arms and legs. The children, especially, crowded around Veronica, with the smallest urged on by the elderly. She reached into the sack of oranges, and beaming a smile, she handed them out to the children one at a time as each came forward and mumbled their thanks.

She gestured for one of the old men to hand out the apples for her. Then she called one of the women to her and gave her the sack of root vegetables. "Dorothy, make a big pot of stew out of these for dinner for the Court." She slipped the woman a sovereign coin and lowered her voice, but Merritt overheard. "Take this to the market and buy as much meat and bread as you can to add to the stew, all right?"

With her eyes glistening with gratitude, the woman nodded and carried away the sack toward what Merritt assumed was the building's makeshift kitchen somewhere at the back of the lot.

He stared at Veronica as she continued to hand out the fruit, struck by her sympathy and kindness. It wasn't only a pretense for him either, as none of the people seemed surprised by the act, which meant she distributed food like this regularly.

Grudgingly, he was beginning to think perhaps Clayton might be right about her. Not about her innocence—he'd yet to see anything that contradicted what he knew about that—but about her good character. He knew a lot of good people who had been forced into breaking the law. Perhaps she was one.

Yet he was still a long way from trusting her.

A boy who couldn't have been more than three or four was

urged forward by his mother. "Go on," the woman ordered. "Go thank Miss Roni."

His round face turned red as he shyly mumbled, "Thank you, Miss, for the new coat."

Veronica knelt down in front of him to bring her eyes to his level. She gave him a bright smile as she fussed with the lapels of the too-large wool coat that draped over his small frame like a tent. "You are very welcome, William."

"And for the boots and gloves, too," his mother reminded him.

"Too," he repeated softly.

"I'll find a hat for you next, shall I?" To seal her promise, Veronica tousled his bright red hair. "I think I deserve a hug in reward, don't you?"

He hugged her. She wrapped her arms around him, then brought her mouth to his ear and whispered something Merritt couldn't hear. But William nodded. Satisfied, she let him go.

"Go see Mr. Thurman in the Burr Street market," Veronica quietly told William's mother as she rose back to her feet. "He's got a bundle of clothes waiting for you."

The woman shook her head. "Really, Miss, I can't accept—"

"I didn't." Veronica nodded toward Merritt. "*He* did."

Clearly, the woman didn't believe her, yet she told him, "Thank you, sir."

"It was nothing," he admitted, the ironic truth of which made Veronica smile. Apparently, he'd purchased more from the clothing stall in the market than his own set of workman's clothes.

When the last of the apples were handed out, the crowd disappeared back behind the makeshift sailcloth walls. Veronica began to walk away, but Merritt stopped her with a tug on her arm.

He lowered his mouth to her ear so no one could overhear. "You buy clothing for children?"

"I buy all kinds of things for everyone, when whatever they need can't be acquired any other way."

In other words—stolen. But the defensive way she uttered that explanation and the reminder of who she was didn't lessen the kindness at the act's heart. He pressed, "Why would a criminal who pled guilty to theft spend her own money to—"

"This way," she interrupted and pulled her arm away from him to move on. "There's someone I want you to meet."

Their conversation was over. For now. But he certainly didn't plan on letting this go, not when he had so many unanswered questions.

He followed her through the fluttering sheets and up a set of wide, sturdy steps at the rear of the building. No one they passed paid him any attention. But then, she'd dressed him to fit in.

When they'd left the Armory that morning, Veronica had kept to her word. She'd taken him shopping, but not to a tailor. Instead, she'd brought him to the local market. There, among its produce stalls and livestock, she'd found a seller of old clothes and searched through the piles of castoff dresses, shirts, trousers… Mostly, the articles were of fine quality, and Merritt recognized the work of some of Bond Street's best tailors. He wasn't surprised. Clothes were usually given to servants when their employers no longer wanted them; those servants then sold them to the rag and bone man for whatever pennies they could to supplement their low wages. As was their contracted right. But somewhere in the pile of castoff finery, she'd managed to find a pair of workman's trousers and a coarse brown waistcoat, stained shirt, and jacket that was slightly too large across his shoulders. Then she'd rubbed them all on the ground to dirty them up and make it look as if he were a manual laborer, like someone who was part of her world.

They reached the top floor of the old warehouse where two large men stood guard. The men nodded their greeting to Veronica, then coolly stepped in front of Merritt to block his way.

"I'm taking him to meet Filipe," she informed them.

The guards nodded. Then, without warning, they pounced.

They grabbed Merritt and shoved him up against the wall. One of the giants held him pinned in place, his face pressed into the boards and his arm twisted behind his back, while the other searched him for weapons. He knew not to fight them.

The guard found the knife strapped to Merritt's left forearm, slid it free of its sheath, and tossed it to the floor. It stuck in the wooden plank by its blade with a dull *thunk*. The guard signaled that Merritt was clean of weapons, and the other man released him.

The two men stepped back to let them pass.

They walked on, with Merritt shooting the guards a dark look as Veronica led him past a series of storerooms toward the rear of the building.

"You could have warned me about that," he grumbled as he rubbed at his shoulder.

A sly smile curled her lips. "And miss all the fun?"

One of the storeroom doors had been left open, and he glanced inside. Barrels, crates, and sacks of all sizes sat stacked inside, all of them sporting different marks and brands from various warehouses.

"Some of the people who live here are thieves," she explained quietly, noting where his attention had gone.

"Like you?" Her criminality grated at him, although he couldn't say why it should matter. After all, he was around criminals every day, including those who had committed far worse crimes. Except that with her, it did.

She wisely ignored his baiting question. "They break into warehouses and ships across the city, take whatever goods they can, and bring them here for temporary storage."

"That's what you were sent to Newgate for, wasn't it?" He matched her low voice. "Stealing from a warehouse."

"Any cloth and food are distributed immediately to people in the rookery," she continued, not answering. "That's one of the conditions of being allowed to live here in the Court of Miracles—if they're able, they have to be willing to hand out goods to those who need them."

"And face the consequences in court if they're caught," he mumbled.

"It's a risk they're willing to accept to have a safe space to live, with a roof over their heads and food in their bellies."

Was that why she participated in the thefts, to keep herself off the streets? Or did she do it because she enjoyed the thrill of breaking the law? God knew she'd seemed to enjoy their sparring last night as much as he had.

"If they don't want to help, they're free to leave. No one's kept here against their will."

"Including you?"

She didn't answer. Her gaze remained straight ahead.

"And the goods that aren't cloth and food?" He pivoted the conversation. "What do you do with those?"

"They're scattered across stalls at the local markets and sold, and the profits are handed out to people in the rookeries to pay for rent or to buy bread and milk." They stopped in front of the last door. "The men only target those merchants and lords who can afford to lose a few goods, and they never take the entire lot."

"Taking from the rich to give to the poor?" he muttered. "Who are you trying to be—Robin Hood's merry men?"

"Yes." She knocked on the last door. "And now I'm going to introduce you to Robin Hood."

She shoved it open.

Like the rest of the warehouse, the whitewashed room was flooded in sunlight. Pieces of old but serviceable furniture sat scattered throughout, including an old stove in the corner with its pipe snaking up through a hole in the side wall. The same sailcloth that served below as walls hung here as drapes on the windows, although unlike the rest of the windows in the warehouse, these were protected by sets of iron bars. The same bars Merritt had glimpsed on the windows in the storage room.

But it was the man who stood in front of the windows who dominated the space. Tall and solidly built, with a Mediterranean complexion and curly dark-brown hair, he gave rapid-fire orders to the two men who were with him, men just as large as the two who guarded the stairs.

He looked up when they entered, his expression freezing for a beat before he smiled at Veronica. Then he slid an assessing look over Merritt from head to boots.

"Filipe," Veronica called out to him as she came forward, "am I interrupting business?"

"You are never an interruption." He took her hands and kissed both her cheeks in greeting. His mouth lingered at her ear as his eyes narrowed on Merritt over her shoulder. "And you've brought a friend."

Merritt tensed. The protective way the man said that…was he jealous? Was that why Veronica lived here, because the man was her lover?

He released Veronica and strode toward Merritt. His hand was outstretched, although certainly more to check that Merritt wasn't palming a weapon than in greeting.

"Filipe Navarre," the man introduced himself.

"The King of Saffron Hill," Veronica added in explanation to Merritt. "You'd said you'd heard of him last night when we met."

He'd said no such thing. Apprehension tightened his gut. What game was she forcing him into? Yet he played along and confirmed, "I did."

Filipe smiled, although not with pride but chagrin. "Being known is not a benefit in my business." His tight smile turned icy. "And who are you?"

Merritt's mind blanked. Damnation, he *really* needed to work on that secret identity.

"This is Mr. Herbert," Veronica piped up, saving him. In a way. "First name Fitz."

He clenched his jaw. Damn that little minx.

"He's a porter on the docks. I ran into him last night when I was stalking for Fernsby. That's why I was late returning this morning. We had a long talk, and I couldn't get away." Her eyes gleamed with private amusement at his expense. "It was almost as if he were holding me prisoner."

He wanted to throttle her.

"So why did you bring him to me?" Filipe asked. "I don't need a porter."

"But you do need a porter who has information about what goods will be arriving to the warehouses and when," she answered. "That information could prove valuable."

Filipe flicked a glance at Veronica as he considered her explanation. "We don't pay for services, Herbert. We expect honor among thieves here." In his voice, Merritt caught the same accent that faintly colored Veronica's. So familiar...yet he couldn't place it. "I'm certain Roni told you that. So why would you want to help us?"

He glanced at Veronica, waiting for her to jump into the conversation and once more prod him along in the direction she wanted him to go in this dangerous game she was playing.

But she didn't. She simply waited silently with Filipe for his answer.

Cold realization poured over him like a bucket of ice water. Not a game—*a test*. And if he didn't pass it, he wouldn't walk out of this place in one piece. Most likely the two guards at the stairs would slit his throat with his own knife.

Lesson learned the hard way. He'd never underestimate her again.

"I have a big family and little pay." He spun the story, drawing on the setup she'd given him and careful to make his pride sound wounded at having to ask for help. "At the docks, the companies don't give a damn whether your family starves or not, but they still expect you to break your back moving their goods." And just the right amount of bitterness. "I'm tired of having to choose between bread and rent."

He didn't glance at Veronica directly and kept his focus on Navarre. But from the corner of his eye, he could see her lips twitch. The infuriating little hellcat was enjoying this.

"My wife grew ill and can't take in mending or washing now," he explained. "The loss of that blunt hit us hard."

"I'm certain it did," Navarre mumbled, his face too inscrutable to tell if he believed the story, while beside him, Veronica's eyes danced with amusement. "How many children do you have?"

"Eight."

She cleared her throat to hide a laugh.

His voice cracked just a bit as he added, "And two wee ones already in the churchyard."

Her laugh strangled in her throat. Merritt knew that part of the story would prove too close to reality for her comfort, as most children born in the rookeries and slums didn't live to see their fourth birthday.

"I can't find the means to feed and clothe them, and I don't want them out on the streets, fending for themselves. I don't want to sell my boys into apprenticeships or the girls into service, of any kind."

The shine in her eyes dulled, and all her amusement at testing him vanished. The grim truth behind what he was saying hit her visibly. That was the real lot of most poor families in London— their children forced into becoming chimney sweeps, washer-women, scullery maids, night soil men...prostitutes.

"Miss Chase told me about the Court of Miracles, how you help those who are willing to help others." When Merritt saw Navarre's gaze flick to Veronica, he knew the man believed him. "So I want to negotiate a trade. I'll share with you what I learn about ships' manifests and warehouse contents, and you'll let me move my family here. All of them. They're young and small yet. They won't take up much space." When Navarre seemed to waver, Merritt added, "They won't be any trouble, I promise."

"I'm certain they won't be." Navarre hesitated, and fear burst through Merritt that his story hadn't been believable enough— then the man gave a decisive nod. "We'll give it a try. Settle your family here first, then we'll meet and talk. You'll have no worries about your decision." He slapped Merritt on the back as he walked away to rejoin the other man and resume their interrupted conversation. He sent Veronica a smile over his shoulder. "As long as Roni guarantees your character, that is."

Merritt sliced her a glare angry enough to scald.

But the little minx simply smiled. "I do. Thank you, Filipe."

"Yes," Merritt seconded, "thank you."

"No need. Give your gratitude to Roni." He turned his attention back to the previous conversation.

"Oh, I'm certain I will," he muttered, which only widened her smile.

She gestured for him to follow her from the room. "I'll introduce him to Ivy," she called out to Navarre, "let her find a place for his family and explain to them how everything works here."

Navarre distractedly grunted his agreement. He'd already dismissed Merritt from his mind in favor of more important business.

As soon as the door closed behind them, Merritt grabbed her elbow and pulled her to a stop. "Is that why you brought me here?" he seethed, lowering his mouth to her ear so his anger wouldn't be overhead by the two giants guarding the stairs. "To test me?"

"Oh no. That was merely a delightful bonus."

When the two guards glanced down the hall at them, she smiled and slid her arm away. She walked on and made him fall into step beside her.

"If you're going to infiltrate this world, then you have to do it from within. What we just did creates a history for you and a set of people you can point to here who are willing to swear to your identity. You have to have that before anyone will trust you."

"But you said there was no trust in your world."

"Exactly."

He stopped her at the top of the stairs. Turning to the nearest guard, he gestured at the floor. "May I?"

The man nodded.

With a grimace, Merritt yanked his knife out of the floorboard. He sheathed it in his sleeve as he followed her downstairs.

"But you trust Navarre," he said quietly over her shoulder.

"With my life."

Dark irritation corkscrewed through him. Yet it wasn't jealousy. *Couldn't* possibly have been, not for someone like her. He'd spent his adult life fighting criminals and upholding the law. Still, a bitter heat grated unexpectedly at his gut at the thought of any intimacies between her and Filipe Navarre, and it compelled him to ask, "Are you and he…?"

"Like brother and sister?" An inscrutable expression slipped across her face as easily as the clouds gathering once more over the city, blocking out the sunlight and turning the warehouse gray. "Yes. We grew up together in Portugal."

Portugal…so *that* was the accent he heard coloring her voice.

"I consider him to be my brother. Just as I consider everyone here to be my family."

That was why she hadn't fled London when she escaped from Newgate, he realized. She couldn't leave her family here, just as he could never leave his father or the men of the Armory.

She stepped off the stairs onto the first floor and called out through the sea of gently moving sailcloth, "Ivy!"

A soft voice answered. Veronica smiled with affection as she followed it through the sailcloth maze, with Merritt trailing after her.

A young woman of no more than fifteen or sixteen pulled back one of the sheets and stepped out to greet Veronica with a big hug that broadcasted her worry.

"Where have you been?" the blond girl scolded. She possessed a grace and regal bearing that belied the threadbare clothes she wore, although she'd done her best to alter them to resemble the current fashions donned by society women, right down to the ribbon at the high waist of her dress. "When you didn't return on time, I was worried something had happened to you."

Something *had* happened, but Merritt knew Veronica wouldn't divulge where she'd been. Or why. Instead, she eased Ivy's worry by tenderly brushing a stray curl from the girl's forehead.

"I met someone last night." She nodded toward Merritt and sent Ivy's attention to him.

Big brown eyes slid curiously over him. Then her face lit up, and dread spiraled through Merritt to his boots. He knew that look—she wore that same expression as marriage-minded mamas who were looking to add a barrister to their families.

"He's very handsome," Ivy tried to whisper privately to Veronica. "I think he likes you."

But Merritt heard every matchmaking word and fought back a sardonic smile. *Like?* What he felt for Veronica Chase was raw lust flavored with disdain, irritation, frustration—nothing anywhere close to *like*.

"He's married," Veronica corrected. To Merritt's relief, she'd fallen easily into playing along with his fabricated tale. "And he likes everyone. He's a nice man." His chest warmed at the compliment, although that sentiment was undercut when she added, "But he carries a knife."

The girl shrugged her slender shoulders, as if men with knives were the most ordinary thing in the world. The sun rose in the east, rain fell down, men always carried knives…

"You have yours with you, of course?" Veronica asked casually, like an older sister making certain her sibling hadn't forgotten her pelisse against the cold.

With a nod, the girl lifted her skirt to reveal the sheath she wore strapped to her stocking.

Merritt blinked. He shouldn't have been surprised; he knew the everyday dangers faced by people who lived in the rookeries. Yet the sight of an innocent, pretty girl so nonchalantly checking for her knife… *Good God.*

"Ivy, this is Mr. Herbert," Veronica introduced, somehow managing to keep her lips from twitching with laughter at his expense. "He's going to be moving his family into the Court. His very large family." At that, she gave up all hope of hiding her amusement and laughed aloud. "Filipe wants you to find a place for them and explain the rules."

"Of course. Welcome to the Court of Miracles, Mr. Herbert."

The smile the girl gave him was purely angelic. If she were a gentleman's daughter, men would be fighting to marry her and give her a life of luxury and ease. But here she'd be lucky to live to see her twenty-fifth birthday.

He cleared his suddenly tight throat. "Thank you."

Veronica took Ivy's upper arms and turned the girl's attention back to her. "There's something else." She cast a quick look around to make certain no one else lurked nearby, watching them or listening in through the sailcloth. Then she reached beneath her leather bodice and withdrew a small bag of coins. She placed it in Ivy's hand. "For you, for your sister and her baby."

Ivy's face fell at the kindness, and her eyes glistened instantly with unshed tears. "Oh, Roni! You really don't need to keep—"

"I want to," she interjected, cutting her off before Ivy said more than Merritt was obviously meant to hear. She lowered her voice, but he could just make out the words. "It's to go directly to the rent and for bread and milk for the baby, understand? Your sister's husband isn't to touch one farthing of it." She placed a kiss to her forehead and whispered what Merritt *certainly* wasn't meant to hear: "If you or your sister give him even so much as a ha'penny, you'll never receive more, understand?"

Ivy nodded and threw her arms around Veronica's neck. Gratitude beamed on her face.

"Now put that away in your pocket, and go visit the landlord and baker before it rains again," Veronica ordered. She released the girl with an affectionate squeeze of her hands. "And make certain you leave well before her husband comes home and finds you there. You know how he can be."

The girl's expression darkened with fear, reminding Merritt of a dog that had been beaten. But only for a moment before she hugged Veronica again and tucked the bag into the hidden pocket in the folds of her skirt, safely out of sight. She gave a parting wave in afterthought to Merritt as she bounced toward the stairs, then down through the warehouse to the street.

Curiosity pricked at him, and he scrutinized Veronica, taking another assessing look at her. Food, coats and boots, now rent money… She protected the people who lived here as if they truly were her blood family, along with Fernsby, who got half her thief-taking earnings to begin with.

Merritt would have admired her for her generosity if he didn't suspect she'd broken at least half a dozen laws to do so.

She stepped to the end of the makeshift hall and pulled back a curtain of sailcloth used as a door, one that separated off the rear corner of the warehouse. Through the gap in the cloth, he saw her living quarters. The small space was crowded by an old velvet chair, a narrow bed, and a tall armoire with brass locks that were shiny from frequent use. He knew why. Where society ladies kept their accessories, Veronica Chase kept her weapons. Not an armoire but an armory.

"What next?" he asked when she turned to face him.

"You'll return to the Armory and wait for me there." She

shrugged out of his greatcoat that he'd given her earlier and handed it to him, then blocked his way so he couldn't enter her room. "I'll come for you tonight."

He nearly laughed. Did she think he was that daft? "And I'm supposed to just leave you here, to trust that you won't decide to renege on our deal and flee London after all?"

"Yes. You are." She flung the curtain closed.

Five

THE WATERMAN'S BOAT SKIMMED ACROSS THE THAMES toward a set of cement steps leading up from the river. Unease moved inside Veronica as fast as the river beneath them and swirled like the eddies they were gliding through just west of London Bridge.

Around them, the city felt alive in the midnight darkness. She could feel it humming like electricity despite the layer of drizzle and fog that continued to press in upon its streets and squares for another night. Something was coming, awakening in the darkness—she could feel it in her bones the way old sailors felt oncoming storms. And not a little part of it had to do with the man sitting beside her, who would certainly love to wash his hands of her as soon as possible. After all, he'd made no attempt to hide his contempt about the thief he thought her to be.

The boat's bow scraped against the embankment wall as the waterman expertly guided it to a sideways stop at the base of the steps.

Merritt hopped out of the boat, then reached down to help her.

She hesitated. There would be no turning back once she stepped onto the stairs with him. But that was the rub, wasn't it? In her life, there was never any choice of going back.

With resolve, she slid her hand into his and allowed him to bring her to her feet in the gently rocking wherry. Then she hitched up her skirt and stepped up onto the stone ledge.

"I wasn't going to toss you into the Thames, you know," he muttered, misunderstanding her hesitation.

No, just back into Newgate. But she would never admit to any uncertainty in front of him. Instead, she slyly smiled from behind the voluminous hood of her cape and lied. "I was contemplating tossing *you*."

That he would certainly believe. But when he returned her smile with a grin of his own, its warmth seared through her as much as his hand that still rested at the small of her back. The heat of his palm bled through her cape and dress and into her flesh, and her heart fluttered recklessly.

"As if I didn't know that." He turned back to toss the waterman a coin and ordered the man to wait for them, then took her elbow to guide her up the rough steps. "With every row of the oars from Blackfriars."

She pulled in a deep breath of relief. They were back to distrust. *Good.* Distrust she knew how to handle, knew to expect nothing from it but disappointment. After all, suspicion had kept her alive in the past, and it would keep her alive after she'd received her pardon. And long after Merritt Rivers was gone from her life.

"This way." She gestured across the street at the dimly lit tavern.

Although to call it a tavern was being generous. It was a mix of gambling hell, gin palace, and brothel, all crammed into a small building that had seen better days under the rule of the Stuarts. But its riverside location made it the perfect haunt for criminals, porters, and sailors to stumble into, waste away whatever blunt they'd managed to earn that day, and then stagger back out at dawn, many right into the Thames for an icy-cold dunking. It was also the perfect location for Filipe and his men to keep watch on the wharves. That was how she knew the place.

In the past eighteen months since leaving Portugal, she had been here only a handful of times. But that was enough to establish her credibility among its clientele, and as the sister of the King of Saffron Hill, she could come and go as she pleased without fear of being accosted. Any man foolish enough to try would find himself spiked on London Bridge. *If* enough of him remained once Filipe was done with him.

Yet tonight, inexplicably, she felt even safer with Merritt.

As he led her inside, she fanned an assessing look over him. He still wore the workman's clothes she'd found for him that morning, with all his weapons cleverly hidden from sight. She took comfort in that. The plain dress and cape she wore gave little room for weapons of her own, and she felt vulnerable with only a single knife strapped to her right calf.

"Welcome to the King's Arms," she drawled. She scanned the smoke-filled room around her, searching for anyone who—

Danker.

Her eyes narrowed on him as he sat at the card table in the rear of the tavern, his back to the corner so he could see whoever came through the door. So no one could sneak up behind him and slit his throat. Danker had his fingers in every simmering illegal pot in London from prostitution to smuggling to child slavery. If anyone had heard rumblings of who was behind the riots, it would be him.

Yes, he would do. Nicely.

She signaled to the bar wench for a glass of whiskey as she moved through the crowded room with Merritt following closely behind. He was so alert and ready to respond to any attack that she could feel the tension dripping from him.

She stopped at the table. Danker looked up from his cards.

She gestured at the pile of coins and banknotes. "I hope you're winning."

"Always." He swept his gaze over Merritt, then turned over one of his cards and tossed another coin into the center of the table. His opponent folded and left. "I see you've brought a guard dog."

She slid a half-hooded glance over her shoulder at Merritt, her only acknowledgment that he was there. She gestured at the chair across from Danker. "May I?"

He waved a hand, and she sat. Merritt remained on his feet directly behind her. His right hand held his left wrist, his fingers only inches from the handle of the knife hidden up his sleeve.

A guard dog indeed.

"I need information." She lowered her voice so it wouldn't drift beyond the table. "Everyone knows you have the best."

"I suppose that would depend upon the information." Danker's voice was little more than a wheezing, rough rasp. Most likely, that was due to a lifetime of smoking and drinking. And to the scar that circled his neck where the noose that failed to kill him had cut into his throat and crushed his windpipe. "What do you want to know?" He reached for one of the coins and tossed it to the bar wench as she placed a glass of whiskey on the table in front of Veronica. "And how much are you willing to pay for it?"

She raised the glass in a toast of thanks, then took a sip. "What do you know about the recent riots and who's behind them?"

A crocodile smile spread across the man's face, ghoulishly mirroring the scar at his throat. He leaned back in his chair and nodded at Merritt. "You can't expect to be given that kind of information in front of a stranger."

"He's not a stranger." She kept her gaze fixed on Danker, her face impassive. "He's a barrister in league with the Home Office." The truth was too ludicrous to resist. "What's not to trust?"

Danker laughed. The wicked and hellish sound vibrated at his vocal cords like a rusty blade scraping over a metal file.

"You know me." This time, she took a healthy swallow of her drink. "Do you think I'd bring along someone I don't trust with my life? Someone Filipe wouldn't trust with me?"

Danker pinned him beneath an assessing look. "He's a Miracle Worker?"

Miracle Workers...the nickname that had been bestowed upon Filipe's men. She'd expected that question, which was why she'd taken Merritt to the Court of Miracles that morning to introduce him to Filipe and why she hadn't warned him to leave his knife behind. She'd needed the guards to remember him, and they'd never forget a man with enough spine to carry a weapon to pay homage to the King. She'd carefully constructed that incident so if Danker asked around about Merritt after they left the tavern, any suspicions about his true identity would be quashed.

"Mr. Herbert is a new recruit." There—she'd worked in the name. Another way for Danker to place Merritt in the Court. And as a bonus, another chance to irritate Merritt. "He's helping with a matter for Fernsby."

Danker knew she'd taken up work as a thief-taker, as did most of the men around Filipe. The idea of honor among thieves was a myth, and they were willing to overlook what she was doing as long as she went after the petty criminals who existed on the fringes of their world. As long as she left them alone and didn't interfere in their business.

But if she ever crossed that line, she would be a dead thief-taker.

"Fernsby! That old bastard?" Danker let out another rasping laugh. "Still paying him off for that favor, are you?"

Her spine stiffened. For the first time, she wished Merritt had waited outside. She didn't want him to know anything about that. "You mean like the way you have yet to repay me for the favor I did for you?"

That silenced Danker. If the tavern weren't so dark, she might have seen steam roll off his bald head.

"I stumbled across a couple of rioters the other night and took one of them," she explained, falling easily into her story and suffering no guilt at lying to Danker. "When Fernsby delivered him to the watchhouse, the constable offered twice the reward if we could provide the names of the men who instigated the riot. Money's not so common in the Court these days that I'm willing to pass up easy blunt. So what can you tell me about them? What have you heard?"

Danker twirled a coin between his stained fingers. "Only rumors. Nothing specific, mind you."

"Of course not," she drawled, not bothering to hide the sarcasm.

"But there's talk of a man named Smathers who's been paying former soldiers to attack the city. He's the one you and Fernsby need to take for the reward."

"Why soldiers?" Merritt interrupted.

"Why not soldiers?" Danker's gaze darted over her head to Merritt. "They need the money and can't find work, yet they're physically strong and loyal and follow orders without question." He sneered pointedly. "And they know how to keep their silence."

"What do you know about Smathers?" Veronica pressed, drawing his attention back to her when she felt Merritt's irritation begin to simmer.

"Nothing much." He dropped the coin onto the table. "An old soldier himself recruiting men down at the east wharves."

"Where?"

"The Ship's Bell."

She knew that tavern. It made this place look like a Mayfair garden club in comparison.

"He pays the men to meet at a specific place and time—ten o'clock at Paternoster, midnight at All Hallows."

Times and places where two of the recent riots had started. Her heartbeat spiked. They'd found their connection to the riots' leaders.

"Once the signal's given, the men move forward through the city wherever they want to go and stop at an agreed upon time." He gave a toothless grin of admiration. "Destruction by appointment."

Yet none of it made sense. "Why would he pay men to riot? What is he gaining by it?"

Danker shrugged a crooked shoulder that had taken the brunt of too many lost fights. "Don't know."

"What are they told to attack?" Some kind of pattern or target might give her a clue about why. And who.

"Don't know. Don't care." He formed the coins into small stacks in front of him, preparing for the next round of cards. "That's all I can tell you." He leaned back in his chair and fixed a deadly stare on her. "I trust this means my favor's been repaid."

"Only if it proves valuable, Danker. I would hate to think you've sent me on a wild goose chase." She enjoyed one last gasping swallow of whiskey before she stood, then smiled coldly at him. "Or what it would mean about the way I'd collect from you then."

With that threat still lingering in the smoke-filled air between them, Merritt escorted her from the tavern.

Six

MERRITT STOPPED VERONICA AT THE TOP OF THE RIVER STEPS with a touch to her arm. Below in the watery shadows, the waterman waited with his wherry to return them upriver.

They had a name now for one of the men connected to the riots, had a location where he'd been recruiting rioters. But details about that conversation with Danker pricked at him. He wanted to be able to trust her, yet there was too much she was keeping hidden.

He leaned down to bring his mouth close to her ear. "Danker said you'd repaid a favor. What favor?"

"There's more currency in the rookeries than blunt, especially among those who don't have ready access to pounds and pence. We also have a barter system of sorts." She paused to fuss with her cloak as if to bundle up against the cold for the boat ride. "If I do a favor for someone, I can call for one in return." She tugged at her kid gloves. "I did a favor for Danker last year. His horse was stolen from its stable, and I found it and returned it. Tonight, he paid me back."

"Not that favor," Merritt clarified. "The one Fernsby did for you."

She stiffened. "It was nothing important."

"Why don't I believe you?"

She arched a brow at him over her shoulder. "Because you possess an overdeveloped sense of suspicion and mistrust?"

"Or because you're hiding the truth. What favor?" He had no intention of continuing toward the wherry until she provided answers. "Newgate is nice at night, don't you think?"

His threat was clear. So was the aggravation in her voice as she grudgingly admitted, "Fernsby helped me during my trial, so now I'm obligated to help him."

"A thief-taker helped a criminal in court?" And pigs flew. "I've witnessed more trials than I can count, and I've never once seen a thief-taker work to prove someone innocent."

She mumbled into the shadows, "Who said he was trying to prove me innocent?"

She tugged her arm free, flipped up her hood, and started down the steps before he could stop her again.

Oh no. That little minx was going nowhere until he had answers.

He darted down in front of her and blocked her path on the stairs. "What do you mean by that?"

Now level with his, her eyes gleamed in the darkness from beneath her hood. He could practically see the thoughts spinning through that sharp mind of hers as she tried to come up with an explanation he would believe. He didn't doubt for one moment that the little minx wouldn't lie to him to keep her—

She cupped his face between her hands and kissed him.

Surprised, he caught his breath as her warm lips touched his. The kiss was nothing more than a feathery tickle, a soft whisper so light that he found himself leaning toward her to increase the pressure beyond this mere teasing. *Sweet Lucifer.* She tasted of wine and adventure, spiced oranges and exotic places…*danger*. And he drank her in.

Her lips were soft and supple as they caressed his. Amazement swept through him that she should be so delicate beneath the hard surface she showed to the world, that he could taste an uncertainty in her that suggested a deeper vulnerability. The intrigue of her simply captivated him.

She was kissing him merely to distract him. No other reason. He wasn't arrogant enough to believe otherwise. Yet that didn't stop his blood from heating as the pressure of her lips increased, as the kiss turned hungrier and more demanding. Nor did it stop the faint groan that rose from his throat when she brushed one hand down his chest while the other slipped behind his head. She sifted her fingers through the hair at his nape in long, slow caresses that scraped her fingertips provocatively into his scalp.

His heartbeat jumped at that unwittingly erotic touch. She might be vulnerable down deep, yet the hellcat in her was never far from the surface.

As if to prove that, she took his bottom lip between her teeth and bit. The sharp nip pulsed straight to the tip of his cock and shocked all sense from his mind, just long enough for her to slip past him and glide down the steps to the safety of the wherry. She smiled brightly at the waterman as he gave her his hand to help her into the boat and onto the front bench as if she were a helpless miss.

Merritt felt like a damned fool.

But she wasn't getting away that easily. With a grin, he sauntered down the steps after her.

She refused to look up at him as he stepped into the rocking wherry and sat close to her on the bench. *Very* close. Nor did she look at him when he slipped his left arm behind her to grasp the edge of the seat and bring himself even closer. But he heard the hitch of her breath, as soft as the water lapping against the wooden boat.

Aware of the waterman at the rear of the boat as he pushed them away from the steps and took up the oars, Merritt lowered his mouth to her shoulder and murmured through the fabric of her hood, "That was a pleasant kiss."

"You're welcome."

His lips curled into a half grin. "I wasn't thanking you."

"You should." She kept her face straight ahead, her attention riveted on the dark ribbon of river stretching before them. She didn't dare to dart him even half a glance from beneath her hood as she added, "Obviously, being kissed by a woman isn't a common occurrence for you."

"You'd be surprised."

She sighed heavily. "Very much so."

He refused to rise to her bait. "And you often go about kissing men on watermen's stairs, do you?"

"Doesn't every woman?"

"None I've ever known."

"Then you've been spending time with the wrong women."

"Very much so," he repeated her words with the same mocking sigh. "As I said, that was a pleasant kiss, but not pleasant enough to make me forget about Fernsby."

"You were thinking of Fernsby while kissing me?" Her brows shot upward. "I don't know whether to be offended or shocked."

"Believe me." He reached up to push back the side of her hood, then brought his mouth to her bare ear and purred, "When you were kissing me, I was definitely thinking about you."

She gave a short laugh. "Why on earth would you do that?"

"Because you're beautiful."

She turned her head sideways to stare at him, for once stunned into silence. Instead of the cutting reply he expected, she stiffened, and he could almost feel the speeding of her pulse. Apparently he wasn't the only one affected by that kiss.

He took advantage of the moment by caressing her bottom lip with his thumb. His gaze fell to her mouth as he outlined her lips with his fingertip. She quivered in response.

"That copper-colored hair of yours that you let fall wild and untamed, those piercing green eyes…that creamy smooth skin…"

He wasn't lying. Not one word. She *was* beautiful, and tonight she glowed brighter than moonlight in the soft halo of the waterman's lamp. Even knowing who she was and why they were together, he couldn't resist touching her and caressed his knuckles over her cheek. She was simply too addictive to ignore, too tempting to resist.

She inhaled sharply but made no move to stop him. "The way

I wield a sword?" she added sardonically. Tonight, she was waging battle with words, but the facetious tone she'd clearly aimed for died beneath her breathlessness.

"Especially that." He touched her lips. "You are beautiful, Veronica. And you know it, too."

"What's wrong with that?" Her warm breath tickled his fingertips in an almost-kiss to his fingers. "A woman should use every weapon at her disposal."

"Not with me."

"*Especially* with you."

She'd meant that as nothing more than a declaration that battle lines had been drawn, yet the seductive murmur heated his loins and made him ache.

"Not with me," he repeated firmly, although more as a reminder to himself of who they really were, why they'd been forced together. A reminder that fell on deaf ears when he trailed his fingers down her throat and had to stop himself from letting them drift even lower. "What favor did Fernsby do for you?"

She swallowed, and that gentle undulation moved deliciously beneath his fingertips. "I wasn't hanged or transported."

"I'm to believe a thief-taker convinced the court that you're a criminal with a heart of gold?"

"There are far—" She choked off when he strummed his thumb over the hollow at the base of her throat where her pulse beat wildly. She pulled in a jerking breath to find the strength to ignore his touch as she began again, "There are far more unusual things."

"Hmm…unicorns, mermaids, fairies…"

"Barristers who prowl the city streets at night."

He froze, his thumb halting in midcaress.

"You've seen my world. You know who I am." Her voice emerged as a low and throaty purr that vibrated into him as she pressed, "But who are *you* in the daylight, Merritt?"

"No one important."

Her eyes gleamed as she brought her mouth to his ear and gave his earlobe a sharp nip in punishment. "Liar."

The pleasure-pain of that bite reverberated through him. Merciful God, he wanted nothing more at that moment than to have her mouth on him. Everywhere.

When she edged herself away and flipped her hood back into place, he realized the bite wasn't his punishment—the loss of her was.

But he wasn't ready to surrender the moment just yet. "I'm only a barrister, day and night." He once more slid back her hood and brought his mouth to her ear, allowing nothing between his lips and her skin. "But you find barristers attractive, don't you?" When she parted her lips to give that absurd question the putdown it deserved, he interjected with forced sobriety, "It's the gown and wig. Drives all the women wild."

She kept her gaze straight ahead at the river and the few lights that began to dot the wharves as they drew closer to their destination at Blackfriars. Only a slight twitch of her lips gave away that she was fighting down laughter. "Well, you know what they say…"

For a million pounds, he couldn't have resisted asking. "No, what?"

"It's not the size of a man's gavel that matters." She turned her head to look at him, bringing her lips tantalizingly close to his. "It's how he pounds it."

Sweet Lucifer. Longing sizzled through him so fiercely that his toes curled in his boots. He'd never wanted a woman more in his life than he wanted Veronica at that moment, even knowing she represented everything he'd sworn to fight against. Thank God the waterman stood only a dozen feet behind them, or he would have made love to her right there in the wherry, taking her twice before they reached the opposite bank.

"But barristers don't have gavels, do they?" She slid a glance between his legs that made his cock jump. Feigning acute disappointment, she sighed. "Pity."

He grimaced, chagrined. But before he could volley back a barb of his own, she reached up to touch his chin and keep him turned toward her. He froze beneath her touch.

"Who *are* you, Merritt Rivers?" she murmured. Her eyes narrowed on his face in unfettered curiosity. "I don't believe for one second that you're nothing more than an ordinary barrister."

This was not the conversation he wanted to have with her. Although, to be honest, it wasn't talking that occupied his thoughts. "I told you. I'm a peer of the realm."

Her lips twisted. "Are you indeed, Mrs. Fitzherbert?"

He grinned. Perhaps a secret identity had its benefits after all.

As if knowing she'd not gain any more information from him on that score, she dropped her hand and scooted away. Only a foot of distance separated them on the bench, but damnation, it gaped like a chasm.

So he moved closer. He simply couldn't help himself and slid his hand down the rear edge of the bench behind her until her shoulder nestled against his chest.

"By day, I truly am a barrister, complete with silks and peruke, poring over my law books and winning in court," he admitted.

She scoffed softly at that but couldn't move away. She'd reached the side of the boat, with nowhere else to go but into the drink. "You can't always win."

"But I do. I'm a very good lawyer." He dared to nuzzle his lips against the tender flesh behind her ear. "My father is a barrister, too, like his father before him."

"An entire family of corruption and vice, I see." But her mocking emerged as little more than a breathless whisper.

He smiled against her ear. "A herd of criminals. You'd fit right in."

"Thank you," she muttered. When her cheeks flushed, he

didn't know if it was from his teasing or from the way his warm breath tickled the side of her face. Not that he truly cared which.

"I'm also a former soldier, terrible card player, and bad dancer." He followed that confession with a soft kiss to her neck. "Painfully ordinary, I'm afraid."

"No, you're not. I've seen you fight. You're—"

"Boring." This time when he kissed her neck, he followed it with a light lick across her soft flesh. A shiver trembled through her. "Dreadfully boring."

"And at night," she panted out as he traced his tongue along the outer curl of her ear, "you prowl the streets…dressed head to toe in black…armed to the teeth… Why?"

"To help people."

Surprise flitted across her desire-flushed face.

He bit back a groan at the spicy-sweet taste of her as he brought his lips to the corner of her mouth, knowing the ambrosia waiting to be claimed within. He somehow found the clarity to ask, "You find it hard to believe that I want to help people?"

"Yes." Her lips tickled against his as she answered, "I do."

"Because I'm a barrister," he murmured, sliding his mouth along her jaw to suck at her earlobe. "And you don't trust barristers."

"I don't trust anyone," she admitted yet tilted her head to give him access to her neck. "Especially you."

Instead of being insulted, Merritt smiled. Even now, he could feel her arousal beneath the waves of shivers that passed through her, could feel her growing desire in the quickening of her breath and the parting of her lips. She might not trust him, but she ached for him as much as he ached for her.

"Liar," he scolded and bit her ear just as she'd done to his. The soft gasp of pleasure that tore from her jolted through him like lightning, straight down to the tip of his cock. *Jesus.* He sucked in a deep breath to steady himself. "If you weren't a criminal and I weren't a barrister…"

"What?" she challenged breathlessly. "What would you do?"

The temptation was too much, and he brought his mouth to her ear. "Before or after I stripped your clothes off?" he asked. "With my teeth."

Her hand tightened on his arm. "After."

That single word spun through him with a streak of liquid heat. If he hadn't already wanted her... "Before or after I licked my tongue over every deliciously bare inch of you?"

"After," she breathed and dug her fingertips into his sleeve and the muscle beneath.

"After I laid you down and feasted my fill of you?" He swirled his tongue in her ear, mimicking what he would do between her legs.

She bit back a whimper. "Yes."

"I'd simply ravish you."

She lost her breath, and as her sharp inhalation shuddered into her lungs, she pulled back, wide-eyed and lips parted, as if she simply couldn't fathom him or the effect he had on her. God knew he didn't understand it himself. She was a confessed criminal, and when this mission was over, she'd be given a pardon and set free—an insult to everything he'd dedicated his life to.

Yet he inexplicably yearned for her, in a way he hadn't wanted a woman since Joanna.

"What would you do, Veronica?" he prompted when she continued to stare at him, searching his face but not finding any answers. But of course she wouldn't. He had none to give.

"I—I'd—"

She cut herself off, despite the way she stared hungrily at his mouth. What he'd wanted to hear, desperately, with every aching inch of him... *I'd let you.*

"I'd rather not," she whispered.

The bow of the wherry tapped the watermen's stairs, and they came to a sudden stop, jolting him with barely a fraction of the force that her soft words had just punched into his gut. Merritt tore his eyes away from her haunted face to glance up—Puddle Dock. They'd arrived.

She scrambled out of the boat and onto the steps before he could stop her. But then, he was in no condition to stand up and help her without embarrassing both of them. Biting back a frustrated curse, he had to let her go.

Seven

VERONICA LIFTED THE TANKARD OF ALE TO HER MOUTH AS SHE once more swept her gaze around the crowded tavern. And took a passing glimpse at Merritt.

Ah, the lovely Mrs. Fitzherbert, exactly as expected.

He sat on the other side of the Ship's Bell from her, attempting to blend in with the crowd of dockworkers and porters that filled the seedy and dank tavern fronting the river. Well, as much as he could, she supposed, given how striking he was. Even wearing stained and torn workman's clothes, he clearly stood apart. He was simply too tall, muscular, and downright dashing not to.

When he took a bored perusal around the tavern, his gaze slid right past her with no flicker of recognition.

She'd have been surprised if he'd spotted her, dressed as she was tonight as a man, right down to the shaggy facial hair she'd affixed to her upper lip and cheeks with actors' gum. She'd bound her breasts beneath a man's worsted waistcoat and donned men's trousers, too, along with a workman's shirt, braces, and plain neck-cloth. She'd even rolled up a flannel and stuffed it into her trousers to resemble a cock.

But the knives she wore up both sleeves were real.

She knew Merritt would be here tonight, chasing down the man Danker had told them about. Just as she was. But after the way they'd parted last night, she wasn't yet ready to face him again. That was why she'd disguised herself, going so far as to flirt with the bar wenches for good measure.

Cowardly, she supposed. But he'd rocked her to her core last night with his heated murmurs and kisses. She needed time and distance to clear from her head the wicked—and utterly tempting—images he'd put there and set her focus back where it belonged. On her pardon.

But sweet heavens if her lips didn't tingle at the sight of him!

Her own fault, really. She'd started the kissing, only to startle him into forgetting about Fernsby, but then he'd repaid her in kind—no, his reprisal was worse, fogging her mind of everything except how wonderful his kisses were, how strong and solid his body against hers. For a moment, she'd nearly surrendered and floated away with him into the darkness, to let him do to her all the wanton things he'd suggested…until her sanity returned and she remembered exactly why the two of them were together.

It certainly wasn't for bedsport.

Yet even now she wanted to spread herself beneath him and let him satisfy the insistent ache he'd put between her thighs, which had begun to throb faintly at the thought of his body covering hers.

Idiot. She scowled at herself and gulped down a healthy swallow of ale. The need arising inside her wasn't because she'd been too long without a man. Wasn't because she wanted a few hours of distraction from the mess her life had become. Wasn't even just simple lust or curiosity about how it would feel to have him moving inside her. No, it was so much worse than that!

It was because she'd never met another man like him, one who was so much her match, physically and mentally.

Unfortunately, he was also the same man who possessed the power to put her back into prison.

"Gentlemen, your attention!"

A scruffy man at a table in the center of the room pushed to his feet and raised his tankard into the air to address the tavern. Hoots and jeers went up as the clientele attempted to shout him down. Half the crowd paid no attention at all, which meant they were used to him and his speeches.

On the other side of the room, Merritt leaned back in his chair in feigned boredom and stretched out his long legs, as if settling in for an evening's entertainment.

"If you are as tired as me of seeing the corruption and vices of those connected to Westminster—and especially to the palaces—"

In other words, Prinny. The regent's popularity had plummeted since the end of the wars; so had that of the royal dukes. With increasing reports in the papers of how much money was being spent on clothes, grand parties, and palaces, the entire monarchy had been tainted and weakened. Or simply gone mad.

"Of immoral princes committing all kinds of sins and crimes on the backs of our good soldiers and officers—"

That brought in the Duke of York and his mistress, along with more shouts and calls from the crowd. This time, they agreed with him.

"What does it matter to us what princes do in their glittering palaces? Why should we care if lords and ladies dine on pheasants and the finest drink from golden plates and goblets? After all, what difference does it make to our bellies what goes into theirs?" The sarcasm dripped from the man's voice as he began to win over the crowd. "Even if nothing is going into our bellies at all these days?"

Curses went up at the Corn Laws and the treatment of smugglers.

"We are taxed to death and forced to pay outrageous sums just for a loaf of bread to feed our families. The roofs over our heads are barely capable of keeping out the wind and rain—when we can afford a roof at all—while Prinny sleeps 'twixt satin sheets on down with his mistresses!"

He was skillfully agitating the crowd but not to the point of sedition—not yet.

"We're not lazy. We want to earn our way. But where are *our* feasts, *our* good pay for an honest day's work? Where is a good day's work to be had at all for hard-working men and women like us, and with His Majesty's former soldiers bearing the brunt of the stick? Those good men fought for England and St George. They deserve better!"

A patriotic roar went up, followed by the stomping of feet and the pounding of tankards on the tabletops.

Merritt frowned.

The rabble-rouser noticed and jabbed a gnarled finger at him. "You, sir—you have a problem with giving thanks to those men who risked their lives for English freedom?"

"Is that what we risked them for?" Merritt drawled. "And here I thought it was because we enlisted, being paid for our service and knowing full well what we were getting ourselves into."

The man's face turned red. "Freedom isn't free, my friend."

"Actually, it is. That's what the word means."

The speaker gaped at Merritt, not knowing how to reply. Clearly, he'd never been challenged like this before. Veronica would have enjoyed the spectacle if she didn't find herself fearing for Merritt's safety in a room filled with very large, very patriotic, and very drunk men.

"True soldiers who've been in the heat of battle don't give a damn about all that stuff and nonsense you're spewing," Merritt continued. "When cannon fire was booming like thunder and balls were whizzing past my head at Toulouse, I didn't stop to think about how much freedom costs—or any of that other meaningless fribble that people love to spout off as truisms, as if saying that nonsense makes you more patriotic than everyone else. Nor did I give a damn what parties Prinny was throwing or what mistress he was tupping when I was fighting hand-to-hand at Waterloo, up to my ankles in blood and bodies."

The tavern crowd quieted, duly chastised. Their snickers and jeers died away into uncomfortable silence.

Merritt's eyes gleamed in a piercing mix of fire and ice. "I risked my life so Englishmen could continue to have the right to a parliament, to have an honest trial by jury, to have their property and liberties protected." He smiled then, an expression so intense that Veronica felt the power of it slither down her spine even as she sat half a tavern away. "I fought so men like you can stand in public and openly criticize the crown without fear of being hanged for it, as long as you don't stray into sedition." His smile turned impossibly icier. "And you would *never* do anything seditious, would you, Mister…?"

The man's jaw worked as he checked his anger. "Smathers."

Roni's heart stuttered. *It was him.*

"And no," Smathers spat out, "I would never do anything seditious."

"Glad to hear it. Because you should be damned grateful that freedom *is* free." Merritt signaled to the stunned bar wench to bring him another tankard of ale. "Because you and the rest of this country could *never* repay the debt that soldiers and sailors are owed for giving you the right to stand there and make an arse of yourself by ranting about not enjoying the same pheasant dinners and satin sheets as a prince."

The tavern fell completely silent at that. Every person who had cheered Smathers on now sat staring into their drinks, ashamed at their behavior yet still simmering with resentment at the monarchy.

"Of course," Merritt added as he tossed a coin to the barmaid, tipping generously for the watery ale, "the Duke of York and his mistress can both rot on London Bridge as far as I'm concerned."

Everyone in the place guffawed and called out in agreement at that. Except for Smathers, who glared murderously.

But the man took a deep breath to shove down his anger and raised his tankard back into the air. A forced smile gripped his face.

"Who's with me, then?" he called out, falling back on script and ignoring the exchange with Merritt. "Who wants to discuss with me what can be done to make England a better country?"

So *that* was how he recruited the rioters…agitate the room over

Prinny, remind the men that they were overworked and under-paid, and then pull them aside to pay them to riot. All according to plan.

Except for tonight. Thanks to Merritt, jeers and laughs answered Smathers now. A few hands waved dismissingly as the crowd turned their backs to him and continued their conversations and flirtations that he'd interrupted.

Smathers's face flushed scarlet. He kicked back his chair, which fell to the floor with a crash, slammed down his tankard, and stomped from the tavern. Hisses and laughter rose in his wake.

Veronica left on his heels, following out the door and into the rainy night. She half jogged after him as he hurried down the street and away from the tavern, then turned into the first intersecting street.

She halted on the rain-drenched cobblestones and watched as Smathers climbed into a waiting carriage. Not just any carriage either. Highly glossed ebony paint, uniformed coachman and two tigers, a fine matching team of black horses…an aristocrat's gold crest decorating the black panel. What the devil was a man like Smathers doing stepping into a carriage like that?

As she started forward, her hand snaked up her sleeve for her knife—

Strong arms grabbed her around the waist and swung her off the ground in a circle, pulling her away from the street and into the dark shadows lining the storefronts. She made a desperate grab for her knife, only to have her hand knocked away.

With a cry of angry frustration, she stomped her foot down hard and caught the man in the right instep. A curse tore from him, but he didn't let go. He pushed her into the recessed door-way of the dark shop and grabbed her by both wrists. Before she could see his face in the shadows or fight back, his powerful body shoved forward into hers. He pressed her flat against the door so she couldn't punch with her fists. He pinned her arms above her head and her hips immobile beneath his.

"Stop struggling, damn it!"

Merritt. *Of course.* Which only made her struggle harder. She yanked her arms to free herself, but he refused to loosen his grip.

"Let me go!" Her hips were pressed so tightly between his and the door that she couldn't find the room to lift a leg to kick him. "He's getting away!"

"Good."

"*Good?*" She strained to look past him at the carriage, but she couldn't see around his broad shoulders.

Yet she heard the quick clip-clop of horse hooves against the pavement as the carriage sped away into the night. Frustration pounded just as loudly inside her.

"I have to stop him," she seethed through gritted teeth. "You're getting in my way!"

"Because all you'll do is catch him."

"A pretty damn good start, if you ask me."

"Someone's funding those rioters. A man like Smathers doesn't have the money for it, which means he's working for someone else. Whose carriage did he get into?"

She glared at him, unable to answer.

"The Earl of Malmesbury's," he answered for her. "And no, we wouldn't have caught both him and the earl together. So I had to stop you before you gave our plans away and before you got yourself hurt." He lowered a pointed gaze down their bodies as they were pressed together against the wall and added huskily, "Any way I could."

His velvety drawl wrapped itself around her, spiking both her pulse and the stirring ache at her core. She thanked God that he couldn't read her mind, or she would have embarrassed herself with the wanton thoughts roiling around inside her head at that moment. None of which was helped by the delicious sensation of his body held against hers, the tension rippling through the hard muscles of his shoulders and arms, the wicked press of his hips into hers.

"I know the Earl of Malmesbury, and believe me when I tell you the earl's not inside that carriage." Every breath he took brushed his rising and falling chest scandalously against hers. "It's October, and Malmesbury is a hundred miles away at his country house, gleefully blasting to death every bird in a ten-mile radius. So who else has been giving Smathers money, who was in that carriage—" His gaze fell to her mouth, and despite the beard, he stared at her with a heated longing that spilled through her like liquid fire... until he frowned. "And why on earth are you dressed like a man?"

"You wear a gown and wig to court," she shot back. "Why do *you* dress like a woman?"

He wisely ignored that, if not for the irritated twist of his lips. "You almost pulled off your disguise. Anyone else in that tavern would never have noticed."

That he'd figured it out irritated the blazes out of her. Her disguises always worked, always kept her safely hidden—until him. "How did you know?"

"I would know you anywhere. Even as a man."

He shoved his hand inside her breeches, and heated longing flared instantly between her legs, so strongly that she bit back a rising moan. But instead of caressing her as her traitorous body yearned for, he fished out the rolled-up cloth and tossed it away.

He lowered his head until his eyes were level with hers. Warning announced in their blue depths that he wasn't in the mood for games. "What the hell were you thinking, coming here alone?"

───────────

As Merritt waited for her answer, his mouth lingered so close to hers that the short hairs of her fake beard tickled his chin. How he'd managed not to give himself away tonight when he'd first spotted her he'd never know. He'd almost missed her beneath the beard and large hat she'd used to cover her copper hair and with the way she'd seemed as at ease as any other man in the tavern. But her eyes gave her away—cat-like green pools that shone brightly enough to pierce even in the dimly lit tavern. Eyes that had haunted him from the moment he first saw them.

Even now, they burned like brimstone.

"If you had let me catch him, we could have stopped the riots," she protested. "Isn't that what you want from me?"

"They'd be stopped only temporarily." He couldn't bring himself to step back. The magnetic pull of her was beyond his understanding. "A man like Smathers is easily replaced. We have to find out who's been paying him, and we can't do that if he's in prison or swinging on the gallows."

"He can be questioned if he's in prison. He can be bribed with a lesser sentence if he cooperates."

She explained that as if he knew nothing about the law, rubbing at his lawyerly pride. "In my experience, a man like Smathers will die before he willingly volunteers information, because he knows the men he works for will kill him if he does."

"And in *my* experience, a man will do just about anything when he's desperate."

Without warning, she shoved against him with all her strength, twisted him around in a circle, and pushed him back against the door. She pinned his arms at his sides and leaned in to press her hips against his, the way he'd done to her.

Electricity crackled through the damp night air around them, so palpable that it stirred the hairs at his nape. He could easily push her away—he had the physical advantage. Just set her back, move her away…except he didn't want to. Especially when she tilted her face up toward his, when he heard the quickening of her breath and felt the tightening of her fingers around his wrists.

"What about you?" The husky challenge transformed her voice into a low purr as she stared longingly at his mouth. "What are you desperate for, Merritt?"

The truth tore from him—"You."

She rose up and seized his mouth in a blistering kiss.

Unable to stop himself, he grabbed her around the waist and yanked her to him, hips to hips, chest to chest, as he hungrily devoured her kiss. Desire sparked a wildfire between them.

This was what he'd craved from her last night, this taste of her passion that he'd longed to have. He just hadn't expected a beard.

With a whimper of capitulation, she opened her mouth, and he thrust his tongue between her lips and claimed the sweetness waiting within.

Her arms snaked up around his shoulders to pull him closer, and he slid his hand behind her neck to hold her head still as he changed his ministrations. No longer the seeking plunges of his tongue that delved into the warm recesses of her mouth, but now relentless and fierce thrusts to selfishly claim all the pleasure he could. She trembled against him, her fingertips digging into the hard muscles of his shoulders in silent encouragement for him to give her even more.

He groaned. *Gladly.*

His hands swept up her body to her chest—and froze. No breasts whose fullness he could caress, no nipples to tease. Only then did he remember that she'd bound herself for her disguise, and disappointment panged in his gut.

As if sensing his frustration, she grabbed his hand and shoved it behind her, against her arse.

"Here," she whispered, granting this small compensation. "Touch me here."

He rubbed his hand over her round bottom, and she inhaled sharply against his mouth. Emboldened, he captured both full lobes in his hands and squeezed them. The rough caresses he gave her turned her breathing shallow and ragged. He squeezed again, and a shudder of raw yearning sizzled through her.

His hands slid up her back to draw her even closer, until her soft lower belly pressed deliciously against his hardening cock. Her pulse raced beneath his fingertips as he brushed his hand down her throat, claiming whatever touches of bare skin he could around the men's clothing. All the while, he continued to kiss her, to tease at her mouth and bite at her bottom lip, doing his damnedest to drive her wild. The same as she was doing to him.

Breathless, she tore her mouth away to gasp for air and fell bonelessly against him, her cheek resting against his shoulder.

He brushed his thumb across her bottom lip. It was still wet and swollen from the bruising kisses he'd given her in an attempt to match the ferocity of her desire. "Veronica, that was…"

"Completely out of line," she finished hoarsely. "My apologies." She confessed in a whisper, "I simply couldn't help myself." Then she pulled back and forced a smile, one that did little to hide her surprise at what they'd just done. "Barristers drive me mad, remember? All those thoughts of gowns and wigs…and thumping gavels."

Despite her teasing, she placed her hand to his chest, right over his pounding heart. She stared up at him with slightly parted lips, waiting for him to make the next move and decide what other pleasures they might share tonight.

Sweet Lucifer, he wanted them all. And repeatedly. Yet he couldn't stop the troubled thoughts about her past that spun through his head, that kept him from scooping her into his arms and carrying her off to the nearest bed. Or simply taking her right here against the door.

A man and woman strolled out of the darkness and through the bank of fog toward them. Merritt slipped his hand behind her neck and drew her head down against his chest so they wouldn't see her face.

Only after they'd passed did he realize he'd hidden her not because she looked like a man but because he simply wanted to protect her. Just as he'd have protected any society miss in his daylight world.

But she wasn't a society miss. She was a convicted criminal with knives up both sleeves and a stark reminder that the night-time darkness inverted everything.

She lifted her head to look up at him and whispered, "What do we do now?"

With a frown, he thoughtfully ran his fingers through her beard. "We hunt down whoever was riding in the Earl of Malmesbury's coach tonight with Smathers."

"That's not what I meant."

"I know." She meant the attraction between them, that primal pull that flared and sizzled every time they were together.

But he sure as hell wasn't going to talk about *that*. Instead, he took her arm and led her out of the shadows and into the street, thanking God for the chilly, foggy air that dampened his lust.

"I don't know who was in that carriage," he explained as he waved down a hackney. "But our hunt just crossed over from your world into mine."

An old carriage stopped in front of them. The rain-wet jarvey at the ribbons didn't bother to tip his tall felt hat to them.

"You took me into the Court of Miracles and taught me how to move through your world." He opened the door and stepped back so she could climb inside, then barked out directions to the driver as he swung up after her. "Now it's time I teach you about mine."

Eight

VERONICA PEERED PAST MERRITT AS HE JUMPED OUT OF THE hackney and held the door for her. She stared up at the building, unable to believe her eyes.

"A brothel?" Blinking in confusion, she stepped to the ground. "You brought me to a *brothel* to teach me about your world?" Placing her hands on her hips, she slid him a dubious glance. "What kind of world do you live in?"

He wisely ignored that. "This isn't just any brothel." He nodded toward the plain-looking town house that could have passed for any other terrace house in the west end, if not for the crowd of gentlemen gathered on the footpath and the large man standing on the small portico, guarding the door. "This is the finest brothel this side of Covent Garden."

"That doesn't mean much."

"This neighborhood is the heart of respectable society, I'll have you know. Almack's is just down the street."

She repeated in a dry mutter, "That doesn't mean much."

With a grin, he tossed a coin to the jarvey and sent the hackney away. "You'll change your opinion once you meet Madame Noir."

A masculine shout of distress echoed from one of the upstairs rooms, loud enough to drift out into the street. It was followed immediately by the snap of a whip and a woman's voice. "Do as I tell you!" Another crack of the whip. "Don't make me use the spurs!"

Veronica silently arched a brow.

"You'll like her." He took her arm to lead her toward the door. "She's…unique."

But Veronica refused to budge. She hated the bubbling jealousy in her belly that made her ask, "And how do you know Madame Noir and this place?"

"Business only, I assure you."

Her brow arched higher.

He grimaced. "Not *that* kind of business."

She wasn't certain she believed him, although a foolish part of her heart desperately wanted to. "Why are we here?"

"Madame lives on the fringe of society. She knows how to move between worlds and behave both among the lower classes and the *ton*."

The front door opened, and a gentleman left the town house. Before the door closed, Veronica caught a glimpse of the crowded entry hall, heard music coming from the front parlor, and smelled the scent of jasmine, tallow candles, and musk. Beyond that door, the house pulsed with life and debauchery.

"What does any of this have to do with catching rioters?" she muttered.

"Not rioters," he corrected. "The men behind the riots."

Well, that was as clear as mud. She cocked her head, waiting for further explanation.

"Madame Noir might be the center of attention here because that's what this place demands of her. But she also knows how to *not* draw attention to herself while moving among society. If anyone can teach you to do the same, it's her." When she looked at him in confusion, he bluntly explained, "She's going to tutor you."

Surprise strangled her. "*Pardon?*"

"If we're going to find out who was in Malmesbury's carriage, we'll have to place you into society and keep you there as long as it takes, all without drawing attention. Madame's going to teach you how."

She gaped at him. "You're mad!"

"Says the woman behind the beard," he drawled.

"I might be wearing a beard, but I'm not daft enough to step inside a brothel to learn society stuff and nonsense that—"

"Oh yes, you are."

Without warning, he pulled her floppy hat down low over her ears and grabbed her around the waist. He tossed her over his shoulder like a sack of flour and started toward the front door at a quick pace before her shocked brain could think to fight back.

But when it did, she let loose a volley of kicks and punches. "You rotten son of a—a *barrister*!"

He smacked her bottom. "Behave."

The man guarding the door stared wide-eyed at the spectacle they made as they approached the town house.

"We're here to see Madame Noir," Merritt informed the man.

Without any questions, the guard opened the door for them and stepped back to let them pass amid shocked looks by the gentlemen gathered in the entry hall and outright laughs by the women.

The heat and smells of the busy brothel engulfed them, as did the noise, most of which came from the parlor leading off the entry hall. The room was filled with men waiting their turn to go upstairs, and they were being entertained in the meantime by scantily clad, flirtatious women and a musician playing the pianoforte.

But it was the woman at the center of the room who caught Veronica's attention.

Tall and willowy with ebony hair and piercing green eyes, she wore a tightly fitted, low-cut gown of green velvet beneath a delicate overlay of gold filigree that only added to her imperial presence. So did the rubies decorating her throat and wrist. Although she was slightly older than the other women present, she sparkled in the lamplight far more brightly than the rest. She could only have been one person—

"Madame Noir," Merritt called out to her.

She turned from the group of men surrounding her and faced him. "Snake."

Veronica twisted just enough to mumble, "You really do make a memorable impression on people, don't you?"

He smacked her on the bottom again. Hard.

"While I appreciate the business, especially from the likes of you," Madame practically purred as she glided toward them, "there's an extra fee if you bring your own partner and no discount for bringing a man." She gestured a gloved hand at the two of them. "Although I daresay I would never have suspected your proclivities ran that way."

Veronica would have paid a hundred pounds to see the look on Merritt's face! But the rascal must have simply grinned rakishly in response, given the consternation that visibly gripped Madame.

"Actually, we were looking for you," he told her. "Can we go somewhere private?"

"Well, now you're proving much more interesting." She slipped past them toward the stairs. "Follow me."

Merritt carried Veronica upstairs. Every jarring step bounced her roughly on his shoulder and swirled thoughts of sweet revenge through her head. As they passed the first floor landing, she could hear all kinds of noises coming from the maze of small rooms that had been sandwiched into the floor plan wherever they would fit.

"Your timing is extraordinary, Snake," Madame called over her shoulder as she led them up to the second floor, her hand trailing gracefully along the banister.

"Why is that?" Merritt replied casually as if carrying a man through a brothel over his shoulder was an everyday occurrence.

She guided them onto the top floor landing and down the hall. "Because I thought of you just yesterday."

"Did you?"

"I saw a lawyer trapped up to his neck in mud in the Thames. The tide was coming in, sure to drown him."

"What did you do?"

She unlocked and opened the door to a set of rooms overlooking the street. "Nothing, of course."

"Of course," he drawled.

"After all, you know what they call a dead lawyer." She smiled as she stepped back to let them pass inside, a wide and toothy crocodile smile. "A good start."

"You're right," Veronica said to Merritt, laughter at his expense coloring her voice. "I *do* like her. A lot."

With a scowl, he dropped her unceremoniously onto a gold settee with a spine-rattling bounce.

She sat up and glanced at the room around her. Undoubtedly, they were in Madame's private suite, decorated extravagantly with lengths of purple silk draped across the walls and a gold brocade settee and chairs. A Chippendale armoire stood between two bay windows, with a writing desk and dressing table both positioned to catch the sunlight that would have fallen through the windows during the day. A set of walnut doors most likely led to her bedroom and dressing room.

Madame closed the door, shutting out the noise of the brothel. Then she folded her arms over her bosom and turned toward Merritt. All amusement vanished from her face.

"Now," she ordered, "tell me why you're here."

"I want to hire your services."

"No."

The bluntness of that made him grin. "But I thought you did anything your customers requested."

"*Almost* anything." Madame eyed Veronica askance. "*Not* him."

Veronica rolled her eyes. Rejected by a brothel madam...*lovely*.

"It's not what you think." He bent down and tugged at Veronica's beard. The adhesive gum gave way, and the beard pulled off. Her hat came next, revealing her hair in a knot at the top of her head.

Madame's arms fell to her sides. Taking a long, assessing

glance over Veronica, she murmured, "Well, aren't you just full of surprises?"

Merritt grinned at the backhanded compliment. "Madame Noir," he introduced, "may I present to you Miss Veronica Chase? Miss Chase, this is Madame Noir, the proprietress of Le Château Noir."

"A pleasure," Madame purred.

"Is it?" Veronica countered, her impudence earning a smile from the woman. "After all, you keep calling him Snake."

"Because that's what he is," she explained. "A barrister in a brothel." Her eyes narrowed at Merritt. "A snake in my henhouse."

He shrugged and casually sat back on the rolled arm of the settee. "A man who can have her business shut down for violating the Disorderly Houses Act."

She nodded at Veronica. "See my point?"

"Yes, I do." So no cause for being jealous after all. From the way she'd greeted him, Madame would have preferred to have *him* up to his neck in the tidal Thames.

"Madame Noir is special," Merritt told Veronica, continuing with the introduction. "She's a skilled businesswoman who used to be a highly sought-after courtesan in the Viennese court and a favorite of the Holy Roman Emperor."

"Please," Madam scoffed but didn't attempt to hide her pleasure at the compliment. "Francis was neither holy nor Roman nor imperial." A nostalgic smile rose on her red lips. "But he *was* good with a sword."

Merritt nudged Veronica with his shoulder and murmured, "Your kind of man."

"If I only had a sword now," she muttered.

Madame turned her attention to Veronica. "And you are…?"

She smiled. "A thief-taker."

"Of course you are." Madame's lips twisted in dark annoyance. "The reptiles are multiplying."

"Then best to deal with us as quickly as possible and send us on our way," he replied.

"Very well." Madame let out an impatient sigh. "What do you want?"

"The use of your skills." Merritt pushed himself off the arm of the settee and crossed to the little cabinet in the corner, opened the glass doors, and reached inside to help himself to a bottle of cognac. Veronica didn't let herself contemplate how he'd become so familiar with Madame's private rooms as to know where she hid her liquor. "Miss Chase is going to be attending a society soiree in two days." He pulled out the stopper and splashed the caramel-colored liquid into a crystal tumbler. "I want you to prepare her for it."

Madame laughed. "You want me to be a *governess*?"

"I want you to teach her all the niceties and manners she'll need to know to make her way through the evening without drawing unwanted attention to herself. She doesn't have to shine. She just can't cause any noticeable offenses." He smiled at her over his shoulder as he returned the decanter to its place. "If anyone can teach her that in such short time, it's you."

That little bit of flattery worked its magic to settle Madame's ruffled feathers. A bit. "What kind of event?"

"A ball. At Carlton House."

"You're mad!" Veronica accused breathlessly as she shot to her feet, shocked by his plans. "Everyone in society will be there."

"And the more people who are in attendance, the easier it will be for you to blend into the crush. I'll take care of securing the invitation and providing an escort and carriage for you." He pointed his glass at Madame. "You'll make certain she's dressed properly and knows what to expect."

"And in return?" Madame pressed.

He shrugged. "I promise not to have your business shut down, your property confiscated, and you transported to Australia."

"How generous of you," she drawled sarcastically.

"I'll also reimburse you for all expenses for whatever gown and accessories you deem she needs, plus an additional twenty percent for your trouble."

Madame blinked in surprise. Then she repeated, this time agreeably, "How generous of you."

"You are not to tell anyone about her and our plans," he warned. "Understand?"

She feigned offense that he'd suspect her of doing such a thing. "Discretion is my business."

"How odd. I thought your business was prostitution."

"Snake," she purred, her red lips stretching into a saccharine smile.

"You have two days to turn Miss Chase into this year's oldest debutante." He lifted his glass to Madame in a toast, then took a healthy swallow of the cognac. "Best get started."

Nine

"No, no," Madame interrupted, drawing Merritt's attention to the two women as they practiced their fan language. "A graceful turn of the wrist—*graceful*. Every move you make with a fan should be fluid and elegant. Try again."

Merritt glanced up from the newspaper he was reading in the gold brocade chair near the fireplace. He'd remained at Le Château Noir for the night's lessons to ensure that Veronica didn't attempt to escape—or that Madame didn't attempt to turn her into a courtesan.

But as he watched Veronica awkwardly flick her wrist in jerking movements, he also found it greatly amusing.

Madame crossed her arms in frustration and muttered, "I think you'd rather be wielding a sword."

Merritt's mouth twisted in private amusement. She had no idea.

Or...perhaps she did. After all, the first thing she insisted Veronica do before starting their lessons was to change out of her man's clothes—including removing the two knives hidden up both sleeves.

Once Veronica was safely ensconced in a proper corset, chemise, and dress of sprigged muslin, the lessons had begun. First with the basics. The *very* basics...how the carriage would arrive at Carlton House, who would take her wrap, how the master of ceremonies would check her invitation and announce her, where to find the refreshments and retiring rooms. Veronica had absorbed that information quickly.

But the fan work was giving her fits.

"Maybe you *should* give her a sword instead," Merritt muttered.

"It's Carlton House after all. You can never be too certain what Prinny's up to there." He turned the page of yesterday's newspaper. "Or how you might have to defend yourself."

"Speaking from experience, are you, Mrs. Fitzherbert?" Veronica attempted to punctuate that by snapping open her fan, only to send it flying halfway across the room. She scrambled to fetch it. "Drat it!"

Merritt grinned and stretched out his legs to settle in for the next round of entertainment. This was better than Vauxhall!

She placed her hands on her hips. "I'm more than capable of protecting myself."

"I've no doubt of that." He raised the newspaper to read to the bottoms of the columns. "I've witnessed many battles among society ladies. The reticule brigade is as deadly with their parasols as a French bayonet charge."

She slapped her closed fan onto his newspaper and pushed it down. Leaning over him, she parried the ivory and silk fan in the air like a rapier. "No matter how many lessons and gowns you force onto me, I'm *not* one of your society ladies." She stabbed him in the chest with the fan. "Remember that."

His pulse raced at the fight in her. "How could I ever forget?"

She bobbed him under the chin and on the tip of his nose with the agility of a fencing champion, then stepped back before he could snatch the fan away.

"Miss Chase," Madame scolded in exasperation. "Engaging a man in a sword fight is not the way to capture his attention."

He wryly arched a brow. "I've always found it effective."

A spark of private amusement danced in Veronica's eyes.

Sweet heaven. A fierce fighter wrapped in soft sprigged muslin and satin ribbon trim…she was the perfect paradox. And the perfect temptation. He shifted uncomfortably in his chair.

"There are better ways to flirt with a man." Madame paused for emphasis. "Without letting blood."

Veronica tilted her head and studied him as if he were some kind of exotic creature on exhibit at the Tower menagerie. "Are there? Hmm. I wonder what they could be."

Oh, *that* did not bode well. Neither did the way she moved forward to sit on the chair arm, then leaned in to give him a very pleasant view down her dress. *If* he'd have allowed himself to look. But he wisely kept his eyes fixed on hers, not because he was a gentleman so much as from wariness about what the little minx might do next.

"After all," she mused, running her fingers up his jacket sleeve, "what powers could a small, defenseless young miss like myself—"

He laughed at the absurdity of *that*!

"—have over a strong and dashing man?"

When she squeezed his bicep, he strangled on his laughter. *Defenseless?* The woman was downright deadly.

"Why, I don't know the first thing about men." She brushed her hand over his shoulder to his neck, then played with his neckcloth. "I don't even know how to properly tie a man's cravat to put it on." Her fingers slipped beneath the cloth to tease across his bare neck and sent his pulse spiking. "Or untie it to take it off." She offered in a throaty murmur that twined through him, "Perhaps you'd like to show me?"

He stared at her, unable to think of a decent retort. Oh, he wanted to show her things all right. But only half a dozen or so involved tying a neckcloth, and none could be described in polite conversation.

"So," Madame succinctly acknowledged, "we don't need to spend time on teaching you flirtation."

Veronica laughed and sashayed away, expertly flitting her fan.

Damnable woman.

With a flip of the pages to straighten them, he forced his attention back to the newspaper. He scoured it to glean whatever new information he could about the riots and the crown's response to them. So far…nothing.

"I don't suppose you know how to dance."

Madame's question caught Merritt's attention.

So did Veronica's answer. "Actually, I do."

That surprised him. She didn't learn to dance where she'd learned to fight. She was well educated, certainly—the way she spoke proved that. But dancing was an altogether different sort of education.

He narrowed his gaze on her over the top of the paper. She was far more than a common thief. What *exactly* was her past? Where did she come from that her life was such a bewildering puzzle? And how on earth did a beautiful woman who knew ballroom dances end up in Newgate?

"In the morning, I'll arrange a review lesson for you," Madame said, "once the pianoforte player is through playing in the drawing room. We're certain to find a gentleman in the house who can partner you and show you—"

"*I'll* partner her," Merritt interjected in a half growl.

Both women stared at him in surprise, as if he'd transformed himself into a goat. Then Madame arched a knowing brow at his jealous reaction. Bloody hell.

"I don't want her to have any contact with gentlemen," he explained, his voice inexplicably rough.

Which only sent her brow higher.

Bloody, *bloody* hell. "We're keeping her identity a secret, remember?" A lie. The truth was he didn't want her to be in another man's arms, even for a dance lesson. "Your clientele comes from all levels of society. I don't want anyone who might be present at the ball to see her here."

"Of course not," Madame assured him in a purring voice that told him she didn't believe one word.

He reached for another copy of the *Times* on the table beside his chair, shook it out, and held it up in front of him. Most likely, this was the first time in history that twelve sheets of paper had ever functioned as a shield.

He scanned over the page—and stopped. A story about the riots filled the last column of page two, reporting that plans had been made by Whitehall to call in the militia to put down the unrest if it continued. He tightened his jaw. That was exactly the worst thing the crown could do. The rising price of not just bread but everything necessary for day-to-day living and lack of jobs had pushed the poor to the brink. Sending in soldiers against British citizens would only enflame the situation and entrench the rioters even more. The only way to end the unrest then would be for the soldiers to inflict such harsh brutality and slaughter that Londoners wouldn't dare to riot again.

The Home Office would callously do exactly that.

He bit back a curse. The clock was ticking now. He had to find the men responsible for the riots before innocent blood was shed.

He looked across the room at Veronica as she gave up learning the language of the fan and gleefully tossed it away. As she turned, she caught his gaze and frowned at his troubled preoccupation. He gave her a reassuring smile, which only seemed to distress her more.

A commotion went up from the hall—banging and thumping mixed with a woman's voice raised in unbridled cursing. In French.

"Ah! That must be Madame Barnaud." Madame smiled at Veronica and crossed to the door. "I've convinced her to make your gown. She's the best French modiste in all of England. But don't you dare tell her I said that," she grumbled, "or the woman will start charging double." She flung open the door with an ingratiating smile. "Madame Barnaud! How good to see you again."

The women exchanged air kisses to each cheek.

"How have you been?" Madame Noir purred as she stepped aside to let the woman into her rooms.

"*Terrible!*" Madame Barnaud heaved out a long-suffering sigh. Then with a wave of her hand, she launched into a diatribe in French about worthless shop girls and assistants, aristocracy who never paid their accounts, and the rising cost of fine Chinese silk.

Merritt glanced at Veronica, who stood demurely at the side of the room and watched the dressmaker's arrival. A knowing smile tugged at her lips, indicating that she understood every word. So she not only knew how to dance, she also spoke French, and not just that drawing room fribble taught to society misses either but real French. Her past just blossomed into an even bigger mystery.

"Thank you for coming on such short notice." Madame Noir took the woman's arm and turned her toward Veronica. "This is the reason I sent for you. Miss Chase. She needs a very special gown."

Madame Barnaud raked an assessing look over Veronica from head to toe. "You are to attend a grand soiree, correct?"

"Yes."

"With the snake," Madame Noir confirmed with a dismissing wave of her hand in Merritt's direction.

He smiled widely in acknowledgment.

Ignoring him, Madame explained, "We need you to dress her. For Carlton Place."

"Hmm." As Madame Barnaud circled Veronica to evaluate her from all angles, she gestured at the footmen waiting in the hallway to bring inside the three trunks she'd brought with her. Following in the wake of the footmen and trunks came a very tired-looking mouse of an assistant who had obviously been roused from her sleep in the dead of night. "Supper or ball?"

"Ball," Madame Noir answered for her.

"Will she dance?"

"Most likely."

"Satin?"

"Of course."

"Husband hunting or status climbing?"

"Neither," Merritt interjected from behind his newspaper, interrupting the volley. "I want her to be invisible."

A flare of surprise crossed Madame Barnaud's face. Surely,

none of her aristocratic clientele had ever asked for that before. Then she narrowed her eyes at Veronica and gave a sharp nod, accepting the challenge. "I possess those skills."

She snapped her fingers, and the timid assistant rushed to open the trunks and unpack them. In a matter of moments, every spare piece of furniture in the room was covered with an assortment of ball gowns and accessories of all kinds.

"There isn't time to make a new gown," Madame Barnaud explained. "I have brought several that can be altered. But such rapid work will cost…"

"Price is no concern," Madame Noir assured her, sliding a victorious smile at Merritt. "None at all."

With a roll of his eyes, he pretended to return his focus to the newspaper, yet he surreptitiously watched Veronica as she let the two women consult between themselves about what she should wear. Her attention had been captured by a sage-green gown decorated with thousands of tiny cream-colored pearls that the assistant had placed across the back of the settee. More than admiration for the dress crossed her face, more than appreciation for the detailed embroidery on the delicate bodice—it was a melancholy longing for things that her life in the Court of Miracles could never provide.

His chest panged for her. He bit back the impulse to tell the two Madames to make a second dress for her.

Madame Barnaud snapped her fingers again. Her nervous assistant raced to fetch the stool from Madame Noir's dressing table and put it in the center of the room.

"Now." She directly addressed Veronica. "You. Here." When Veronica blinked, puzzled at what the woman wanted, Madame Barnaud clapped her hands together sharply as if scolding a misbehaving dog and pointed at the floor in front of the stool. "There—now!"

Veronica did as ordered and came forward, although judging

from the irritation and embarrassment coloring her face, she would have loved to have shackled the woman with her handcuffs.

Madame Barnaud took a yardstick and tapped Veronica on the shoulders to make her lift her arms. Immediately, the assistant darted forward like a border collie. The girl's fingers unbuttoned her bodice with lightning speed, then grabbed the hem of the dress and stripped it up Veronica's body, over her head, and off, all before Merritt could think to look away.

He sucked in a mouthful of air at the unexpected sight of her. She stood there in short stays and a chemise that hid little from the light of the lamp behind her, which silhouetted her curves through the thin cotton. Instantly, she covered her bosom with crossed arms, but that did nothing to hide the outline of her long legs beneath, the curve of her hips, the dark patch of feminine curls between her legs—

God have mercy. He raised the newspaper high enough that he couldn't see over the edge and did his best to summon what few tendrils of gentlemanly manners were left inside him. At that moment, in the brothel's warren of rooms, women were in stages of undress far more revealing than Veronica, yet none of them could have affected him the way that fleeting glimpse of her just did.

More snapping of fingers. "Remove that corset."

An image of a bare-breasted Veronica filled his head, and he shifted in his chair as his trousers tightened uncomfortably. He didn't dare lower the paper to take the look at her that the scoundrel in him craved.

Snap, snap! "The chemise, too."

Which meant she would be wearing nothing except stockings if she—

"And the stockings."

A heated ache began to throb at his crotch.

"Fortunately, she has a full bosom," Madame Noir commented.

"Enough for a very snug gown, one cut lower in the new Parisian style, don't you think?"

Yes. Yes, I do.

"And a thin waist, shapely hips," Madame Barnaud mumbled, "nice round bottom…"

Very much round. And nice. And luscious. Perfect for a man to run his hands over, to squeeze and clench—

He blew out a hard breath and kept the paper high. Although if they kept this up for much longer, it wouldn't be the newspaper that was raised.

None of it was helped by the fact that he was sitting in a brothel. That even here on the top floor and in an isolated part of the house, he could hear the faint grunts of masculine exertion and the practiced female moans in response echoing from the rooms around them. That the musky odor of sex mixed with the scent of perfume and tallow candles to create a lingering aroma of debauched pleasure.

Madame Barnaud ordered, "Stand up on the stool."

The thought of Veronica posed naked on a pedestal, like a statue of Venus—

His cock jumped.

Enough. He slapped down the newspaper and vaulted to his feet, keeping his gaze carefully focused on the Aubusson rug on the floor. He stalked toward the door, well aware of all four sets of female eyes staring at him in bewilderment. He didn't dare glance their way.

"Morning has arrived," he explained to the floor. "I'm leaving. To work."

From the corner of his eye, he saw the blackness of predawn still darkening the window and felt like an idiot.

"To catch some sleep," he amended quickly. "Then work."

There. That should be a good enough explanation, as opposed to the real one—that if he didn't get the hell out of there, he'd grab

Veronica in his arms like some beast and drag her onto the nearest bed, to hungrily take her the way every inch of him burned to do. Gentlemanly manners and rioters and Scepter all be damned.

"Don't let her leave," he ordered the floor. "Keep her away from sharp weapons. And for God's sake, put some clothes on her before she dies of cold!"

He slammed the door shut with a bang.

Ten

"Are you finished with me?" Veronica tugged the sprigged muslin dress into place and quickly fastened up its buttons herself before the women could once more strip her bare. By now, though, there wasn't a part of her that hadn't been measured, traced, and recorded.

Madame Barnaud held up the long list of notes she'd made during the fitting. Her eyes narrowed as she scanned it. "I believe so."

Thank God. And not a moment too soon.

With a tired sigh, Veronica turned toward the bay window to gaze out at the breaking dawn while behind her, the two women launched into their final business negotiations. A flurry of back-and-forths in rapid French regarding last-minute details over her ball gown, right down to whether she should have bows on the tips of her satin slippers and if her matching wrap should be lined with velvet or fur. In the end, the velvet lost to Madame Noir's insistence on using only the finest materials Mr. Rivers could afford.

Veronica frowned. *Mr. Rivers* had fled over two hours ago. She didn't know whether to take his parting orders to cover her nakedness as an endearment or an insult.

Would she ever understand that man?

Beyond the glass, the city was awash in golden light, the bright sunlight chasing away the blues and grays of the rainy night. The only visible clouds clung low to the distant horizon, white fluffy bunches that looked like puffs of wool against a blue blanket and portended a warm fall day. Instead of welcoming the sight, she felt dread tighten in her chest. No rain meant the possibility of another riot tonight.

Below, King Street was quiet, as if taking a moment to catch its breath before the day began. So was the brothel. The gentlemen had all left by the cover of darkness, although more likely done to miss the morning congestion of carriages on the city's main avenues than because they cared who might have seen them departing Le Château Noir. The women had all eaten breakfast and gone to bed, to lose themselves in a few hours of rest and privacy before the next round of men began to arrive after sunset. Even the pianoforte player in the drawing room had finished for the night and gone home because Merritt wasn't there to partner her for dance lessons.

She was more disappointed at that than she wanted to admit. They'd already done a dance of sorts that first night with their swords, so she knew exactly how skilled his footwork, how light his movements. He was a natural-born athlete, and she'd looked forward to dancing with him. But the women had rattled him to the point that he'd had to flee. Veronica had struggled to keep from laughing at the stiff way he'd hurried from the room, newspaper raised like a blinder to the side of his face and his gaze glued to the floor.

It was also endearing. She'd never met another man who wouldn't have stared shamelessly as she undressed.

Despite his weapons—and being a lawyer—Merritt was a gentleman at heart. That made this all so much worse. It should have been easy to hate a man who reminded her at every step that she'd falsely been branded a criminal, who held a pardon over her head like the sword of Damocles. Yet she'd sneaked a glimpse beneath his façade, and what she was beginning to feel for him was far from hatred.

Madame Barnaud turned away from Madame Noir and clapped her hands, signaling that all the decisions regarding the clothes had been made. She gestured to the footmen to take the repacked trunks downstairs. Her exhausted assistant let out a long sigh, grateful to be able to slink away after the footmen, while the two women charged ahead into the thick of financial negotiations.

It was almost like watching a play, Veronica mused, enacted by two very well-rehearsed actresses. They'd arrived at the final act.

"The ball gown is your top priority," Madame Noir reminded the modiste. "It must be done by five in the afternoon tomorrow."

Madame Barnaud feigned insult that she couldn't alter a dress by then, even one as delicate and fine as the green satin and gold filigree creation Veronica had coveted since the assistant pulled it from the trunk. "It will be done, along with all the accessories."

"Good. I also want to order more dresses for Miss Chase."

That captured Veronica's attention. What the devil was Madame planning?

"Three day dresses and all the necessary accessories," she ordered.

"But I only need the one gown," Veronica interrupted.

Madame Noir rolled her eyes at her as if she were a cake of a girl. "My dear, you will need far more than that." Then she ignored Veronica and instructed Madame Barnaud, "All in the finest muslin, all in the latest fashion, and none of that pastel nonsense worn by unmarried misses. Deep colors that command attention. I want her to glow when she wears them."

That wasn't at all what was needed. Veronica knew how to do reconnaissance, and glowing certainly wasn't part of avoiding attention. "I don't think—"

"Along with a green kerseymere coat dress for carriage rides in the park."

She blinked. *Carriage rides in the park?* Who exactly did Madame think she was?

Cold realization sank through her. Madame thought she was a mistress. *Merritt's* mistress. After all, they'd given her no reason to think otherwise.

She bit her bottom lip. "I think you misunderstand why—"

"She'll need a walking dress, too, and a good pair of half boots."

"Actually, I don't need any of—"

"Four sets of night rails and matching dressing gowns, two for winter and two for...*not* winter."

Madame's lips curled into a smile, and not just at the sexual innuendo. Every time Veronica attempted to interrupt her and decline the dresses, Madame added more to the list, which Madame Barnaud dutifully listed in her little account book.

Oh, that woman! Veronica didn't know whether to shake her at the trouble she'd cause for her with Merritt...or hug her for it.

"And all the accessories she'll need for each outfit—gloves, reticules, hats, parasols, wraps, shoes, stockings...everything you can think of. Oh, and fur muffs."

"*Muffs?*" Veronica choked out in disbelief.

"Of course." Madame blinked as if the answer were obvious. "Winter is coming."

"Of course," Veronica repeated in a stunned mumble.

"Charge Mr. Rivers for payment," Madame ordered. "He keeps a small town house at the west end of Red Lion Square. Send the accounting for everything there."

He *used* to have a town house, Veronica amended silently with trepidation. Once the tally was delivered, he'd have to sell it to settle the debt.

Madame Barnaud smiled like the cat who'd gotten into the cream. "Everything will be finished within the fortnight. I'll assign extra seamstresses to work on it."

And undoubtedly charge Merritt double for the additional expense. Despite a prick of guilt, Veronica knew not to argue or the two women might just decide that she also needed a riding habit. With a matching horse as an accessory.

Madame Barnaud paused with the pencil tip resting against the page and glanced up at Veronica. "And the direction where the finished goods should be sent?"

Veronica hesitated. A swift sting of shame pierced her, so strongly that the blood drained from her face.

She couldn't—simply *couldn't*—admit that she lived at the Court of Miracles! Not after the way the two women had fussed over her as if she were a real lady, as if she deserved satin ball gowns and fur-lined wraps. She couldn't bear to think of how they would look at her if they knew the truth about her current life, if they ever discovered what she'd done in her past—

"Have them sent here," Madame Noir interjected. She crossed to Veronica, nudged her over in front of the dressing table, and turned her toward the mirror. "That way, she can try them all on and have any last-minute alterations done right here." She gathered Veronica's hair and lifted it onto the crown of her head, then pulled loose a few tendrils to frame her face. Madame studied the style as if trying it out for the ball. "Don't you agree, Miss Chase?"

She looked at her reflection in the mirror. A stranger in pretty muslin and upswept hair stared back. No, not a stranger—the woman she wanted to be. The woman she once thought she *would* be until her life all went so horribly wrong. Sophisticated, urbane, feminine, cultured…someone who had worth and measure. Someone who mattered to the world, rather than one of the fleas it seemed always to be trying to shake off.

For a few precious moments, she could reject the unwanted existence fate had thrust her into. She could let herself believe a new life was possible…

"Yes," she answered a bit breathlessly. Then she added more boldly, as if daring the woman in the mirror to contradict her, "I think that would be lovely."

"Perfect." With a knowing smile, Madame released Veronica's hair and stepped back to show Madame Barnaud from the room.

The modiste departed with a flurry of air kisses and goodbyes in French that came from the streets of Marseilles and not the Parisian courts where the woman claimed to have been employed before fleeing the revolution. She might have fled France, but it wasn't from the Louvre. And it wasn't to escape the guillotine.

"Thank you for all that," Veronica told Madame Noir once the woman had left.

"It's nothing. A little gift for you, that's all."

One at Merritt's expense. "Mr. Rivers won't be amused when he sees the tally."

She smiled wickedly. "And *that* is my gift to myself." She turned her back to Veronica and gestured at the row of tiny buttons that kept her tight bodice in place. "You can repay me by unfastening me. But no straying hands," she warned over her shoulder, "or I'll have to charge you extra for the pleasure. I like you, but business *is* business after all."

"Of course." Her lips twisted wryly. Veronica could see beneath the woman's surface now. All bluster and conceit…the toughness she showed the world was nothing but a façade.

Oh, Madame was mysterious, certainly. There was no doubt of that. Or how carefully she must have crafted that pretense over the years, as carefully as she'd decorated both the room around them and herself to create the perfect image of exotic sensuality.

But she also wasn't the woman she claimed to be. Veronica could see that as easily as her own reflection in the mirror. Merritt—and, apparently, most of English society—had been hoodwinked. She was no more a former courtesan to the emperor than a nun.

A knock rapped softly at the door.

"That will be my maid with the breakfast tray." The last button slipped free, and Madame walked into her bedroom. "Let her in, and help yourself."

Veronica did as requested. The maid set the tray onto the tea table in front of the settee and arranged small plates of food around a silver chocolate pot, bowl of strawberries, and rack of toast.

Heavens, Madame must have thought she was feeding an army…or expected Merritt to return and join them for breakfast.

She could have saved herself the trouble. Merritt wouldn't be returning any time soon, Veronica knew. Not until dusk at the earliest, and then only to check on the progress of her lessons. Or, more likely, to see if she'd fled.

"Will that be all, my lady?" the maid asked.

My lady. A warm sensation spun low in her belly. Veronica wasn't a lady, not by any means. Yet she couldn't bring herself to correct the maid because she enjoyed the sound of it too much. Just as she'd enjoyed being fussed over by Madame Barnaud and dressed in fine silks and velvets.

"Is there anything else you'd like?"

Not to be woken from this dream. Veronica smiled her gratitude. "This is fine, thank you."

Madame swept back into the room and settled onto the stool in front of her dressing table. She'd changed into a peacock-print silk dressing gown, cinched at her slender waist.

"Good morning, ma'am." The maid began to take the pins out of Madame's hair, letting it down carefully. "Cook sent up strawberry tartlets for you. She knows they're your favorite."

"How thoughtful of you both."

Veronica pretended to study the breakfast dishes as she surreptitiously watched from the corner of her eye as Madame interacted with her maid. Gone was the hard façade she'd shown Merritt earlier. So was the steel-spined businesswoman she'd been with Madame Barnaud. Now, she looked like any other Mayfair society woman going through her morning routine and overseeing her household. Except that her household was a brothel.

"I'll wear the yellow day dress when I wake this afternoon," Madame instructed. "And the blue-and-gold velvet gown this evening."

"Yes, ma'am." The maid removed the last pin and set them onto the dressing table.

As she rose gracefully to her feet, Madame combed her fingers through her hair to shake it loose over her shoulders. She nodded at Veronica. "Miss Chase will be our guest for the next two days. Have a room prepared for her, and please see that all her needs are met."

"Yes, ma'am." A curious glance in Veronica's direction followed, but the maid knew not to ask who she was or why she was here. Questions were dangerous in a brothel.

"That will be all, thank you." Madame dismissed her by reaching for the chocolate pot and giving the molinet a quick twirl to whip up the chocolate. "I'll send for you in a few hours when I'm done napping. You may come for Miss Chase when her room is ready."

"Yes, ma'am." The maid drew the heavy drapes in the adjoining bedroom so Madame could sleep away her morning, as she most likely did every day. She sketched a curtsy to both women and left.

"You seem surprised," Madame commented, holding out the cup of chocolate toward Veronica. "Didn't you think I have a maid?"

She accepted the chocolate with a sting of chagrin. "I didn't expect uniformed servants."

"I keep a full staff here." Madame reached for one of the strawberry tartlets. "Maids, footmen, housekeeper, butler." She took a bite of the tartlet and gave an appreciative sound. "And the best cook this side of Piccadilly."

Prodded by Madame, Veronica helped herself to one of the berries. The tartness of the berry followed by the sweet velvet of the chocolate—*divine*. Luxuries she never would have expected to find in a brothel.

"This place is my business, but it's also my home and the home of the other women who work here." Madame finished the tartlet, her lips nearly as red as the strawberry filling. She delicately brushed the crumbs from her fingertips, then reached for the chocolate pot to pour a cup for herself. "I keep it just as I would any other house in Mayfair, including making certain I have the staff necessary to run it properly and ensure it remains a safe haven for everyone who lives here."

"Other brothels don't do that."

"Other brothels don't cater to the same level of clientele that I do." Pride laced her voice.

"Is that why Merritt keeps threatening to shut you down?" Veronica cast a glance out the window at the row of buildings lining the opposite side of the street, one of which housed Almack's. "You're awfully close to their world."

"Mr. Rivers is a mere nuisance, although he certainly has the power to do exactly as he threatens." She warned quietly, her gaze intense, "Do not underestimate that man."

Veronica had already learned that lesson.

"I do as he asks because it's in my best interests to remain on the favorable side of a barrister, not because of his threats." Madame's red lips curled slowly. "And he's *very* entertaining."

Yes. Veronica had learned *that* lesson, too. Quite well.

"London is full of women who have no choice but to sell their bodies to survive. Here, I provide a place for them." Madame gestured a hand to indicate the house around them. "But make no mistake—I am first and always a businesswoman. But my business also helps the dozen or so women I'm able to hire, women who would still be forced to sell themselves but otherwise not have anyone to offer support. In exchange for a portion of their earnings, I let them live here in comfortable rooms and ensure they have everything they need, including security, clothing, food, and servants to take care of them and the house."

Veronica thought of the Court of Miracles, how she and Filipe worked to provide the same for the people who lived there. "So they're family to you?"

"Of course not." Madame sent her a bemused look. "They're my employees. They're business assets, and a woman in my business always takes care of her assets."

"Yes," she mumbled against the rim of the cup as she took a sip of chocolate, hiding her amusement. "I suppose she does."

"It's quite simple. I offer them protection, and in return, they offer me their loyalty."

In that, Madame was no different from Filipe. He had made his way through the world by constructing a web of favors and opportunities that allowed him to profit from others as they profited, just as she had. He'd also carefully crafted a persona that allowed him to hide the truth of his past, just as she had.

Veronica stared down into the dark puddle inside the cup. "Merritt said you were at the court of the Holy Roman Emperor."

"I was. Vienna before 1806 was simply amazing." Madame's eyes brightened with a faraway gleam. "Such grand palaces, gardens, fountains—music everywhere, even drifting from open windows as you walked past on the avenues below. Ladies wore wide dresses of shimmering satins, and distinguished gentlemen donned their red heels, all vying to be noticed at court."

"How lovely." Veronica paused as she traced a fingertip around the rim of her cup. "But while you might have been at the Viennese court, you weren't a high-ranking courtesan."

She raised her eyes in time to see a stunned expression flash across Madame's face. *Caught.*

"I'm not judging or accusing," she amended. "It doesn't matter to me what you did in your past. We all have our secrets." The surprise in Madame's eyes darkened inscrutably. "But I would like to know how you came to be here, how you created a better life for yourself than the one fate gave you."

"Tit for tat," Madame purred, having corralled her surprise behind the mysterious air she cultivated. Then she attacked— "Who are *you*?"

"I told you." She carefully sipped the chocolate, more to hide any stray emotions that might be visible on her face than because she wanted a drink. "I'm a thief-taker." *Of sorts.*

"Hmm." The disbelief in that single sound resonated as loudly as cannon fire. "And where do you live? It isn't Mayfair."

"Saffron Hill. At the Court of Miracles." Setting the unwanted chocolate aside, she summoned what shredded dignity she possessed and lifted her chin to boldly meet the woman's gaze. "I'm certain you've heard of it."

Madame's eyes narrowed as she studied Veronica, the rim of the cup poised at her lips. "You might very well be a female thief-taker. After all, I've also heard rumors that fairies exist." She lowered the cup and reached for a piece of toast. "You might live in Saffron Hill now, too, but you certainly didn't come from there."

"What makes you think that?"

"You possess a continental accent beneath flawless English, and I didn't teach you about society manners so much as simply provide reminders of what you'd already been taught." She waved the toast at Veronica. "The way you talk and move, how you know how to dance and curtsy and hold yourself—how you know French. Oh yes." Her eyes sparkled at Veronica's surprise. "Your facial expressions were quite clear whenever Madame Barnaud spoke. You understood perfectly everything she said."

There was no point in denying it. "Every word." Veronica paused before adding, "She's not from royal Paris, you know. She's lying about her past."

"So are you. But she makes fine dresses, so I'm willing to live with her lies." Madame nibbled at the toast, but the tone of her voice was deadly serious. "Why should I be willing to live with yours?"

"Because I make fine dresses," she quipped.

Madame's lips curled in amusement.

"And because neither of us seems to have a choice."

Madame's smile faded. "Who *are* you?"

"No one important."

Madame set the unfinished toast onto her plate. "Ah, but Mr.

Rivers seems to think you are." She reached for the chocolate pot to refill her cup and mused, "I wonder what he knows about your past."

Very little. And I intend to keep it that way. "About as much as he knows about yours."

Madame paused in midpour. The threat was subtle but clear.

Veronica was done sparring. Now she went for the heart. "You see, I've known courtesans my whole life. I know how they move through daily life and society, how they conduct their business. I would assume one would have to be good—*very* good—to succeed in Vienna, in the presence of the emperor himself, no less." She paused for emphasis, the beat of a sword thrust. "And the good ones never end up in brothels. Not even running them." *Touché.* She selected a coveted strawberry tartlet from the plate. "Who are *you*?"

Madame brought the cup to her lips and smiled against the rim, her cat-like eyes gleaming as she repeated, "No one important."

"Well then. It would be a shame if Merritt's time was wasted by learning the truth about the pasts of two women who aren't at all important." Veronica popped the tartlet into her mouth. "Don't you think?"

Madame's smile widened against her cup, and their gazes met for a long moment, each recognizing the other's power to inflict damage and knowing they were both on equal ground. Oddly enough, respect blossomed between them because of it.

"I agree," Madame finally answered.

The tension eased from her shoulders, and Veronica pressed, "I don't want to know the truth about your past, and I don't really care who you were then." But she *was* desperate for other information she could use to pull herself out of the hell her life had become. "What I'd like to know is how you ended up here, a place I'm assuming is far better than wherever you came from." She leaned forward and lowered her voice, almost pleadingly, "How did you do it? How did you take control of your life?"

"Very carefully." The enigmatic answer carried a finality with it. Apparently, the mysterious woman had no intention of disclosing anything about her past, including that.

Madame turned away from the breakfast tray to sit at her dressing table. She set down the cup of chocolate and picked up a bottle of lotion, poured out a dollop on her palm, and rubbed her hands together.

She looked at Veronica in the mirror. "Mr. Rivers isn't the kind of gentleman who takes a mistress. Certainly not one from Saffron Hill."

That stung, more than she wanted to admit. But then, didn't the truth often hurt?

Madame didn't lower her gaze as she rubbed the lotion over her face and neck. "How did you become involved with him?"

"Very carefully," Veronica repeated dryly.

A knowing smile stretched tightly across Madame's face. "A barrister with a thief-taker...yes, I'd wager so." She sensuously rubbed the lotion down her neck and beneath her dressing gown. "Mr. Rivers is a young bachelor of the *ton*, so God only knows what kinds of idiotic ideas are passing through his head about you." Then she rubbed the lotion over both forearms, and Veronica was struck by how porcelain her skin was. But then, Madame obviously didn't spend a lot of time outside during sunlit hours. "*You*, though, have a tendre for him." Her eyes gleamed with wicked amusement. "Or for parts of him, anyway."

Veronica knew better than to answer anything to that.

"You're doing quite well for a woman from Saffron Hill," Madame purred. "In addition to whatever other agreement you've struck, you've gotten a new wardrobe from him and an invitation to Carlton House to meet the regent."

The thought of both made Veronica uneasy.

"What else do you want from him, hmm?" Mischievousness danced across Madame's face as she brushed out her hair. "Make a wish, and we'll do our best to make it come true."

"I want nothing else from him except the payment he's promised," she answered carefully.

"Good. You'll suffer less grief that way."

Taking her eyes away from Veronica's reflection in the mirror, Madame set down the brush, stood, and walked back to the tea tray. "I like you, Miss Chase, so I will give you the best advice I can."

"Which is?"

"Do not set your heart on that man." Madame contemplated Merritt the same way she did the tea tray apparently—as if he were simply another part of a buffet to sample. "He is a gentleman in every way, and it's the true gentlemen who are capable of wounding the deepest because they never lead you astray, never lie to you, never take advantage. Yet they also never give their hearts. Oh, they'll give their attentions, their money—their bodies eagerly, certainly. But their hearts they always keep to themselves."

"Then it's a good thing I don't want his heart," Veronica countered, not daring to let herself consider if she were lying to herself.

Ignoring that, Madame selected a hard cinnamon biscuit and murmured, "I know from firsthand experience the impossibility of wanting a man who is out of reach." She studied the biscuit in her fingers. "People see what they want to. A woman in fine satin must be special, a woman in worsted wool is not…but the exact same woman, in fact, when all that's changed is the packaging. They assume the person you are on the outside must match the one on the inside." She glanced around the room, as if taking in not just this suite of rooms but the entire brothel around her, the long years she'd spent building up her business, and how far she'd come from whatever hell she'd once crawled through to arrive here. "When the two might be nothing alike."

Madame snapped off a bite of the hard biscuit between her teeth.

"Merritt Rivers is a barrister above reproach," she continued, "a man who should have been recognized as a war hero but wasn't, yet not for lack of trying. A friend to dukes, earls, and all kinds of important, upstanding men, the likes of which would never darken my door. While you…" She tossed away the rest of the unwanted biscuit and flicked the crumbs from her fingers. "You come from a den of thieves."

No. Veronica might have ended up there, but that was *not* where she came from. She could take pride in that part of her past at least.

"So leave the snake alone, or you might just get bit," Madame warned gravely. "And not at all in a pleasurable way."

Eleven

MERRITT OPENED THE HEAVY WALNUT DOOR TO THE SECOND floor law chambers he shared with his father near Lincoln's Inn and stopped in the doorway. He blinked.

"Well," he muttered as he stepped into the room, "that's something you don't see every day."

Slowly, he approached the full-sized tailor's wickerwork mannequin standing in front of his desk. *Good God.*

The form was dressed in a new set of barrister's robes. Not just any robes either, he recognized immediately as his gaze swept over the mannequin. A black silk gown that fell to just below the knees with its flap collar and long, closed sleeves, a black bar jacket with its long tails and turned-back cuffs marked by three buttons...and to finish it off, a set of new breeches, silk stockings, and the most frilly jabot he'd ever seen in his life—all of it capped by a snow-white horsehair wig with curls hanging at the sides and down the back. *This* regalia was special, denoting rank as surely as a duke's four ermine stripes.

These were the robes of a King's Counsel.

A note card was pinned onto the mannequin's faceless head where its nose should have been. His father's elegant handwriting informed him that word had arrived last night, that his father wanted to be the first to congratulate—

Tossing the note onto his desk, Merritt collapsed into his chair.

"Christ," he muttered, "I've been made a silk."

He stared at the regalia. His father must have paid a small fortune to have that made—far more than the ball gown Madame Barnaud was making for Veronica. After all, *this* gown was from Ede & Ravenscroft, the most exclusive tailors of regalia in England. They numbered among their clientele nearly every peer of the realm, every barrister and judge, most men in Parliament, and an occasional archbishop.

Of course, in his pride, his father would have ordered the best. Had done so months ago, apparently, to have the whole thing waiting here like this.

Sadly, this would only be the start. As the list of names of those barristers selected as King's Counsel hit the chambers at all the Inns of Court, it would be as if a royal wedding had been announced—the popping of champagne, parties one after another, the ceremony itself at Westminster when the next Parliament convened…

Merritt wanted no part of it.

When he'd first begun to study law, becoming a KC had been his dream—to take the silks, to follow in his father's footsteps as a barrister and eventually as a judge. The long nights of study, countless days in the Old Bailey, and hours spent poring over court records had seemed worth it at the time, all of it laying the foundation for the life he'd wanted.

But then everything changed, and that old life simply wasn't enough. Frustration burned in his chest. What good was prosecuting criminals and applying justice after the fact, after innocents were hurt or killed?

His gaze drifted to the framed watercolor hanging on the wall between the two windows, between his desk and his father's. A landscape of the sea at Brighton on some forgotten summer afternoon…whitish haze lying over the gray-blue water until it was almost impossible to tell where the sea ended and the sky began, a stretch of pebbly beach in tans and browns across the bottom of the canvas. Far from exciting. Ordinary. Done by an amateur artist who had braved the wind, the relentless sunshine, and the bite of salt air to capture that moment in time. Done by Joanna.

He stared at that painting and was borne back into the past to that night when another riot had terrorized the city. To the night when Joanna had been killed.

No matter how tightly he squeezed shut his eyes, he couldn't stop the images from swimming behind them... A mob of rioters swarming through the midnight streets near Covent Garden, coaches trapped in the melee, their carriage surrounded by a group of men and women who rocked it violently back and forth while the driver did everything he could to keep the team from trampling into the crowd. The fear on Joanna's face, the scream that tore from her when the carriage door ripped open and they were dragged outside into the street. The sickening helplessness that bubbled up even now like bitter acid on his tongue that he could do nothing to stop them.

She'd tripped as she'd tried to run away. She fell, hit her head against the cobblestones—

No. That was a goddamned lie. But that was what he let everyone believe because it was less painful than the truth. That one of the rioters had slammed a hammer into the back of her head.

He clenched and unclenched his hands as the images barraged him. They grew more distant, more faded with each passing year, until their edges blurred as if looking at them through a rain-streaked window. Distorted. Smeared. Still he forced himself to remember everything about that night, not because it was his last glimpse of the woman he'd loved but because it was his punishment.

Five years later, the ghosts haunted him as much as ever. No matter that he'd dedicated his daylight hours to bringing justice to men who harmed innocent victims. No matter that he patrolled the city's streets night after night like some wraith prowling through the darkness. Always, he saw the scarred face of the man who'd killed her, whose features had been seared into his mind. Always, Merritt hunted for him.

Only during the past few days had that unending circle of darkness changed, when he'd been with Veronica. When he hadn't thought of Joanna at all.

With a curse, he shoved himself out of the chair and began to pace. But there wasn't enough room in the book- and paper-strewn chambers to burn off the agitation boiling inside him. It was Veronica's face he saw now when he closed his eyes, not Joanna's. It was her scent and softness that he craved, her arms where he wanted to seek both pleasure and comfort. The guilt was eating him alive.

A sharp knock rapped at the door only a heartbeat before it was flung open. Instinctively, Merritt's hand dove for the knife beneath his sleeve.

"Well, well," Clayton Elliott called out as he strode into the chambers. "If it isn't the newest King's Counsel. And all along I thought you were nothing more than a poor excuse for a former soldier."

The tension eased from Merritt's body, and he let his hand drop away. He was in no mood for Clayton's teasing, yet he welcomed the distraction from his own dark thoughts. "Shouldn't you be out doing Home Office business and saving England from itself?"

Clayton grinned and wisely ignored that. "I just heard the news this morning." He set a bottle of Kopke port onto the desk and announced, "I've come to celebrate with you."

"Or commiserate," Merritt muttered, nodding toward the mannequin.

Clayton raked his gaze over the new court regalia and let out a low whistle. "Congratulations, Cinderella. You're all set for the ball."

Merritt grumbled, "Thanks."

"Actually, I think this might be a great idea." Clayton folded his arms over his chest as he circled the mannequin and pretended to study it. "You can send this into the Old Bailey in your place. They'll all welcome a barrister who doesn't talk." He muttered, "God knows I would."

Merritt gave a faint chuckle. He appreciated what Clayton was attempting to do. During the time they'd served together, they'd become as close as brothers, and Clayton knew him well enough to know how Merritt would react to the news and so had come bearing liquor. *Thank God.* "The court dress is a gift from my father."

"He's proud of you." Clayton propped a hip onto the corner of the desk. "So are all of us at the Armory."

Merritt's chest tightened. He didn't want attention called to him among the men there. He didn't mind having their respect for his fighting abilities, but this was completely different. Most of the men who were part of the Armory were still finding their way since leaving the army and returning home. Some still hadn't secured respectable employment. He didn't want to remind them that he'd picked up his life right where he'd left off, while they hadn't.

He didn't want to remind *himself* of that either. Yet he murmured, "Thank you."

"Don't thank me," Clayton warned. "The Duchess of Hampton and the Countess of Sandhurst have already started planning a celebration for you." When panic registered on Merritt's face, Clayton clarified, "Just a small affair. You and your father, the men of the Armory…" He grinned at Merritt's expense. "And every barrister practicing at all four Inns of Court."

"Good God." Merritt grimaced. "I need a drink."

He crossed to the bookshelves that covered the side wall of the chambers and were filled floor to ceiling with thick legal tomes.

"When you become a judge, you'll need an entire distillery," Clayton added.

"Not enough whisky in all of Scotland for that," he muttered beneath his breath. He pulled down a volume that was half a foot thick and reached behind to the store of fresh glasses and half-empty bottles of liquor his father kept hidden there. He didn't have to glance at the tome's title to know. Blackstone's *Commentaries on the Laws of England.* As his father always said, any dive into the legal system should always be followed by a stiff drink.

"But you're getting a dashing new wardrobe," Clayton reminded him. "From the looks of it, you'd think barristers were as prissy about their dress as all those unmarried misses at Almack's."

"Ah, that's where you're wrong. The parasol contingent has nothing on the Inns of Court." Merritt pulled two glasses from their hiding place and carried them back to his desk. "When you get all of us together in our black silks, it's like a murder of crows."

He opened the bottle of port and poured out the fig-colored liquid.

"You have more robes coming soon, don't forget."

His hand jerked at the reminder, splashing drops of port over the rim of the glass and onto the desk. His baronial robes. *Good Lord.* He'd blocked that from his mind.

"You'll need at least two sets, you know. A parliamentary set for gatherings of peers and another for coronations."

Twisting his lips, he frowned as he finished pouring and set down the bottle. "I only need coronation robes if the monarch dies."

"*If?*" Clayton repeated. "It will happen eventually, you know."

Merritt handed over one of the glasses. "Isn't it considered treason to discuss the death of the monarch?"

"Technically, we're discussing fashion." Clayton raised his glass in a toast. "Here's to dressing you like a peacock!"

"Thanks," he grumbled. "Nothing like friends to make a man feel better."

Clayton grinned with brotherly affection.

Merritt took a healthy swallow of port and let the rich liquid cascade smoothly down his throat. *That* he could easily take comfort in.

He sank back onto his desk chair and muttered into his glass, "Parliamentary robes, coronation robes, coronet, ermine… Good God." He gestured at the mannequin. "That's why my father bought those. He knows I have to buy the other robes and was most likely afraid I couldn't buy these, too, on my income."

"That you *wouldn't* buy them, you mean," Clayton corrected, "and so try to avoid becoming KC."

"Would that work with being a baron, too, do you think?" he asked with mock sincerity. "Because if I don't have a robe, I can't assemble with the other lords, and I could just go on with my life as if none of this stuff and nonsense ever happened."

"Except for one small thing." Clayton leveled his gaze on Merritt. "The judge."

His father. He blew out a hard breath.

"Your father's proud of you," Clayton said quietly. "If for no other reason than that, let him have these moments. He deserves them."

"I know." He lifted his glass. "To the Honorable Mr. Justice Rivers."

"Hear, hear." Clayton followed in the toast by taking a long swallow. Then he gestured at Merritt across the desk with his glass. "Seriously—why aren't you out celebrating?"

"I came here to work." When Clayton's brow arched up at that, Merritt glowered at him in annoyance. "I do have a real job, you know, and bills to pay." He counted them off one finger at a time. "Town house lease, stabling fees, ticks at various chophouses and stores—"

"Gold coronets and ermine robes," Clayton interjected, fighting back a laugh at Merritt's expense. "All the usual household expenses."

Merritt shot Clayton an irritated scowl. Then his gaze fell to his desk and the papers and files stacked there, and he admitted seriously, "I've neglected my work over the past few days and came here to catch up."

"Hmm. And speaking of Miss Chase—"

"We weren't."

Clayton crooked a knowing grin and took a sip of port. "I expected you to have her on a short leash. Where is she?"

"Le Château Noir."

Clayton choked on the port. Wiping the back of his hand across his mouth, he forced out, *"Where?"*

"You heard me." He kicked his feet onto the desk. "Our investigation into the riots has taken an interesting turn."

He took a moment to fill Clayton in on the meeting with Danker, Smathers's speech at the Ship's Bell, the Earl of Malmesbury's carriage, and his plan to use the regent's ball to discover who might have been inside the carriage. He conveniently left out everything else.

Clayton swirled the last of the port in his glass. "I'll post a man to the Ship's Bell. It's unlikely Smathers will return there, but perhaps someone else will take up recruiting in his stead."

"It takes a lot of men to populate a riot," Merritt mumbled into his glass. "Smathers can't be doing this alone. We should consider other taverns where former soldiers might gather."

"I might be able to reassign half a dozen men or so, put them into the streets, see what they turn up."

"Let's talk to the men in the Armory, too, especially Nate Reed. He's still in the horse guards and might have heard rumblings among the soldiers about other rabble-rousers."

Clayton thoughtfully swirled the port in his glass. "You think Malmesbury's behind the riots?"

"I don't know." But he was damned well going to find out.

"Then we'd better hurry. The Home Office has soldiers waiting at the ready to put down the riots by force if they continue."

Dread filled his chest. "Under whose command?"

"Major-General Horatio Liggett."

"Liggett?" Surprised, he kicked his feet to the floor and sat up at the ludicrousness of that. "You're certain?"

Clayton finished off the last of the port in his glass. "Heard it this morning from the Home Secretary himself."

Of all the men Merritt would have picked to put in charge of the militia, it wouldn't have been Liggett.

Like a good portion of the officers in His Majesty's army, Liggett had earned his rank by purchase, not merit. Liggett's command with the Scots Guards had been mostly unimpressive, neither disastrous nor triumphant and, in the end, making little difference to the outcome of the wars. A general of middling competency at best, he'd been promoted far beyond his skills because he was the son of a duke. A man without a bone of true leadership or military ability anywhere in his body.

"Nothing's wrong with him as a general," Clayton commented with that uncanny ability he had to read Merritt's mind.

"Nothing's right with him either," Merritt countered in a low mutter. "And an odd choice to bring in to put down a riot."

"A good choice actually." Clayton frowned. "What other general do you know who would eagerly fire on his fellow Englishmen?"

True. Liggett wouldn't hesitate to shoot down his former brothers-in-arms.

"And they didn't bring him in," Clayton added. "Liggett approached Whitehall to offer his services, and the War Department agreed to temporarily reassign his regiment."

"To put down civil unrest?" Merritt was dumbstruck. The Scots Guards instead of the militia? That was like hitching a Derby thoroughbred to a plow to turn a field—a complete waste of skill. And dangerous. Because the Scots Guards were some of the best fighters the British army had ever produced. If those men were turned loose on a crowd… "God help the rioters."

"We won't have to worry then about figuring out who's behind the riots then because all our leads will be dead."

Merritt glanced out the window at the sunny day. Unless more rain came, he feared there would be another mob tonight. If so, soldiers would be sent into the streets, the riots would be put down by force, and any chance he had of finding a connection to Scepter would vanish with the dawn.

So would any chance Veronica had of earning her pardon.

He frowned into his glass. "What do you truly think of Miss Chase?"

"That she's hiding the truth about why she was arrested and that she has better connections to London's underworld than most Home Office agents."

"No, I mean—" He grudgingly clarified, "What do you think of her…as a woman?"

"I don't."

Merritt glanced up in surprise. "When have you ever not noticed an attractive woman?"

"When she's wielding a sword," Clayton shot back. "A man tends to live longer that way. She's not the sort for me." He gestured at Merritt with his glass before setting it aside. "You, however, might have met your match."

He blew out a dark laugh. "I don't think so."

Clayton sent him a look of disbelief, as if Merritt had sprouted a second head but hadn't noticed, then slipped off the desk and stood. "It's back to Whitehall for me, and off to the ball with you, Cinderella." He gestured at the mannequin as he crossed to the door. "At least you've already got the gown."

"Very funny," Merritt muttered.

Clayton paused to glance back. Admiration for his friend shone on his face.

"Congratulations, Merritt," he said sincerely, his voice full of warmth. "You finally have the future you've always wanted."

As he stepped out the door, Merritt's gaze wandered back to Joanna's painting. He tossed back the rest of the port in his glass, leaned his head back against the chair, and squeezed shut his eyes.

No, I don't.

Twelve

Veronica glanced up into the dark night sky as the bell of St Sepulchre's Church struck out the midnight hour. What she noticed most, though, wasn't the time but the sky.

The night sky shone clear as glass. A field of stars and full moon lit the city streets so brightly that they cut through the foggy haze that always hovered over London. She certainly didn't need any of those fancy gas lamps that lined the avenues in the exclusive parts of London to make her way. Nor did she want even this much light. After all, there was safety in darkness.

She glanced into every dark alley and narrow passageway she passed, hunting but not finding. Yet she knew Merritt would be out here somewhere, because the same bright and clear night that made her hunt for him go more easily also increased the odds of another riot.

He hadn't returned to Le Château Noir as she'd expected. The afternoon had slid by without him. Then evening had fallen, and the gentlemen had begun to arrive. Yet still no Merritt. Even Madame had seemed a bit preoccupied by his absence, although that was most likely due to her own worries regarding him. After all, the cat that caught the mouse was always the one the unfortunate mouse never saw coming.

So when nine o'clock came and Madame had to turn her attention fully to running the house and accommodating her clientele, Veronica left. She'd returned to the Court of Miracles, donned her fighting clothes, and headed into the night after him.

"How hard is it to find one man in a city this size?" she muttered sarcastically to herself, knowing she was looking for a needle in a haystack yet had to try anyway. One sharply witty, interesting, and dashing man. One who knew how to wield a sword as if it were an extension of himself. One who made her insides go molten with only a glance and a grin.

One unlike any she'd ever met before.

Blowing out a recriminating breath at herself for letting him get under her skin, she headed southeast and quickened her pace through the rabbit warren of streets in Cheapside and Walbrook where he would most likely be. She wasn't worried about him. Heavens, why would she be? The blasted man was more than capable of taking care of himself. But if he'd gone after Smathers or Malmesbury, or if he'd done something even more foolish like circle back to speak to Danker again without her—

She halted and held her breath, cocked her head, and listened. The little hairs at her nape stood on end.

From a distance of several streets away, she could just barely make out the faint but familiar noises. Raised voices echoing off the stone buildings, the smashing of wood, a shattering of glass—*a riot*.

Her heart jumped into her throat. It knew before her head that she'd find Merritt there in the thick of it. Damn foolish men! Equal parts concern and exasperation grated at her as she raced toward the commotion.

On any other night, she would have remained behind the mob, to linger at the rear to capture those opportunistic men who weren't part of the protests but used them to commit crimes. In the confusion of the melee, they could easily burglarize shops and warehouses, break through shutters and windows of houses to snatch whatever they could, and escape into the chaos of the mob. Easy pickings for a thief. *Very* easy pickings for a thief-taker.

But tonight, she raced ahead. She circled through the alleys and passageways to bring herself dangerously close to the front of the riot and to its leaders because that was where Merritt would be. With every panting breath and thumping heartbeat, she kept her eyes peeled for him.

A scream cut through the night. Her hand darted to the short sword at her side, and she sprinted toward the sound.

Merritt.

He stood halfway down one of the dark alleys that angled away from the main street. Lit by a stray slant of moonlight, his blade flashed as he held it in front of him and kept at bay four large men positioned around him in a semicircle. Behind him on the ground, a young woman with her dress half-torn from her body cowered against the stone wall.

Worry for him wrapped around Veronica's spine. He'd rushed to place himself between the woman and her attackers. But he'd also backed himself into a corner at the end of the alley, cut off from the street and escape. The four men advanced in slow, swaying steps like a pack of circling wolves.

"Mrs. Fitzherbert," she called out from the mouth of the alley to alert him that she was there. "We really must stop meeting like this."

Glancing past the men, his gaze collided with hers. His fierce expression sliced into her like a shard of ice and ripped her breath away. It was a look of pure vengeance.

He tore his attention back to the four men as they continued to circle in front of him. They ignored her, most likely believing she was nothing but a weak woman who wouldn't interfere, and kept their focus on Merritt as they looked for any weaknesses in him. *Futile.* He possessed none.

"Leave," he ordered through clenched teeth. "Go home before I give you the justice you deserve."

One of the men laughed.

Veronica commented sardonically, "Good to see you've got everything under control."

His lips twisted into a strained smile. "Just giving them a false sense of confidence before I put them in their place."

"And here I thought you were about to get your arse kicked."

He flashed her a crooked grin, which knotted all the tiny muscles in her belly.

Then he lunged, so quickly the movement was almost a blur. He slashed the tip of his sword across the closest man's arm, through his clothes, and into the muscle beneath.

The man bit out a venomous curse and clamped his hand over his arm. Blood seeped between his fingers.

Instead of attacking again, Merritt retreated farther back into the alley and past the woman who still sat huddled and sobbing in the shadows along the wall. The men followed after him like trained dogs.

Knowing what Merritt wanted her to do, Veronica darted forward. She took the woman by the arm and yanked her onto her feet. "Run!"

But the woman only sagged back against the wall and pressed a fist to her mouth, too terrified to move.

Veronica grabbed her shoulders and gave her a fierce shake. "*Run*, damn you!"

With a gasping sob, now just as terrified of Veronica as the men, the woman stumbled backward a single step. Her terrified eyes darted toward the street and escape. She pulled in a deep breath and ran.

Merritt stopped his retreat and flashed his sword in the moonlight, to let the light catch the blade and remind those four damned fools of exactly how sharp it was. But the idiots thought they had him trapped and didn't retreat. Instead, they raised their clubs and started forward. One of the men snatched up a discarded bottle and smashed it against the wall.

With a grimace of aggravation, Merritt lunged and easily knocked the broken bottle from the man's hand. This time, he didn't retreat. He struck, stabbing his blade into the man's shoulder and driving the tip of his sword an inch deep.

The man howled in pain and fury. But he was smart enough to run away before Merritt could strike again.

He pointed his sword at the man to his left, who'd rushed forward when his comrade had fallen back. Merritt stopped him at the tip of his sword. "You want to have a go next?"

"Or would you rather fight a girl?" Veronica called out, stepping into the middle of the alley behind the remaining two men.

When they glanced over their shoulders at her, she pulled both knives out of her sleeves in a single cross-armed movement. And smiled.

The men's eyes widened, then glanced between Merritt's sword and her knives. They were beaten and knew it. They stumbled backward, carefully slid past Veronica, and raced out of the alley.

Veronica lowered her knives to her sides with feigned disappointment. "Guess they didn't want to fight a girl after all."

"God knows I wouldn't," Merritt answered dryly. "You girls fight dirty."

A low thrill tingled through her as he stalked toward her, and she replied huskily, "What fun is there in playing clean?"

A hungry look darkened his face, and the tingle turned into a full-out throbbing. He moved his gaze predaciously over her, the way a wolf might contemplate its prey. Right before he devoured it.

He stepped forward and slowly backed her up against the alley wall. She flattened herself against the bricks, with her arms raised to her shoulders and her hands still fiercely grasping both knives as if her life depended upon it. When he stopped in front of her, she turned her face away and squeezed her eyes closed to shut out the temptation he presented. She didn't dare let herself step into his embrace.

She swallowed. Hard. Madame Noir was right, Veronica knew that. He was the absolutely worst man in the world for her to desire. She and Merritt? A convicted criminal and a barrister? A thief-taker and a gentleman? She'd have to be mad to let herself even consider such a thing.

Yet knowing that didn't stop her from wanting him.

He placed his hands flat on the wall on both sides of her shoulders and lowered his head close enough to hers that his warm breath tickled over her cheek. He didn't touch her, yet she was certain the front of his body thrummed with electricity from her nearness as much as hers did from his. He murmured, "You came looking for me."

"Yes," she whispered.

"Worried about me, were you?"

She could practically taste the self-pleased smile on his lips. "Never."

"Liar." His low chuckle rumbled into her. He cajoled in a husky voice, "Look at me."

Unable to resist, she opened her eyes and somehow managed to lift her chin in defiance, despite pressing herself flat against the wall. She didn't dare touch him, not even an accidental brush of bodies. One touch… God have mercy, she'd be lost.

"You're not kissing me," he pointed out.

"Brilliant observation," she drawled with all the sarcasm she could muster. She wore it like armor to keep him at bay. "I'm sure the army appreciated your finely honed reconnaissance skills."

Ignoring that, the devil leaned closer until his lips almost teased at hers. "Why aren't you? This is usually when you grab me and kiss me."

She scoffed. "Someone has a high opinion of himself."

"I speak from experience."

"And I speak from common sense when I tell you that you're not nearly as attractive as you believe you are."

She expected him to laugh at that, too. Instead, he stroked his thumb along her jaw. "But you want to kiss me."

So very much! "What I want is my pardon and for you to—"

"To let you kiss me."

He'd twisted her words, the same way he was twisting an aching knot low in her belly. "That isn't it at—"

He grazed her earlobe with his fingertip, and a shiver sailed through her, proving her a liar. "So why aren't you?"

She caught her breath at the simple question. Why *wasn't* she? Her mind spun like a whirlwind but was unable to latch onto any viable reason except for a truth she didn't want to face. That she would never mean anything to him except as a help in stopping the riots.

"Kiss me, Veronica," he murmured. Each word pulsed a ghost pain from his lips that hadn't yet been brought against hers. "Let go," he urged her breathlessly. "Let go of whatever is holding you back and surrender."

He turned his head slowly each way to glance at the knives she still clutched in her hands, so hard that her fingers ached. Her heart pounded wildly in a heady mix of apprehension and anticipation, so fiercely that she was certain he could feel it even though their chests weren't touching.

"Let go."

His velvety voice wrapped around her with its temptation. He was the devil himself, come to claim her soul… Yet she opened her hands, and the knives fell away to clatter against the stones at their feet.

With a pleased smile, he whispered against her mouth, "Now surrender."

A whimper of capitulation rose from her throat—

An explosion reverberated through the streets. The ground shook, and a flash of light pierced the darkness in the street beyond the end of the alley.

Veronica startled with a gasp. Merritt grabbed her to him and protectively shielded her between his body and the wall. Their racing hearts beat off the seconds until they were certain the attack was over.

She lifted her head from his chest. "What was that?"

He glanced over his shoulder into the street as the noise from the riot increased, and he let out a curse. "A declaration of war." He looked back at her, staring longingly at her mouth as he ordered with an aggravated breath, "Stay here."

He ran out of the alley toward the explosion.

Stay here? *Absolutely not!*

She snatched up her knives and raced into the street after him, only to halt in her steps. Her mouth fell open at the sight of the crowd—no, not a crowd. A complete mob. Uncontrolled. Violent. *Good God.*

This was nothing like what she'd seen of the riots before. Men, all in their twenties and thirties and armed with hammers, shovels, pikes, and clubs, moved through the streets seemingly without reason or focus. They randomly destroyed whatever they came across...barrels, crates, shutters, windows, lamps. There were no leaders at the front to direct the crowd or keep them moving forward, no shouts or rallying cries that gave cause to their protest. Their sole intent was to harm and destroy. Directly in the mob's path, flames from the explosion leapt high into the night and engulfed the building adjacent to the Bank of England.

A chill slithered up her spine as unbidden memories of Portugal and the wars flashed before her eyes...scenes of death and destruction that had no purpose except to lay carnage to the land, of men who took gruesome pleasure in butchery and demolition. The similarities between tonight and her last days in what had once been her homeland struck her like a slap. She remembered how the men who'd ridden in advance to terrorize the villages and countryside had given way to the armies, which in turn had given way...to hell.

Cold perspiration beaded across her forehead despite the hot flush of her cheeks, and her heart pounded so strongly that her chest hurt. She couldn't catch her breath, couldn't move. All she could do was stand there, watching and reliving those last horrible moments before her mother—

"Look there!" someone cried out near the burning building. "A soldier with a sword!"

Panic swirled through the crowd as one by the one the rioters spotted Merritt, who had raced toward the burning building to make certain no one was trapped inside. Their surprise turned to rage, and shouts and curses rolled through the mob. A group of men waved their weapons in the air and started toward him.

A desperate need to protect him flared inside her. Defying his orders, she raced toward him and straight into the heart of the riot.

"Merritt!" Calling his name so he would know she was behind him, she pulled her sword from its sheath. She wheeled around to face the advancing group and positioned herself between him and the men. "We have to get out of here!"

"There might be people trapped inside." He shielded his face against the heat with his left arm and started toward the door. "I have to check."

And get himself killed in the process. If the flames didn't do it, then the mob would. "No one's inside. Look at the windows! If anyone were inside, they would be at the windows, calling for help."

The men hurried closer, their anger at Merritt—and now also at her—flaring with each step. She brandished her sword and cut a swathe through the air in warning. She wouldn't hesitate to strike them down.

"We have to leave—*now*," she pleaded. The men would be upon them in moments. She and Merritt were too greatly outnumbered this time to fight them off, and these men wouldn't frighten away like the ones in the alley. "Merritt!"

He lowered his arm and stepped back from the building, still staring up at it, still searching its façade for any sign of anyone who needed his help. Finally, he turned to face her, and the overwhelming relief that blossomed in her chest nearly undid her.

But the first group of men had reached them. With her sword

in her right hand and her knife in her left, she crouched in a fighting stance and slashed at the men to keep them back. Her blood pounded like a drum in her ears, every inch of her alert and tense, ready to attack.

Merritt moved into his own battle position behind her. Back to back, they faced the men who now surrounded them. They were both acutely aware of the other's every step and swing of their blades.

"At my order," he told her over his shoulder, "lunge, attack, and retreat. Follow me down the street as fast as you can run, understand?"

"Yes." She swung her blade at a man with a pickax who'd come too close and forced him to jump back.

Her heartbeat pounded off the wait—

"Now!"

He lunged and sliced his blade across the arm of the nearest man. Veronica followed less than a second behind, cutting with her sword into two of the men's legs. The rest of the group charged, and Merritt and Veronica slashed and stabbed indiscriminately as they lashed out at whichever man their blades could reach.

Merritt pulled back in retreat, grabbed her by the wrist, and yanked her through the gap they'd cut through the encircling pack of men. "Run!"

But a few of the attackers gave chase. Merritt steered her down one dark street after another and darted with her through passageway after passageway. Yet the men pursued, determined to catch them and kill them.

Without warning, he slid to a stop in front of a narrow wooden door to an old abandoned building and rammed his shoulder into it. The door gave way with a loud splintering of wood and slammed open against the inside wall. He yanked her into the building, then kicked the door shut behind them. They were sealed together in the darkness.

Merritt flattened himself against the wall between the broken windows where the slants of moonlight that shone into the building couldn't reveal them. His arm went around her like an iron band and pulled her tightly against him, out of sight from the street.

He lowered his mouth to her ear and warned, "Don't move."

She didn't dare to even nod as she stood frozen against him, pressed tightly to his chest.

The men ran past. They chased after shadows down the street and away.

Veronica and Merritt continued to stand unmoving and silent as the minutes slipped by. The roar of the riot grew into a distant din as the mob moved into a different part of the city. Her ears strained to catch any sound of the men who'd chased them, yet all she could hear in the darkness was the mingling of her breath with Merritt's and the fierce thumping of their racing hearts.

Her blood coursed hot through her veins, not helped by the rapid breaths she sucked deeply into her lungs. Every inch of her tingled and pulsed, but only part of it came from being chased.

She wanted him—dear God, how much! She physically ached with arousal to possess him, for him to quench the yearning that he'd flared inside her since the moment they'd met. A yearning he'd only increased to blazing wildfire during all the time they'd been together since.

But her feelings for him were so much more than simple physical desire. She needed him, the way she needed air to breathe, the way deserts needed the rain. The way she'd never needed a man before in her life.

He couldn't be hers, never completely. Her head knew that. *Her heart* knew that. But right here, at this moment, he belonged to her. She would take however much of him she could claim and somehow make that be enough.

"Merritt," she murmured, thanking God that the darkness hid the true depth of her emotions for him on her face.

Then she shifted away from him to sheath her weapons, reached down to unbutton his breeches, and sank to her knees.

———

Merritt stared down at her as she freed his cock from his breeches, closed her lips around him, and then…*bliss*.

He inhaled sharply in surprise, and every muscle in his body stiffened. This was so much more than the kisses and caresses he'd attempted to cajole from her in the alley. This was—*Sweet Lucifer*. But he couldn't find the will to stop her. Didn't *want* to stop her. The blood that pounded in his veins was too heated to tamp down, the pleasure she stirred inside him too much to resist.

When a soft whimper from her throat vibrated against his cock, the breath he'd caught poured from him in a long, ragged sigh, and he knew he was lost.

He couldn't see her face in the shadows, couldn't see his hardening length slipping in and out of her hot, wet mouth. But he could feel it…every delicious slide, every teasing flick and swirl of her tongue over his tip, every graze of her teeth.

She sucked—

The sensation shot through him and straight out the top of his skull like a lightning bolt.

His hips bucked. "Jesus!"

But she held on, refusing to release him. Instead, she clung even more tightly as if she couldn't bear to let him slip away. The soft suction of her mouth increased its intensity as her hand slid up his thigh. It slipped beneath his breeches to cup his balls against her palm and lightly tease him with her fingers the same way her lips teased his cock.

A groan tore from him. What she was doing was incredible by itself, but added to the excitement of the night and the openness of their location, less than a stone's throw from the street…*God have mercy*.

He dropped his sword with a clatter and shoved both hands deep into her hair. Leaning back against the wall, he held her head still as he began to pulse between her lips in small, controlled thrusts.

In response, she slid her hands behind him to clasp both of his buttocks and squeeze with each hard suck. Her cheeks hollowed with every great pull, with every attempt to take him as deep into her mouth as possible.

He shook violently as he fought for control. His fingers dug into her scalp, and his thrusts came faster now as he moved between her lips. He couldn't stop the growls and groans that spilled from him.

She moaned as she experienced her own shudder of joy.

"Veronica," he uttered hoarsely in warning, giving her one last chance to stop.

But she didn't pull away. He jerked his hips, and when release fired through him and he gushed into her mouth, she drank him in. He slumped back against the wall to gasp for breath, but even then, she didn't release him until she'd claimed every drop.

Finally, she pulled back and let his flaccid length slide slowly through her lips.

He sank bonelessly down the wall to the floor, knees bent and shoulders slumped, as residual pleasure undulated through him.

Slowly, Veronica rose to her full height and stood in front of him like a goddess at whose feet he was worshipping. Fitting. Because this dark angel had certainly brought him to his knees.

"Veronica," he whispered breathlessly. His sex-fogged brain was unable to put words to the sensations spinning through him, all his doubts and troubled thoughts warring with the elation she'd just given him. "What we just did…"

His voice trailed off into the shadows. For the life of him, he had no idea what to say, unable to admit that tonight was the most amazing encounter he'd ever had with a woman that hadn't ended with him inside her. That he wanted nothing more than to forget who she was and why fate had brought them together.

But he couldn't. The past could never be forgotten.

His voice ached with grief and regret as he rasped out the truth that both of them knew in their hearts. "That can never happen again."

Thirteen

"AND JUST WAIT UNTIL YOU SEE THE GARDENS! THEY'LL SIMPLY take your breath away!"

Veronica smiled at the exuberant young woman sitting across from her in the carriage. Mrs. Claudia Trousdale, the woman Merritt had chosen to accompany her to the ball.

He'd sent her a note telling her that he'd taken care of all the arrangements, that she was to dress for the evening at Le Château Noir and wait for a carriage to arrive to take her to Carlton House. She'd done as asked, but she hadn't expected such a luxurious town coach and beautiful team of matching horses to whisk her away like Cinderella to the ball. Or the young woman who waited inside who would serve as her guide through the evening's perils.

Claudia introduced herself before Veronica even had the chance to sit down, insisted Veronica call her by her first name, and then barely paused for breath during the short ride to Carlton House as she crammed in as much information as possible about what Veronica could expect from the evening. Most of it, though, was simply gushing about how exquisite the royal house was and why the party was being thrown. And names. Lots and lots of names and titles that simply flitted right over her head.

"And of course, as soon as we arrive, I'll introduce you to my brother, Marcus, and his wife." Claudia paused only long enough to glance outside the window. The flickering gas lamps that lined the drive confirmed they'd finally wound their way into the long line of carriages that snaked slowly toward the front of the grand building, despite the bells in the nearby church now striking only eight o'clock. "But perhaps you know them already—Marcus and Danielle Braddock, Duke and Duchess of Hampton?"

Veronica stifled an amused laugh and replied casually, "No, I don't believe I do." As if she were in any position to know a duke and duchess! And not just any duke, either, but the man second only to Wellington in being England's greatest hero in the wars. "The general is your brother?"

Claudia craned her neck for a better view toward the front portico to gauge how far they were from arriving. "Yes. And I love him dearly." The carriage's progress had now stalled completely. She frowned as if contemplating if they should leave the carriage and make a run for it on foot. "But that doesn't mean there aren't times when I want to send him back to France."

Veronica smiled. She liked Claudia. A great deal.

"Marcus often forgets that he's no longer a general and tries to order the Braddock women around." She slid Veronica a long-suffering look. "It never goes well for him."

Veronica's lips twisted. "I can imagine."

"Merritt served under him in the army, you know. In the Coldstream Guards. Merritt and Brandon Pearce and Clayton Elliott—they're all like family to us. Which was why I was so happy to do this favor for him tonight and accompany you."

Her chest panged at the mention of Merritt's name. She hadn't seen him since the riot, although thank God she hadn't, because she had no idea what she would say when she finally did. *I hope you don't mind that I went mad, dropped to my knees, and…*

"To attend this celebration in particular," Claudia rambled on, "to welcome Prince Gorchakov and Count Wittgenstein to England—and all the other foreign nobles in attendance, too— oh, this is going to be the event of the year!"

Or how shamelessly I enjoyed it and very much want to do it again.

"Everyone will be talking about it right through the holidays and into the next Parliament."

You've gotten under my skin, and I have to find a way to push you out before you destroy me.

"And to think that we're among the lucky few thousand who are favored enough to attend!"

Veronica snapped out of her reverie. "Few *thousand*?"

"Oh yes!" Claudia nodded vigorously and set the ostrich plume in her coiffure bobbing. "All the cream of English society will be there."

That wasn't Veronica. But neither was a barrister for that matter. She frowned. "I don't understand. How did Merritt secure invitations for us?"

"He sent the palace your name as his guest." Claudia shrugged, as if invitations to royal balls were everyday occurrences. But then, for the sister of a duke, they most likely were.

"But why was *he* invited in the first place?"

An odd mix of bewilderment and curiosity crossed her face. "You don't know?"

Apparently not. "Know what?"

Claudia began to answer but then hesitated, as if thinking better of whatever she was about to say. Finally, she explained, "Merritt's father is a High Court judge. One of the most respected and powerful in the entire empire."

Her stomach plummeted. He'd told her that his family had worked in law for generations, but he'd never mentioned that his father was a High Court judge. Fate was surely laughing at her! No wonder Merritt judged her so critically. It was in his blood.

Sensing Veronica's sudden unease, Claudia reached across the compartment to put her hand over hers. "Don't be worried about tonight. We're all here to help you if you need us. Especially Merritt."

Oh, he wanted to help her all right. Right back into Newgate.

"Just enjoy yourself and have a grand time," Claudia urged and squeezed her hand. "When else will you get to drink this much fine champagne and devour all the truffles you can eat?"

Veronica stifled a laugh at the irony. When indeed?

"Oh, I almost forgot!" Turning her head from one side to the other, Claudia removed her beautiful teardrop-shaped pearl ear-bobs and held them out to Veronica. "These are for you, to finish off your outfit."

Claudia's generosity stunned her. "I—I couldn't possibly wear them."

"But you simply must. They'll go perfectly with your gown."

Veronica's eyes stung at the gesture. Obviously, Merritt hadn't told Claudia the truth about her, or she never would have offered to loan jewelry to a woman whom society believed was a criminal.

"I might lose them…" And never be able to replace them. "I can't accept." But how much she wished she could! Temptation to reach for them itched at her fingertips.

"But you have to! I told Merritt I'd—" Claudia broke off and bit her bottom lip. When she started again, her eyes and voice were pleading. "As a friend—that is, I hope we'll become dear friends—it would mean a great deal to me if you would wear them. I'll retrieve them from you in a few days." Her eyes gleamed mischievously. "Until then, consider them yours."

Not wanting to offend her, Veronica reluctantly accepted them and placed them on her ears. She was struck by how perfectly the teardrop pearls matched her gown.

Claudia glanced out the window. "Our turn." She let out a long sigh. "Finally."

The carriage stopped directly in front of the wide portico inside the courtyard. A uniformed footman in the regent's elaborate gold-trimmed velvet livery rushed down the wide steps to flip the step and open the door for them. With a quick bow, he reached inside to help Claudia to the ground. Then he turned back for Veronica.

The moment her slipper touched the gravel she knew she'd been swept away into a magical world. Where else could she have been, all wrapped up in satin and fur and pearls, surrounded by the glow of flickering lamps and the shimmer of crystal decorations? Bright music drifted through the large double doors that stood open wide in welcome to the sumptuously dressed guests who streamed toward the grand house. No, not a house—a palace, where she was a guest of the Prince of Wales.

Goose bumps dotted her skin. Dear heavens, she'd slipped into a fairy tale!

"This way." Claudia took her arm and guided her toward the steps as their carriage rolled away behind them to make room for the next arrivals.

Veronica pulled in a deep breath to tamp down the excitement crackling inside her and did her best not to gawk at the spectacle surrounding her. She was playing a role tonight, she knew. Just as she knew the only reason she was here was because Merritt and the Home Office still dangled a pardon over her head.

Perhaps for a few minutes at least, she could do as Claudia had urged and simply enjoy the wonder of the grand ball unfolding around her. Perhaps she might even be able to convince herself that she belonged here.

Inside the entrance hall, a uniformed footman checked their invitations and then welcomed them to Carlton House with a curt nod of his head. They handed their wraps to a second footman with one hand and accepted glasses of champagne from the silver tray of a third footman with the other. Even the bubbles in her glass seemed to sparkle more splendidly than she'd ever seen in champagne before, and the taste of them popping on her tongue—*divine*.

They pressed through the crowd gathered around the grand entrance and ventured deeper into the series of reception rooms. Yards of silk and shining crystal decorated tall windows and walls, freshly cut flowers filled large urns and vases, chandeliers glittered nearly as brightly as the jewels that covered the ladies…and over it all, the sweet scent of beeswax candles mingled with the soft strains of violins and cellos.

The rooms unfolded like a maze, each more elaborate and fantastical than the next.

Veronica moved her gaze around the enormous green drawing room that had been decorated to resemble a forest. A tall fountain done up like a waterfall spilled dark-blue water into a shallow stream that circled the edges of the room and was filled with large goldfish and floating candles. Her lips parted incredulously. Goldfish... *Good heavens*. Where did one find that many goldfish in London? How did one even think of that idea in the first place? But as her gaze followed the stream around the room, she knew it was simply the most marvelous thing she'd ever—

Merritt. Her eyes landed on him in the crowd, and the sight of him took her breath away.

Standing straight and tall beneath the glow of the chandeliers, every inch of him revealed the regimented former soldier he'd once been and the respected barrister he'd become, from his broad shoulders beneath the black kerseymere jacket all the way down to the polished shine of his shoes. She was certain he'd carefully chosen every piece of his finery tonight to emphasize his place in London society...the dark-blue silk waistcoat that matched his eyes, the ruby pin in his snow-white cravat, the white breeches that tightly hugged his muscular thighs. Only his dark-brown hair, left in an unruly mess of thick waves, hinted at the rebel beneath the façade.

God have mercy. She'd never seen him look more powerful and confident, not even when he'd been wielding a sword. The sight of him nearly undid her.

But it was his smile that captivated her, that easy grin that crinkled the corners of his eyes as he laughed at something said by one of the men with him.

When he saw her, he froze. Only for a heartbeat's pause, yet long enough that their gazes locked. This time when a smile curled his lips, she knew it was for her and her alone, and an ache of longing corkscrewed itself deep into her core.

This is only a dream. She pulled in a deep breath to calm her spiking pulse as his gaze dropped over her to slowly assess how her satin gown draped over her body, how her hair was pinned in a riot of misbehaving curls on her crown. His smile deepened. *Tonight isn't real.* A low heat began to simmer in her belly, and he prickled goose bumps across her bare skin everywhere he looked. *Only a dream...*

Please, God, don't let me wake up!

His eyes never left her as Claudia led her through the crowd toward him and the small group of friends gathered around him. She barely heard Claudia introduce her to her brother, Marcus, Duke of Hampton, to his wife, Danielle, and to the Earl of Sandhurst and his countess, because with every thumping heartbeat, she was aware only of the heat of Merritt's gaze on her as he waited patiently to claim her for the evening as his guest.

When he finally did, taking her hand and bowing over it, she wasn't prepared for the tingle in her fingertips that spread up her arm and landed heavily in her breasts.

"Miss Chase." His deep voice fluttered through her. "You look absolutely enchanting this evening."

His words were merely empty flattery in front of his friends. Her head knew that, yet her foolish heart yearned for it to mean so much more.

"And where is the judge?" Claudia craned her neck to search through the crush. "I want to introduce Miss Chase to your father."

Veronica's knees turned to jelly. She wasn't at all prepared for that!

"Father's here, but he's lost somewhere in the party," Merritt explained. "The last I saw of him, he was cornering the Duke of Chatham into making a donation to the Foundling Hospital. We'll have to make introductions later."

She eased out a silent sigh. *Thank God.* More nervousness percolated inside her at the thought of meeting his father than it had at meeting the duke and earl.

"Good, you've got champagne." The duchess nodded at Veronica's glass. "We can make toasts." She held up her own flute and explained, "Tonight, while the rest of the party is celebrating the Lithuanian contingent, we're celebrating something even better."

"And what is that, Your Grace?"

The duchess beamed. "Merritt has been named King's Counsel!"

Merritt dropped his gaze to his glass and said nothing as he watched the bubbles escape to the surface.

"You have?" Veronica's chest warmed with genuine happiness for him, even if the news only widened the chasm between them. "That's wonderful."

His gaze raised solemnly to meet hers. "Is it?"

"Isn't it?"

"Doubtful."

"Not at all."

"A mistake."

She lifted her glass to toast him. "Well deserved."

He smiled faintly, surrendering the argument although obviously not at all convinced.

Suddenly, she was aware of everyone's curious stares moving back and forth between her and Merritt, as if they were watching two actors onstage. She quickly took a sip of champagne to cover her self-consciousness, although she supposed tonight they were exactly that—two people playing out their parts.

The Earl of Sandhurst lifted a brow. "Do you two often converse like that?"

"Yes," they answered with simultaneous sighs of aggravation.

Their gazes immediately darted to the other, which drew a small smile from Veronica and a frown from Merritt.

"Well then." The Duke of Hampton raised his glass, offering the toast his wife had started. "To Merritt Rivers, the best KC in the empire."

Merritt's lips twisted as he reluctantly joined in by lifting his glass, but he corrected, "Next to my father."

They all smiled at that and drank both to his father and to him, yet Veronica noticed the distraction darkening his face. God help her, she noticed *everything* about him. But then, when a man was this dashing, how could any living woman not?

"And what are we toasting?" An elegantly dressed older man with silver-gray hair approached the group, welcomed by all with warm smiles.

Except by Merritt, who suddenly stiffened and paused grimly before lowering his glass.

"Even with the *ton*'s rapid channels of gossip," the man continued affably, "you couldn't possibly have heard of my success in twisting an additional thousand pounds out of Chatham for the hospital."

Claudia beamed and rested a familiar hand on the man's arm. "Merritt's recognition as King's Counsel, of course!"

"Well, then I've arrived at exactly the right moment." The man snagged a glass of champagne from a passing footman and lifted it into the air. "To Merritt and all he's worked so hard to accomplish." His eyes glistened. "We're all so very proud of you."

Merritt grimaced into his glass. "Thank you, Father."

Veronica's breath strangled. *Father?* Only Merritt's hand shooting out to take her by the elbow and steady her kept her from sinking to the floor. How could she not have noticed immediately the similarities between the two men? The same build, same bright eyes, same jaw—

"How thoughtful of the regent to throw you a party to celebrate." The same sense of humor.

She slid a curious glance over the judge, and this time, she easily noted the commanding presence shared by the two men, their dashing charisma, and their undeniable good looks. A peculiar sensation struck her that she was staring at Merritt twenty-five years into the future.

His father caught her staring and crooked her a grin. Good Lord, the two men even shared the same smile!

He held out his hand toward her. "I don't believe we've met."

And if there were a God, He would make the earth open up and swallow her right then so they wouldn't ever have to.

"Father, this is Miss Veronica Chase," Merritt introduced, seemingly no more happy about the meeting than Veronica. "Miss Chase, may I introduce my father, the Honorable Mr. Justice James Rivers?"

Slipping her hand into his, she somehow managed to sink into a short curtsy without her jellied knees dropping her to the floor. "A pleasure to meet you, sir."

"And you, Miss Chase." The judge sketched her a short bow before releasing her hand. "I hope you're enjoying yourself this evening. First time to Carlton House?"

Veronica blinked. Who exactly did this man think she was? She slid a sideways glance at Merritt for answers about what he'd told his father about her, but his stoic expression gave no help.

So she answered truthfully, "Yes, it is." Then the devil inside her made her add, "And most likely my last."

"We should all be that fortunate," the judge murmured with a wink.

Veronica smiled. She liked him. Of course, though, he made her as nervous as a mouse cornered by a cat. Yet there was something about him that she found endearing.

"And your family?" he asked, politely striking up conversation. "Are they here tonight as well? I wonder if I know them."

Only if he frequented the docks and rookeries...but then, didn't his son? "Perhaps you've encountered them in your judgeship."

"Ah, so your family's involved with the courts and law?"

Her lips curled. "You could say that."

Beside her, Merritt smothered a curse only she could hear and tossed back the rest of his champagne.

"If you'll all excuse us," he interjected before his father could ask her more questions—and before she could give more answers. "I'd like to take Miss Chase for a turn through the party." He placed his empty glass onto the tray of a passing footman and held out his hand to her. "Shall we?"

A tingle spread up though her from her toes. She knew he'd only asked in order to separate her from his father, yet wild horses couldn't have stopped her from accepting this invitation. Not tonight, not in the middle of her fairy tale. So she slipped her hand into his, to willingly be swept away.

Placing her hand on his arm, he led her away from the group. His friends' and father's curious stares surely followed after them.

"Your friends are lovely," she commented in a voice just low enough not to be overheard by anyone standing nearby in the crush.

"They're like family to me. I'd be lost without them."

"And your father is quite impressive."

"He means the world to me." He paused in front of the attendant positioned at the end of the room to change out her almost empty glass of champagne for a fresh one. "They all do."

She mumbled her thanks as she took the glass and raised it to her lips, eyeing him carefully over the rim. "What did you tell your friends about me?"

"The truth." He led her deeper into the party. "That you're a legal associate who's helping me uncover information about the riots."

Not *quite* the truth. "And what did you tell your father?"

"Nothing."

She kept the sting of that from registering on her face by lifting the glass to her lips and taking a long swallow. Of course he wouldn't have said anything about her. She might be dressed like a princess, but Merritt still saw her as nothing more than a criminal.

After all, that was the only reason she was here. So she changed the conversation back to business. "What do you want me to do tonight?"

"Lady Malmesbury is in attendance." He nodded at an acquaintance in the crowd. "I want you to get close to her and find out who was in the Malmesbury carriage three nights ago."

"Is that all?" she muttered sarcastically. "Might as well ask me to dance with the regent. I have just as good a chance of doing that."

He slid her a sideways glance. "If you're not up to the challenge, then I suppose we can call off the evening."

And your pardon along with it. The words lingered between them as clearly as if he'd spoken them aloud.

"No, I can do it." She'd *never* let him think her weak. Not him of all men. "But I have no idea who Lady Malmesbury is."

"I'll point her out to you when I see her. She's here. The men at the door confirmed it when I arrived." His eyes swept over the crowd. "You'll approach her at an opportune moment, make conversation, and uncover what information you can." He paused. "But don't take any risks."

She nodded. "Because it would put your mission in jeopardy."

He admitted quietly, keeping his attention straight ahead, "Because I don't want you to be hurt." Before her surprised mind could process that, he swiftly—if blatantly—changed topics. "Quite the party, isn't it? Let's circle through the rooms so you can see more of the place."

They moved farther into the party and through each of the reception rooms that held a specific form of entertainment for the guests...rooms for cards and games, picture galleries, dining rooms, a separate music room where a quartet played unnoticed by the guests. She could barely take it all in. Of course, her attention wasn't helped by having Merritt at her side, stealing most of her concentration away without even trying.

Finally, they arrived at the ballroom and the beating heart of the party. Somewhere within this crush was Lady Malmesbury, she was certain…along with the prince regent, a foreign prince or two, the Duke of Wellington, the prime minister, every peer in the Lords, and most everyone who served in Whitehall. Nervousness flared inside her and ricocheted out to the ends of her fingers and toes.

She didn't belong here. With every passing heartbeat, she waited for someone to point at her, call her out for a fraud, have the footmen remove her—

As if reading her mind, Merritt placed his hand over hers on his sleeve and reassuringly squeezed her fingers.

Her nervousness ebbed. He might never let her into his trust, but he had faith in her skills as a thief-taker and spy. She would let that be enough for now.

They joined the end of the long line of people waiting to be announced by the master of ceremonies so they could enter the room and officially join the party. As they inched closer to the front, Veronica peered into the ballroom, which seemed to shimmer in a sea of satin, silks, and jewels. Beautiful gold and crystal chandeliers as large as carriages cast their candlelight onto the room, revealing what appeared to be all of English society and an army of uniformed attendants in old-fashioned powdered wigs. From its balcony on the other side of the room, a full orchestra played strains of dance music, and floor-to-ceiling mirrors reflected the dancers as they glided past.

Finally, they reached the head of the line. As Merritt handed their invitations to the master of ceremonies, he leaned down to bring his mouth close to her ear. "There's something I need to tell you about the introduction that's about to be made."

An amused smile teased at her lips. "What's that? That you truly are Mrs. Fitzherbert after all?"

"No." He straightened and grimaced into the ballroom. "Something much worse."

The master of ceremonies thumped his staff loudly against the floor and called out, "Miss Veronica Chase…and the Right Honorable Lord Rivers!"

Fourteen

MERRITT STEELED HIMSELF AS VERONICA WHEELED TO GAPE at him. "*Lord* Rivers?"

"I'm a baron," he answered grimly and took her arm to lead her into the ballroom.

"You're a lord?" she repeated as if she couldn't fathom what that was. "A *lord*?"

"Stunned the daylights out of me, too, I daresay," he muttered and guided her forward toward the dance floor.

"A baron—"

"It wasn't my idea to become one."

"—who sits in the House of Lords."

"Unwillingly." He grimaced. "If it helps, it's only a title without any land."

She stopped him with a sharp tug to his arm. "No, that doesn't help."

Damnation. He supposed he deserved this, but why did she have to keep staring at him as if he'd just attempted to kill the king? "If you'll remember, I told you the night we met that I was a peer of the realm."

She arched an accusing brow. "You also told me that you were Mrs. Fitzherbert."

True. He was beginning to dislike that sharp mind of hers. "There was no reason to tell you about the barony that night."

"So you waited until right now?"

"It gave us entree to the ball and an opportunity to question Lady Malmesbury."

Her brow eased down at that bit of far-fetched logic as her lips hardened into a tight line. God help him, he wanted to kiss her mouth until it softened.

"Until a month ago, I was nothing but an ordinary barrister."
He gave a frustrated roll of his tight shoulders beneath his jacket.
"Believe me, if I could have refused the title, I would have."

"Why didn't you?"

"Because it means a great deal to my father." And he would
do anything for the people he loved. Even become a goddamned
peer.

She blinked, not quite able to understand all he was revealing.
God knew he barely understood it himself. "But—but how can
you work as a barrister and be a baron?"

"Very carefully." He'd never spoken truer words in his life.

"And one who prowls the city streets at night with a sword?"

He fixed her with a grave look. "*Very* carefully."

When she opened her mouth to challenge him, he took her
arm and led her around the perimeter of the room.

"Baron, barrister, King's Counsel—*none* of it matters, don't
you understand?" He leaned down to speak privately into her ear,
as if they were just another flirtatious couple among the crowd,
trying to decide whether to dance or sit out. "When people are
dying in the streets, what does any of that nonsense matter if innocents can't be saved?"

She didn't look at him, even though he felt her tense on his
arm. In her heart, he knew she agreed with him.

"That's why you're working with Clayton Elliott and me to learn
about the riots," he explained, "and why we're here tonight—to
stop innocent victims from being hurt. That's all that matters. The
rest of it is merely costume."

She nodded tightly but kept her gaze straight ahead as she
asked, "Is that what I am tonight—a convict in a costume?"

"No." What she was tonight…*simply breathtaking*.

But he didn't dare let himself go there. She was emblematic
of everything he'd spent his life fighting against, and he couldn't
forget that. No matter that Clayton doubted her guilt, no matter

how selfless she'd been with the people in the Court of Miracles. No matter how alluring she was.

So he lifted her hand to his lips to place a kiss to her fingers and answered instead, "You're my secret weapon."

She laughed at the unexpected comment, just as he'd hoped, and the tension between them faded. Apparently, distraction worked just as well in ballrooms as in sword fights.

"Are you ready for tonight?" he pressed.

"I was a lot readier before I knew you were a baron." She sent him a chastising glare that would have done a governess proud. "You should have told me before."

"And have you refuse to come? Never."

The little hellcat had the audacity to look offended.

"It was hard enough preparing you for tonight." He stopped them at the edge of the dance floor. Only a few yards away at the head of the room stood Prinny and what seemed like half the crowned heads of Europe. She didn't belong here, he knew that. But his gut certainly felt as if she did. "I couldn't risk having you flee at the last moment."

"I wouldn't have done that, not after you'd gone to so much trouble."

Guilt pricked at him. When she said things like that, he wished he could trust her more than he did. "Madame prepared you well, then?"

"She taught me not to spill my drink, not to flirt with the footmen, and how to curtsy to anyone who looks important and call them 'my lord' and 'my lady.' Is that what you mean?" She slid him a mischievous look. "*My lord.*"

"Perfect," he grumbled and stopped her before she could drop into a low curtsy that would have done the queen proud. "She's prepared you to be a housemaid."

With another laugh, this time at his expense, her red lips curled into a teasing smile that tingled down through him to his crotch.

"What Madame couldn't teach me, she made up for in contingency plans," she explained. "All kinds of strategies to keep me from drawing attention to myself. Is it working?"

"No. Everyone is staring at you."

She glanced around at the crowd and caught half a dozen people watching her. "Because I've done something wrong already?"

He frowned, not at all happy about it. "Because you're beautiful."

He couldn't help looking into her green eyes as he said that. But damnation if the little minx didn't stare boldly back, her eyes gleaming as heat flared once more between them. Desiring her was becoming as routine as breathing.

"And because none of them have any idea who you are," he added. "Which makes you not only stunning but also mysterious."

"Apologies," she said in a throaty rasp that only cinched tighter the knot she'd already put into his gut. "Next time, I'll blacken an eye and knock out some teeth, shall I?"

Next time. There wouldn't be a next time. Tonight was singular, and he wasn't prepared for the disappointment that panged sharply in his chest at that realization. "Just try to fit in, all right?"

She cast her gaze to the end of the room at the royals and heads of state. "Does this mean you won't introduce me to the regent? I've always thought Prinny so debonair. Maybe he'll dance—"

"Let him get his own girl." He covered a surprising prick of jealousy by adding cheekily, "After all, he has an empire full of them."

"Now, now, Mrs. Fitzherbert! What a thing to say about—"

"The pleasure of dancing with you tonight belongs to me." He took the glass from her hand, tossed back the remainder of the champagne, and handed it off to a passing attendant. "Princes be damned."

Her mouth fell open, for once stunned silent. He opportunistically seized the moment to pull her onto the dance floor and into a waltz.

When she finally found her voice, she warned, "I think that was treasonous."

"Well, you know us barristers." He quirked a grin. "Always a seditious lot."

He twirled her in a circle and kept turning her against all rhyme and reason until she fell laughing against his chest. Then he took her into proper position and promenaded her across the floor.

Good God, she was lovely, dancing as fluidly as she wielded a sword. Yet every sweeping step was graceful and utterly feminine, made even more so because he'd witnessed firsthand the other side of her. That fierce woman warrior who even now lurked beneath the soft satin of her gown.

He'd never met another woman like her and knew he never would again. She was as singular as this night.

Damn it that his attraction for her wasn't merely physical, that it was so much more than mere beauty and mystery. It was her sharp mind that had him eagerly anticipating every bantering conversation with her, along with a bravery he'd rarely witnessed outside the men he'd served with in the wars. He'd seen her interact with the people at the Court of Miracles and knew how she took care of them, and her loyalty to Fernsby went beyond whatever favor he'd done for her; she was caring for an old man who would have otherwise died on the street.

But he'd also read the court report of her trial with his own eyes, knew she'd pled guilty. According to the evidence, Veronica was a criminal, no matter how much he wished she wasn't.

Yet none of that kept him from wanting her.

Sensing the unease in him, she asked quietly, "Why do I have the feeling sometimes that you're not happy with me, like now?"

"I wanted you to blend into the crowd tonight," he dodged. "And you certainly do not blend."

Unable to help himself, he dropped a heated glance down her

front, as far as he could while still leading her through the waltz. God only knew what wolfish expression darkened his face, but it was fierce enough that she shivered in his arms.

"That's not what I meant," she corrected in a husky voice, evidence that she was just as affected by the dance as he. "You tease me and spar with me, in every way, yet you don't seem to like me very much."

Not *like* her? Sweet Lucifer, he nearly laughed! She had no idea… He lowered his mouth as close to her ear as the waltz allowed. "A woman who insists on having her way with me in dark alleys? A man would have to be dead not to like that."

She eased away from him, and her green eyes darkened. No amusement was visible anywhere in her at the teasing flirtation that was meant to distract her.

"Even now, after spending so much time together," she said quietly enough that he could barely hear her over the orchestra, "you still believe that I couldn't possibly be anyone except a criminal, that I deserve to be scorned."

He said nothing to defend himself.

"It must be so easy in your world," she mused somberly, "where everything is black or white, guilty or innocent, with no blurring of the ground in between. But believe me that the world is filled with shades of gray." She looked away. "Whether we like it or not."

The waltz ended, the orchestra finishing with a flourish of notes. The dancers all circled to a stop with bows and curtsies.

When Veronica began to move off the dance floor, he stopped her with a touch to her arm. She stiffened but didn't turn to look at him.

And thank God she didn't when he lowered his mouth over her shoulder and admitted, "I did feel that way about you, when I first learned who you were and what you'd done." He didn't release her even as the other couples around them moved off the floor, even when he saw her bosom rise and fall with wary breaths at his confession. "You *were* nothing to me then but a criminal who deserved to be used, who didn't warrant my concern. And certainly not my respect."

"And now?" she asked breathlessly.

"I don't know what to think." He confessed in a low voice, "Except that I can't stop thinking about you."

Fifteen

VERONICA GLANCED OVER HER SHOULDER AT MERRITT, AND his haunted expression stole her breath away. She could read the truth in every emotion that stirred on his face and in the intensity with which he stared at her...desire, the hesitancy to trust, and warring confusion.

"If I told you I was innocent," she whispered breathlessly, hesitating at each word over the enormity of what she was asking, "if I could convince you of it..." *Would it make a difference to you? Would you look at me just once as something other than a creature to be scorned?*

But if she convinced him, she'd be offering up Filipe to the flames in her place. More—she'd have to reveal everything from her past. *Everything.* And then she'd no longer be a woman to be scorned but one to be despised.

"Never mind." She blinked rapidly as she walked away before he could see any glistening in her eyes.

But the frustrating devil wouldn't let her escape her misery and strode after her to once more take her arm and be the perfect model of a society gentleman escorting his partner from the dance floor.

"Perhaps," he admitted reluctantly, "you could try."

Her heart somersaulted. Oh, the foolish thing! Agreeing on *perhaps* was nothing more than an empty illusion, as ephemeral and unrealistic as the goldfish in their drawing room stream. Their two worlds clashed and always would. No fairy-tale evening could change that.

Yet knowing how much it cost him to soften even that little bit toward her, she nodded and lied, "Perhaps I will."

Wordlessly, he took her hand and lifted it to his lips to place a kiss to the backs of her fingers—

He froze.

Veronica followed his gaze across the room. "What is it?"

"The woman in the dark-blue dress with the white ostrich feather in her hair." He lowered her hand. "Lady Malmesbury."

Reality crashed into her dream like an ax blow. She pulled in a deep breath. The fairy tale was over.

Knowing what she had to do, she slipped her hand from his and walked on without him. She moved casually through the crowd toward the countess without a single glance back.

Lady Malmesbury excused herself from her conversation with an older woman in a bright orange turban and walked out of the ballroom. The countess headed toward the main reception rooms—rather, toward the series of anterooms and closets that served as retiring rooms—and Veronica followed. Gladly so.

After that conversation with Merritt, she needed a moment to herself to catch back the breath he'd stolen and ease the nervous flutters stirring low in her belly. Not butterflies, nothing as delicate as that. These were roiling rapids that threatened to sweep her off her feet and carry her away. *Never* had she been as torn about anyone as she was about him.

But there was no help for it. There was no way to shore with him.

Veronica stepped into the retiring room shortly after the countess, then paused to glance around the room. Dressing tables adorned with tortoiseshell brushes, powders, and rouge pots lined one wall, and a red velvet settee sat against the other. A large screen separated off the end of the room from where the soft rustle of fabric tattled on where the countess had gone. Two women inside the room who were chattering up a storm over the most recent on-dit fell silent as they raked their gazes over Veronica, then excused themselves from the room, leaving her alone with the countess. *Perfect.*

A few moments later, Lady Malmesbury emerged from behind the screen. The distracted frown on her face from adjusting her skirts turned into a faint but pleasant smile when she saw Veronica, who suddenly busied herself with adjusting her stocking.

"Surely, the combination of long skirts, tight corsets, and having to use the jordan is an invention of the devil," Veronica tossed out in an attempt to establish friendly banter.

"Most likely just a man's," the countess corrected, falling into easy conversation as she sat at one of the dressing tables to check her hair.

"Fascinating party, isn't it?" Veronica fussed with the hem of her gown. "I've never seen anything like it." That was the God's truth.

"This is your first time to Carlton House."

Not a question, and her heart missed a beat. Of course a countess would recognize that Veronica didn't belong here. "Yes, it is."

"Well, now that you've arrived in England, you should know the parties here are unlike anything you're used to on the Continent."

Her tense shoulders eased down. Lady Malmesbury hadn't recognized her for a fraud. She'd thought Veronica was part of the foreign contingent. Warm pleasure spread through her that someone as high ranking as a countess thought she belonged here.

She played along and thickened the Portuguese accent she normally worked to quash. "How so?"

"No sense of restraint, for one." She frowned at her reflection and reached for the tiny ceramic rouge pot. "I've always found that tendency ironic in the prince regent, given the usual reserved nature of the English."

Veronica smiled, having thought just that herself. "I understand it is unusual to have such a grand party at this time of the year."

"It is. Most balls are held when Parliament is in session and the aristocracy are all in town. It's shooting season now, so most everyone is away at their country houses until after the new year."

"But you are not. You are in London."

"Only as of yesterday afternoon. I was in Brighton until then."

So…it wasn't Lady Malmesbury who was in the carriage outside the Ship's Bell. "And your husband?" She grimaced at a nonexistent tear in her hem. "Why is he not in the country?"

"Oh, but he is." The countess dabbed the red pigment lightly onto her lips. "Malmesbury would never give up an opportunity to hunt, not even to meet the prince of Lithuania. He left London as soon as Parliament ended and refuses to return until January."

Just as Merritt had said. But if neither Lord nor Lady Malmesbury were in London, who was in the carriage?

"That cannot be," Veronica muttered. "I am certain I saw a carriage bearing the earl's crest two or three days ago." An ironic smile tugged at her lips. "The baron who was with me said it was yours."

Lady Malmesbury stiffened, her fingertip pausing as she smeared the rouge over her bottom lip. Then she smiled tightly. "I'm not the only woman in London who has a carriage marked with the earl's crest." She wiped off her hands on a towel and shoved the rouge pot away as she muttered caustically, "Malmesbury's like a hound that pisses around his kennel to mark his territory. He loves to put his mark on all he possesses."

Veronica noted the feminine hostility with which she'd said that, the underlying wounded pride…

A mistress.

The countess rose from the bench and pulled on her long white gloves with as much dignity as she could muster. Without another word or glance at Veronica, she left the retiring room, as if afraid she might see amusement on Veronica's face at her predicament. Or pity.

Veronica pulled in a deep breath to calm herself. A mistress! Or a mistress's carriage at least. She'd gotten the information from the countess in the most improper, terrible way, but the prick of guilt that brought was overshadowed by the realization that they had their next link in their investigation.

She hurried toward the door. When Merritt heard about this—
A woman's reflection in the mirror startled her. She halted.

For a moment, she didn't recognize herself in the elegant styling
of her hair and the length of neck and nape it revealed, the drape
of her satin gown as it fell from her tight bodice to her slippers, the
long white gloves that stretched to her elbows. Her life had given
way from satin to steel since her mother died, and she'd forgotten
what it was like to dress so elegantly, to move through the world
of the aristocracy. The woman in the mirror wasn't who she truly
was anymore, yet every inch of her longed to be her again. The one
who enjoyed grand parties beneath shimmering chandeliers, who
strolled in the morning sunlight down wide avenues, who rode in
fine carriages through the park.

The woman Merritt thought was beautiful and mysterious.

She'd stepped into a dream, right down to the delicate pearl
teardrops at her ears. Veronica smiled at her reflection as she
reached up to touch one. Claudia said they'd complete her outfit,
and she'd been right. As if they'd been chosen specifically with this
gown in mind—

A harsh sound of self-recrimination fell from her lips as the
truth struck her. Oh, she felt like a complete nodcock! They
looked as if they'd been chosen for this dress because they had
been. By Merritt.

"You devil," she whispered as she caressed the earbob. "You
wonderful, surprising, and utterly frustrating man."

Perhaps, that was what he'd said. That perhaps she could convince him, that perhaps he was receptive to being convinced. The
pearls might very well have been his first concession toward seeing
her as something other than criminal, as a woman as fine as the
other ladies in attendance tonight.

This was an opportunity she fully planned on seizing. Because
she *was* just as fine as they were, just as deserving of Merritt's
attentions.

Her soul ached to be part of his world with a longing she'd never felt before. It should have been hers…the glamour and sparkle and magic of nights like this, along with the calm and security that such a privileged life bestowed long after the party ended and the candles were extinguished. After all, she'd been part of this world once, before it was stolen from her.

Tonight, she might finally have her chance to reclaim the life she'd been meant to have. *Perhaps.*

Hope blossomed in her chest as she hurried from the retiring room. When she entered the ballroom, she stopped to catch her breath and cast a searching glance around the crowded room for Merritt. Her pulse spiked when her eyes landed on him as he stood so casually yet confidently at the side of the room, talking and laughing with his friends.

With a slow smile, she whispered to herself, "Mrs. Fitzherbert."

But then the crowd parted. The moment lasted only a heartbeat but long enough for her to gain a good look at the people standing with him. A duke and an earl, a duchess and a countess, a High Court judge, distinguished society gentlemen and beautiful ladies…surrounding a man who was both a baron and King's Counsel. All of them distinguished and regal, all of them possessing power and status.

None of them like her.

An invisible fist crushed her chest, and all hope squeezed out through its fingers. Perhaps…*not.*

Oh, what a fool she was to think she could ever be one of them! Madame Noir was right. She didn't belong here. The door to this world had shut to her over a decade ago and would never reopen. No matter how finely she dressed, no matter how many lessons she subjected herself to, she was still an outcast. And now always would be.

Merritt looked up and caught her staring. When he smiled at her across the room, the realization of all she could never have sliced into her like a blade.

She couldn't move, couldn't breathe. It took every ounce of strength she had to simply stand there and return his stare without breaking into tears.

His smile slowly faded into a frown. He knew something was wrong, she could read his concern on his brow, yet he didn't have any notion of the truth. And she fully intended to keep it that way. To see his look of disbelief that she would even consider a future in his world, to hear him laugh at her—worse, to see his pity for her… Dear God, it would end her!

She sucked in a deep, ragged breath and willed herself to be strong. The night was at an end, as was their mission now that she knew who was in the carriage with Smathers. Only a few minutes longer to endure. Then it would all be over, and she'd go back to doing what she'd always done before—whatever it took to survive.

He excused himself from his friends and made his way through the crowd to her. His concerned frown deepened with every step.

"Veronica, are you all right?"

When he reached for her elbow, she moved away. She couldn't have borne his touch!

He dropped his hand to his side. "What's wrong?"

"I know who was in the carriage," she answered instead, gladly steering his attention away from her and onto their mission. "Malmesbury's mistress."

"A mistress?" Incredulity colored his voice.

"She has access to a carriage bearing the earl's crest."

"Are you certain?"

"Yes," she bit out angrily, clinging to the sliver of pride she still possessed. "I'm very good at gathering information. Do not doubt that."

He stiffened at the unexpected change in her. But what did she care if she'd offended him? He was lost to her.

"I'm not doubting you. I know exactly what you're capable of." The narrowed look he sent her was a reminder of all he knew about her—rather, all he *thought* he knew. He didn't know half the truth! "But why would a mistress want to start riots, and where would she find the money to pay the men?"

"I don't know," she said in a hoarse whisper, trembling as shivers sailed over her skin. Being this close to him was unbearable, and she needed to leave. *Now.* "And I don't care. I've done what you've asked of me. My role in this is over."

She hurried away as quickly as she could through the crush of bodies, out of the ballroom and into the circuit of reception rooms that had seemed so magical to her before. Now she recognized them as nothing but hollow fantasy, and they closed in around her until she struggled to breathe.

Desperate for air and heedless of where she was going, she accidentally smacked into a man's shoulder. She staggered back, mumbled an apology—

"Veronica." Merritt grasped her elbow from behind to steady her. His mouth lowered to her ear, and she shook from the concern that filled his deep voice. "What is wrong?"

She didn't dare look over her shoulder at him. "I'm—I'm—" she stuttered. Her mind whirled to latch on to any excuse to flee. "I'm not feeling well."

"Did something go wrong with Lady Malmesbury?"

More than he'd ever know! Yet she shook her head and lied. "No. I just—I don't feel well suddenly." From the way she trembled uncontrollably and the pallor that surely gripped her face, he had no reason to doubt that. "The noise and heat, all the people... I need to leave."

"Then you shouldn't be alone. I'll escort you home."

She bit back a laugh. *Home?* She had no home! Not a real one. Fate had taken that from her, too. "I can make my own way."

Yet the frustrating man didn't leave her side, keeping his firm hold on her arm and his other hand at the small of her back as he guided her through the party toward the front entrance. "Then I'll make certain you make your own way safely."

They reached the entrance hall, and he requested her wrap from the footman, who hurried away to fetch it. An eternity passed until the man returned with the beautiful length of fur and velvet, an eternity in which Merritt stared at her with troubled concern and unwittingly grew the ball of pain that twisted like gnarled metal inside her belly.

When he took the wrap from the footman and placed it over her shoulders himself, she nearly burst out of her skin.

"I don't need an escort," she shot sideways to him as he persisted in following her outside into the night and down the wide front steps. Oh, why wouldn't he leave her alone?

He kept pace with her as she practically ran alongside the line of waiting carriages, out of the courtyard, and into the avenue. "Dressed as you are tonight, yes, you certainly do."

"It's just a dress. I'm the same person beneath it as I've always been. The same woman who wears leather and steel to patrol the streets." The truth of that stung. *You can take the girl out of Saffron Hill…*

"Only if you've got a sword hidden up your skirt," he drawled.

"Wouldn't you like to find out?" she grumbled.

"Wondering about that did make waltzing with you very intriguing."

With a frustrated cry, she halted on the footpath just past the wrought iron fence and stared at the seemingly endless line of carriages that snaked out of the courtyard and spilled into all the surrounding streets. Her exasperation boiled over. How was she supposed to find a hackney amid all these? And for heaven's mercy, *why* wouldn't Merritt leave her alone?

She wheeled on him as her anguish bubbled to the surface. "You have to let me go—*please.*" Her voice choked in a plea for understanding. "I don't belong here."

In the darkness, she couldn't read the emotions that flicked across his face. *Thank God.* This would be the last time she would ever see him, and she didn't want her last memory of him to be colored by his pity for her.

"Veronica," he whispered and reached to touch her cheek. "What is—"

"Major Rivers!" A booming voice rang out.

Merritt spun around to place himself in front of her, and his hand dove to his sleeve and the knife he kept there. But that protective gesture only clawed anguish deeper into her heart.

A large man swaggered down the footpath toward them. As he emerged from the shadows, Veronica saw his blood-red uniform and the glint of medals on his chest.

"You *are* Major Rivers, correct?" the soldier pressed. "Haven't seen you in two years."

Merritt relaxed slightly, yet his concern for her remained and was evident in the glance he sent her over his shoulder before greeting the man. "Yes, General, it is." He held out his hand and corrected, "Or it was. I sold my commission after Waterloo."

The man slapped Merritt on the shoulder as he shook his hand. "A great loss to the British army."

"A great loss to the French, I'm afraid," Merritt drawled.

The teasing self-deprecation earned him a laugh from the general, but Veronica knew Merritt well enough to recognize that his joking was forced. Something about the way he'd tensed, how his expression hardened... Merritt did not like this man.

He stepped back to take Veronica's arm and bring her to his side. "General, may I introduce you to Miss Veronica Chase? Miss Chase—" He paused. Only a heartbeat's hesitation, but she noticed. "Major-General Horatio Liggett."

Liggett clicked his heels in exaggerated formality, then gave her a shallow bow and a wide smile. The man was certainly in a good mood, and he hadn't yet reached the party. "Miss Chase, a pleasure."

"General." As she dropped into a curtsy, she took a sideways glance at Merritt. Based on his expression, *not* a pleasure at all. And no longer any of her concern. Her heart still begged to flee and put this night behind her. "If you two will excuse me, I'll just go—"

"Stay," Merritt whispered into her ear. He tightened his hold on her arm and refused to let her leave.

Liggett smiled politely at Veronica, and she forced one in return so he wouldn't see her distress. But she couldn't stop the shiver that swept visibly over her. He was just another guest of the regent's, just another of the many important and powerful men who would crowd into Carlton House tonight, yet an inexplicable chill swirled down her spine at meeting him.

Merritt dragged the general's attention away from her by asking, "So you're attending tonight's party?"

"Not of my own choice. Damnable royal affairs," Liggett grumbled as he nodded toward the palace. "But every field marshal, the War Secretary, and even Wellington himself are all here tonight. If I want my orders, it seems I have to mix business with pleasure."

"What orders would those be?" Merritt forced out a good-natured ease that belied his tension. "Last time I checked, we'd won the wars."

"And now we must win the peace." The general glanced across the courtyard at Carlton House, all ablaze with light and pulsating with music and laughter. His smile never changed, but Veronica sensed the same tension in him that radiated from Merritt. "And regain the faith and trust of all Englishmen by showing strength and resolve, not frivolity, wastefulness, and weakness."

"How do we do that exactly?" Merritt asked.

"We begin by putting down the riots."

He squeezed her elbow in a silent signal. *This* was why he'd wanted her to stay.

"Those are my orders," Liggett explained. "I've been brought in to stop them before more damage is done."

"So why aren't you out tonight? Good weather for a riot, I would think…not that I know about those things."

Veronica fought to keep from rolling her eyes—and kept looking for any opportunity for escape. Military matters were none of her concern. Not anymore.

"There won't be a riot tonight," Liggett assured him.

"You're awfully certain."

"I'm awfully good when it comes to matters of civil unrest. Soldiers will be positioned to stop the next mob when it takes to the streets." He smiled smugly, as if the potential for lost lives was of no concern. "And I'll be there to lead them."

"With restraint, I hope."

"With necessary force. I have the authorization to use all resources at my disposal." He glanced at Carlton House with disdain. "While the regent has been wringing his hands over the Riot Act and been afraid to engage the rioters, Whitehall has been as decisive as I have. Mark my words, these riots *will* be stopped, and Londoners will once again feel safe in their homes and on their streets."

"How safe will the rioters feel to have their own countrymen firing upon them?" Merritt challenged quietly. "There will surely be innocents among the crowd who are there only to have their voices heard."

The general's face turned hard. "There are other ways of being heard. Any innocents among the crowd know the crimes they're committing by taking part, just as they know the consequences."

"I hope you're right, General." But Merritt's voice lacked all conviction.

"I will be *proven* right." Liggett dismissed the conversation with a nod and a stilted bow to Veronica. "Miss Chase, it was indeed a pleasure to meet you."

"And you, sir." Her eyes fell onto an unusual piece pinned to the general's chest, one crafted of metalwork and enamel that was half-hidden among his other medals. It was a pin in the shape of a key that she couldn't remember seeing on any other British officer she'd ever come across, and God knew she'd come across plenty during the wars. "That's a very interesting medal you have there—that key."

"This?" He glanced down at his chest and flicked it dismissively. "Just a symbolic piece."

"And what does it symbolize?"

"The keys to the kingdom." His smile faded, and he pulled at his gloves to bring them into place on his wrists. "My apologies, Rivers. I just learned about Miss Gordon. Damnable shame, that." He shook his head. "Damnable shame."

Merritt froze. Not one muscle moved, not even to breathe. He'd turned to stone.

"She was a fine woman with a bright future," Liggett continued. "How terrible that you weren't able to protect her."

Merritt lunged. His left hand went around the general's throat as he shoved the man backward against the wrought iron fence. He pinned Liggett there while his other hand drew back into a fist. He slammed it into Liggett's face, again and again—

"Merritt, no!"

Veronica grabbed his arm as he pulled back for another furious punch despite the blood that already oozed from the general's mouth. Merritt wrenched his arm to shake her off, but she refused to let go. Instead, she shoved herself between the two men, physically stopping him with her body.

He paused to gulp down great lungfuls of air and stared at her blankly in his fury, as if he didn't recognize her.

She pushed him back several steps to give Liggett room to slip away from the iron bars. Her hands grasped Merritt's arms to hold him back. His tightly clenched fists and the rippling hardness of the muscles beneath his jacket terrified her. He was more than capable of killing the general with his bare hands if she hadn't stopped him.

"You'll regret that," Liggett promised. He scooped up his hat from the ground where it had fallen and wiped the blood from his mouth onto a handkerchief he'd pulled from his pocket.

The rage cleared from Merritt's eyes, if not the darkness that still gripped his face and kept every muscle in his body taut and ready to spring. His fists remained clenched as he spat out, "Doubtful."

Liggett jabbed a finger at Veronica. "Keep him under control, or I'll call for someone who can."

"Yes, General," she agreed quickly. Her hands tightened on Merritt's shoulders to keep him from doing something even more stupid, like attacking Liggett a second time as he walked away.

When the general was safely surrounded by the crowd at the front door, Veronica's gaze darted to Merritt. He stood as still as a statue and watched Liggett's back until he disappeared up the steps and into the house. His breath came forced and agitated, every inch of him metal-stiff. Blood had splattered across his waistcoat and breeches, and it gruesomely matched the ruby pin in his cravat.

"Merritt." Confusion spilled through her. "What on God's earth…"

When he didn't look at her, still lost in whatever dark thoughts were swirling inside his head, she reached up to cup his cheek against her palm.

He flinched at her touch and looked down at her. A murderous rage simmered in him that she'd never seen before.

She knew it had nothing to do with the riots. "Who is Miss Gordon?"

He stared at her for a long, terrible moment in which her troubled heart pounded off the passing seconds. Then he answered quietly, guilt thick in his voice, "My fiancée."

An electric shock jolted through her, followed immediately by a strike of jealousy so hot that she winced. He was…*engaged*?

"I—I don't understand," she breathed out, in her shock unable to speak any louder. Her hand trembled with confusion as she reached up to touch the earrings he'd given her. "Then why isn't she here tonight? Why didn't Claudia mention her?"

He looked away as the answer tore from him. "Because she's dead."

Sixteen

WITH A FIERCE GROAN, MERRITT SWUNG THE SWORD WITH ALL his might and sliced it into the sawdust dummy in the Armory's training room. He pulled back the blade and swung again. Pain shot up his exhausted arm and landed in his chest from straining the tight muscles all along the right side of his body. He welcomed the pain. Craved it.

Deserved it.

The now dull blade lodged deep in the dummy, slicing through the leather casing and sawdust fill to stick into the wooden post in the very center. Panting hard from the past hour's exertion, he wrenched the blade to twist it loose, then stepped back to do it again. And again. And again...and would keep attacking until he'd purged all the burning anger and churning emotions inside him.

Damn Liggett for mentioning Joanna! The bastard had no business talking about her. Certainly not at that moment, not when Merritt needed to focus on the riots, when he needed to figure out who was behind them and why—

When he was standing next to Veronica, wanting her more than he'd wanted any woman in his life. Including Joanna.

His shoulders slumped with recrimination. That was why he'd attacked Liggett, why he'd wanted to murder the bastard right there in front of Carlton House. For the first time since Joanna died, he hadn't been thinking of her.

He'd been thinking of another woman.

He dropped his arm to his side, the tip of the sword pinging softly against the stone floor, and scoured his free hand over his face. Veronica...*Christ*. He'd managed to dodge all her questions about Joanna and put her into a carriage to send her away, then came straight here. He'd taken time only to shrug out of his jacket and roll up his shirtsleeves before he'd picked up a sword to physically beat down his guilt and confusion.

But the look on her face! She'd wanted answers he simply wasn't willing to give.

What was he supposed to tell her? *My fiancée is dead because I wasn't able to protect her.*

He sucked in a mouthful of air and lunged at the dummy again. *She put her faith in me, but I failed to be the man she needed, a man who would keep her safe.*

He hacked the blade against the leather now in wide, sweeping swings of his arm as if the sword were an ax. *And if you put your trust in me, the same might just happen to you.*

Too dull now to cut into the leather, the blade simply bounced off the dummy. Merritt let out a furious growl and pounded at it with the sword's pommel, striking again and again. Each jarring blow shot an agonizing jolt of pain straight up his arm and into his chest.

"I think it's dead," a deep voice called out from behind him.

Merritt wheeled around to find Marcus Braddock, Duke of Hampton, standing in the doorway to the training room. Behind him stood Brandon Pearce, Earl of Sandhurst. Both men still wore their evening finery, most likely coming straight here from Carlton House. And neither man was someone Merritt wanted to see at that moment.

Marcus came forward and frowned at the destruction Merritt had unleashed upon the dummy. He twisted around his fingers a strip of leather that had been hacked from the covering.

"I'll replace it," Merritt told him.

"And who replaces you?" Marcus asked quietly. He released the leather casing and gestured toward the sword. "Seems you're bent on self-destruction these days."

The accusation irritated like hell. "You're wrong."

"I'm not. You're out every night prowling the streets and rookeries where even the night guard refuses to go because it's too dangerous."

"I'm capable of taking care of myself." *More* than capable. For God's sake, hadn't he dedicated nearly every waking moment of the last five years to fighting so he would never be caught off guard again? To prove it, he turned toward a second sawdust dummy a few feet away and stabbed it with his sword.

"You put yourself needlessly at risk night after night, neglecting your friends and family, ignoring your work—"

"*Not* ignoring it." In anger, he flayed the dummy. The dull blade snagged and ripped the leather casing instead of cleanly slicing, but he didn't care. Nor could he stop the punishing pain and fatigue that flooded through him with each slash and stab. "I did my job tonight." Another jab into the dummy, this one coming so hard that the blade bent as he stepped forward to thrust it into the leather and sawdust. He panted out between harsh breaths, "Malmesbury's mistress—it was her carriage that collected Smathers." He attacked the dummy from all sides now, taking long running charges at it, only to fade back to attack again. He crouched low in his stance, and his thighs burned. "That was my charge for the evening, and I succeeded."

"And publicly attacking a decorated general without provocation on the regent's front doorstep?" Pearce called out from the doorway. "Was that part of your charge, too?"

"No. *That* just felt damn good." In a spinning strike that dropped him onto the balls of his feet, he swung the sword in a complete circle and struck the dummy from the side. "The bastard deserved to be punched. You both would have done the same."

"No, we wouldn't have." Marcus crossed his arms in a commanding stance that had shaken fear through his enlisted men. "So what set you off like that?"

Merritt gritted his teeth and lunged. He stabbed the tip of the sword firmly into the leather, only to retreat three steps and lunge again. His frustration powered a fierce slash to the dummy's legs. "That's none of your business."

From the corner of his eye, Merritt saw Marcus stiffen, his demeanor growing impossibly more imperial. *Good.* Merritt loved the man like a brother and trusted him with his life, but this time, Marcus had overstepped.

"You attacked Liggett and then left without one word of explanation to any of us, including your father," Marcus reminded him. "Is that none of our business, too?"

"I'd finished all that needed to be done there and sent word to Clayton at Whitehall." The burning ache in his muscles and lack of breath in his lungs nearly overwhelmed him. Still, he fought on. He needed to purge every last piece of fire from inside him. "No reason to stay any longer."

Merritt swung his sword—

"No reason to stay with Miss Chase any longer, you mean," Pearce called out.

His sword missed its mark. It sailed through the air with a blow so strong that it propelled him forward after it. He stumbled to find his balance and remain on his feet.

Panting both for breath and to keep down his anger, he turned to face his best friend. "Exactly. Her part of the investigation is over." He swiped his arm across his face to wipe away the stinging sweat that fell into his eyes. "I don't need her any longer."

Pearce scoffed. "That's a damn lie if ever I heard one."

Merritt attacked. He charged across the room and forced Pearce back against the wall. He held him pressed there at sword point, the tip positioned beneath his chin.

"You bastard! You, of all people, have no right to say anything." The cold rage inside him worked to replace the anguish that had compelled him here in the first place. "I told you about Joanna's death in confidence, and you broke my trust."

"You told me because it was two days before Waterloo, you were foxed off your arse, and we all thought we were going to die in a hail of French cannon. And I told Clayton because I was worried about you." Pearce irritably batted the sword away with his arm. "I still am."

"We both are," Marcus interjected.

Wanting them to leave him alone, Merritt insisted, "I'm fine."

"Another damn lie," Pearce muttered.

This time when Merritt pointed the sword at his throat, Pearce grabbed it from his hand and threw it away. It landed with a tooth-jarring clatter against the stone floor.

"This has to stop," Marcus ordered. "Whatever it is that's driving you to take these risks, to behave so unlike yourself, it has to stop. *Now*. You're worrying Clayton, Pearce, me, our wives—" Marcus blew out a harsh breath. "For God's sake…you're worrying *your father*."

Merritt turned away to snatch up the discarded sword and to hide the guilt on his face. "My father isn't worried about me."

"More than you realize."

He crossed to the small table pushed up against the stone wall and grabbed a fresh towel from the stack. He rubbed it over his face. "I've given him no reason."

"He knows about your nighttime patrols."

Merritt froze, the towel resting against his damp nape. His father *knew*?

"He approached us about it at the party when he'd heard what you'd done to Liggett. He admitted that your focus has slipped during the past few months, that he worries about how you go out into the city at night, that you seem constantly distracted."

"But he doesn't know why," Pearce interjected.

"He thinks it's because of the war," Marcus continued. "Because you're having trouble adjusting to life back in London as a barrister after five years of being a soldier." He paused soberly. "But it has nothing to do with that, does it?"

Merritt shrugged and dropped the towel to the floor. "I think five years of sleeping in the mud and rain, eating spoiled food, and fearing for your life at every turn could make a man—"

"It's because of Joanna."

He wheeled toward Pearce. His jaw clenched so hard that his teeth ached. "*Do not* mention her."

But Pearce wasn't cowed in the least and simply crossed his arms over his chest as he leaned against the wall, as if settling in for the rest of the night. "It's because she was killed in a riot, and now you're doing everything you can to stop anyone else from being hurt in one."

They had no idea about the darkness that drove him, about what really happened the night she died. But if they wanted to believe that was why he wanted to stop the riots, he'd gladly let them.

"Yes," he lied and set the ruined practice sword onto the table with a thud. "You've figured it out." He leaned back against the table, assuming the same crossed-arms stance as Pearce. "So now there's nothing more for you to worry about, and we can end this conversation."

"No, you're wrong," Marcus said thoughtfully, not to Merritt but to Pearce. "It's not about his late fiancée. At least not completely." He paused, his eyes narrowing as he studied Merritt. "It's about Miss Chase."

Merritt's pulse spiked. They were meddling too close for comfort now. "Miss Chase is no longer my concern," he drawled to deflect their prying.

"And that's the problem, isn't it?" Marcus leveled a hard gaze on him. "Because you very much want her to be."

"An escaped convict with a King's Counsel?" Merritt scoffed, yet the truth cut deep. "I'm a barrister, not a fool. If my behavior is worrying my father now, how happy do you think that news would make him?"

"How happy would it make *you*?" Pearce countered quietly.

"Miserable." That was the God's honest truth. If he couldn't protect a woman as predictable and conventional as Joanna, how on earth would he ever be able to protect someone like Veronica?

"Good. Because that would be a marked improvement." Marcus came forward and picked up the sword, then frowned at the ruined weapon. "Because where you are right now is self-destructive and dangerous, as if you're set on getting yourself killed and won't give up trying until you've succeeded."

Merritt let out a laugh. "I'm not being—"

Without warning, Marcus lunged, bringing the flat side of the blade against Merritt's chest and holding him in place against the table. Marcus pushed the blade hard into his waistcoat with both hands.

Merritt froze, knowing not to fight back against the former general.

"You're no good to anyone like his," Marcus bit out, his gaze as piercing as a shard of ice. "Not to your father, not to the Home Office, certainly not to the men of the Armory or to me. And not to Joanna's memory."

With a hard push, he released the blade and stepped back, leaving Merritt to catch the sword as it fell.

"You're not only placing our mission against Scepter in jeopardy," Marcus warned, "but your own life as well. So put the past behind you and move on before it destroys you and all you care about."

"I *am* moving on," Merritt shot back, the anger inside him flaring once more. This time at himself. "For God's sake! What do you think I'm doing with the riots?"

"Trying to save Joanna," Pearce answered quietly.

His words pierced Merritt's chest as easily as a saber. For a moment, he could do nothing more than remember to breathe.

"And you'll never be able to." Pearce pushed himself away from the wall and came slowly toward him. "No matter how many riots you stop, how many rioters you arrest and put behind bars, how many innocents you save—she's gone, and you can never bring her back. You're not grieving anymore, but you haven't yet let go of her either. You haven't let yourself move on, and you'll never be happy until you do."

And how the hell do I do that? Merritt's anger at himself turned into fury at how helpless he felt, how out of control in his own skin. He knew why guilt and anguish ate at his gut every waking moment, why it gave no quarter against the nightmares that plagued him.

Except when he was with Veronica.

When he was with her, he didn't think about Joanna or the man who killed her. He didn't remember the guilt that had rained down upon her parents when he'd told them she was dead or his grief at the future that had been stolen from him. What he felt was...alive. For the first time in five years.

Damn the world that it was Veronica! A woman who lived among the worst of London's underworld and represented everything he'd sworn to fight against. A woman who was the complete opposite of Joanna, in every way.

And damn himself that he couldn't stop wanting her. And not just in his bed but also in his life.

"You're no good to anyone like this," Marcus repeated quietly. "Come to terms with it, Merritt. And quickly. Before other people are hurt—including you."

That was the problem. Because no matter how hard he tried, he couldn't find a way to end it.

As Marcus turned away to leave the training room, the outer doors of the Armory screeched their familiar grating of metal upon metal. Clayton Elliott strode inside.

"You'll never guess what I learned tonight," he announced as he crossed the octagonal room to the side table that held the

Armory's collection of liquor. "I just returned from the Horse Guards. Thought maybe Nate Reed or one of the other men might have information—"

He sensed the thick tension pulsing between the three men and stopped. His hand froze in midreach for a bottle of whiskey.

Clayton quirked a brow. "Am I interrupting something?"

"Not at all." Marcus joined him at the side table to pour himself his own glass and nodded toward the ruined sword in Merritt's hand. "Merritt was in the process of destroying the training dummies."

"I see," Clayton muttered as Merritt laid the sword aside on a chair, then began to roll down his sleeves to cover the bruises on his forearms that he'd given himself tonight. But wisely, Clayton knew not to question further. "It's good you're all in fighting condition, then." He finished pouring his drink and took a healthy swallow before explaining, "I found out some interesting information about General Liggett."

Merritt ignored the troubled looks Marcus and Pearce sent him. "What's that?"

"Liggett volunteered to put down the riots."

"That's not surprising." Marcus frowned. "He's ambitious."

"But he's not a fortune teller," Clayton corrected. "His letter to Whitehall offering his regiment's services to deal with the mob arrived the morning after the first riot."

Pearce amended with a shrug, "He's *very* ambitious."

"And over a hundred miles away in Lincolnshire when he sent the letter." Clayton lingered at the side table to top off his glass. "The Royal Mail's good, but not good enough to stop time."

A cold chill raced through Merritt. He murmured, "He knew about the riots before they happened."

"Because he's been in communication with the men behind them," Marcus added.

"Through Malmesbury's mistress?" Shaking his head, Merritt

tugged at his waistcoat and sleeves to bring them back into place. "I have no idea how she's involved, but it's not because of Malmesbury. The man's incapable of staging riots from his country seat in Yorkshire, nor would he care unless the mob somehow improved pheasant hunting. So what connection does the mistress have to Liggett?"

"I think we should pay her a call and find out," Clayton decided. "First thing in the morning."

Pulling in a fortifying breath, Merritt slid his gaze around the circle at the men he considered to be his brothers, these men whom he trusted with his life. They needed his help and wanted to help him in turn. For that, he would always appreciate them.

But he couldn't bear remaining here a moment longer. He'd go out of his skin if he did. The walls were closing in upon him, and he couldn't sit still. He needed to patrol, burn off energy, clear his head—*now*.

"Then I'll be back at dawn." Merritt snatched up the jacket he'd tossed over the back of the sofa and walked away, out of the Armory and into the night.

Seventeen

THE TIGER OPENED THE CARRIAGE DOOR AND STEPPED BACK.

Veronica paused in the doorway, her eyes raised to the hulking warehouse which stood bleak and cold in the darkness. The Court of Miracles. The closest thing she had to a home.

And the last place she wanted to be.

But she'd already had the driver spend the last hour driving in circles around west London as if patrolling from the back of the carriage instead of on foot and still in her ball gown. She'd told herself that she needed a glimpse of the city to see what was happening tonight. But there was no riot, not even a stirring of one, and no reason she could fathom why there wasn't. The sky was crystal clear, the moon bright—the perfect night for destruction. She'd puzzled long enough on her drive that every quarter of an hour or so the driver would call down to ask if she was ready to head to her destination, and always, she asked him to continue driving on instead so she could view more of the city.

The simple truth was that she didn't want to go home. She wanted to stay as long as she could in tonight's swirling magic of music, bubbling champagne, glittering lights, and gowns. With Merritt.

But the inevitable end had arrived. The fairy tale was over.

She mumbled her thanks to the footman and stepped onto the muddy ground. Her beautiful slippers sank halfway into the filth. She grimaced. Ball costumes were not made for life in Saffron Hill.

She paused to hand up a coin to the driver in gratitude. Instead of hiring a hackney for her, Merritt had placed her inside one of the grandest carriages she'd ever seen, right down to its matching team of four horses and the tigers in their blue velvet livery. With a glance at the unfamiliar insignia on the door, she asked the tiger, "So you work for Lord Rivers, then?"

"No, ma'am."

Well, thank goodness for small—

"His Grace the Duke of Hampton."

Her shoulders slumped as she muttered, "Of course." Just another reminder of how very different their two worlds were. Merritt was best friends with dukes and earls; she stood in filth nearly up to her ankles. "You're out on an adventure tonight, then. I suppose the duke doesn't frequent neighborhoods like this."

The tiger laughed. "You'd be surprised what that duke gets up to, ma'am, him and his friends."

Her heart bounced painfully. "Like Lord Rivers, you mean?"

"Aye. He's unusual, that one."

Veronica couldn't stop the smile that pulled at her lips as she muttered beneath her breath, "You have no idea." She handed the tiger a second coin. "Thank you."

He gave a quick nod, then swung up into his perch at the rear of the carriage. He pounded on the roof to signal to the coachman, who flipped the ribbons and started the team forward.

Veronica watched until they disappeared from sight around the corner, not wanting them to see her enter the old warehouse and report back to the duke where she'd gone. She might be dressed like a princess, but she lived like a pauper.

"I still have my pride," she whispered to herself as she walked up the steps. What little of it was left.

She pushed at the old door, but the heavy thing wouldn't give. Someone had closed it up too tightly against the night. She had no choice but to lower her shoulder and shove into it as hard as she could. The door gave way, the creak of old hinges accompanied by the faint tearing of fabric against the splintered wood. The sound sickened her.

She looked down at her shoulder and the ripped gown. Her

heart would have broken at the damage if it hadn't already been ripped in two tonight.

She closed the door behind her and paused a moment to take in the building around her. Silent, still, and dark, despite the dozens of people crammed inside for protection against the night. There was no difference between this derelict building and countless others like it scattered across London where the poorest of the poor sought refuge.

"Except that I live here," she breathed out, barely loud enough for a whisper. She'd never been ashamed of this place before and the friends she'd made here who were like family to her. Until tonight.

Now it had become just another reminder of the glaring difference between her world and Merritt's.

Best that it had, too, she decided as she squared her shoulders and walked through the maze of sailcloth walls. Because she had to find a way to cauterize the wounds that had been sliced into her heart and go on with her life.

Merritt was gone now, slipping away as easily as if he'd never been there at all. But the hole he'd unknowingly left would take a very long time to fill. If ever.

When she rounded the top of the stairs, she saw a figure standing in the makeshift hall. The woman's white night rail blended with the sailcloth like a ghost in the fog. A tingle swept down her spine, fading only when the girl's face emerged from the shadows.

"Ivy," Veronica said quietly, not wanting to disturb the rest of the small village inside the warehouse. "It's the middle of the night. You should be asleep."

"I thought I heard something...an odd noise..." With a troubled frown, Ivy glanced down the hall. Not finding whatever she was searching for, she brought her gaze back to Veronica. Her big eyes grew impossibly larger. "Why are you dressed like *that*?"

Veronica grimaced. Ivy routinely saw her coming and going in her leather and metal-studded patrolling clothes, complete with sword and knives. Yet it was a satin gown that made the girl gape at her as if she were a bedlamite.

"What's wrong with this?" Veronica stepped past her and hurried toward her room before someone else came out from behind the sailcloth walls and saw her. "I think it's beautiful."

"It is." Ivy fell into uninvited step behind her. "It truly is breathtaking. It's just…" Veronica could picture in her mind the way the girl was surely biting her bottom lip as she trailed along behind her. "*Why* are you in it?"

Veronica rolled her eyes. "Sheep herding."

When she tossed back the piece of cloth that served as her door, she glanced over her shoulder and saw Ivy's chastising expression. But even Ivy's angry hands on hips in her best irritated governess pose couldn't keep Veronica from glimpsing the fleeting flash of wounding on the girl's face.

Guilt stung her, and she apologetically let out a long sigh. "If you really must know." She held open the cloth to gesture for Ivy to follow her inside. "I went to a ball. With a prince."

"You're lying. Ladies from the Court of Miracles don't go to parties with princes."

Wasn't that the awful truth? "Fine, then." She let the cloth drop into place and retreated into the space that served as her room, calling out over her shoulder, "I won't tell you about the palace and all the fine dresses and shimmering jewels I saw."

The panel flung open. "A palace?" Ivy's mouth fell open. "You were at a *palace*?"

Veronica smiled at how the girl had so easily taken the bait. "I was at Carlton House at a grand ball thrown by the prince regent himself."

Ivy stepped inside and let the cloth fall closed behind her. "The regent was there? Did you see him? Did you get to meet him? What's he like? Oh, tell me!"

The young woman practically bounced with excitement. Curiosity and awe lit up her pretty face, framed by her loose, golden hair. If Ivy had been the daughter of a lord—or even a merchant of the middling sort—she would have been declared an Incomparable, with gentlemen waiting in line for the opportunity to court her. As it was, she would be lucky not to be forced into prostitution just to survive.

But not if Veronica could help it.

That was the first thing she wanted to change as soon as she received her pardon and could make an honest living. She wanted to find good positions in households and shops for the young women who lived here and apprenticeships or naval positions for the boys.

"Unbutton me, and I'll tell you." Veronica removed her fur-trimmed wrap, turned her back to the girl, and gestured at her bodice. When Ivy came forward to undo the tiny pearl buttons, she continued, "Actually, I didn't get to meet him. There were simply too many people at the party."

"Oh." Disappointment dripped from the girl's voice.

Veronica allowed herself to feel one last rush of pleasure about the evening. She smiled at Ivy over her shoulder and admitted, "But I did waltz with a baron."

"Did you?" Ivy's fingers flew to undo the tiny buttons. "Was he dashing?"

"Utterly."

"What did he look like?"

Veronica's lips curled in ironic amusement. "A bit like Mr. Herbert, I'd say."

"Oh, he's very handsome then!"

She murmured, mostly to herself, "*I* think so."

"Tell me everything," the girl pleaded. "And don't leave out a single detail."

She laughed. "If I do that, we might be here longer than I was at the ball!"

"And what's wrong with that?"

The buttons gave way, and her bodice loosened. "Nothing, I suppose." After all, there would be no patrolling tonight. No reason not to stay right here until morning, pleasing the girl with stories. Ivy had so few other amusements in her life that Veronica couldn't bring herself to deny her this one. "Well, to begin, I rode to Carlton House in a fine black carriage drawn by two beautiful bay horses."

The girl heaved out a sigh of romantic longing and sank down onto Veronica's pallet bed, settling in like a child for a bedtime story.

"Once we arrived at the palace, there was an army of uniformed footmen in the finest livery and powdered wigs just waiting to serve us, complete with gold trim on their velvet jackets and boots shined so well that I could see my reflection in them." With that captivating description, she pulled up one of the loose floorboards to fish out the key to her armoire. "And those were just the servants. You should have seen the guests. The place was a flood of satins, silks, and kerseymere." She crossed to her armoire, unlocked it, and opened wide the doors. Inside, she kept all her most precious possessions safely under lock and key, including her sword and knives. "The light blazed from a thousand shimmering candles in the chandeliers overhead, and everywhere I looked, women were draped in diamonds and rubies and wore tall ostrich plumes in their hair."

"And pearls?"

A slow smile crossed her face as her fingers touched the earbobs. "Yes, those, too."

"Tell me about the baron you met. Is he special?"

"Very much so." *Too much so.* Her smile faded. "He told me that he was once a soldier. Undoubtedly, he was a hero in the wars, although he would never admit to being such a thing. He's far too modest for that."

She removed the earbobs and placed them into a secret drawer with its own separate lock. She had to return them to Claudia as soon as possible, and all the while, she would have to pretend with the woman that she didn't know they were a gift from Merritt. All the while, she would have to pretend that her heart wasn't breaking. But she simply couldn't keep them.

"He asked me to dance with him and bowed to me as if I were a grand lady," she said quietly. She prayed Ivy couldn't hear the sadness in her voice. "And the way he waltzed, to be in his arms, it felt…"

"Perfect?" the girl guessed.

No. It had felt like coming home.

Veronica took a moment to gather herself as that realization twisted grief through her that she would never be there again. Then she pulled in a deep breath, pasted a smile on her face, and turned around. "It felt like I needed more dance lessons before—"

She froze as icy fear darted through her bones.

Ivy no longer sat on the bed. Instead, she stood next to the sailcloth wall; a man behind her held a knife to her throat. Terror gripped the girl's pallid face, and she was too frightened to scream or cry for help. In the slant of moonlight that fell through the window, Veronica could see the glistening tears of fear on her cheeks.

"Let her go," Veronica demanded as coolly as possible.

"I will," the man answered in a low voice, "if you come with me." The sailcloth stirred around them in the nighttime drafts like a crowd of ghosts. "I won't hurt the girl if you do."

"No," Veronica countered, turning so she could slowly reach her hand behind herself into the open armoire without him seeing. "You want to hurt me instead."

"I only want to talk to you."

As if she were foolish enough to believe that! Her fingers crept slowly along the edge of the shelf. "About what?"

"The riots."

Her hand touched the hilt of a small knife. "What do you care about those?"

"You're sticking your nose into places it don't belong," he warned. "I need to find out why."

Slowly, she closed her hand around the knife. But helplessness turned to acid on her tongue that she was too far away to save Ivy. There were too many steps between Veronica and the man to cover in the split second it would take for him to slit the girl's throat. All Veronica could do was hope for an opportunity to move close enough to strike.

"What does it matter to you?" she pressed, hoping to distract him. "Who paid you to come after me? Was it Malmesbury's mistress?" She remembered Merritt's belief that someone else was orchestrating the riots, someone far deadlier... "Or was it Scepter?"

The man froze for only a beat, yet long enough to convince her that her guess was correct. Fresh fear enveloped her. *Good God.* All this time, she'd thought Merritt and Clayton Elliott had been exaggerating about Scepter's involvement, that the group couldn't possibly be connected to the riots.

"Come with me," the man offered, "and I'll let the girl go."

"Let the girl go," Veronica countered, "and I might come with you."

"Go on, then." He jerked his head toward the flap in the wall. "You go first. I'll follow."

Veronica slipped the knife from the shelf as she slowly turned toward the door as if to carry out the man's orders. Her hand nestled unseen in the folds of her gown, with the handle of the knife clasped against her palm and the blade pointing back up her wrist toward her elbow.

She stopped and shook her head as if changing her mind. "And have my back to you so I won't know when you've stabbed a knife into it or reached around to slit my throat? I don't think so." She was at least half a dozen feet closer now. Close enough that she might just be able to strike before he could hurt Ivy. She took another step toward him. "You'll have to do better than that."

He grinned a devilish smile. Slowly, he moved the edge of the blade back and forth beneath Ivy's chin. "I don't have to do anything. I've—"

"Please!" Ivy cried, her voice shattered with terror. "Please let me go!"

Veronica moved forward. "Ivy, it's all right—"

"This has nothing to do with me!" The girl's frantic voice rose higher in mounting panic. "Let me go!"

Veronica took another step. She stood so close now that she could lunge and be on top of the man before he could react. Her hand tightened around the knife. She shifted her weight to the balls of her feet in preparation to spring, for a powerful right thrust to that soft spot between the man's ribs and hips—

A long blade sliced through the sailcloth, into the man's back, and out through his belly.

He spasmed, jerking violently as his hands fell away from Ivy. The girl tumbled to the floor as his mouth opened and blood spilled out. Then the sword yanked back free of his body, and he fell forward, dead before he hit the floor.

"Ivy!" Veronica dropped her knife and ran forward. She fell to her knees on the floor and pulled the wailing girl into her arms.

A hand reached beneath the sailcloth and lifted it out of the way. Filipe ducked beneath it and stepped into the room. He paused at the man's feet as a thick, red puddle oozed around his boots. Matching blood dripped from his sword. Filipe poked him with the toe of his boot to make certain he was dead.

The attacker's shirt had pulled back when he slid to the floor and revealed marks on the side of his neck. Through the shadows, Veronica could just make out a tattoo—

Her heart lodged in her throat. *A key.* The same symbol she'd seen on General Liggett's uniform.

"He was here after you," Filipe muttered and kicked the man again. Hard.

"Yes." She pressed Ivy's head against her shoulder as the girl fought to choke back her terrified sobs.

His dark gaze lifted slowly to meet Veronica's. "God only knows how many people he could have hurt while looking for you."

"Yes," she whispered, self-recrimination pulsing through her as painfully as the sound of Ivy's cries.

"He was here because of the riots." Filipe wiped the sword over his thigh to clean off the blood, then spat on the man. "Not because of thief-taking."

"Yes." She tightened her arms around Ivy to gather what little resolve she could and admitted, "I've lied to you. The past few nights…I haven't been out catching criminals."

"What have you been doing?"

She confessed softly, "Working for the Home Office."

The expression of betrayal that tightened his face pierced her. He was a brother to her, the only person left from her childhood who loved her. And she'd deceived him.

"Their agents caught me a few nights ago while I was patrolling for Fernsby. They knew I'd escaped from prison." She smoothed back Ivy's hair and placed a kiss to the girl's forehead, equally to console herself as much as Ivy. "They offered me a pardon if I cooperated with them to find the men responsible for the riots."

He paused to absorb her confession, then he asked quietly, "So that Mr. Herbert you brought here—is he a rioter or a Home Office snitch?"

"A barrister." Telling Filipe anything more would put Merritt in danger. "He's going to secure my pardon when the mob's leaders are found."

Filipe gestured a hand at her gown. "Did he dress you up like this, too?"

"Yes." Her heart broke at the torn and blood-stained gown that had once been so beautiful. She'd danced with Merritt only a few hours before, but now, the ball seemed a lifetime ago.

Filipe stared at her for a long while as if trying to find the sister he knew inside the woman at his feet. Then he gave up, as if she were a stranger to him. His resignation filled her with guilt and desolation.

He pointed his sword at the body that was still bleeding out onto the floor. "Your presence here endangers the entire Court."

"I know." Just as she knew in her gut what was coming next—

"I want you to leave."

The quiet words pierced her. She bit the inside of her cheek, calling on the pain to keep all emotion from her face.

"Until the riots are over, until you're done with the Home Office," Filipe ordered, "you cannot be here. Men are after you. Our friends won't trust you." He shook his head. "*I* can't trust you."

She sucked in a mouthful of air. *Exile...*

"I want you to leave. Tonight. Take whatever you want." He paused as if wanting to say something more. But he looked away and finished, "Don't come back until you're invited."

A knot of emotion strangled in her throat. Unable to speak, Veronica nodded tightly.

"Come, Ivy." He reached down to take the girl's arm, pulled her gently to her feet, and slipped his arm around Ivy's still shaking shoulders as she continued to sob. As he led her away, he nodded silently at the body.

Clean up your mess. The words lingered as palpably as if he'd uttered them.

Veronica's eyes blurred with unshed tears. She met Filipe's gaze for only a beat before he flipped back the sailcloth and left the room. Ivy never looked back.

Her chest convulsed as she pulled in shallow, quick breaths and pressed the heels of her hands against her eyes. She wouldn't cry. She *wouldn't*! She wouldn't let anyone hear one sound of the agony and desolation that gripped her. Hadn't she already learned that lesson, so long ago and at such a high price? Tears solved nothing. Crying only made a woman appear weak and helpless, only invited ridicule and abuse.

But the tears came anyway, falling hot and silent, faster than she could wipe them away. She wrapped her arms around her middle and folded over herself onto the floor as she cried out her wretchedness in silent, shaking sobs.

She couldn't stay. She had to leave before Filipe returned. Despite the pain that churned inside her, her arms and legs were numb as she shoved herself to her feet and reached down to grab the dead man under his arms, to drag him toward the hall. She gritted her teeth, pulled hard, and shuffled her feet backward toward the sailcloth flap. She grabbed it and threw it out of the way.

From the corner of her eye, she caught a movement on the other side of her room. She froze, taking several terrified beats to realize it was her own reflection in the mirror.

A strange woman gazed back, her face ghostly white and her hair collapsing down the side of her head. Blood was everywhere… puddled on the floor, streaking the ripped sailcloth behind her, splattered across the front of her gown…*marking her*. And at her slippers lay a dead body.

Her stomach churned until she thought she might be sick, until she had to place a hand against her belly to keep from casting up her accounts. This was what her life was now. That image captured in the mirror all she represented…

Death and destruction.

Good Lord, what had she become? What kind of monster had fate turned her into? Lonely, hopeless…

She didn't want this life. She'd never belonged here with Filipe among his cronies and the Court, should be glad she no longer had an obligation to be here for all that his father had done for her. She didn't belong to the night and to the death and pain it wrought—

Her eyes blurred until the gown's reflection in the mirror was nothing but a green smear. Nothing but a stained and ruined reminder that she didn't belong to society either.

She belonged nowhere in the world.

The stab of isolation and loneliness struck her so powerfully that a strangled sound tore from the back of her throat.

Dear God—she had no one! No one to take her in. No one to give her comfort.

Except…perhaps one.

Eighteen

MERRITT LAY IN HIS BED AND STARED AT THE DARK CEILING, unable to sleep.

After an hour of patrolling—actually more of an hour of solid running in an attempt to lose the ghosts that chased him tonight—he gave up and came home to a dark and silent house. But sleep was proving impossible.

Being here was worse than being at the Armory. How his friends had confronted him tonight was infuriating as hell and none of their damn business. But here, his own thoughts haunted him, with no escape.

He turned onto his side and punched at his pillow.

He shouldn't have come home tonight. He should have stayed on the streets. He should have gone back to the Ship's Bell and dug deeper for any leads on Smathers. He should have been watching Malmesbury's mistress—hell, he should have gone to Madame Noir's if nothing else. Not to enjoy the girls but simply to find distraction in Madame's sharp insults and baiting. *Anything* to distract him from the riots, Joanna's ghost, and the temptation of Veronica Chase.

Damnation! He flopped over onto his back and draped his forearm over his face. Dawn was still hours away. Maybe he could go to the nearest inn, rent a horse, ride out for air and—

A soft creak from the staircase split the silence.

The tiny hairs on his arms stood on end. He held his breath and strained to listen, waiting for another creak, another footstep on the stairs. He employed no live-in servants, and the housekeeper who kept the small town house for him and cooked his meals had left at dusk, just as she always did, and wouldn't be back until morning.

Slowly, he reached beneath the bed for the knife he kept there. Another creak. This time from the top stair.

He didn't make a sound, didn't move except to close his hand around the knife handle. Every muscle tensed with readiness to spring.

The door handle jangled, and the door opened slowly. The figure paused in the frame, silhouetted by the moonlight—

"Veronica," he whispered, releasing the knife.

He couldn't believe his eyes as she stepped into the room and silently closed the door behind her. She looked otherworldly standing there in her ball gown like a ghost draped in shadows. Her face was hidden by the darkness, except for her piercing eyes, which shone with intensity.

She didn't move, as if not quite believing herself that she was there.

"Is something wrong?" He sat up as concern tightened in his chest. "Are you all right?"

"I'll be fine." With that cryptic answer, she slowly reached up to remove the pins from her hair. She slipped them free and tossed them away, unwanted. Each pinged quietly against the floor in the silence of the house.

When she ran a hand through her hair to loosen her tresses, Merritt felt the smooth glide of her fingers from across the room. It shivered through him with a liquid heat.

Which did nothing to ease his worry at her unexpected visit. "How did you get inside?"

"A wicked and wild wind." She stalked slowly toward him. Each silent step tingled his naked skin beneath the bedcover that draped over him from the waist down. "It blew open the door and invited me in."

Sweet Lucifer. He was dreaming. He *had* to have fallen asleep and was dreaming...

She stopped at the foot of the bed. "Do you want me to leave?"

Leave? Good God, no! But he coolly shrugged a bare shoulder and somehow kept his voice from cracking with need. "You can stay if you'd like."

"I'd like."

So would he. Sweet mercy, so very much!

And yet... "But there's a price to pay if you do," he told her quietly. His heart pounded at the terms of surrender he was offering, terrified she wouldn't accept them. He wanted her to reveal more to him tonight than her body—he wanted to learn her secrets. "The truth."

She stared at him for a long while, silent and still, as if her heart was debating with itself over whether she could put her faith in him.

Trust me, Veronica. Please trust me...

Then she reached behind her for the row of tiny buttons at her back. Her gaze never left his as she tore them open with a small tug. That soft rip shot through him, straight down to the tip of his stiffening cock.

"My surname isn't Chase." Her voice emerged as soft as the shadows around them. "It's Chaves. I was born in Portugal." She slowly slipped the dress's cap sleeve off her left shoulder and bared it to the shadows. "I'm the daughter of the Count of Redondo." With her other hand, she pushed down the opposite sleeve, and the bodice sagged loosely over her bosom. "My mother was his mistress."

Understanding fell through him. That was why she'd learned so quickly from Madame Noir how to behave at the ball, to carry herself, to properly greet everyone she might meet. Why she was so well educated.

But that certainly didn't explain everything. So he remained perfectly still and let her continue, knowing even the smallest movement or softest word would silence her.

"She was only his mistress, not his wife, but he cared for her and provided well for us. Fine clothing, grand houses and carriages…all kinds of wonderful things." She slipped her arms out of her dress. "Until the French and Spanish invaded and destroyed everything."

She let go of the gown.

The air slid from his lungs as easily as the satin slipped through her fingers and down over her hips to puddle on the floor around her feet. She stood before him in her underclothes, their whiteness making her seem even more ethereal.

"They burned down our home and killed my mother." She stepped out of her slippers and took a single step forward in her stocking feet, leaving the gown behind. "They almost killed me— *would* have killed me if not for Jabir. He was a career soldier, a mercenary working for the Portuguese. He felt sorry for me and took me away with him."

Merritt stared at her as she gave her soft explanation. He was afraid to say anything for fear she would vanish back into the night, like an apparition.

"I was still a child, not yet ten. But the country had been invaded, the cities destroyed, the countryside was unsafe… Redondo had fled for Italy, and I had no one to turn to for help. No one but Jabir. He raised me as if I were his own daughter, right along with his son."

"Filipe," Merritt guessed quietly. She'd said the man was like a brother to her, but that confirmation didn't stop the jealousy from burning in his gut.

She nodded and reached behind her to tangle her fingers in her short corset's lace. "Jabir taught me about weapons and how to fight. He needed someone Filipe could spar against for practice, but I was the better fighter." A proud smile teased faintly at her lips. "I still am."

She pulled the lace free. The corset loosened and dropped to the floor, followed by her petticoat. With every discarded piece of clothing came another confession.

"During the wars, we had no choice but to work for the Spanish and the French. For the enemy. I became a mercenary, too, just like Jabir and Filipe, working alongside the soldiers in all kinds of reconnaissance missions." A small hesitation before she admitted, "I killed men when I had to in order to survive."

Her arms dropped to her sides as she let him look at her, her soul bared nearly as much now as her body. She stood in front of him in nothing but shift and stockings. In the slant of moonlight, he could just discern the curves of her full breasts and hips, the patch of curls nestled between her thighs.

"When the Allies finally arrived, we switched sides and worked for them until the Peninsula was freed. Then the war moved north into France and went on without us." She bent over to reach beneath her chemise for her stockings, her hair falling forward in a fiery curtain that hid her face. But she couldn't conceal the pain in her voice. "By then, we'd been separated. Jabir was dead, Filipe had already left for England, Redondo was God only knows where... and I had no reason to stay. So I followed Filipe to London to start a new life here." Her shoulders trembled as she untied the stocking and rolled it down her leg, over her foot, and off. "I was wrong." The stocking slipped through her fingers to the floor. "I'm just as trapped here as I was in Portugal."

She fell silent as she removed the second stocking, rolling it off her leg and dropping it away with its mate. She wore only a thin, sleeveless shift now, yet she possessed all the dignity of a queen as her intense gaze held his through the shadows.

"When the Winslow warehouse was broken into last year, one of Filipe's men was captured and gave testimony against him. I had to save him...for all his father had done for me, for all he does for the people of Saffron Hill." Her hand trembled as she ran it through her hair, to sift the silky curls away from her forehead, just as she was sifting through the dark memories. "So I persuaded Fernsby to claim he'd caught me outside the warehouse that night, to testify that it was me who led the raid and that Filipe wasn't even there." Her hand fell to her side. "I went to prison to protect Filipe and the Court of Miracles. I sacrificed myself so he could remain free."

She was innocent. Exactly what Clayton had believed from the beginning and what Merritt had been unwilling to accept. Until now.

"I never did what I claimed in court. I was never at that warehouse—nor at any warehouse. I've never been part of their activities. Please believe me." Her voice was haunting as she whispered so softly that he could barely hear her, "I need you to believe…"

He held out his hand and rasped out hoarsely, "I do."

Veronica's heart pounded as she crawled onto the bed and slowly made her way toward Merritt on her hands and knees. Her eyes never broke contact with his. Dear God, how much she wanted this night with him, more than she'd wanted anything else in her life—

No. That was a lie.

What she wanted more than anything else was the chance at a future with him. But that would never happen. She could never be his in the daylight world.

But here in the dark, *he* could be hers. If only for the night.

"I think you should know," she warned as she moved up the length of his body, "I might not be a criminal, but I'm also not an innocent."

"And I think *you* should know," he warned in return, "neither am I."

She stopped and blinked. Only Merritt could tease like that at a time like this. With all the emotions the events of tonight had set churning inside her, she didn't know whether to laugh or cry.

But she knew she loved him.

"Good," she purred and continued up his body.

When she reached his waist, she pulled away the blanket that covered him. She held her breath, then dared to look down.

He was completely naked, and the sight of him thrilled her. *Magnificent*, that was the thought that popped into her head as she raked her gaze over his lean and muscular body. His manhood lay against his thigh, already half erect even though she had yet to touch him. What would happen when she did? How hard and large could she make him? How much pleasure could she give?

Teasingly, she trailed her fingertip down his length, from the nest of dark hair at his abdomen to the round tip—

With a soft curse, he jumped beneath her touch and sucked in a mouthful of air.

His reaction only emboldened her to do it again, this time closing her hand around his thick girth and stroking up and down until she drew a groan from the back of his throat. Every slide of her hand made her revel in how the softness of his skin contrasted against the steely hardness beneath.

Not pausing in her slow strokes over him, she used her free hand to lift her shift out of the way so she could straddle him. Tonight, every bit of this wonderful, amazing man would be hers to take pleasure from and give pleasure to in return. *Never* had she found any man who was as much her equal in every way as Merritt— physically, emotionally, mentally. And tonight, she planned on showing him exactly how much.

When he tenderly touched her cheek, she took his hand and guided it down between her legs to the feminine folds that ached to possess him. His long fingers caressed her in smooth, slow glides that stirred the heat inside her until she trembled just as much as he did. Until she was slick and hot with evidence of her desire for him, until she quivered with shameless need.

His intimate touch was more than she could bear, yet still not enough. When he grazed that sensitive little nib buried in her folds, a throaty moan tore from her. She wanted him inside her, *needed* him there, both body and soul.

"Merritt," she whispered and gently pushed his hand away so she could rise onto her knees, pointed the tip of his erection against her throbbing core like an arrow, and lowered herself over him.

She shuddered with pleasure as his hard length slid deep inside her. He filled her so completely that for a moment, she could do nothing more than sit still and let her body adjust to his. She closed her eyes and concentrated on the feeling of holding him inside her, to brand the delicious sensation on her mind so she could carry it in her memory long after he'd disappeared from her life.

Wonderful... It was so wonderful to be with him like this that her eyes stung with emotion. But when she opened them and gazed down into his, his desire for her nearly undid her.

Tonight, he would be her rock to keep from falling away. Making love to him would be a benediction, and he would give her absolution. He would give her the strength and resolve she needed to go on. Without him.

She cupped his face between her hands and leaned in to kiss him, granting herself this lingering taste of him before she let go completely of her heart and made love to him.

She began to pulse her hips against his in small but eager thrusts. He murmured her name and clasped her hips to help guide her in their quickening tempo as she rocked herself over him. These small plunges and retreats were nothing but a tease of what she knew would come, of the desperate desire brewing in both of them that would eventually be satiated beyond the edge of control. But even now, her body tingled from the small jolts of electricity that pulsed into her belly, from the way the tiny muscles inside her deliciously clenched and released around him.

"Jesus!" He sat up, startled, and his hips froze beneath her. He craned his neck to stare at her side where his hand rested on her hip, where dark stains had seeped through her dress into the white cotton shift beneath. "*Blood.* What the hell happ—"

She kissed him, then rasped out against his lips the terrible confession, "Not mine."

For a long moment, he didn't move as understanding of what she meant fell through him.

She felt his shock fade into acceptance as his lips slowly relaxed against hers. But only for a moment before his kisses turned hungry and fierce, hot and openmouthed, as if he knew the absolution she sought in him for everything she had done, and not just tonight but for years before.

Yet the initiative had to be hers to take. So she broke the kiss and pushed him down onto his back. She peeled her shift up her body, over her head, and off, exposing herself completely to his gleaming eyes.

The heat of his gaze raked over her. He stirred up goose bumps across her skin and drew her nipples into tight points. When he caressed her breasts with his hands, a whimper of such unbearable need escaped her that she shuddered.

Unable to restrain herself any longer, she placed her palms flat on his chest and rode him hard and fast. His pulse pounded wildly beneath her fingertips, and she dug them into his muscles as the pleasure grew inside her. With every forward slide up his abdomen, she felt the loss of him inside her, only to give a soft moan of joy when she slammed back and brought him once again inside her to the hilt.

Tossing back her head, she welcomed the swelling need that overwhelmed her as her body spasmed around his. All the muscles inside her clamped hard around his length, and her thighs shook uncontrollably as they clasped like a vise against his hips.

Pleasure pounded through her, from that place of pulsating heat where their bodies joined straight out through the top of her head. She cried out as bliss overtook her, only realizing after she'd collapsed upon his chest that she'd screamed his name into the darkness. An unconscious attempt to brand him onto her soul.

His arms tightened around her as she struggled to regain her breath. The decadent pleasure washed over her in waves. All of her tingled, all of her belonged to him. In her heart, she knew she always would.

He buried his mouth in her hair and whispered between panting breaths, "Are you all right?"

Unable to find her voice, she nodded against his shoulder.

"Did you enjoy that?"

Enjoy? Her soul laughed! The shattering had been so much more than mere enjoyment. Yet she nodded again.

"Good." Not withdrawing from her, he flipped her onto her back and pinned her arms against the mattress over her head. His eyes bore into hers with a look of such wicked intensity that she trembled. "My turn now."

Her heart leapt into her throat. She couldn't move except for a small wiggle of her hips that only served to elicit a groan of wolfish pleasure from him. "Merritt, if you—"

He thrust into her with a hard swirl of his hips that pressed his pelvic bone against her already sensitized sex and ripped her breath away. He prompted devilishly, "If I what?"

He did it again, and stars flashed before her eyes.

"If I make love to you slowly and relentlessly, for hours and hours and hours?"

He darted his head down to lick at her nipples, and every teasing flick of his tongue drove her mad. She could do nothing more than moan out his name in soft protest and intense yearning.

"If I told you how much I want you to surrender to me, to give yourself to me in every way?"

He took her nipple between his lips and suckled, long and hard and worshipping, until her breaths came in panting gasps.

She arched her back off the mattress to bring herself even tighter against his mouth.

"Because that's what I want, Veronica." He placed a tender kiss to her nipple. "I want you to surrender to every pleasure I plan on giving you."

The only reply she could manage was a shuddering whimper of capitulation.

He reached down to slip his arms beneath her legs and hook them over his biceps. Then he placed his hands flat onto the mattress at her shoulders. When he locked his elbows, he rolled her high onto her upper back beneath him and lifted her hips completely from the mattress. In this new position, she had no choice but to wrap her arms around his neck and cling to him as he began to move inside her.

Each plunge and retreat created a seesawing motion that rolled her back and forth along the length of her curled spine, from her shoulders to her buttocks. With each long and smooth rocking motion, he went impossibly deeper inside her until she felt as if she might slip completely beneath his skin and become part of him forever.

She let go of his shoulders and grabbed for the headboard. "I can't—I can't hold on..."

"Then let go," he ordered huskily as he released her legs and let them wrap around his waist, to hold him clenched in the cradle of her thighs. "Let go and claim your pleasure."

He placed his hands on the headboard next to hers for leverage and began to thrust into her hard and deep as he relentlessly drove them both toward release. His muscular body was covered in a sheen of perspiration in the moonlight as he worked like a piston, plunging and retreating into her tight warmth without pause.

"Let go," he whispered hotly into her ear. "Surrender to me, Veronica. Let me give you this joy."

He swirled his hips against hers, and the tender motion

threatened hot tears at her eyes. She let go of the headboard to encircle her arms around his neck—

And let go of her control. She broke beneath him with a swell of such shuddering joy and anguish that she shattered like glass from the intensity of it. She clung to him, burying her face against his neck and blinking hard to fight back the tears.

His arms went around her to pull her close. He took two more long and deep thrusts. Then he pulled out of her and slid his length between their pressed bodies. He shuddered with a low groan. His hips jerked, and a warm wetness seeped across her abdomen. His buttocks clenched as he strained to empty every drop of himself.

When he was finally spent, he didn't ease his hold around her even as he struggled to regain the breath she'd stolen. No move to release her, no move to shift away…only his mouth sliding down to her ear to whisper a single word—

"Bliss."

With that, she was lost.

Nineteen

DEAR GOD, SHE WAS BEAUTIFUL. MERRITT COULD BARELY believe how much. So much so that he couldn't stop touching her.

Luckily, he didn't have to.

He lazily caressed his hand over the soft curve of her hip as they lay on their sides in his bed, facing each other. Her skin was deliciously soft and warm, her eyes intense as they returned his stare. She was fierce, his little minx, and just as turbulent and passionate as he'd imagined. But now he also saw a vulnerability lurking beneath her strong façade, the same one that had brought her to him tonight and convinced her to bare herself to him, body and soul.

Tracing an invisible pattern along her outer thigh, he frowned. "Not that I'm complaining, but—"

"You'd better not."

His lips curled into a smile. "But how did you know where to find me?"

Her head rested on her folded arm, allowing her hair to fall across the mattress as if someone had spilled a bolt of copper-colored silk. "Madame Noir told me." Her turn to frown. "How does Madame know where you live?"

"Not because she or any of her girls have ever been here, I assure you." Was that jealousy he heard in her voice? God help him, but he liked the sound of it. "It's her business to know things like that. A good soldier," he said as he trailed his gaze down her front, "always knows where the enemy is."

"I'm not your enemy anymore."

And *that* was wounding he heard this time. "You were never my enemy." He placed a light kiss to her lips. "You were a challenge and surprising as hell." *And the most unique woman I've ever met in my life.* "You were a puzzle I couldn't solve. Until tonight." Another kiss to her lips, this one lingering before he eased away. "Thank you for trusting me."

"I didn't know if you would listen," she whispered. "You could have turned me away."

"And miss the chance to see what weapons you might have hidden beneath your skirts? Never."

He slid his fingertips lightly up her arm in an attempt to appease himself with this small touch. It wasn't working. He so much wanted to bury himself between her thighs again that he burned with it.

A faint smile teased at her lips. "You're quite the lover, Mrs. Fitzherbert."

His chest warmed at the compliment. A man could certainly do worse than being told things like that. He grinned arrogantly. "Well, thank—"

"No wonder the regent is so infatuated with you."

His grin twisted into a grimace, and he finished in a dry drawl, "—you." He slapped her playfully on her bare bottom. "Thank you."

She laughed, the lilting sound musical in the shadows. Apologetically, she reached up to caress his cheek. Her affectionate warmth heated through him and made him long for all sorts of things he had no business wanting. And damn himself, he wanted far more with her than physical pleasure.

But other matters had to be addressed first.

He placed a kiss to her fingertips, then held his breath. "Whose blood is on your dress?"

Her laughter died.

He didn't mean to upset her. But it was either venture down this path or declare that he loved her, and this path had less chance of giving them both apoplexy.

He frowned at the flash of pain on her face. Perhaps not.

"A man came after me tonight at the Court of Miracles." Her voice was so low that he could barely hear her.

Christ. He'd put her into danger, and self-recrimination pierced him. "Because the men there learned who I truly am?"

"No. This man wasn't one of Filipe's. He was there because of the riots." She placed her hand flat against his chest and right over his heart. "He knew I'd been asking about them." Her fingertips curled into his muscle, and her gaze pinned there, avoiding his. "He came to kill me."

He clamped his hand over hers and squeezed her fingers. Hard. As they trembled in his, he'd never felt more helpless in his life except for the night Joanna died. *Damnation!* Would he ever be able to protect the women he cared about?

"What happened?" he urged quietly.

She shrugged a bare shoulder. "He didn't succeed."

"Obviously." Her nonchalance did nothing to untie the roiling knot of worry in his belly. He took her chin and gently lifted her face until she looked directly at him. "What happened, Veronica?"

She blew out an aggravated sigh. "The man was in my room—in my corner of the warehouse, that is," she corrected. Her gaze traveled around his bedroom. The unspoken comparison between there and here, her life and his, was tangible in that glance. "He was threatening me, holding Ivy at knifepoint…"

As she casually rushed past specific details, icy fear licked knowingly at the backs of his knees at what she wasn't admitting—she'd been lucky to escape with her life.

"Filipe heard us and killed the man." Another shrug, as if death were as commonplace in her world as buying eggs in the market. She'd admitted tonight that she'd killed men in the war, but… *Jesus.* "Then I disposed of the body."

"How?"

"I left it in a nearby alley."

"That's how you got blood on you," he murmured, and she nodded.

The life she must have led to be able to dismiss such horrible things so lightly, the inner strength she must possess to simply keep going—good God. He'd never met another woman like her.

"Who was he?" He laced his fingers through hers to keep her hand on his chest and searched her face for answers. "Had you ever seen him before?"

"No. I would have remembered him." Her gaze dropped to their entwined hands. "But he had a tattoo—the same key design as the pin General Liggett was wearing on his uniform. Do you think they're connected?"

"Most likely just a coincidence." Liggett might have been a deplorable human being, but sending an assassin after a woman wasn't his style. There was no glory to be won in it.

"But you'll check into it."

Not a question, he noted. Already she knew him well enough to realize he planned on doing exactly that. But troubled thoughts warred inside him…pleasure that they'd grown so close, doubts that he could keep her safe.

So he answered the only way he could, by reassuringly touching his lips to hers.

"I'm sorry about the dress," she said softly, embarrassed. "I know it cost a great deal. I'll find a way to repay you for it—and for all the other clothes." She rolled over onto her back and whispered up into the darkness, "But it might take a while."

He shifted over on top of her. "They're a gift. Keep them and wear them. Or sell them and use the money to buy yourself what every smart woman longs to have."

"What's that?"

He grinned. "A new sword. One to match every dress." He nuzzled the side of her neck in an attempt to distract her from the darkness of their earlier conversation. "Like bonnets."

She laughed. That wonderful sound once more wound around him like a silk ribbon, tying him to her. He knew then that she would be all right. *Thank God.*

But her laughter died away. "I had to leave everything behind at the Court when I left." Guilt filled the silent pause. "Including the earrings you gave me."

Somehow he managed to keep his face passive. He shouldn't have been surprised that she'd figured it out, a woman as sharp as she was. Yet he feigned ignorance. "What earrings?"

The chastising look she shot him would have done a nun proud. "You might be an amazing lover, Mrs. Fitzherbert, but you're a terrible actress. I know you plotted with Claudia to give them to me. What I don't understand is why." She reached up to touch his cheek, a caress of gratitude edged with frustration. "Was it because you didn't want to be known as a barrister who gives jewelry to criminals?"

That stung. Yet he deserved it for not trusting her sooner. "I wanted you to have them, that's all."

"Why didn't you just give them to me yourself?"

"You've been away from society for too long." He feigned exasperation with a long, loud sigh. "You have no idea how dangerous it is for a bachelor to give jewelry to an unmarried miss."

From her expression, she wasn't falling for his act. "Even a baron?"

"*Especially* a baron." To distract her from taking the conversation in the direction of his peerage, he trailed his hand lazily down her body and thrilled when he elicited a tremble from her.

She arched wantonly into his touch. "Well, I won't hold the ruse against you."

"No," he countered in a wicked voice and slipped his hand between her legs. "Please hold everything against me." When his fingers grazed against the sensitive nub buried at the top of her folds, her hips bucked. He growled appreciatively and nipped at her ear. "*Everything.*"

He wanted her, and he would have her again before morning broke—repeatedly, if he had any say in the matter.

But for now, he didn't want to overwhelm her and slowly pulled his hand away. At the whimper of loss that fell from her lips, he nearly relented and made love to her again right then. Instead, he gave her a long, lingering kiss that promised more to come and rolled onto his back beside her to tuck her protectively into the hollow between his shoulder and his chest.

He'd never been happier in his life.

Her lips tickled against his chest as she whispered, "That was the most wonderful gift I've ever been given."

His pulse spiked. She wasn't talking about the earbobs.

No. *Now* he'd never been happier.

She rose up onto her elbow and stared down at him. "Filipe knows the truth about you." Concern edged her voice. "I had to tell him about the riots and the Home Office, about you and the pardon."

"Doesn't matter." Not when he and the men of the Armory had less than twenty-four hours to stop the slaughter Liggett had planned for the rioters. Exposing his identity to the King of Saffron Hill meant nothing in comparison.

"It does matter," she corrected. "We might still need his help."

We. Not *you.* Most likely nothing more than a slip of her tongue, but he couldn't allow her to continue thinking she would still be involved with stopping the riots. Her role in this was over. He wouldn't place her in danger again.

"The investigation is moving in a different direction now," he dodged and reached up to loop a ginger curl behind her ear.

She stilled, then replied knowingly, "One that doesn't involve women in ball gowns, you mean."

Or one wielding swords. "Yes."

"So it's all over, then."

The finality of her whisper was cutting, but he didn't regret his decision. If anything happened to her…dear God, it would end him. "You'll receive your pardon. Clayton will make certain of it."

"I don't care about that."

"You should. A pardon gives you the chance to start over, free and innocent." He paused, coming as close as he dared to declaring his feelings when he murmured, "To permanently make London your home."

Her face fell as if he'd struck her. Good Lord, what had he said wrong? He reached to caress her cheek—

She edged away. "No, I—" When he frowned, she explained, "London can't be my home now."

Now…after they'd made love, or after he'd placed her life in danger? Either answer would devastate him. "Why not?"

"I've been cast out of the Court of Miracles," she confessed with a touch of shame. "Filipe ordered me to go. That's why I came here tonight. I'm leaving London." Her voice cracked. "I wanted to say goodbye."

She slid off the bed and slipped through his fingers.

Twenty

VERONICA COULDN'T BEAR TO LOOK AT HIM AS HE SAT ON THE edge of the bed and waited patiently for her to explain, so she moved around the room to pick up the pieces of clothing she'd discarded as she'd bared herself to him. She had to keep busy for fear of glimpsing the bewildered look that was surely on his face, and for fear of rushing back into his arms and begging him to make love to her one last time.

She wouldn't argue, cry, beg—she wouldn't do any of those things silly misses did because of love. She simply didn't have it in her. But she did have her pride, and she would never let him see how much anguish churned inside her.

She picked up the shift and saw the blood stains. Just another reminder of how her real world was destroying the fantasy he'd created for her tonight. There was no hope for her here. Or for them.

"Explain," he finally ordered, quietly but brooking no refusal.

"I have to leave London," she repeated.

"Why?"

"I can't stay."

"You can. London's your home now."

"Not the one I want." Exasperation slammed into her. He didn't understand at all.

"Once you have your pardon, you—"

"And you, Merritt?" She wheeled on him as she unleashed the truth. "Will I ever have you?"

As soon as the question passed her lips, she regretted it. Shame and embarrassment surged into her chest, right up her neck and into a hot flush in her cheeks. She was such a cake! To even venture the idea of wanting a life with him, when he'd most likely thought nothing of her beyond the end of his bed—no, not a cake. A damn fool.

Yet she somehow found the resolve to not look away as he silently returned her gaze with a stunned one of his own.

But when his confused expression melted into guilt and grief, her heart melted with it.

"Don't worry," she assured him. "I'm not some goose of a society girl dreaming of marriage. I know how impossible you are for me. I've known it all along."

Unable to bear whatever he might say to try to console her—and knowing he couldn't contradict her—she turned away and pulled on her shift. A thin barrier that did little to protect her.

"A foreign lord's bastard daughter with a respectable baron, a King's Counsel with a confessed criminal…" Even as she said the words, the impossibility of it crashed over her. She covered the slump of her shoulders in anguished acceptance by fussing with the shift's straps. "A pardon would make no difference to any of that."

None. His career would still be ruined, his barony turned into a laughingstock, and his reputation destroyed. Perhaps his father's right along with his. And her as a baroness—simply laughable!

"I didn't come here tonight to try to persuade you differently." *I came here because I love you. Because I needed to bare my soul to you just as much as I wanted to bare my body, to draw on your strength and resolve. Because I needed you the way I have never needed another man in my life.* She shrugged. "I wanted to be in your bed. That's all."

At that blatant lie, she bent over to slip on her stockings and blinked hard. Once. That was the only emotion she would allow herself. She'd accepted that tonight would be their only intimacy, knew she had to live on without him…yet, oh God, how much it hurt!

She hesitated as she reached for her stays. How would she ever put them on without his help? She choked back a sob. How would she manage to survive at all without him?

"As I said," she forced past the knot in her throat, as much to convince herself as him, "I came to say good—"

"You're right, Veronica. You are impossible for me," he admitted hoarsely. "But not at all for the reason you think."

The grief in his voice thundered through her. So did the realization that he was standing right behind her, having come up silently until he stood a handful of inches away. She held her breath, not daring to move.

"Her name was Joanna Gordon." The wretched sadness in his voice chilled her to the bone. "She was my fiancée."

"You don't have to tell me about her," she whispered. "I don't need to know."

Didn't *want* to know. How could she bear to hear about how much he'd loved another woman, even a dead one, when his musky scent still lingered on her?

"Her name was Joanna," he repeated. He took her shoulders and drew her back against him. "We'd grown up together. Our parents were longtime friends, and a marriage was expected." He slipped his arms around her and buried his face in her hair. "She was a good and kind woman, pretty, well educated. The perfect sort to be a barrister's wife." He paused. "And I loved her."

Harsh jealousy sliced into her.

"She died before we could marry."

"Merritt," she pleaded for mercy, "I don't need to—"

"We were coming back from a party and were caught up in a riot. The carriage was overturned, the doors ripped open. She was pulled out into the street by the mob." He sucked in a pained breath. "They killed her—*he* killed her. A man with a hammer struck her in the back of the head as she was trying to crawl away."

She shuddered in his arms. To have seen his fiancée killed like that... *Good God*. A tear of grief for him slid down her cheek.

"Christ! I felt so helpless." His agony was palpable, and he tightened his arms around her as if afraid she might be torn from him just as Joanna had been. "I couldn't keep her with me inside the carriage, couldn't fight them off... I wasn't the man she needed to keep her safe."

"There was nothing you could have done." Yet even as she breathed out the words, she knew he wouldn't believe them. He'd been punishing himself since that night, and there was nothing she could say that would bring him peace. But she loved him enough to try. "You were in the wrong place at the wrong time. No one could have stopped what happened. It wasn't your fault."

He shook his head. "I failed her that night." His voice ached. "And I've been failing her ever since."

Icy realization of what he meant sank over her. She turned in his arms to search his face. His expression was hardened by guilt and shame, and by something else so cold and dark that it made her shiver.

When he said nothing, simply holding her gaze with that same terrible expression, she knew why he'd put himself at such risk, why he rushed into the heart of the riots—

He was chasing a ghost.

Her blood turned cold. No...not chasing. "You've been *hunting* him."

He released her and turned away. Not looking at her, he yanked on a pair of trousers tossed over the back of a chair and began to pace the room. He scoured his hand over his face as his shoulders tightened visibly.

"That's why you went into the army, too, isn't it?" she guessed, but she knew she wasn't wrong. "Not to learn to fight but to learn to hunt."

The fighting, the swords, the knives...prowling the streets, stopping the riots—it all made dreadful sense now. So did the futility of what he was attempting to do. He wanted to prove to

Joanna's memory that he loved her, that he would find her killer and put everything to rights.

But the task was impossible. That healing would *never* come.

"I went into the army so I could get away from London and all the memories here. Learning to fight was simply a bonus." He paused in front of the cold fireplace and stared down at it. "The day I left for the Continent, I went to the churchyard and placed flowers on her grave." He paused, a single heartbeat of agonizing silence. "That morning should have been our wedding day."

She ached to reach for him, to wrap her arms around him and ease his pain, but she knew he'd only push her away. He wasn't ready to be comforted.

"When I had the chance to learn to fight, I took it—every type of fighting, every weapon I could get my hands on, every master boxer and fencer who was willing to teach me." He reached for the iron poker but stopped short before jabbing it into the ashes, as if he simply needed the solidity of it in his hand. Like a weapon. "I swore to myself that I would never be helpless again. I mean to keep that promise."

"From what I've seen," she murmured, "I think you've achieved it."

"Not at all." He replaced the poker and turned away from the fireplace to slowly approach her. His mouth twisted ruefully as if at some private joke she didn't understand. "Even now, after all the training and fighting, I still can't protect the people I care about."

He reached out and touched the blood stain on her shift. She sucked in a sharp breath.

"*That's* why you're impossible for me, Veronica. Because I can't protect you." He cupped her face between his hands and placed a tender kiss to her forehead, his lips lingering there as if he, too, yearned for all they could never have. He rasped out, his voice raw with guilt and dread, "If I lost another woman who was in my care…it would end me."

She whispered painfully, "Merritt—"

Without warning, he jerked back and cocked his head toward the door. His body tensed, and Veronica felt his heartbeat jump beneath her hand as it rested on his chest, her own pulse immediately matching his. Quick fear licked at her toes.

"What's—"

He tapped his finger against her lips in a warning to keep silent, then pointed at the door.

She held her breath and listened, straining to hear over the pounding rush of blood in her ears—

A footstep on the stairs.

His eyes darted down to hers. A low warning glowed in their dark depths... *Someone's in the house.*

He pulled her silently to the bed, gestured for her to lie down, and stretched out next to her.

"Don't move," he mouthed as he gently put her head down onto the pillow where she could pretend to be asleep.

She nodded. If the intruder was only a burglar who wanted to rob the house, he most likely wouldn't harm them as long as he thought they were asleep. But the ball of fear in her belly held little hope for that.

Someone had come after her tonight to kill her. Now they were coming after Merritt.

He turned onto his back at the edge of the mattress. With his left arm lying across his abdomen, he reached beneath the bed with his right. Then he lay still.

The footsteps drew closer. Not one set but two. From the hitch in his breath, Merritt realized that, too. But neither of them moved, keeping their eyes closed and pretending to sleep even as the intruders moved steadily toward them.

A stretch of silence came as the men paused on the landing, followed by the opening of the door to the other room. A few seconds passed as they looked inside, then the door closed.

Her heart lurched into her throat. Not burglars. *Hunters.*

The door to their room opened with a soft click, followed by the same pause as before. But this time, the quiet shuffling of fabric and boots as they entered revealed that the two men had found what they'd been looking for. Merritt, asleep in his bed.

But they hadn't expected him to have company.

"Look at that," one whispered to the other.

The second man drawled, "A pretty little present."

Veronica forced herself to breathe slowly and evenly. She pretended to be asleep, yet every one of her senses came alert, her muscles ready to spring.

"Don't even have to unwrap it," he joked.

"Used gift."

"Still tasty, though. And a fun treat after our work."

She opened her eyes, unable to keep them closed a heartbeat longer. The two men stood silhouetted by the frame of the open door, one wide and hulking and the other slender but tall. A slant of moonlight revealed the steely flash of knives.

"You take him," the smaller man ordered and pointed his knife at Merritt. "I'll take the whore."

The big man nodded and started toward the bed.

Merritt sprang. He slashed with his knife in his right hand as he spun in a half circle and kicked his leg. His foot plowed into the shorter man's chest and sent him staggering back. Then he dropped into a crouch and slashed with his knife at the other man. The blade sliced through the man's trousers and into his calf.

The attacker let out a howl of pain but somehow found the lucidity to strike back and lunged forward on his good leg to thrust the knife at Merritt's shoulder.

Merritt dodged the blow, dropped his shoulder, and charged forward like a bull. He slammed his shoulder into the man's midriff and threw him backward halfway across the room. The two men grappled, their knives flashing in the moonlight.

The smaller of the two men recovered and came at Veronica.

She rolled off the bed and darted to the fireplace to grab the iron poker. When she brandished it in front of her, the man laughed, only for a groan of pain to escape when she swung and caught him on the boney edge of his hip. He lunged. She jumped to the side and stabbed the poker forward like a sword. But the dulled tip didn't puncture the man's clothes and simply bounced off the hard flesh beneath as if she'd never touched him at all.

Panting hard from exertion and fear, she retreated slowly but kept the poker gripped tightly in her hand. Her heart pounded so hard that each beat jarred against her breastbone and ricocheted painfully. So did the slap of iron in her ungloved palm as she swung the poker again, this time in a wide arc that hit his shoulder with a dull thud.

"You bitch!" he bellowed.

With a fierce cry, she swung again. The iron poker caught him on the side of the head and dropped him to his knees.

He remained on all fours on the floor at her feet, stunned and breathless. His chest heaved as he gasped for breath. When he tilted back his head and looked up at her, his rage-filled expression made her gasp.

Before she could swing a second time, he snarled and flung himself at her. He grabbed her by the legs and tossed her to the floor, then climbed on top of her to pin her down. He clutched her throat.

She kicked and punched, but he was too large and heavy. She couldn't shove him away! No scream left her lips, only a soft gargling as he squeezed her throat. She couldn't see around him to find Merritt, had no idea if Merritt was still fighting. Or if he was still alive. All she could hear was the deafening roar of blood in her ears with every pounding heartbeat.

He drew back the other hand that still held his knife and flashed it in front of her face.

He lowered his face close to hers. So close that she saw the jagged scar marking his cheek and smelled the stench of his hot breath. "I'm going to gut you for that."

He lowered the tip of the knife toward her belly.

An arm shot around his neck. The bicep flexed hard like steel as the man was yanked off her and flung against the wall so hard that the room shook from the impact. The air whooshed from his lungs.

Merritt pinned the man to the wall and shoved his knife blade under the man's chin. Blood splatter covered Merritt's bare chest and dripped down his thighs.

Yet the bloodied sight of him wasn't nearly as terrifying as the look of sheer hatred that gripped his face.

"You won't hurt her again, you bastard," he seethed. "You won't take her from me again."

He pulled back his arm to slice the man's throat—

"Merritt, no!" Veronica cried out. "We need him alive!"

He whipped his head toward her and stared at her as if he were staring at a ghost… No, she realized as icy fingers wrapped around her spine. Not at a ghost. *At Joanna.* He wasn't with her; he was lost in his memories from five years ago. That horrible night had blended into this one for him, and she had blended into Joanna.

He shook his head hard, but when he glanced at her again, there was no recognition in his eyes.

The attacker shoved him back and slashed his knife. Merritt darted to the side to avoid the sharp blade.

The man raced from the room. His boots pounded hard on the steps as he fled from the house and out into the night.

Merritt started after him—

"No!" she called out, terrified of what would happen to him if he left.

He halted and looked over his shoulder at her. The murderous set of his face shuddered through her, strangling her throat in shock and preventing her from calling out to him again.

Then he ignored her and chased after the attacker in cold-blooded pursuit.

Veronica fought to catch back her breath and slowly crawled to her feet, leaning back against the wall for support. The iron poker fell from her hand and clanked against the floor. Six feet away lay a dead man.

She shook violently as her heart pounded out every second Merritt was gone. Her deep and labored breaths burned her lungs at the realization of why he'd chased after the attacker. Not to capture the man to interrogate him for answers but to kill him, to take revenge for this night the way he hadn't been able to do five years ago.

You won't hurt her again… You won't take her from me again… Again.

He didn't mean her.

Merritt reappeared in the doorway, dripping blood onto the rug and still clasping the knife in his hand. His face was set hard as stone, and his bare chest heaved with exertion.

"You killed him, then?" she breathed out, unable to find enough voice to even whisper.

He shamefully shook his head.

Thank God. She slumped back against the wall as the terror of losing him fled.

He dropped his knife and hurried to her. He ran his hands over her, not to comfort her, she knew, but to check for wounds. Finding none, he cupped her face between his blood-sticky hands and pressed his lips to her forehead.

"I'm not hurt," she told him, desperate to ease the turmoil pulsing from him. The same anguish roiled inside her. "I'm fine. He didn't hurt me."

A rush of relief flooded from him so intensely that it seeped into her.

"And you?" She reached up to touch his brow and the deep cut there that trickled blood down his face. "Dear God…Merritt!" She dropped her gaze over his body and nearly cried out. So much blood! "Are you all right?"

He gave a curt nod and slipped his arms around her to draw her against him, heedless of the blood.

She buried her mouth against his shoulder and whispered against his hot skin, "You left me…" *You left me to chase after a dead woman.*

"He was going to kill you," he justified simply.

His words fell through her with an icy tremor, and not because of what might have happened to her. He'd killed one man tonight to protect her, had almost killed a second. Yet she knew he hadn't truly been saving her at all.

He'd still been trying to save Joanna.

He loosened his hold on her and stepped back. She flashed numb as she watched him kneel down beside the dead man, his face inscrutable, his every movement carefully controlled. Emotionless. The man she'd made love to was gone; in his place was a cold and detached hunter.

"That man who attacked you tonight," he called out to her over his shoulder. "You said he had a tattoo. Where?"

"The left side of his neck."

He grabbed the dead man's shirt and ripped the collar back. A key-shaped tattoo marked his skin. "Like this?"

She nodded.

"The same one as on Liggett's uniform," he bit out grimly.

He let go of the man's shirt and stood. Without explanation, he crossed to the armoire, flung open the doors, and pulled out two shirts, waistcoats, breeches, and sets of braces. He kept one set of clothes for himself and tossed the second onto the bed over her ruined gown.

He nodded at them as he stepped up to the washstand in the

corner. "Put those on." He poured water into the basin and began to wash. "And hurry."

Fresh fear rose inside her. "Why? What are you going to do?"

With water dripping down his face and turning the water in the bowl blood-red, he pinned her with a gaze of fierce resolve. It was unlike any she'd ever seen from him before, so intense that it shivered like a cold wind across her skin and slammed her heart into her throat.

"I'm ending this," he promised. "Tonight."

Twenty-one

WHEN MERRITT OFFERED HIS HAND TO MADAME NOIR TO help her out of the carriage, she glanced up at the sandstone town house, then slid him a sideways look. "Where have you brought me, Snake?"

"Somewhere interesting," he assured her as he led her to the footpath. "Besides, you're getting paid for your time. And quite well, too."

Madame sniffed and turned away at that reminder that she was nothing if not mercenary.

He reached back into the carriage for Veronica, although she certainly didn't need his help. But he wanted to hold her hand in his, if only for a few fleeting moments, to buoy him up for what was to come. He couldn't stop the twist of worry in his gut that she was here. But she'd refused to go to the Armory where he could set guards to protect her.

She'd changed from his ill-fitting clothes into her battle outfit, complete with weapons, that they'd retrieved from the Court of Miracles. Thankfully, Filipe and his men had done nothing to stop them from collecting her belongings, including the pair of earbobs she'd slipped into her pocket when she thought Merritt wasn't watching.

"You pulled Madame away from her business," Veronica reminded him. "The least you can do is tell her why we're here."

"I will," he conceded and escorted the two women to the front door. "When the time is right."

He pounded the brass knocker and waited. The town house wasn't dark. Lamplight glowed behind the closed shutters in the front windows.

They were expected.

The door opened a crack, and Clayton Elliott peered out, one hand on the door handle and the other beneath his jacket on the pistol he kept there. He silently stepped back to let them inside.

"You know Veronica," Merritt mumbled in introduction to Clayton.

He nodded at her. "Nice to see you again, Miss Chase."

"And this is the illustrious Madame Noir of Le Château Noir." Merritt took Madame's arm and led her forward. "Madame Noir, Major Clayton Elliott."

"Madame." Clayton sketched her a bow.

"A pleasure to meet you, Major." Her interested gaze traveled over him. "*Very* much a pleasure." She smiled flirtatiously and held out her hand. "And to what do I owe this pleasant meeting?"

"Merritt didn't tell you during the carriage ride?" Clayton grinned and accepted her hand in greeting. "I'm an undersecretary with the Home Office."

Snatching her hand away, she muttered icily beneath her breath to Merritt, "You duplicitous little snake! To bring me here like this, to meet—"

"He's the one paying you for your time this evening," Merritt calmly informed her.

"In that case, my price just doubled." She plastered a false but bright smile on her face for Clayton. "How may I be of service, Mr. Elliott?"

Clayton glanced over his shoulder into the dining room where a woman sat tied to a chair. Merritt knew without being told... Malmesbury's mistress.

"The woman who lives here has information I need," Clayton told her. "We'll be questioning her tonight."

"Torture," Madame purred delightedly. "How delicious! I'm quite good with whips and spurs."

Clayton slid a dubious glance to Merritt, then cleared his throat. "Hopefully, it won't come to that."

"Pity." Madame sniffed.

Wisely, Clayton didn't reply. "I'll be conducting the questioning," he told them in a low voice so they wouldn't be overheard. Then he turned his attention to Merritt. "While I'm talking to her, I want you and Miss Chase to search the house for any evidence that connects her to the riots, no matter how small. Madame Noir, I would like you to linger a few feet away and listen in to what she has to say."

"Why should I do that?"

"You know women."

"I know *men*," she corrected pointedly. The no-nonsense look she leveled on Clayton would have done a governess proud. "Before I take one more step, I want to know what's going on here and who that woman is. Snake has told me nothing."

"Snake?" Clayton puzzled.

"Me." Merritt grinned. He slipped his arm familiarly around Madame's shoulders and gave her an affectionate squeeze. "Madame and I have a close and loving relationship."

She arched a brow. "Is that what you call continuously threatening to send me to Australia?"

"No relationship is perfect."

She pushed his arm away and scowled irritably.

"She's Charlotte Jones," Clayton explained, ignoring their antics. "The Earl of Malmesbury's mistress and someone we think is involved with the riots. Do you know her?"

"No. But I'm always interested in meeting new colleagues." She nodded toward the dining room without blinking an eye, as if seeing a bound woman was an everyday occurrence. From what went on at Le Château Noir, it most likely was. "Shall we begin? I need to return soon to my guests."

"Of course." Clayton gestured politely. "After you."

As Madame walked past, she trailed her hand suggestively down Clayton's arm.

He froze and stared after her for several long seconds, then turned to shoot Merritt a questioning quirk of his brow.

"She'll be useful," Merritt promised. "Trust me."

"And how exactly do you know her?"

"Don't ask," Merritt muttered.

He took Veronica's arm to lead her toward the stairs to start their search.

"I want to speak with you," he told her quietly. "We need to talk about what happened tonight."

She cast an uncertain glance as Clayton walked into the dining room with a friendly smile for Miss Jones and pulled a chair up in front of hers to begin his interrogation. "Now isn't a good time."

"When we were attacked tonight—"

"Merritt, please. Not now." A plea for mercy filled her voice, as if she knew what he was about to say. And couldn't bear it.

She slipped her arm away and hurried up the stairs before he could stop her.

Biting back a curse, he had no choice but to let her go. For now. But she couldn't avoid him forever. One way or another, the battle they'd started the night they met would finally end.

"Miss Jones," Clayton began casually, as if the two of them were discussing nothing more important than the weather, "why don't you tell me about your relationship to Lord Malmesbury? He keeps you in very comfortable circumstances here."

Pulling in a patient breath, Merritt walked into the adjoining parlor and began to search it. He looked for anything that would tie Charlotte Jones to Liggett, Smathers, the riots…Scepter. Every drawer and its underside was checked, every locked cabinet pried open with the tip of his knife and searched.

Meanwhile, Madame Noir helped herself to a cup of tea from the tray resting on the dining room table. Then she leaned back against the doorframe between the dining room and the parlor and settled in to observe.

That was Madame, all right. Merritt grimaced as he shut the door of the parlor closet after finding nothing of importance inside. Always her own sovereign. What he wouldn't have paid at that moment to have her locked in a room with the prince regent. God only knew which one of them would come out alive.

Taking his lead from Madame, Clayton poured a cup of tea, then untied Miss Jones's arms. If Merritt were a betting man, he'd have wagered in the book at White's that one of Clayton's men had tied her up just so Clayton could be the one who compassionately untied her. A twisted knight in shining armor, complete with sugared tea and biscuits.

Thank God Clayton was on their side.

"Here, Miss Jones." Clayton's expression softened with concern as he handed her the teacup. "I find that tea always makes things better."

The woman hesitated, then gave a jerking nod. Her fingers trembled as she reached to accept the tea.

"I want to help you, I truly do," Clayton cajoled in a soft voice. "But I need more information to prove your innocence."

As Merritt stepped up beside Madame, she rolled her eyes at Clayton and muttered against the rim of her teacup, "And I thought *you* were the snake."

Merritt's lips twisted. "Clayton's very good at getting the information he wants."

"Hmm." She lowered her cup and listened.

Clayton continued, "We know you're involved with General Horatio Liggett, that you've been spending time with him." He paused a beat. "Intimately."

Miss Jones's eyes widened. "How do you know that?"

Oh, he *was* good, Merritt reflected. Because Clayton *hadn't* known. The connection had been a wild guess until just now.

Her shoulders shook as she admitted, "The general and I have been...close."

Merritt glanced at Madame, happy to be proved right about

Clayton's interrogation skills. But she kept her gaze pinned to Miss Jones.

A sob tore from the woman. Her cup clinked softly against the saucer as she set it down, as if afraid in her distress that her shaking hand might spill it.

"I-I only did…as Malmesbury…asked of me," she choked out between sobs. Her slender shoulders hunched forward, her gaze guiltily fixed on her tea as it rested on her knee. "He asked me to… to take the general into my bed."

That last was said so softly that Merritt could barely hear her. But Madame heard and frowned.

Miss Jones pulled in a shuddering breath. "To settle an old debt between them."

"And that's how you came to know the general?" Clayton asked understandingly. He took a handkerchief from his pocket and handed it to her.

She nodded and dabbed at her eyes. "When the general came to my door, he had a letter from Malmesbury instructing me to make him feel welcome." She paused, holding the bit of linen against her nose. "I knew what Malmesbury meant."

"Are you certain he meant that?"

"This is how I make my way through the world, sir." She gave him an indignant look that he would doubt her. "Pleasing Malmesbury is what keeps me from starving on the streets."

Madame's frown sharpened.

"Has the general been staying here with you?" Clayton asked.

"Heavens no!"

"Then who's been using your carriage?"

She blinked. "My carriage?"

"It was seen three nights ago in front of the Ship's Bell near the Strand. A man who has been connected to the leaders of the recent riots was seen climbing inside. The question I have is who was he meeting inside your carriage?"

"It wasn't me." Her face turned white. "It must have been the general. He'd asked to borrow the carriage, so of course I let him." She took a comforting sip of tea, but her color didn't return. "He was here at Malmesbury's behest, and I am not foolish enough to deny a request from an old friend of the earl's. But I don't know where he went or what he did. I don't know anything about the riots."

Clayton's face remained inscrutable. "Liggett didn't tell you that he's been given orders to use his soldiers to put down the unrest? That innocent men and boys might be killed in the clash?" He paused just long enough to draw her full attention to his next question. "Or that he knows the men who are responsible for starting them?"

"No, he never…" She pressed the back of her hand against her lips and whispered her confession through her fingers. "I saw him for only one night, for a few hours at most. I wanted to please Malmesbury, that's all…just please my protector."

Clayton put a concerned hand on the woman's arm to comfort her. She sobbed into his handkerchief.

Madame shifted closer to Merritt. "She's lying. Her relationship with the general isn't at all what she claims." She muttered against the rim of the cup as she raised it to her lips, "Oh, she's a good actress—very good, indeed. But she's lying."

Merritt narrowed his eyes on Miss Jones. "How do you know?"

"I know men, remember?" She nodded over her teacup at Miss Jones. "What man—and a general no less—would lower himself by using the carriage of another man's mistress? And a mistress he'd tupped only because that man was in his debt?" She shook her head at the idea. "None I've ever known, and I've known all kinds."

No, she'd been *intimate* with all kinds. And for that hard-won experience, Merritt was willing to hear her out. "If he'd already visited her bed, what would he care as long as the carriage was convenient?"

She slid him a look as if he were a bedlamite. "All those years you spent studying the law yet learning not one thing about men…" She gave a long-suffering sigh at the waste of it, then explained, "After intimacy is exactly when a man strives to show off how manly and powerful he is. Trust me. He'd walk his boot soles thin before he allowed himself to be seen in the carriage of another man's mistress."

A low warning prickled at the backs of Merritt's knees, and his gaze flicked back to Miss Jones. If she was lying, then—

"Merritt?" Veronica called out from upstairs. "I think you should come up here." A short pause, then far more firmly, "*Now.*"

He hurried up the stairs and found her in the front bedroom. The door to the old servants' passageway that was meant to blend into the paneling and wallpaper of the bedroom's walls stood open wide. Veronica stared inside.

She mumbled, "I think the Home Office might be interested in this."

"Then grab it," he said as he entered the room. "Clayton's nearly done interrogating Miss Jones. We'll take it away with us in the carriage."

Both of her brows rose in incredulity. "We're going to need a bigger carriage."

Merritt came up behind her and peered over her shoulder. He blinked. "Good God…"

The space that had once been used by servants to come and go unseen had been filled with shelves stacked full with small bags of coins, banknotes, account books, and various goods that hungry and poor men living on the streets would find to be a godsend. All of which Merritt had no doubt was meant to pay former soldiers to riot.

"I think we've found the person who's been giving money to Smathers," he muttered and picked up one of the small bags of coins. They jangled softly as he bounced the bag on his palm.

"I should say so." Veronica turned to face him, leaning a

shoulder against the wall. "But why would Miss Jones be involved with riots? And how did she acquire all this money?"

"I don't know." He tossed the bag back onto the shelf and closed the door. "But I bet we can find out."

"There's something more." A grim tone edged her voice. "I also found this in her jewelry box."

Veronica held up a necklace, letting it fall from her fingers by its long chain. A large pendant in the shape of a key dangled from its end. The same symbol that had been tattooed on the men who had attacked them tonight.

The same symbol that connected all of them to Liggett.

———————

Veronica followed on Merritt's heels as he hurried downstairs to Clayton. He put his hand on Clayton's shoulder and leaned down to speak quietly into his ear.

Clayton's gaze swung from Merritt to Miss Jones, where it narrowed with such intensity that Veronica shivered, even on the other side of the room.

Merritt surreptitiously slipped the wadded-up necklace into Clayton's hand and retreated to Veronica's side as she lingered with Madame Noir.

"Miss Jones." Clayton leaned back in the chair. "Is there anything about your story that you would like to amend?"

Her face twisted into grief at not being believed. "I've told you the truth! You can ask General Liggett. He'll tell you the same. Go on—go ask him yourself."

"Oh, I'm certain I will." Clayton kicked out his long legs in the posture of a man who had nothing to lose. "But first I want to give you the chance to clarify your details. After all, memories can get rather blurry, can't they? Let's start with this." Clayton held up the necklace. "Liggett has a pin just like this pendant."

"He probably does since he gave that one to me. That necklace is nothing more than a cheap token. He most likely gives them away to women like ha'pennies to children." She swiped at her eyes. "I told you. Liggett means nothing to me except as a way to appease Malmesbury."

Madame Noir let out a tired sigh. "I really do not have time for this."

She coolly walked into the dining room, handed her teacup to Clayton, who scrambled to his feet in surprise, and stepped straight up to Miss Jones. Then she stunned them all by slapping the woman.

With a gasp of surprise, Veronica started forward, but Merritt stopped her with a hand to her arm and a shake of his head not to interfere. Clayton, too, was smart enough to stand back out of the fray.

"Listen to yourself, for heaven's sake," Madame said calmly and leveled a hard look at Miss Jones. "You are lying to protect a man who is willing to kill innocent people. Do you really think he cares about you, a woman he's used only to further his career?"

The woman's hand rose slowly to her red cheek. For the first time since the interrogation began, real tears watered her eyes.

"There was no message from Malmesbury about any debt needing to be repaid." Madame punctuated that accusation by crossing her arms over her chest in an imperial pose that Veronica was certain she used at her business to maintain the peace. "Lies. All of it. All said to protect a man who doesn't deserve your sympathy."

Miss Jones stared at her, saying nothing. But her bottom lip quivered, and Veronica thought she might just let out a true sob.

"You foolish girl." Madame shook her head with grim disappointment, as if Miss Jones had betrayed all of their sex. "At the very least, Malmesbury will find out that you've been cheating on him and will cast you out." She leaned forward, placing her hands on both chair arms. "And he *will* find out because I will make certain of it when I offer my services in finding him a new mistress."

Miss Jones glanced desperately at Clayton, begging silently for help. But this time, her tea-bearing knight wisely stood back and did nothing.

"At the very worst, you'll be implicated in the riots and if not hanged at Newgate then surely transported to Australia, where you'll wish the crown had had the mercy to hang you after all." Madame shook her head. "Do you really think the Home Office is here to play games?"

"No," Miss Jones whispered, barely louder than a breath, and grew deathly pale.

"The only thing preventing any of that from happening to you is Mr. Elliott." Madame smiled at him conspiratorially, although knowing her, it was to gauge if she could demand double payment for her unexpected services tonight. She took the necklace from him and looped it around Miss Jones's neck. "So if I were you, I'd cooperate and tell him the truth. Otherwise..." Madame trailed her forefinger around the woman's throat. "This necklace of yours will surely be replaced by a noose."

Miss Jones stared at her, knowing she'd been bested. With a fierce cry born of fear and rage, she threw her teacup as hard as she could against the wall. It smashed against the blue wallpaper and fell to the floor in a shower of black tea and shattered china.

"Fine," she seethed, the anger that pulsed from her so palpable that Veronica could feel it from across the room. "I'll tell you what I know. But if I do, you don't arrest me." She jabbed an accusing finger at Clayton. Her murderous gaze swung to Madame, as did her jabbing finger. "And *you* don't tell Malmesbury."

"The Home Office agrees to your terms," Clayton answered with a calmness born from years spent on the battlefield. "And you, Madame Noir?"

"Deny myself the fun of informing Malmesbury?" Yet she

acquiesced as she tugged her long black gloves into place. "Very well." She sighed with disappointment. "I'll keep my silence."

Veronica breathed her own sigh of relief. They were making headway. *Finally.*

"My work here is done." Madame retrieved her teacup and finished the last swallow, then handed her cup and saucer to Merritt as if he were a footman. "I'll see myself home."

As she glided toward the entry hall, she stopped in the doorway and turned back to rake a blatantly suggestive look over Clayton.

"I'm assuming you'll pay me for my services in person, Mr. Elliott." A smile teased at her red lips. "I'm *very* much looking forward to it."

Clayton replied to her challenge with a rakish grin. "So am I."

She called over her shoulder as she sauntered toward the front door, "Perhaps next time, you'll let me use whips and spurs."

Clayton's smile faded as the door closed after her. He arched an incredulous brow at Merritt.

"I told you she'd be helpful," Merritt replied.

Wisely not replying to that, Clayton turned back toward Miss Jones, took his chair, and spun it around before sitting directly in front of her. He straddled the seat and rested his arms across the back in a no-nonsense position that announced he'd just transformed from questioner to interrogator.

"We found the money and goods you're keeping upstairs to pay men to riot. We know you've been doing it since the riots started, long before Liggett arrived in London," Clayton explained in a low and steely voice. "Why?"

"Because the general asked me to." Hatred for Clayton blazed in her eyes, but she understood the deal she'd struck with him and grudgingly answered, "Horatio has been my lover for the past six months. Malmesbury doesn't know, of course."

"Of course," Clayton drawled. "So Liggett brought you into his plans, gave you a closet full of money, and sent you out to recruit men to lead the riots while he convinced Whitehall to put him in charge of putting them down."

Her belligerent silence confirmed his assumption.

"And now he's planning one last riot tomorrow night to unleash his soldiers against the mob. Why?"

"Because this country's leadership is weak and spoiled, and when Liggett puts down the rioters, he will prove that he's a better man than the regent. That he's a strong, natural-born leader who cares about protecting England." Her eyes flared with a light in their depths that was almost fanatical in its intensity. "Because something needed to happen to make the government wake up and do what's best for England."

"Doing what's best for England is arranging for soldiers to slaughter their own countrymen?" Merritt challenged angrily, unable to keep his silence. "Is that what this whole plot is about—for Liggett to arrange for a riot tomorrow night simply so he can fire upon them? For God's sake, he'll slaughter them!"

"Didn't the same thing happen during the wars?" she shot back. "Generals starting battles in which our soldiers were fired upon? The slaughter of Englishmen for the greater good?"

Veronica squeezed Merritt's hand for him to keep his silence. No matter how much they despised this woman, they needed the information she possessed.

Miss Jones pinned her gaze on Merritt. "Too many good men died in the wars, and for what—to preserve the English way of life?" she mocked. "So the same royal leeches and aristocrats could remain in power? So they could continue to make their fortunes on the backs of the poor who work themselves to exhaustion just to afford a loaf of bread? From where the rest of us sit, that way of life isn't worth preserving. Social and political upheaval is the only way for people like me to rise."

Veronica grimaced. She was certainly telling the truth about *that*.

"But you're wrong about the riots. The last one isn't planned for tomorrow. It's scheduled for this morning, just before dawn, while all those European princes are still in town and can see how weak our regent is, how mad our monarch." With a vengeful smile, she leaned back in the chair. "And you're too late to stop it."

Twenty-two

"SO WHAT'S OUR PLAN?" MERRITT CALLED OUT TO PEARCE AND Clayton as the loud jangle of the Armory's iron doors announced their arrival.

They were back where they'd started. Back at the Armory, back to trying to find a way to stop the riots.

Except that now, Veronica was no longer the enemy.

His gaze flicked to her as she stood at the massive fireplace and stirred up the coals for the light and warmth a fire would provide. He wanted her here because he wanted her to be part of the planning and because he wanted her at his side for however tonight would eventually play out. But mostly because she wasn't safe anywhere else. That was why they'd left Miss Jones's town house as soon as they'd learned of Liggett's plans, before Clayton had even finished interrogating the woman—to put their men into place. Even now, men were guarding his father's house, and a messenger had been sent to the Court of Miracles to tell Filipe to put more men on watch. Merritt would protect the people he cared about tonight, no matter what he had to do to ensure it.

Pearce and Clayton exchanged concerned glances as they strode into the room, with Pearce going directly to the sideboard and its waiting bottles of liquor.

"Miss Jones admitted who's been giving money to Liggett to fund the riots." Clayton stopped in front of Merritt, his haggard face grim. Merritt knew before he'd spoken the name—"Scepter."

"That doesn't make sense," Veronica interjected and returned the poker to its stand. "From what Merritt's told me, Scepter wants a controlled revolution." She walked slowly toward the men. "Yet riots are the exact opposite of that. They're unpredictable."

"But bringing in soldiers isn't," Clayton countered. "That's their endgame. Not the riots and the civil unrest they cause but the show of strength in putting them down."

"All the credit for the success of it given to Liggett," Merritt added.

"And all the blame for doing nothing placed squarely onto the regent," Pearce finished.

"We learned something else from Miss Jones." Clayton passed a grim look between Merritt and Veronica. "Liggett sent those men to kill you because he realized you were on his trail, and he didn't want anything to interfere with his plans."

Merritt didn't look at Veronica, doing his best to hide all traces of his worry and concern for her. "That's why they all had the same symbol…the pin, the tattoos, the pendant—they were all in league with Liggett."

"They were all in league with Scepter," Clayton clarified. "We think the key is the group's symbol, like a secret password they use for immediate recognition of one another."

"The keys to the kingdom, that's what Liggett called it," Veronica murmured. "I thought it was a religious reference."

"Not religion," Clayton corrected. "Revolution."

Merritt's blood turned to ice. "This means Scepter has infiltrated the military."

"The military, the Home Office, Parliament…" Clayton blew out a harsh breath. "We can't assume anything is out of their reach."

"Except the monarchy," Pearce muttered from the other side of the room as he raised his glass to take a sip.

Merritt turned to stare at him as an icy revelation struck him. "The monarchy—the regent," Merritt muttered. "That's what we keep hearing from the members of Scepter we've managed to find so far. That the regent is weak and corrupt, the monarch mad."

Clayton interjected quietly, repeating Miss Jones's words from the interrogation, "And England lacking the strong leadership it needs."

Merritt's heart skipped. "Liggett said the same. That the government was indecisive, that England needed a show of strength and resolve instead of wastefulness and weakness." A sickening, bitter taste of acid covered his tongue. "He didn't mean putting down the riots. He meant overthrowing the regent."

A curse fell from Clayton's lips, and Pearce set down his drink. A grim silence settled over the men. In their entire lives, their most sacred duty had been to the monarchy and army. Now, Scepter was plotting to destroy even that.

"But Liggett, of all men?" Pearce shook his head. "Does Scepter really think it can make Horatio Liggett into an English Napoleon?"

"No," Merritt answered quietly. "And they don't have to. Liggett is just their current pawn. They'll employ others like him to keep demonstrating over and over how weak the regent is, how corrupt, how destructive for England. And eventually, when the time is right, Scepter's men will declare that the regent is just as unfit as King George, that he needs to be removed and a new monarch installed. Voices will call out from all levels of the government and the military." He stared grimly at the floor. "Who will be there to stop them from overthrowing the House of Hanover?"

"One of the royal dukes," Pearce interjected firmly. Disbelief filled his voice that they were even having this conversation. "Especially if he's the one Scepter's picked to replace the regent."

"Not if Scepter can't trust any of the royal dukes to do their bidding," Merritt explained. "They'll want a puppet ruler in place, not just a change in monarch. They'll declare that every one of the royal dukes is as mad as their father, as unfit as their brother—emotional hysterics and breakdowns, fits of rage, publicly flaunting mistresses, committing scandal after scandal, and spending the country into poverty. They'll put a new monarch in place. One they can control."

Clayton added grimly, putting voice to what they were all thinking, "A second Glorious Revolution will be born."

"And we only have until dawn to stop it," Merritt reminded them.

Pearce came forward. All three men stood in a circle, shoulder to shoulder, as they'd done on the battlefields of Spain and France when they needed to strategize. The familiarity of the gathering and the shared purpose behind it warmed through Merritt. These men were his brothers, a family formed in the fires and blood of battle, and he would lay down his life for them.

"So where do we start?" Pearce said.

"*How* do we start?" Clayton shook his head. "For God's sake, to stop this, we'd need our own army to replace Liggett's or a riot we can control."

Merritt and Veronica said in unison, "I can get us—"

Realizing what they were doing, they both stopped and turned toward each other.

"An army," Merritt finished, his chest warming as he held her gaze beneath his.

"A controlled riot," Veronica added, a slow smile crossing her face.

Pearce and Clayton exchanged bewildered looks. Then Pearce threw up his hands. "I don't even want to know how."

"Miracles," Veronica answered enigmatically.

Merritt shrugged. "And a little kidnapping." He removed his jacket, tossed it aside, and rolled up his sleeves. "But first, we're going to need General Braddock."

"This is madness," Marcus Braddock, Duke of Hampton and former general with the Coldstream Guards, declared to the men as he finished listening to their plan.

From across the octagonal room where she leaned back against the wall and did her best to go unnoticed, Veronica silently agreed.

Dawn was only a few hours away. According to Clayton and Pearce, soldiers from the Scots Guard were already positioned in the streets behind makeshift barricades. Liggett would arrive soon to lead them in firing on the rioters. And Scepter would be one step closer to revolution.

Marcus Braddock knew it, too. That was why he shoved himself off the arm of the sofa where he'd been perched for the past half hour and began to pace the length of the main room of the Armory. Brandon Pearce had had the unfortunate task of rousing the duke from his warm bed and out of the arms of his wife to bring him here, while Merritt and Clayton had remained behind to concoct their plans.

If the men of the Armory didn't get themselves killed—with several rioters and soldiers right along with them—it would be a miracle.

But everyone in the room also knew this was the only workable plan they had.

"So let me see if I understand this correctly." The duke paused in his pacing to cross his arms over his chest. "We've got a monarchy to rescue, a riot to put down, Scots Guards to immobilize, and only three hours left to do it."

"That's about right," Merritt confirmed.

"And this is our plan—kidnapping, mutinying soldiers, and starting a riot of our own?" Marcus gestured a hand at the Armory around them, indicating all they'd plotted out tonight. "Crossing both the Home Secretary and War Department to protect rioters?"

"Well," Clayton grudgingly acquiesced, "when you put it that way—"

"Yes," Merritt finished resolutely.

Marcus blew out an aggravated breath and shook his head. "Defeating Napoleon was easier."

Yet his eyes gleamed at the sense of purpose the four men now shared, something they'd all missed since the wars ended.

"Then call out the Coldstream Guards, General," Pearce said quietly. "Every man who was under your command will still lay down his life for you."

Marcus dropped his arms to his sides as he looked thoughtfully between the three men standing with him. All three were still just as loyal to their former general as he was to them.

"You all know your parts in this and have agreed to do what must be done?" He paused meaningfully and pinned Veronica with a look over his shoulder. "Including you, Miss Chase?"

"Yes, General," she answered, as any good soldier would.

Her pulse spiked to be included, no matter how improbable their plans, but also because of the dark glance Merritt darted at her across the room. From the way his jaw tightened, he wasn't at all pleased at her answer.

Marcus gave a decisive nod. "Then we'd best get started."

He turned on his heel and left the Armory to prepare. Pearce and Clayton knew their roles in how the rest of the night would play out, right up until the breaking dawn, so they followed after. Their roles in the plan had commenced.

The iron doors clanged shut behind them.

When the last metallic rattle died away, Merritt turned toward Veronica. She'd been aware of every glance he'd given her during the past hour, but now his stare prickled electricity through her to the ends of her hair—which then stood on end when he began to stalk toward her—because she knew…

The next battle of the night was about to begin.

"You don't have to do this," he said mildly, a soft deception of the knockdown brawl she knew was brewing. "This isn't your fight."

"It's become my fight." *Because of you.*

"You can stay here until it's over. You'll be safe inside the Armory."

"I'll be safe fighting beside you."

He faltered in midstep. Only a moment's imbalance, but Veronica noticed. "You might not be," he admitted. "Not in the midst of rioters and soldiers."

Her chest squeezed. *Joanna.* That was what he meant. That he would fail to protect her the same way he'd failed to protect his fiancée.

The woman still haunted him, even now.

Her pulse increased with each step that brought him closer, yet she stood her ground. "Then it's a good thing I'm an experienced fighter." More—she was a survivor, and when this was over, she would continue to survive without him. *Somehow.* "I can take care of myself."

He stopped in front of her, so close that she had to tilt back her head to look up at him, so close that her skin tingled from his nearness. Yet instead of reaching for her as she'd expected, he crossed his arms over his chest in his best impersonation of an immovable mountain.

"So let me be clear then. I don't want you there. Not in the riot, not anywhere near it." His gaze bore into hers. "I don't want you to be part of this."

His rejection of her help took her breath away. She'd expected to vanish from his life after the dawn. But she certainly hadn't expected him to exile her now when the men needed her most. "That's not your decision to make."

"I'm the one who brought you into this mess."

"And I'm the one who decides how I'll leave it," she countered. More truth lay behind that quiet statement than she wanted to admit. "I promised to help you stop the riots, and that's exactly what I'm going to do." There were so many promises in her life she'd never been able to keep, but not this one. This one she would see though to the end. Or die trying. "You need a good fighter with you for this battle, Merritt." She added before he could shatter her heart anew by stating that he didn't need her, "And I'm not your responsibility to protect."

"That's where you're wrong. You are mine to protect."

His words sliced into her. "I'm not yours, Merritt." Her voice cracked at the horrible truth of that. "I never can be."

"Because of what you said tonight?" His eyes darkened somberly. "About a criminal with a King's Counsel? A by-blow with a baron?"

Sadly, she shook her head, knowing the truth now. Peerages and pardons weren't what stood between them. "None of that matters."

"Good. Because you *are* mine, Veronica," he argued gently. "Just as I'm yours. Tonight proved that. That's why you came to me, because you needed me. That's why we made love, because we needed each other. And that's why I don't want you in this fight." He paused beneath the weight of his confession. "Because I couldn't bear to lose you now."

No, not *now*… "Again," she corrected in a whisper, the breathless sound barely audible.

He blinked. "Pardon?"

"Again. That's what you said earlier, when you were threatening that attacker, that he wouldn't take me from you—*again*." Her lips trembled with the pain of it, but it needed to be said. "But you didn't mean me. You couldn't have, because I've never been taken from you." *Because I've never completely been yours to begin with.*

"I meant I wouldn't lose another woman I care about."

Instead of making her soar with joy, his words ripped her apart. "No, you meant Joanna," she breathed out, unable to speak louder for fear of breaking into sobs. "Dear God, Merritt, after all these years…you're still trying to save a dead woman."

He flinched as if the quiet accusation hit him with the force of a punch. His arms dropped to his sides, and a stricken expression gripped his face.

"I'm not her," she forced out hoarsely. "I'm not Joanna."

"I know that." The seductive purr of his deep voice landed with an aching tingle between her legs. "Trust me, Veronica. I know exactly who I made love to tonight."

The rush of loss and sadness overwhelmed her, and she choked as she challenged softly, "And in the heat of the fight afterward? Who were you with then?" She drew in a ragged breath. "Because it wasn't me."

He froze, every inch of him tensing so hard that his surprise radiated into her.

"That's why you ran after that attacker, why you left me alone—because of Joanna." The guilt that darkened his expression pierced her, and what was left of her heart shattered irreparably. "You chose revenge for a dead woman over staying with me."

"Veronica..." Yet there was nothing he could say to defend himself because she was right. They both knew it.

"You cannot protect the world, Merritt. No man can. Accidents happen, missteps are taken—people die. *Good* people die. No one can stop that." Her arms fell to her sides in a gesture of defeat. "And certainly not if you insist on chasing the dead instead of focusing on living. Believe me, I know that better than anyone."

"I will *not* lose another woman I care about because I failed to protect her."

"And I'm *not* Joanna. I'm capable of holding my own in any fight."

"That's the problem." He touched the brass studs on the leather corset she wore like plate armor and admitted quietly, "If I couldn't protect Joanna, a pastel-wearing society miss, what chance in the world do I have of protecting a fighter like you?"

His confession pierced her, so brutally that she flinched.

"They took Joanna from me. I won't let them take you, too."

"You can't lose what you don't have." That reminder emerged barely louder than a whispered breath. "As long as you're still clinging to Joanna's memory, you'll never truly have me. Not in your heart." She placed her hand to this chest, and the strong pounding of his pulse drummed against her fingertips. "Let her go, Merritt." The soft plea to be loved rose up from her soul. "And let me inside."

Anguish cut deep lines into his handsome face, and his broad shoulders slumped.

"I can't let go of her," he admitted starkly, placing his hand over hers. As if he were afraid he would lose her right then. "If I let go, if I turn my back on her—" He choked off, then admitted the awful truth. "I've tried to move on, but always, I get pulled back."

"I know." She'd seen that happen tonight with her own eyes, and just like him, she had no idea how to stop it.

The enormity of all they could never have hurled itself at her with the force of an explosion, and she shuddered, the pain too much to bear.

"But I'm not Joanna," she repeated hoarsely, her throat raw. Yet she knew it mattered not at all how many times she said that. His heart refused to let go of the past.

"Veronica—"

"I'm fighting tonight with you and the men. I'm carrying out my part of the plan." When he began to argue, she cut him off. "I want to do it with your agreement, but I'll defy you and do it on my own if I have to." Desolation warred with her resolve as she admitted, "But I'd so much rather be fighting with you than against you." *One last time…*

He gritted his jaw silently, as if his mind were racing through all possible options for a way to argue against her, a way to convince her to stay behind and let him protect her. He might as well have been chasing the wind.

With no other choice, he gave a grudging nod of acceptance and looked away. He'd lost the battle.

But she'd lost the war. The fortress he'd built around his heart had proved impenetrable after all.

She pulled in a deep breath to gather as much strength as she could. When dawn came, she'd fight at his side, the way she'd come to love. They'd end the riots, stop Liggett, and finish what they'd started. Then she'd leave London. And him.

For the rest of this night, though, he was hers. She wouldn't waste a minute of it.

Slowly, she reached to unfasten her sword belt and let it fall away to the floor around her boots.

His gaze snapped back to her, and the heat in his eyes flamed into a bonfire when she drifted a hand down her front to unfasten her waistcoat. The metal fastenings slipped free, and the leather parted.

He inhaled sharply through clenched teeth. With his gaze fixed on her, she shrugged and let the thick waistcoat slip off her shoulders, down her back, and off. Then she loosened the gusset tie for her breeches at the small of her back.

Her hand went to her corset next, and she temptingly tangled her fingers in the front tie. "Do you want me to stop?"

"No." He swallowed, hard enough that his Adam's apple bounced. "Not if you don't."

"I don't." She did her best to push down her sadness that this would be the last time they would be intimate and smiled as seductively as possible. "I might need your help, though." She glanced down at the corset. "Silly me. I seem to have knotted the lace."

"Damn shame," he murmured as he slowly closed the distance between them. "May I?"

"Yes," she whispered, agreeing to so much more.

He deftly pulled at the tie of the corset. With a long, slow, torturous slide of his hand down her front, from breasts to belly, he pulled the lace free. The stays dangled open, revealing the man's linen shirt she wore beneath.

"There." He stepped back and put several feet between them. "All untied."

She dropped her fisted hands to her sides. Oh, frustrating man! "That's not what—"

Without warning, he grabbed her into his arms, scooped her off the floor, and carried her to the fireplace. As he lowered her onto her feet, he slid his hands beneath the open corset and caressed her breasts through the soft linen. Her nipples immediately tightened into hard, aching points... *Oh, frustrating man.*

He leaned forward to bring his lips to her ear and nibbled at her earlobe as his hands continued to stroke her. "I thought you might be cold."

"Not at all." Despite herself, she couldn't help arching into him, to encourage him to tease even more wickedly at her nipples and stoke the growing ache between her legs. "Actually, I feel...quite heated."

His hands pushed the corset off her shoulders to the floor, then pulled the shirt taut across her breasts. Her dark nipples pressed against the white material. He stared hungrily down at her and said huskily, "My mistake."

She inhaled sharply when he lowered his head and captured her nipple in his mouth through the soft linen. When he began to suckle at her in gentle but persistent pulls, she ran her fingers through his hair and let out a long, shaking sigh. Would any other man ever be able to make her feel this way again, this beautiful and desired? Would any other man stir this much longing inside her with only a caress of his lips?

She trembled with growing pleasure as his tongue laved at her, then moved to do the same to her other breast, leaving a damp circle in the linen. When he bit at her nipple, she cried out softly at the wanton sensation of pleasure-pain he spun through her.

"Then perhaps we should remove some of your clothes before you overheat," he murmured against her breast and placed a soft kiss to its tip.

"A fine idea." But even as she returned the teasing flirtations, she felt the anguish of losing him flood the dark corners of her heart. But wasn't this where they'd always been the most comfortable with each other since the beginning—in the middle of teasing banter and conversation without consequence? This was what she would cling to tonight, this part of him that she loved, and somehow not think of the rest.

His hand slid lower to unbutton the fall of her breeches. Then lower still to slip beneath the buckskin and caress between her legs. Shamelessly, she moaned at his touch. She was already hot and damp there, and she was certain he could feel her desire for him throbbing beneath his fingertips.

He teased his middle finger against the hollow at her core, then slipped it inside her. But it wasn't enough. She craved far more than this small bit of him inside her and longed for him to fill her completely, to end the emptiness that throbbed hollowly between her legs.

"Merritt," she panted out and arched her hips toward him, begging with her body for more of him.

He tucked a second finger inside her tight warmth and wickedly stroked inside her. A soft whimper left her lips, and he smiled in triumph as his mouth darted down to seize hers. As he plundered her mouth with his tongue and lips, his hand continued to pleasure her. Every plunge rubbed his knuckle against that aching point in her folds, every retreat came as an agonizing loss. His free arm snaked around her waist to hold her steady as her trembling increased and her legs grew boneless, as he tightened an invisible coil tighter and tighter inside her toward the breaking point—

She cried out at the expected loss of him as he pulled his hand away from her just as release was about to overtake her. But with a devilish grin, he grabbed her breeches in both hands and stripped them down over her hips.

She stood in front of him, bare in the firelight from waist to ankles and without a trace of shame. She brazenly stroked his cock through his trousers. He was steely hard for her, his bulging erection tantalizingly enormous. When she licked her lips in anticipation, he growled and pulled her to the floor with him.

She wanted him too desperately to take the time to remove her boots and clothes, yet she managed to scramble enough to free one leg from her breeches and spread herself wide to him. "Make love to me, Merritt." *One last time…*

With a groan of masculine need, he tore open the fall of his trousers. He covered her body with his and settled into the inviting cradle of her thighs.

She wrapped her legs around his waist, and the rough scratch of his trousers against the bare flesh of her inner thighs thrilled her with its wantonness. A small cry of pleasure tore from her as he sank inside her, and she welcomed him eagerly, encouraging him with a bite to his shoulder to claim her as greedily as he dared. Deep, powerful thrusts of his body stole her breath away and left her clinging helplessly to him, never wanting to let go.

Locking her ankles together at the small of his back, she arched into him as the breathless release she craved began to overwhelm her. It licked at her toes and fingers, stirred in her hair until her scalp tingled—until *every inch* of her tingled with a fierce yearning she knew only Merritt was capable of satiating. A yearning that went beyond mere physical desire, beyond the melding of bodies…one that made her want to brand him onto her forever.

When she broke beneath him, the shattering of body and soul was more than she could bear. A sob tore from her, and she buried her face against his neck to hide all evidence of her tears.

Twenty-three

A KNOCK RAPPED SHARPLY AT THE TOWN HOUSE'S FRONT door.

"It's about time," Horatio Liggett grumbled as he strode toward the entry hall from the study where he'd been making last-minute additions to the correspondence he was sending to Parliament to inform them that he had the riots under control. It would all be over by dawn. By afternoon, Westminster would proclaim him to be England's most recent hero, and by nightfall, everyone across London would be making comparisons between a man of strength like him and that cowardly buffoon Prinny.

He snatched up his hat and sword from the waiting footman and put them on, then gestured for the man to open the door.

"General." A tiger in a plain uniform greeted him with a small bow. "Your carriage is here, sir."

"Carriage?" he boomed out in surprise. "I didn't ask for a bloody carriage! I asked for a guarded escort."

He shoved the tiger aside and looked out at the street where a plain black carriage waited beside the footpath. Around it stood three horse guards, their uniforms bright red against the dark night.

"General Liggett." The lead officer called out to him with a salute but didn't dismount from his horse. "Captain Nathaniel Reed with His Majesty's Horse Guards. We're here to escort you behind the barricades. It's an honor to guard you, sir."

Well, that was more like it. And exactly the deference he deserved.

Everything was coming together, just as planned. Once he'd left Carlton House earlier this evening, he'd spent the night overseeing the building of the barricades at the eastern edge of

Westminster, where his soldiers would hold their position to keep the rioters from penetrating into St James's and Whitehall. But the mob had been paid well to ignore the soldiers and push through, and the only thing stopping them would be him and a volley of musket fire.

But a carriage? His jaw tightened. "I should be going on horseback, like one of the guards." *Like a general.* Wellington would never have arrived for battle in a carriage, for God's sake!

"The Home Office insisted, sir," Captain Reed answered. "We don't know how many rioters might already be in the streets. It's for your own protection."

"I am a general!" Liggett seethed. "I don't need to be shielded like some green lad."

"The Home Office insisted," the captain repeated. Then he added in a low voice, breaking his officer's demeanor to sound his own personal opinion, "You know how Whitehall is, run by a bunch of spineless men who have never set foot on a battlefield." Reed glanced at the other guards and the men waiting at the carriage and confided, "The guards and I will escort you through the City, per our orders, but we can stop the carriage a few streets from the barricades so you can approach on foot if you'd rather."

"I'd look more commanding arriving on horseback," Liggett grumbled. But walking was the best he'd have tonight apparently. Damn the Home Office! That would be the first thing he'd change under the new regime—put the militia back where it belonged, under the hands of the War Department.

With an aggravated wave of his hand to signal that he was ready, he walked down to the carriage. The tiger held open the door and put down the step as if he were some debutante who needed help stepping into a coach. *That* added insult to injury. But he would find out who in Whitehall had decided to put him in a carriage, and heads would roll.

He sat on the bench and ordered, "Drive."

The tiger shut the door. A few seconds later, the carriage started forward.

Suddenly, the door was flung open, and a man swung inside the compartment. He landed on the bench across from Liggett with a light bounce and slammed the door shut after himself.

He pulled a pistol from beneath his greatcoat and pointed it at Liggett's chest.

"Good evening, General." The man smiled pleasantly. "We've not yet formally met. I'm Clayton Elliott."

Confused rage boiled inside Liggett. "What is the meaning of—"

"Former major with the Grenadier Guards, First Regiment of Foot. Now Home Office undersecretary." The man's smile faded, its disappearance punctuating the easing down of the pistol's hammer. "And the man responsible for ensuring minimal loss of property and life from tonight's riot." He laid the pistol down across his knee but kept his hand on it. "Which means I'm putting an end to your plans."

"What the hell is going on?" Liggett glanced out the window. The carriage was heading in the wrong direction. "Stop this nonsense and take me to the barricades!"

He pounded his fist against the roof to signal to the driver to stop, but the coachman only flipped the ribbons and urged the team into a faster pace.

Liggett leaned out the window and yelled, "Stop this carriage immediately!"

"Apologies, General," the Home Office undersecretary said calmly. "But the men are under my command and have orders to ignore you."

"I am a general. I have the authority to command the Horse Guards." Liggett leaned out the window again and noted that two of the guards had left, leaving only Captain Reed following behind on his horse in a slow canter. "Stop this carriage, Captain. I order you!"

But Reed ignored Liggett's command and rode on.

Shaking with fury, he sat back on the bench and clenched a fist at the man across from him. "Take me to the barricades. *Now.* I have orders from the Home Secretary himself to put down the riots."

"But I am taking you to the barricades," the man said with exaggerated calmness. "And by the Horse Guard escort you specifically requested, to ensure your safe arrival in Tilbury."

"*Tilbury?*" Liggett sputtered. "That's half a day's ride in the other direction."

The undersecretary smiled. "Didn't I mention? You're going to the barricades via Botany Bay."

Liggett's blood grew cold. "You're kidnapping a general, impressing me—"

"Kidnapping...facilitating overseas diplomatic travel..." The man shrugged. "There's such a fine line between the two, don't you agree?" His eyes glinted icily in the darkness. "By this time tomorrow, when you're finally found tied up and gagged in the hold by the sailors I've paid to ignore you until then, the ship will be out to sea and on its way to the South Pacific."

"You're mad! When the Home Secretary learns of this—"

"Of course, they can't keep you in Australia," he mused. "The ship's captain can bring you back immediately—round trip, in about six months. Give or take a month. Or three."

"I'll ruin you for this!" Liggett threatened. "I will end your career and have you hanged."

"Can't do that if you're dead," the undersecretary warned in a low and threatening voice. "You've working with Scepter." The accusation was leveled with deadly certainty. "And we both know what Scepter does to people who fail it."

At that, Liggett's blood turned completely to ice. If he wasn't there to lead the soldiers and stop the riot, if he wasn't there to be the symbol of strength and leadership that the country lacked, if he was no longer needed—

Scepter would kill him.

"So you might discover that you prefer life in Australia to returning to England." The undersecretary leaned casually back against the squabs and kicked out his long legs, settling in for the drive to the docks at Tilbury. "Either way, General, I think it's safe to say that your military career is over."

———————

The steam from Veronica's breath clouded the frigid predawn air. "Are we ready, then?"

Filipe stood just at her shoulder and nodded, turning to face her so that each of them looked in the opposite direction down the street and no one could sneak up on them. They fell easily back into the old ways of battle that his father, Jabir, had taught them all those years ago in Portugal.

"The men have their orders," he answered quietly.

Around them, the City's narrow streets were alive in the darkness, filled with hundreds of people milling about on the cobblestones and along the brick building fronts. All of them were solemn and quiet, yet an excited anticipation pulsed through them. She could feel it buzzing like electricity, all the way down into her bones.

"But will it work?" Filipe muttered beneath his own clouded breath.

"It will." It *had* to work. Tonight would be their only chance. Her *last* chance. She wouldn't let Merritt down.

"It had better. I've called in every favor I had to make this happen," he half mumbled to himself. He added, looking away, "Then I paid twice as many men just to make certain we'd have enough show up."

Guilt pricked at her belly. "You shouldn't have done that. That money could have been given to people who—"

"It wasn't the Court of Miracle's money," he corrected, his gaze swinging back to hers for only a moment before sweeping on down the dark street. "It was my own."

Her heart tugged with gratitude even as she chastised, "You *really* shouldn't have done that."

"Fight fire with fire, I always say." He shrugged a shoulder and tugged at his gloves. "Or in this case, paid rioters with paid rioters."

She arched a brow. "You've never said that."

"Perhaps I should have," he said dryly. "Because that's what we're doing."

Exactly that. They'd created their own personal riot. One they could control.

The plan was lunacy…gather together enough people that the crowd could take on a critical mass of its own, send them into the square to join Scepter's waiting mob, then send their people in a different direction than Scepter wanted them to go. They would direct the riot north, hopefully taking Scepter's people with them, to move them away from the soldiers before letting it fizzle out completely beneath its own lack of momentum and with the help of the night watch. But this plan was also their only option.

She prayed it would work.

"We're as ready as we can be." Her hand strayed to the hilt of her sword. "Now we simply wait for the signal. You'll rush to the front to guide them, I'll bring up the rear, and we'll meet back at the Court of Miracles at dawn."

"No," he said gravely. "We won't."

"Of course we—"

"No." He paused to take a deep breath. "This is goodbye, *querida irmã*." His eyes softened on her with affection. "I know you're leaving the life you had before, just as I know it has nothing to do with the pardon they've promised you."

Her throat tightened. There was no point in denying it. "You're right. I'm not going back to that life." No matter what happened tonight, she had already moved on. "But this isn't goodbye for us. You're still the King of Saffron Hill, still presiding over the Court of Miracles. I know where to find you when I want to say hello." Her voice cracked. "Or when I need you."

"You don't need me anymore. You have your barrister to protect you now." When she began to correct him, he stopped her by taking her shoulders in his hands. "You think I can't see what's between you? You think I didn't notice the way he looks at you, the way you look at him?" He leaned in to place a kiss to her forehead, and she was certain he felt the way she trembled at the pain of parting. "You have a new life ahead of you."

Her heart stuttered. Merritt had told her almost the exact same thing. But claiming that new life also meant surrendering so much—

Her hand clutched at his jacket lapel. "I won't give up my family."

"You have new family waiting for you."

He meant Merritt and the other men of the Armory, Merritt's father, Claudia…but she would lose him. "You're my brother, Filipe," she choked out, not knowing how she was able to speak past the knot in her throat. "I won't let go of you."

"Then it's time that I let go of you. I won't let you sacrifice yourself a second time for me. I couldn't stop you before when you went to prison, but this time, I can." He released her shoulders and put her hand away from him. "I'm leaving England. I'm turning the Court over to Ivy for her to run. My men have been told to look after her and all the people there, to help them the same way we've helped them."

A hollow ache burned in her chest. "Where will you go?"

"Back home to Portugal where I belong." He gave a faint, sad smile. "England was never my dream. It was my father's. I came here to prove myself to his memory. But I've done enough to appease his spirit. It's time now that I satisfy my own. And that you do the same."

She pulled in a deep breath of resolve, hating the thought even as she said, "Then I'll come with you. We'll return—"

"No, *querida*. My future lies in Portugal." His eyes glistened. "Yours lies here."

The bell of Temple Church pealed the hour, slowly striking six times. Each toll reverberated through the streets and jarred into her with as much force as Filipe's words. Blinking hard to gather herself, she glanced in surprise toward the south through the night, as if she could see the bell tower through the impenetrable darkness.

It was time for their riot.

"Now!" Filipe signaled to the crowd milling around them with a wave of his arms. "Let's go!"

Excitement crackled on the cold night air and pulsated through the crowd as they followed his orders and moved off toward the square where Scepter's mob had already formed. Men swung their clubs in the air as they marched, with strict orders to stay far away from the soldiers and destroy as little property as possible while still making it seem as if they were truly rioting. It would be an exercise in controlled chaos.

Filipe turned and walked backward down the street, joining with the crowd to lead them north. "*Adeus, querida irmã*," he called out to her. "Goodbye, my sister."

Then he was gone, disappearing amid the crowd as they headed into the maze of narrow, dark streets.

Veronica stood still, unable to move as grief coursed through her. This parting had been coming for a long while, but knowing that didn't lessen the pain of her loss. She forced herself to drag in a deep, trembling breath.

"*Adeus*, Filipe," she whispered after him into the night.

Pulling back her shoulders, she inhaled a deep breath and steeled herself for what she'd been charged to do tonight. Then she drew her sword and started after the mob, to bring up the rear and keep as many of the rioters moving north as possible.

But half an hour later, part of the mob broke away. A group of two dozen or so men peeled away from the main group and cut down the city streets toward the west. Just as they'd been paid to do.

"Wrong way!" She gestured with her sword toward the north, to round them back together and drive them after the rest of the mob. "Follow the others!"

While several of them rejoined the main crowd, most of the breakaway group ignored her and charged on west toward Westminster…and toward the soldiers who were waiting at their barricades with guns ready to fire.

Veronica watched with sickening frustration. There was nothing she could do to stop them. But she wouldn't give up without a fight.

Clutching her sword, she raced after them.

Twenty-four

THE CLIP OF THEIR HORSES' HOOVES ECHOED OFF THE BRICK and stone buildings as Merritt, Pearce, and Marcus rode from the Armory toward Westminster. Around them, London was quiet and dark as if the whole world had paused to catch its breath in this last hour of night before the sun rose and the day jarred to life. But a low apprehension lingered over it, one that had Merritt's muscles tense with alertness. His horse felt it, too, based upon the way its ears moved uneasily in a constant semicircle, flicking back and forth to catch all the sounds of the night.

From their route west along the Strand, no traces of a riot were visible. London was quiet. Only the usual people prowled its streets, and none of them were the likes of men that Scepter would have paid to lead a mob. But Merritt knew the rioters were amassed and moving through the streets just as the three of them were, and all of them were heading in the same direction—toward the barricades.

Marcus rode lead, dressed in his old general's uniform, complete with officer's sword and pistol, with Pearce following behind and Merritt bringing up the rear. The sight of his two friends stirred such memories that Merritt could almost believe they were once again in the middle of the wars, once again riding to engage the enemy. *Almost.* Because the familiar streets were a stark reminder that they were now fighting battles at home.

So did the sight of uniformed English soldiers standing behind tall barricades that blocked the way at Charing Cross where Pall Mall, Whitehall, and the Strand converged. The exact place where Malmesbury's mistress had told them the rioters were paid to go in their march toward Westminster.

As soon as the soldiers came into view, Marcus kicked his heels into his horse's sides and sent the large black gelding into a canter. He rode straight-spined and tall in the saddle, the perfect image of British command and confidence.

"Attention!" Pearce called out. His old brigadier's uniform was nearly as impressive as the general's as he darted his horse ahead of Marcus to address the men. "At attention!"

The soldiers shifted nervously and glanced among themselves for answers to what was happening. The officers were just as surprised as the foot guards.

Pearce reined his horse into a tight circle in front of the barricade and shouted angrily at the soldiers, "Stand at attention! General Braddock has arrived to take command!"

His shout sent up a ripple of excited murmurs through the group of soldiers, some of whom now craned their necks to see past the five-foot-tall barricade at the two men.

Merritt half smiled to himself. No one cared about him in comparison, and he gratefully slipped unnoticed from his horse in his plain black patrol clothes. Only his sword gave evidence that he was there for a fight.

Marcus stopped his horse directly in front of the barricade, but there was no doubt now among the men about who he was. He ranked second only to Wellington in terms of notoriety and service to England, yet he reigned first in soldiers' admiration and loyalty. They stared with awe, exactly as the men of the Armory had hoped.

"I'm here to replace Major-General Liggett," he announced. Instead of dismounting, he took full advantage of the striking figure he made on horseback and raked his gaze across the soldiers. "Where is your commanding colonel?"

"Here, General!" one of the officers called out as he climbed onto the bottom step of the barricade and saluted. "Colonel Anderson at your command, sir."

Marcus gave a curt nod of acknowledgment. "You were

expecting Liggett. There's been a change in orders." He dismounted and tossed the reins to a private who stood guard at the front side of the barricade. "I'm in command now. You'll follow my orders."

"Yes, General," the colonel snapped out in quick deference. Then he added, "We're thrilled to have you among us, sir."

Marcus strode up to the barricade and climbed over it, then signaled for Pearce and Merritt to follow.

The two men exchanged a knowing glance. There were no orders from the Home Office or War Department regarding a change in command, and not one of the three men still possessed his active commission. But the soldiers didn't know that. And wouldn't know that until after the riot was long over.

"Always better to ask forgiveness than permission," Merritt muttered beneath his breath to Pearce as they climbed over the barricade and landed on the other side.

"You spent years studying the law," Pearce quietly replied, "and *that's* the lesson you learned?"

Merritt crooked a brow. "Can you think of a better one?"

Especially since that philosophy had brought them past the first obstacle in their plan—removing Liggett and putting a man they trusted in charge of the soldiers.

Now he prayed that the second part of the plan would go just as smoothly and the riot would never reach them.

But he also couldn't help a worried glance down the dark street in the direction of the square where the rioters were told to meet, knowing that Veronica was somewhere among them. She was more than capable of taking care of herself, his head knew that. But his heart... That was a different matter completely.

Marcus finished giving instructions to Colonel Anderson and rejoined Merritt and Pearce. Every inch of him exuded power and confidence. All the soldiers around them recognized it, and Merritt welcomed it. There was comfort here among the soldiers with Marcus in command, a unified purpose that had been missing from his life when he'd returned to England. Working with the other men of the Armory against Scepter had begun to fill that void, and Veronica was helping to finally ease the pain of losing Joanna. But would he ever find peace?

"There's another blockade farther up Whitehall," Marcus informed them with hard tugs at his gloves. That same old habit from before every battle in the wars. In a lesser man, Merritt would have said it was nerves. "It's there in case the rioters break through this one."

"They won't." Pearce frowned at the ready muskets slung over the shoulders of the Scots Guards. "They'll be slaughtered by gunfire here first."

"Even so, I want you there. I want to make certain the soldiers behind us don't do something stupid like rush forward to our position and fire on the rioters."

"Or on us," Merritt muttered.

"That, too." Marcus nodded at Pearce. "Go take charge at the second barricade, Brigadier."

"Yes, sir." Pearce saluted smartly and turned on his heel to hurry to the rear position farther down the dark street behind them, shouting out his name and rank as he went. *No one* wanted surprises in the darkness tonight.

"Merritt, you'll remain with me."

"Yes, sir." Instead of saluting, he placed his hand on the hilt of his sword. God only knew the kind of fighting that would be required of them before dawn.

A motion at the end of the street beyond the barricade caught his attention. A handful of men carrying torches in one hand and home-fashioned weapons of clubs and cutlasses in the other stalked toward them from out of the shadows.

"Our plan didn't work," Merritt muttered as the number of men swelled to over two dozen. "They didn't head north."

"Most of them did," Marcus corrected. "These are likely the ones that Scepter paid to lead the riot here, still carrying out their orders like the well-trained soldiers they used to be."

The rioters quickened their pace when they saw the barricade. They shouted at the soldiers and brandished their torches and weapons as they advanced.

Behind him, Colonel Anderson called out, "Ready, men!"

Rifles raised nearly in unison as the first row of soldiers came forward to position themselves. Their muzzles pointed over the barricade's makeshift mound of wooden boards, crates, barrels, and anything else the soldiers had found nearby. Its purpose wasn't to stop the rioters but simply to slow them down just long enough to shoot or bayonet them.

Marcus's sword shot into the air. "Hold fire! Fire only on my order!" He repeated in a powerful command that brooked no question of his authority, "*Only* on my order."

The soldiers tensed as they switched their attention from Colonel Anderson to Marcus, but they held their position, as unmoving as statues.

"I know you want to save the rioters," Marcus said quietly to Merritt. "But my first priority, as always, is to defend Westminster." He slid a somber glance sideways at Merritt, his arm still straight in the air. "I *will* order the soldiers to fire if they charge the barricade."

"Well then," Merritt muttered. "Best not let it come to that."

And it wouldn't. The men were former soldiers who knew what it meant to confront the regiment standing here. They were paid rioters, not suicidal. They would certainly come closer, daring to wave their weapons in the air and threaten the soldiers, shout insults and threats, and perhaps even destroy the front of the build-ings lining the street, but they wouldn't attempt the barricades.

Yet the rioters hurried on fearlessly toward the barricade long after they should have stopped.

Merritt's blood turned to ice as the horrifying realization struck him—they thought the soldiers wouldn't fire on them because they'd been told they wouldn't. They'd been assured that Liggett was in command and wouldn't give the order for the soldiers to shoot, that they'd be allowed to climb over the barricades and march on toward Parliament and St James's Palace unmolested.

Good God. The rioters had been set up for slaughter.

Merritt grabbed Marcus's pistol from his side and leapt onto the barricade. He raised it into the air and fired. The crack of its report echoed off the stone buildings and stopped the stunned rioters dead in their steps.

"Stop this now!" he shouted at them. His voice was nearly as loud as the gunshot. "Go home. Liggett isn't here. He's been replaced by General Marcus Braddock, and you know his reputation. He will not hesitate to fire upon you if you attempt to cross the barricade. You will be killed." He flung the spent pistol down onto the street. "No matter what you've been told about being allowed to pass into Westminster, it will *not* happen."

The rioters hesitated and exchanged surprised looks as they considered his words.

But then one of them shouted back, "He's lyin'!" The man jabbed his spade into the air to punctuate his point. "Just puttin' on a show! They wouldn't dare shoot us."

More cries answered in agreement, and the crowd began to move forward. They still came toward the barricades but now with less determination and certainty than before. Several of the men in the crowd hung back to let the leaders stride on.

At Merritt's feet, the soldiers stiffened their arms as they aimed their rifles.

"Hold your fire!" Merritt yelled at the soldiers and darted to the center of the barricade to put himself directly between their guns and the rioters. As Marcus echoed the command to hold fire, Merritt drew his sword and stretched out both arms to make himself as wide a target as possible. "Does this look like a show to you?" He constantly turned between the two groups to keep watch on all of them and to keep all their attention on him. "What are you going to believe—some man who paid you to come out tonight in a mob or your own eyes?" He pointed his sword at the soldiers. "*Look at them!*"

The rioters stopped again, this time amid mutterings about being paid. The men demanded answers from one another now, and Merritt could clearly distinguish the men who had been paid from those who had simply been caught up in the momentum of the mob. But the mentality of violence still pulsed through them, still made their eyes glow wild, even in the dancing shadows of the torchlight.

"You were soldiers once yourselves," Merritt called out, making his plea directly to the leaders. "You know that these men behind me will follow orders and cut you down where you stand if you dare come any closer. And for what? A handful of coins?"

"We've got no jobs!" one of the men yelled back. "We're starvin' an' the lords in Westminster don't give a damn about none o' us!"

"You're right," Merritt countered. "They don't give a damn about you."

That honest reply set them muttering again with surprised and gaping expressions, as it did to the soldiers at his feet.

"They think you don't deserve their help, that you're nothing but a bunch of lazy, insolent bastards who've returned from the wars to be a blight on English society."

Merritt didn't have to fake his outrage. He'd felt as strongly as they had the sting of coming home to an England that he didn't recognize and that didn't appreciate him, that might have preferred if he'd died on the field in Belgium. Politicians knew how to handle dead soldiers—throw up a memorial and forget. What they couldn't manage were those who had the audacity to survive.

He pointed the end of his sword at the chest of the man closest to him. "If you persist in this—if you attempt to cross the barricade and march on Westminster—then you will prove them right. Is that what you want? To give them proof that former soldiers are no better than vandals and criminals?"

Slowly, the rioters lowered their weapons, but they didn't retreat. Likewise, the Guards didn't lower their guns.

"You were soldiers once—*good* soldiers," Merritt pressed. "Remember how you once gave everything you had for England, how you were willing to die for her and the liberties she gives you? But now you march against her. Are you no better than the French, wanting to strip away all that is good and right from English soil?" His heart ached as he poured out the words, desperate to make them listen. "You've already gotten your coins for your trouble tonight, so now take them and go home. Do *not* give up your lives here in this filthy street."

The rioters said nothing but shamefully looked down at the street. No one made eye contact, least of all with him.

He lowered his sword. "Be good soldiers again and go home. There's no shame in this retreat. You've done what you came here for—to bring attention to your plight. I promise you that I'll make certain your concerns are heard in Parliament, in the law courts, in the papers. Damnation, I'll take them to Carlton House and present them to Prinny myself!" A few uneasy laughs went up at that. "But now, *go home*. Go home to your families if you have them or to your favorite prostitute if you don't—or to your favorite prostitute even if you do." More laughs, less uneasy this time. He knew then that he'd won them over, and he blew out a hard, long breath before adding with solemn finality, "Tonight's fight is over."

The rioters stared at him for several more long seconds. Then they began to move slowly away, back into the dark maze of streets from where they'd emerged. Only a few took swings at the fronts of the buildings and at easy targets like doors, lamps, and posts, until they, too, vanished into the night. All thoughts of attacking Westminster disappeared with them.

Thank God.

His shoulders slumped, and his arm fell to dangle his sword at his side. Never in his entire life had so much depended upon his ability of persuasion. Never once in his entire law career.

And *never* did he want to go through anything like that again.

"Stand down!" Marcus ordered the soldiers, who gladly put down their rifles. Relief rippled through them that the attack had dissolved.

Relief should have streamed through Merritt, too, that their mad plan had worked and they'd stopped the massacre. That for once they'd gotten the upper hand on Scepter. But it didn't. Because Veronica was still out there in the streets, still herding the main mob of rioters toward the north, still putting herself in danger.

He jumped down from the barricade and off into the night after the riot.

And after Veronica.

———

Veronica hurried through the maze of narrow streets at the rear of the riot, her pulse pounding and her muscles burning from being on alert for over an hour now. And damn that dawn was only a mere sliver of light on the distant horizon!

She'd sheathed her sword in favor of one of her knives, but thank God she'd not had to use it. Shouts and threats had been enough to keep the rioters from breaking into the buildings, from keeping innocents from accidentally being caught up in the melee—prostitutes, sellers on their way to their market stalls, dock workers making their way to the warehouses along the river…and a handful of men just like most of the rioters, who'd spent the night at a tavern drinking themselves far into their cups to escape the harsh reality of their lives. A flash of her knife and a quiet threat had been all that was necessary to keep the men in line. But the physical strain and mental fatigue were beginning to wear on her.

Please, God, let this end soon! But she wasn't at all certain that God was watching over them tonight or if evil had taken hold instead.

Their plan was falling apart. Instead of the riot fizzling out beneath dwindling momentum, it seemed to grow as more people joined in from the hovels and makeshift buildings erected in back alleys and courtyards where they lived in squalor. Their frustrations at their daily hand-to-mouth existence had flared, and the riot presented a good opportunity to let out their anger. But Filipe's men were still leading them toward Farringdon and Clerkenwell, toward Saffron Hill and their home territory, where they had knowledge of the lay of the land and could gather reinforcements if necessary.

Yet they weren't moving fast enough into that area of the city where the streets grew so narrow and mazelike that the mob would be scattered and thinned to the point that it would lose its coherence and dissipate. Even now, Filipe's men were forced to join in with stopping the violence, which sparked fights among the rioters themselves. Parts of the riot had become a free-for-all, destructive to property and potentially deadly.

She halted in midstride. An uneasy prick of apprehension tickled at her nape and slid down her spine like droplets of ice water. Shouts were growing louder, the noise of destruction increasing, the streets becoming more and more crowded. And then she saw—

The mob had turned on itself and was moving back toward her. She was no longer at its rear. She'd been caught up in the midst of it and was surrounded.

Knowing how dangerous her position had become, she raced to the edge of the street where doorways might provide protection, where she might find a narrow alley passageway that—

A fierce blow from a club caught her square between the shoulder blades.

The air slammed from her lungs. She staggered forward to keep on her feet and spun around to face her attacker. But a second blow across her chest shoved her backward into a recessed archway, and her back slammed hard against a wooden door. The violent jolt knocked her knife from her hand. Its blade clattered uselessly against the stones at her feet.

Immediately, the attacker was upon her. He dropped his club and squeezed his hands around her throat.

She kicked with all her strength. Her foot caught the man in the groin and shot enough pain through him that he stepped back with a furious bellow. In a slant of moonlight, she saw his face.

"Danker," she whispered, stunned.

He lunged at her again. In the narrow doorway, she had no room to escape. When she kicked again, he dodged the blow, and her foot passed through empty shadow.

"You won't stop this riot." He reached for her throat again, but she threw up her forearm and deflected his hands, just enough that he couldn't squeeze her throat. With her other hand, she punched at his face. She slammed the hard heel of her hand into his cheek and the corner of his eye. He growled furiously but didn't release her. "Bitch! I won't let you interfere."

What was he talking about? "But you helped me, when I came to you for information—you told me about Smathers—"

He dodged another blow to his face, grabbed her wrist, and twisted her arm down to her side so roughly that she screamed in pain. "To get out of your debt! What the hell did I care about Smathers? You think he was the only man recruiting rioters?" He grabbed her forearm and pressed it against her throat as if to crush her windpipe with her own arm. "But you didn't end it there, you and the Home Office. You kept looking, kept digging for more— now I stop you."

She wrenched her damaged wrist away and slashed her fingernails at his face. But she missed when he ducked his head to the side. Instead, her fingers clawed down the side of his face to his neck and pulled back his collar.

A key tattoo. A terrifying horror sickened her.

"Scepter," she panted out as the pressure on her throat grew so fierce that her vision began to turn black and she could barely suck in enough air to keep from falling unconscious. Her hand fumbled for the second knife she kept up her other forearm. "You're one… of them… *Why?*"

"What better way to bring down a monarchy and put our own king in place? What better way to make a fortune from its ruins?" He lowered his face so close to hers that the hot stench of his breath fanned over her cheeks. "And you and your friends won't be able to stop us."

He lunged to bring his full weight to bear against her and strangle her.

With a desperate cry, she yanked the knife free. She swung her arm downward in a quick arc, then up—

The sharp blade sliced into his abdomen.

A surprised groan fell from his parted lips, and his grip around her throat instantly loosened. With a trickle of blood from the corner of his mouth, his face twisted in pain before he toppled against her. She shoved him back, and he crumpled to the stones. Her knife was lodged in his abdomen, all the way to its hilt.

Veronica slumped back against the wall. Her hand flew to her throat as she coughed and gasped to pull air back into her lungs. The black spots that danced before her eyes faded with each deep breath she took, and the pounding in her head subsided as the world slowly stopped rising and plunging around her.

She stared down at the dead man at her feet. She'd trusted him, as had Filipe. Her chest ached, and from more than gasping back her breath. Everything in her world had turned upside down. Who was left for her to trust?

"Veronica!"

Her eyes darted up. A man raced through the mob toward her. His face was hidden in the shadows from the yellow light of the sun rising behind him, but her heart knew...*Merritt*.

When he reached her, he cupped her face in his hands. He turned her head side to side as he frantically examined her for any wounds, then brushed his hands down her bruised neck to her shoulders and torso. When he found none, he seized her mouth beneath his in a blistering kiss that tasted of pure relief. He kissed her long enough to send her heart thumping for a whole new reason, to bring feeling back into her numb limbs and chase away the hollow pang of grief.

He shifted back and glanced down at Danker's dead body. "What the hell happened?"

Solemnly, she moved past him, bent down, and pulled her knife from Danker's body. She paused only to wipe the blade clean on the shoulder of Danker's jacket before rising to her feet.

"All debts have been repaid," she told him quietly, her voice raw.

He nodded as if that cryptic answer explained everything. "Then let's get out of here." He flinched as the sound of shattering wood and glass echoed down the street. "*Now.*"

Twenty-five

MERRITT FOLLOWED ONLY A PACE BEHIND VERONICA AS SHE led them through the crush of rioters. No longer attempting to control the riot or stop the destruction that continued to break out, their only thought now was escape.

The mob had circled back and engulfed them, and hundreds of rioters filled the streets around them. All of them wielded torches and weapons, including the women and the youngest of boys who had joined with the crowd. They attacked the fronts of buildings, smashing shutters and windows, breaking gas lamps, ripping down wrought iron railings, and bashing apart anything they could. Fires had been set in their wake by those among the mob whose frustrations weren't appeased by brute force, while others broke into buildings to steal what they could find inside. Filipe's men had lost control over the riot, and chaos reigned.

Damnation! This wasn't at all what he'd hoped for tonight. Dread and anger rose sickeningly inside him that he couldn't stop it, and he prayed to whatever god would listen that no innocents were hurt, that the only damage would be the destruction of property that could all be replaced. His only consolation was that the mob hadn't attacked the barricades as planned. The slaughter of those lives had been stopped, and tonight's riot would be the last for a very long time to come.

"What happened at the barricades?" Veronica called out over her shoulder as she veered away from two men recklessly swinging cutlasses in the air.

"The soldiers didn't fire," he answered succinctly and glanced behind them to keep an eye on what was happening at their rear. They couldn't afford to have their only path of retreat cut off, not when the way forward grew more precarious with every passing minute.

She stopped and turned back toward him with relief. "Then it's all over now."

With a grimace, Merritt took her arm and pulled her onward with him. "Not even close."

Only when the sun rose high enough for the morning light to fill the streets and chase away all cover of darkness would it end. The City had at least another hour to endure before the mob vanished back into the rabbit warren of alleys and rookeries from which it had emerged, and God only knew how much destruction and violence would be wrought before then.

But this would be the last of Scepter's riots. That much was certain.

"This way." He guided her across the street to a road that ran past Gray's Inn and would take them south to High Holborn Street. From there, it would be an easy trek west to the Armory where she would be safe until—

His gaze landed on one of the rioters directly ahead, and he halted.

Clinging to the shadows at the edge of the street, the man was revealed by the flickering torchlight of two young boys who sped past to catch up to the front of the riot. Only a moment of light shone on his face, but that was enough. The same broad build, the same scar marring the side of the man's face from jaw to temple— God's mercy, *it was him*.

The man who'd killed Joanna.

His heart stopped, the enormity of the moment squeezing around it like a vise. When it jarred to life again a second later, the pain was brutal. So was the need for revenge that consumed him in a wildfire of hatred and grief. He loosened his grip, and Veronica's arm slipped free of his hold as she walked on toward safety.

He turned back after the man. Each step pounded as fiercely as his pulse, both fueled by murderous intent.

"Merritt?" she called out and stopped to turn back for him. "What's wrong?"

"Go on without me."

"No."

"Go to the Armory, Veronica."

"*Hell* no."

He hurled a quelling look at her but continued to walk away. "You'll be safe there. I'll meet up with you later."

"I'm not leaving you here."

"Go!" he snapped out the angry order. This wasn't her fight; it was his alone. It had been simmering for the past five years, but now the need for vengeance boiled inside him. So did the drive to put an end to the years of hunting. And an end to the bastard who'd murdered Joanna. "God damn it, go!"

He turned away from her and the wounded look on her face. Then he broke into a loping jog to move as quickly as he dared after the man without calling attention to himself.

He didn't look back. Veronica didn't understand. He didn't expect her to, but there was no time to explain. He'd promised Joanna that night when he'd held her lifeless body in his arms that he would find the man who killed her, and for every drop of spilt blood, Merritt would cause the bastard pain. Blinding. Insufferable. *Damn him to hell.* Where he belonged.

He sheathed his sword and pulled out his knife. He kept the blade low and unseen at his side and the handle firmly gripped in his palm as he followed the man down the street. His pulse pounded deafeningly in his ears as he drew nearer, and his blood burned hot as it coursed through his veins. Vengeance drove each breath he took. He moved closer to the man, so close now—

He lunged. He tackled the man around the waist and propelled him forward against the building.

But the man twisted out of his grasp. He slammed Merritt into the wall with a fierce shove, then ducked beneath the sweep of the knife as Merritt struck out in white-hot fury. But the rioter didn't dodge the hard punch of Merritt's left fist as he swung it with every ounce of his strength. He caught the man's jaw and snapped back his head, sending him staggering from the force of the blow toward the doorway where the door lay twisted half-open on its hinges from the mob's earlier attack.

With no way to escape down the street, the man darted inside the dark building.

Merritt chased after him. He would *not* get away. Not this time.

Darkness filled the building; the dim morning sunlight and torchlight from the rioters were unable to penetrate through its shuttered windows. Yet the place was alive with shadows and ghosts, and they antagonized him with every step and searching glance he took.

Like the skilled predator he'd become, Merritt tightened his grip on his knife as he moved forward into the darkness. He carefully approached the wooden stairs. The only place the man could have gone was up, and he stalked after him. No capture. No quarter. No trial. *I will kill you where you stand…*

A shadow darted across the top of the stairs, and a dark object hurtled toward him. Merritt held up his arm but not in time to stop the glancing blow of an old wooden cask. It grazed his temple and cut his brow before it slammed into his shoulder. It wasn't enough to stop him but more than enough to escalate his anger.

With a growl, he charged up the stairs three at a time.

The man raced up through the warehouse, and Merritt pursued. The door at the top of the stairs slammed shut in front of him, but he dropped back onto his rear foot and kicked as hard as he could in the center of the panel. The kick broke the latch, and the door banged against the wall so hard that the rusted hinges shattered with a pop as loud as gunfire.

Merritt charged through the door, out onto the roof, and directly toward the man. He lowered his shoulder and plowed it into the man's stomach. He propelled him backward, only for the attacker to find his footing and fight back. They struggled back and forth across the roof with punches landing with dull thuds on each other's bodies, with Merritt unable to find the space to swing his knife and slice the man's throat.

"You murdered her, you son of a bitch!" Like a man possessed, Merritt threw punch after punch with his left hand, slash after slash with the knife in his right, and drove the man against the low balustrade framing the edge of the roof.

He charged relentlessly forward on top of him and forced the man to bend backward over the railing. He shoved his right forearm beneath the man's chin, and his knife blade glinted in the moonlight just inches from the man's throat.

"You killed her," he ground out and shoved his forearm against the man's windpipe. "And now I'm going to kill you."

The man's eyes flared wide as he clawed desperately at Merritt's arm to free himself, but Merritt only stepped closer and forced the man farther back over the balustrade. The man darted a terrified glance over the edge of the roof at the ground two stories below. *Good.* Let the bastard be afraid. Let him experience the same terror as Joanna when she was ripped from the carriage. Let him feel the same pain she did when his body broke against the stones below.

He pointed his knife at the man's belly, drew a deep breath—

"Merritt—no."

The soft voice behind him arrested his hand, and he froze, the tip of the blade poking into the man's gut. *Veronica.*

Her presence slammed into him like a punch. She didn't belong here. She was the present, not the past. "Leave."

"No."

"You're not needed here."

"So much more than you realize." In her short pause, he could almost see her arching her brow in that chastising manner she had. "Did you really think I'd let you go off alone?"

His heart slammed into his throat, but his eyes never left those of the bastard in front of him. The end was so close now that he could taste it, like acid on his tongue. *Why* wouldn't she leave and let him finish this?

"He killed Joanna," he explained hoarsely. "It's him. I finally found the bastard."

Thank God she didn't ask if he were certain, or if he could have possibly made a mistake and caught the wrong man. Five years of memories and nightmares and always seeing that man's face with every stroke of a sword, every punch he learned to throw, every time he sharpened his knives, every step he took through the dark city in his hunt—he knew this man's face as well as he knew his own.

"Now it all ends." Each panting, fear-filled breath the man took pulsed against the tip of Merritt's knife. How easy it would be to simply step forward and plunge the blade deep into his gut. It would be as smooth as slicing into butter, not at all the hard crack of the hammer the bastard had used against Joanna. "He deserves to die."

"Yes, he does." Her voice grew closer. "But at Newgate. *Not* here."

"Here seems as good a place as any." His left hand tightened its hold on the man's throat as he leaned in and dangled the man even farther over the balustrade. With one small push, he would tumble over the edge. "Or on the stones below."

The man's eyes grew wide with terror, and his hands clawed at Merritt's arms to somehow make him release him. But he would *never* let go now. Not when he was only heartbeats from finally driving away the darkness.

"The last time I checked, you were still a barrister." She stopped directly behind him. "When did you also become judge and jury?"

That rankled, more than he would admit. But she didn't understand, could *never* understand—

"Your whole life you've put your faith in the law, in its integrity." Her hand slid up his back to his shoulder, and the heat of her touch sizzled through his clothes and into his flesh. "So put it there now. Arrest him and let the courts bring justice." Her fingers squeezed into his tense muscle, and her soft voice tickled at his ear as she leaned in close to his shoulder, her cheek next to his. "But don't make a mockery of all you believe in because of this man. He doesn't deserve to have that power over you." Her hand slid down his right arm. His muscles trembled beneath the brush of her fingertips. "So don't you dare give it to him."

He shuddered when her hand closed around his on the knife. But he refused to surrender it to her, refused to concede now that he was so close—

"You're a good and decent man, Merritt Rivers. That's why Joanna loved you." Her fingers squeezed his, and she said so softly that only his heart heard, "That's why I love you, too."

Her words shot through him like a bullet, and he shuddered. She loved him… The black revenge that had consumed him for so long lifted like a fog, and in its place came Veronica.

Slowly, he loosened his grip and let her take the knife from him.

As she straightened away, she grazed her lips against his cheek. The warmth of that affectionate gesture blew through him like a whirlwind and left him breathless and trembling. "But you still infuriate the daylights out of—"

Without warning, the murderer lunged.

He shoved Merritt aside and hurled himself away from the balustrade to charge straight at Veronica. Caught off guard, she didn't react fast enough to dart out of his way, nor could she stop his hand as he grabbed for the knife. She attempted to fight back, but she was simply too small, the brute too strong.

He wrenched the knife from her, yanked her in front of him, and placed the blade to her throat. "Move, and I'll kill her."

Merritt went instantly still.

The man began to back slowly toward the steps, taking Veronica with him as a shield. Merritt flashed between hot rage and icy fear, but if he made any move toward them, the man would slit her throat.

"I'm leaving," the killer called out. "Stay where you are until I'm down on the street and out of the building."

Like hell I will. "No." The word tore from him in an animal growl. The warning in his voice was murderous. "You don't get to take away the woman I love."

He met her gaze through the shadows, and the same determination that was on his face was mirrored on hers. There was no fear visible in her, just complete trust in him. He would *never* fail her.

He let the man back across the roof toward the doorway and the dark stairs beyond, and his heart thumped painfully in his chest at every step the man forced Veronica to take with him. But she was smart—oh, she was brilliant! And she didn't fight him, didn't let out a single sob or plea. She knew to go along and wait for the right moment to attack.

But waiting was the last thing Merritt would do.

They moved closer to the dark stairs. When the man reached the doorway, he eased his hold on her and glanced down over his shoulder to find the first step—

"Now!" Merritt shouted and hurled himself toward them.

She simultaneously jabbed an elbow into the man's gut and shoved his arm away, deflecting the blade as he sliced it toward her throat. Her hand dove into her sleeve and slid free her own knife. She stabbed, and the blade sank deep into the bastard's shoulder. A howl tore from him, and instinctively, he stepped back and put himself off-balance.

Merritt plowed into him with his shoulder and shoved him backward. The man cartwheeled head over heels down the stairs. Each bounce of his body came with a sickening thud, and he landed in a crumpled ball on the floor below. But he wasn't dead. An agonizing groan came from him as he found the strength to crawl across the boards as he still attempted to escape.

That bastard wasn't getting away this time. Merritt snatched up the dropped knife and froze—blood stained the blade. He stared at it, knowing…

Veronica.

He spun around and saw her slumped in pain against the doorframe. Her face paled to ghostly white as her trembling hand reached toward her shoulder. When she pulled it away, bright blood covered her fingers.

His worst fears seized him in a block of ice. He couldn't tear his attention away from the wet spot darkening her leather waistcoat.

"Go after him," she urged in a breathless rasp. "Stop him, arrest him…"

He started down the stairs, then halted. The man had pulled himself to his feet and was attempting to hobble the rest of the way to the ground. His left leg was badly twisted, as was his left wrist, and blood trickled from the cut on his brow. But he was still alive and capable of escaping.

The bastard deserved to die. He deserved to be arrested, tried, and strung up by his neck, dangling and kicking until all the life drained from his body. Until Joanna finally had justice and could rest in peace.

But Veronica needed him. As the darkness inside him warred with the light, he knew he couldn't have both. He couldn't save Veronica and still have vengeance on this man. He had to choose— the future or the past.

Throwing the knife away, he turned back to Veronica and caught her just as her trembling legs gave out. He gently lowered her onto the roof and into his arms.

Bonelessly, Veronica sank against him as fatigue and loss of blood overcame her. Pain pounded in her shoulder in such rapid hammer blows that she could only breathe by sucking in sharp gasps through clenched teeth.

"Go," she ordered, unable to summon more than a hoarse whisper. "Go after him—you have to…"

"What I have to do is care for you," he countered as he laid her on her back and tore open her waistcoat. He swiftly untied the stays and pushed them open to reveal the blood-soaked linen shirt beneath.

"It's not serious," she insisted.

In silent argument, he stuck his finger through the knife hole in her shirt and wiggled it at her somberly. Then he grabbed the shirt in both hands and ripped it open to bare her chest.

She gasped. "Not that I mind you…ripping off my clothes." She attempted to pant down the pain. "But this isn't the time nor place."

Her joke fell flat when he flicked a glance at her and she glimpsed the absolute worry etched onto his face.

She squeezed his arm to reassure him. "I've had worse." Although she would have been hard pressed at that moment to say when. "I'll be fine."

Ignoring that statement, which sounded wholly ridiculous even to her own ears, he stripped his own tunic over his head, then ripped off the sleeves. He balled up the rest of the fabric and pressed it against her shoulder to stanch the bleeding.

A bolt of pain shot out through the top of her head, along with a cry from her lips.

Guilt gripped his face as he leaned over to lightly kiss her in what she knew was an attempt to ease the torment.

"When I saw that knife at your throat," he said quietly, his voice raw, "I thought…"

When his confession died away, she finished, "That you would lose me…just as you lost Joanna."

He gave a jerking nod.

"But you didn't." She touched his cheek, heedless of the blood she smeared there. "You saved me."

He looked down at her chest, focusing his attention there, but not before she saw his eyes glisten in the morning sunlight. "I can't bear to lose you."

Anguish rose in her throat. If he uttered the word *again*, she would have died right there. "I'm not Joanna," she said as firmly as possible despite the choking hitch of breath. "I can never be the woman she was." *Respectable, acceptable...*

He snatched up the sleeves and tied them around her shoulder to hold the makeshift bandage in place. "I know exactly who you are, Veronica Chase."

Mercenary, convict, by-blow... When he looped one sleeve under her arm, she gritted her teeth so he wouldn't know how much pain he was causing her. Not just the wound to her shoulder but the one he'd put into her heart. The same one he was now carving deeper.

"You're unlike any other woman I've ever known. I knew it from the moment we met, and I don't mean because you came after me with a sword." For once, he wasn't teasing, and his expression remained bleak. "When Joanna was killed, I couldn't stay in England. I didn't belong here. I didn't belong anywhere."

Her eyes blurred with hot tears. For all her life, she'd felt the same.

He cinched tight the tie around the bandage. "Since I returned, my life has been nothing but hunting—every night, every day... I thought I knew what I was hunting for, why I was out there. But I know now that I was wrong. I wasn't hunting for that man." He admitted quietly, "I was hunting for you."

The pain was so brutal that she could barely keep her breath, and she whispered a plea for him to stop. "Merritt..."

"Now that I've found you, I'm not letting you go. I want a new life, one with purpose. One with you." He tied off the sleeve and slowly lifted his gaze to fix on hers. "Marry me, Veronica."

She couldn't stop a tear from sliding down her cheek. "I have to leave, you know that." She swiped at the tear, and the pain of jostling her arm was nothing compared to the anguish that pierced her chest when she rasped out her hoarse confession. "I care about you too much not to go."

"That's odd. Because I care about you enough to make you stay."

She bit back a cry of desolation. God's mercy, how hard it was to keep her resolve when he said things like that! "I'll ruin your life."

"You'll be giving me a life." He fussed with the bandage. "You'll be pulling me back from the dead."

She sucked in a ragged breath and desperately tried again. "I'll ruin your career."

He shrugged a shoulder as casually as if they were discussing the weather. "It's ruined either way, because if you leave London, I'm leaving my position to come after you."

Her watery eyes widened at that promise.

"I mean it, Veronica. If you go, we go together." As he said that, a determination so fierce pulsed from him that the intensity of it made her tremble. "But I'd sure as hell rather stay right here with you."

Her throat tightened as a second tear spilled free. "You can't—*we* can't." Grief swelled inside her as pitiless as when her mother died. "I'm a convicted criminal… You're a baron, a King's Counsel—"

"Damn King's Counsel." He lifted her hand to his lips and kissed it. "Damn the law." Another kiss to punctuate his words. "Damn the barony." He released her hand and leaned over to stare down at her. "Damn everything else but you and me."

He reached toward her chest. She thought he would touch the

bandage on her shoulder. Instead, he tenderly fluttered his finger-tips over the breastbone that guarded her heart. Her pulse spiked beneath his fingers.

"Marry me and let me spend the rest of my life sparring with you, arguing with you…loving you. I love you, Veronica. I'd be mad not to." He curled a smile for her. "You might just sink a sword into me if I didn't."

A bubble of laughter escaped through her tears.

"I need you, Veronica. And you need me." He traced an invisible pattern over her breastbone. "So let's just admit it and be happy together, all right?"

Heedless of the pain, she grabbed his shirt and pulled him down to her to stare into his eyes. His mouth lingered a hairs-breadth from hers. "Let's get something straight, shall we? I'm strong and independent, more than capable of taking care of myself. I don't *need* you, Merritt Rivers." When he began to argue, she interrupted, "But I very much want to be with you."

He held his breath. "Is that a yes?"

"Yes," she whispered, unable to find her voice beneath the emotions cascading through her, a swirling mix that left her both light-headed and elated at the future now waiting for her. For *both* of them. "I love you, Mrs. Fitzherbert."

He grinned and kissed her.

Epilogue

VERONICA HELD TIGHTLY TO MERRITT'S HAND AS THEY HURried down the front walk of Charlton Place. Large, delicate flakes of falling snow were rapidly blanketing the city and casting a white sheen over the ebony carriage waiting for them, with its uniformed footmen in dark-blue velvet and four matching black horses. On the path leading to the carriage, red rose petals from the Duke of Hampton's greenhouse contrasted brightly against the snow.

Behind them, their friends and family spilled out onto the front portico of the duke and duchess's grand London house. They'd all gathered to celebrate Merritt and Veronica's wedding, and now they waved goodbye and tossed more rose petals into the air. When Veronica paused to glance back, wanting to imprint this scene into her mind forever, Merritt affectionately placed a hand to her lower back to guide her onward. Home was waiting for them.

The footman opened the door. Merritt tossed him a sovereign, and the man nodded gratefully. "Thank you, my lord." Then he sketched a bow to Veronica. "My lady."

My lady. God's mercy, they were married, and she was officially a baroness. The realization struck her with enough force to halt her in her snowy tracks.

Merritt grinned and snatched her up into his arms, eliciting a gasp of surprise from her and laughter from their friends. "Too late now to change your mind, my darling wife."

Wife…another name she would have to grow used to. But this one warmed her down to her soul. She caressed his cheek. "Never."

He placed her into the carriage, then swung inside and closed the door. As the carriage rolled away, they both leaned out the window to wave goodbye.

The carriage turned a corner, and their friends and family vanished from sight. With a sigh, Veronica sat back from where she'd been leaning across Merritt to ease onto the seat beside him.

Strong arms slid around her and pulled her down fully across his lap. "It's cold outside." He took her long wrap of white ermine and velvet and tucked it around her. "Better stay right here and keep warm."

"I'm warm enough." Yet she slipped her arm around his neck and shifted herself closer.

The sage-green bodice of her velvet wedding dress slipped smoothly over the matching satin waistcoat he wore beneath his black kerseymere jacket. He'd looked so handsome and dashing that morning that she'd lost her breath when she saw him standing at the front of the church, waiting for her to join him. To join *with* him, now and forever.

He grinned wolfishly as his hands slipped beneath the ermine wrap and caressed up her body. "Who says I was talking about you?"

She laughed. Dear heavens, how happy he made her! And now they would have the rest of their lives to laugh together, love together, and poke at each other with swords.

"I wouldn't want you to be cold." She pressed herself against him, her breasts flattening against his chest and sending his pulse spiking. When she brought her mouth to his ear, she seductively murmured, "Whatever can I do to make you hot, hmm?"

The tip of her tongue traced the outer curl of his ear in a wantonly suggestive gesture of what she could do to other parts of him if he would let her.

"Oh, I might have a few ideas," he mumbled, his voice thickening with desire. "Starting with a cup of hot chocolate brought to you in bed."

She smiled against his throat at his thoughtfulness, and for a moment, she lost herself in fantasies of leisurely breakfasts in warm beds on cold winter mornings. "I love hot chocolate."

"Oh, it won't be for you. It's for me."

She laughed lightly at his teasing. "For you? Why should you have it all?"

He brought his mouth to her ear. "So I can pour it over your naked body and drink you up," he murmured the wicked promise. "One lingering lick at a time."

A heated sigh of longing escaped her. "I didn't realize I'd married such a libertine."

"Did I shock you?"

"Not yet." She nipped his earlobe in a playful bite that made him suck a mouthful of air between his teeth. "So you'd best keep trying if you want our marriage to be a happy one."

He laughed and buried his face in her hair, holding her close as the snow crunched beneath the carriage wheels and muffled the horses' hooves on the cobblestones. "You have no idea how much I love you."

Oh, she had a pretty good idea. As she'd convalesced at Charlton Place after the riot, he'd refused to leave her side while both her wound and her heart healed. More than that, he'd not gone after the man who'd killed Joanna. But for once, fate had been her friend and made certain that Merritt gave up the hunt, because the man's body was found in a Covent Garden alley two days later, his throat slit from ear to ear. Most likely a victim of Scepter.

As for the others involved with the riots, they'd managed to escape Scepter's wrath. Miss Jones had somehow magically disappeared after the Home Office had finished interrogating her about Scepter. When Veronica pressed Merritt for answers, all he would say was that the Duchess of Hampton was a very resourceful woman.

General Liggett had also vanished. When a storm forced his

ship to seek shelter in the bay at Dakar, he managed to sneak ashore and hide until the ship sailed on. The last anyone saw of him was boarding a ship bound for Barbados. Clayton Elliott was certain he'd never set foot in England again.

The riots and the evil behind them had been stopped. For now. And at that moment, safe within Merritt's arms, all that mattered was how much she loved him.

"Did you have a lovely day?" he asked.

She sighed. "It was perfect."

Truly, it was. They were married at St George's Church in a very small gathering of family and close friends, with Brandon Pearce standing as Merritt's best man and his wife, Amelia, as her matron of honor. The Duke of Hampton's niece, Pippa, practically danced through the church in her role as flower girl, showering red rose petals everywhere, much to the priest's dismay. And Merritt's father escorted Veronica down the aisle, the judge as dignified as ever despite the faint glistening in his eyes.

Even Madame Noir was in attendance. The woman had been genuinely moved by the ceremony, although she would never admit it of course. But Veronica knew—after all, Madame hadn't once referred to Merritt as Snake all morning.

Veronica had barely had time to catch her breath before the ceremony was over, vows made, and the parish registry signed to make their marriage official. Then they were through the church doors, with Merritt tossing coins to the children and poor who had gathered on the steps, and into their carriage, and through it all, inundated by the rest of Pippa's rose petals. By the time they reached Charlton Place, the snow had covered them and all of London in a light dusting. Neither cared. They finally had each other. Nothing else mattered.

The entire day had been nothing less than a dream, and she hadn't felt so loved and accepted since her mother died. Perfect. Wonderful. So very happy.

Except…

"I wish Filipe could have been here," she whispered and nuzzled Merritt's shoulder with her cheek to hide all traces of sadness. Her brother's absence was the only gray cloud lingering over an otherwise perfect day.

"He was there in spirit."

She fiddled with the gold buttons on his waistcoat. "If we ever travel to the Continent, perhaps we can visit him in Portugal."

"Of course we can." He smiled against her hair. "He's family."

"And now I have your father as family, too."

"He already thinks of you as a daughter."

She prayed he was right. Whatever ground she'd lost in the judge's eyes because of her past, she'd made up for by insisting Merritt continue his legal work, encouraging him to become even more dedicated to the law. Now he was working to do what he'd wanted all along—stop the violence before it happened. He was using his connections to establish a professional street patrol and to press for changes in the laws that would work to eliminate the corruption inherent in the arrest and trial process.

But Merritt still couldn't care less about the barony.

Neither could she, although society seemed absolutely fascinated with her and would only become more so now that she was a baroness. Her past had been wiped clean when her legal records had inexplicably all gone missing, most likely thanks to Clayton Elliott, who hadn't been able to hide his grin even as he'd denied having a part in it. As far as the world knew, she'd simply appeared out of nowhere, like so many of the continental aristocracy who had been displaced due to the wars. It allowed her to tell the truth—that she was the daughter of a Portuguese count, albeit an illegitimate one, which only served to make her seem notorious and exotic yet made society keep their distance. Exactly what she preferred.

She tilted back her head in invitation to be kissed. He obliged, giving her a passionate, openmouthed kiss that seared through her all the way to the tips of her toes.

When she tore her mouth away from his to catch her breath, she glanced out the window. "We're going in the wrong direction."

He persisted in placing kisses down her neck as his hands stroked her body beneath the fur. "No, we're not."

She began to tingle and ache as she always did when he caressed her. As she prayed she always would. "Why aren't we going to your town house?"

"*Our* town house," he corrected. "It's our home now, my love."

His words sparked a thrill inside her more powerful than all his kisses and caresses… *Our home.*

"I have a surprise for you first," he murmured. "A wedding gift."

"You shouldn't have."

He touched his lips to hers. "I wanted to." Another kiss, this one lingering heatedly until he groaned and pulled away. "So we'd better stop all this or I won't be in any condition to leave the carriage and give it to you."

"Good idea." She slid onto the opposite bench and put the distance of the cold compartment between them. "Because you're already warm enough, and something tells me that if you grow any warmer, *I'll* be the one with my clothes off."

He flashed her a wolfish grin.

A few minutes later, the carriage stopped. Veronica looked out the window, and disappointment panged in her chest. Her wedding gift was *here*?

"We're at the Armory." She tossed him a dubious glance. "Unless you're planning on tying me to another chair, I don't think—"

"Tying you up is tomorrow night's plan." He grinned devilishly. "And the night after that, and after that…"

When she opened her mouth to give him the scolding he deserved, he flung open the door and bounded to the ground, then reached back for her.

"Trust me, Veronica," he said, suddenly serious. "I think you'll like this gift."

With a deep breath, she placed her gloved hand in his and allowed him to help her from the carriage and across the outer courtyard. The place felt positively medieval in the snow, its gray stones as ominous as the darkening sky above it, especially when he led her beneath the two portcullises and into the dimly lit entry hall.

When they reached the octagonal room of the central tower, she stopped and stared.

"What on earth…?" she whispered, barely louder than a breath as she stared at the group of women waiting for her there.

Merritt leaned down to murmur in her ear, "Your gift. It was their idea."

Her gaze moved over the women, all of them from the Court of Miracles. Sweet heavens… She hadn't seen them in nearly three months, not since the night of the riot when she'd collected her belongings and left, never to return. But here they all were, including Ivy, and all of them stared back at her just as apprehensively.

"What are you all doing here?" she asked, blinking hard. She couldn't believe her eyes! She released Merritt's arm as she stepped forward and held out her trembling hands toward Ivy.

"We missed you. The Court isn't the same without you," Ivy told her, moving tentatively forward. But when their hands touched, the girl launched herself into Veronica's arms for a tight hug, so tight that she squeezed the air from Veronica's lungs. "We need you with us!"

Veronica shot Merritt an aggrieved look over Ivy's head. "But I'm married now. I can't live there with you anymore."

"Not live with us," Ivy clarified as she pulled back. "*Help* us. Help us find a fresh start, like you did."

When Veronica began to shake her head, at a loss for words, one of the other women interjected, "You can help us run the Court to start. Filipe left it to us, but we don't know the first thing about running the place. Ivy tries, but…"

"But there are others who would rather run it," Ivy confirmed. "Men who want to take it over for themselves, use it for their own profits. It should be *ours*, not theirs. You and Lord Rivers can help us keep it."

Veronica darted a glance at Merritt, who wasn't at all surprised by that request. Oh, that devil knew what the women wanted… "You've already agreed to help, haven't you?"

"I bought the warehouse for you yesterday." He casually shrugged a shoulder. "*That's* my wedding gift to you."

She blinked hard, trying to absorb that. "You bought me a *warehouse* for my wedding gift?" She twisted up a sarcastic brow and muttered, "And to think that most husbands so thoughtlessly give jewelry."

He grinned. "Something told me you'd like this better."

She did, blast it. As long as she owned the building, the women and children who lived there would never be cast out into the street. She could fix it up, put in real windows, doors, shutters… walls. No more sailcloth dividing the large floors into living spaces because that was all they could afford but real rooms where they could all be warm, dry, and safe. She could protect them.

But a tingle of apprehension licked at the backs of her knees. That wasn't why all the women were here. They didn't have to come here to tell her about the warehouse. No, Ivy had said they were here for a fresh start, and merely saving the warehouse wouldn't give them that.

She frowned. "You came here for more than just the Court."

Several of them nodded. "We want you to teach us to fight," another woman called out from the back of the group. "To train us to defend ourselves—"

"More than that," another interrupted. "I want to work, make my own wages and way. Fernsby said he needed to find another thief-taker to work with him. That's what I want to do."

"And me," another called out.

"I want to patrol like a watchman—"

"I want to work with reformers—"

"In the courts—"

"The law—"

"Hospitals—"

"However we can, wherever we're allowed to," Ivy finished decisively for all of them. "But we can't do it without you."

Veronica gaped at them, barely able to fathom what they were asking of her. Or how much work it would take, the long hours, the struggle… Most of the women standing in front of her couldn't even read or write, let alone do legal or medical work. As for fighting, some had never touched a knife in their lives except to peel potatoes. Was it even possible to teach them all they would need to learn?

Merritt slipped his arm around her waist and leaned down to bring his mouth to her ear. With that uncanny way he had of reading her mind, he told her privately, "Anything you do to help them will make a difference in their lives, no matter how small. And you *will* be able to help them. I know it."

His confidence in her warmed her like a ray of sunshine. Yet the task ahead was enormous. "I wouldn't even know how to begin."

"You won't be alone. I'll help you. So will the Duchess of Hampton. She has her own organization that she uses to advocate for women, which she calls Angel Wings." He eyed the women in front of them as he slipped behind her and encircled her in his arms. He drew her back against him and murmured the temptation in her ear, "This could be your own group of angels to work with."

"The Angels of the Armory," she whispered. The possibility of it all overwhelmed her too much to find her voice.

"This is what you wanted all along." He nuzzled his cheek against hers. "The chance to make a new life."

"No," she softly corrected him, unable to keep a knot of

happiness from forming in her throat. "The chance to be with the people I love."

When she turned around in his arms and rose up on tiptoe to kiss him, her heart ached to overflowing, and she knew…

She'd finally found the place where she belonged.

About the Author

Anna Harrington is an award-winning author of Regency romance. She writes spicy historicals with alpha heroes and independent heroines, layers of emotion, and lots of sizzle. Anna was nominated for a RITA in 2017 for her title *How I Married a Marquess*, and her debut, *Dukes Are Forever*, won the 2016 Maggie Award for Best Historical Romance. A lover of all things chocolate and coffee, when she's not hard at work writing her next book or planning her next series, Anna loves to travel, go ballroom dancing, or tend her roses. She is a terrible cook who hopes to one day use her oven for something other than shoe storage.

Escape into the passion and adventure of the Lords of the Armory series from award-winning author Anna Harrington!

An Inconvenient Duke

Marcus Braddock, Duke of Hampton and former general, is back from war and faced with mourning the death of his beloved sister. He's sure Danielle Williams knows something about what happened, but the more Marcus digs for answers, the more dangerous things get for both of them, and the only option is to keep Danielle close...

An Unexpected Earl

Brandon Pearce, former brigadier and now the Earl West, is determined to help the girl he once loved save her property and the charity she's been struggling to build. But he'll have to deceive her first...

"Harrington masterfully marries suspense and romance... Readers will be riveted."
—*Publishers Weekly*

A GENTLEMAN NEVER TELLS

Sparkling Regency romance from *New York Times*
and *USA Today* bestselling author Amelia Grey

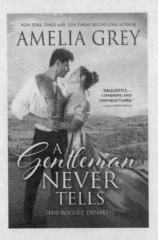

Viscount Brentwood is in London for one reason only: to find the perfect wife to give him sons. He just needs to choose a bride and everything else will fall into place. But the only one falling this season is Lady Gabrielle Windergreen—directly into his arms to steal a kiss. The last thing Brentwood wants is to get caught up in yet another scandal, but it seems whenever Gabrielle is near, scandal is exactly what he gets...

**"Amelia Grey grabs you by the heart, draws
you in, and does not let go."**
—*Romance Junkies*

LADY MAGGIE'S SECRET SCANDAL

Sparkling Regency romance from *New York Times* and
USA Today bestselling author Grace Burrowes

Lady Maggie Windham has secrets…and she's been perfectly capable
of keeping them—until now. When a blackmailer threatens to expose
Maggie's parentage, she turns to investigator Benjamin Hazlit to keep
catastrophe at bay.

Benjamin Hazlit has secrets of his own, including an earldom he never
talks about. However, when Maggie comes to him with innocent eyes and
a puzzling conundrum, he feels he must offer his assistance. But with each
day that passes, Maggie begins to intrigue Benjamin more than the riddle
she's set him to solve…

**"[A] tantalizing, delectably sexy story that
is one of [Burrowes's] best yet."**
—*Library Journal* Starred Review

For more info about Sourcebooks's books and authors, visit:
sourcebooks.com

LESSONS IN FRENCH

Poignant and delightful Regency romance from
beloved, bestselling author Laura Kinsale

Trevelyan de Monceaux and Lady Callista Taillefaire were childhood
sweethearts with a taste for adventure, until the fateful day Callista's father
discovered them embracing and drove Trevelyan away in disgrace. Nine
years later, Trev is back, and as they get embroiled in all manner of mis-
chief, Callie discovers Trev can still make her blood race and fill her life
with excitement. But the secret he's hiding means he can't give her what
she wants most—himself.

**"Kinsale creates magic... I wish for every romance
reader...to experience the singular and extraordinary
pleasures of a Laura Kinsale novel."**
—Lisa Kleypas, *New York Times* bestselling author

For more info about Sourcebooks's books and authors, visit:
sourcebooks.com

A WOLF IN DUKE'S CLOTHING

A delicious mix of Regency romance and shapeshifting
adventure in an exciting new series from author Susanna Allen

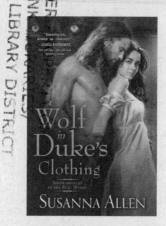

Alfred Blakesley, Duke of Lowell, has long been an enigma. No one dares
to give a man of his status the cut direct, but there's simply something not
quite right about him. What would the society ladies say if they learned
the truth—that the Duke of Lowell is a wolf shifter and the leader of a
pack facing extinction if he doesn't find his true love? So now he's on the
hunt…for a wife.

**"Sparkling wit, scrumptious chemistry, and
characters who will go straight to your heart!"**
—Grace Burrowes, *New York Times* and
USA Today bestselling author

For more info about Sourcebooks's books and authors, visit:
sourcebooks.com